NightZone

Books by Steven F. Havill

The Posadas County Mysteries
Heartshot
Bitter Recoil
Twice Buried
Before She Dies
Privileged to Kill
Prolonged Exposure
Out of Season
Dead Weight
Bag Limit
Red, Green, or Murder
Scavengers
A Discount for Death
Convenient Disposal
Statute of Limitations
Final Payment
The Fourth Time Is Murder
Double Prey
One Perfect Shot
NightZone

The Dr. Thomas Parks Novels
Race for the Dying
Comes a Time for Burning

Other Novels
The Killer
The Worst Enemy
LeadFire
TimberBlood

NightZone

A Posadas County Mystery

Steven F. Havill

Poisoned Pen Press

First Edition 2013

10 9 8 7 6 5 4 3 2 1

Library of Congress Catalog Card Number: 2013933206

ISBN: 9781464200694   Hardcover
       9781464200700   Trade Paperback

Poisoned Pen Press
6962 E. First Ave., Ste. 103
Scottsdale, AZ 85251
www.poisonedpenpress.com
info@poisonedpenpress.com

Printed in the United States of America

To Kathleen

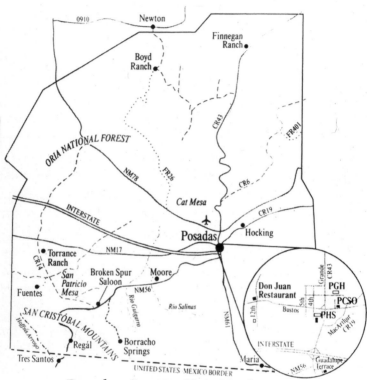

Posadas County, New Mexico

Chapter One

There were several reasons why it made perfect sense to sit on the rim rock of a towering mesa in southwestern New Mexico at one o'clock on a February morning, wrapped in a musty old army blanket and sipping powerful coffee from a chipped ceramic mug. Maybe overly zealous border patrol officers do something similar during stakeouts. Or elk hunters, waiting to hear the first secretive shuffles of a bull elk's hoof. I fit neither category.

Long ago, I had learned that it never worked to toss in bed, twisting sheets in knots while trying to chase away my chronic insomnia. I wasn't one to pop pills or swig hot milk and honey or read a boring book. I couldn't stand the idiocy of late night television. But, on the rim rock of Cat Mesa in the crystalline air, with a panoply of stars from horizon to horizon, I could snuggle down against the limestone boulders that had spent the day soaking up the sun's warmth. Without interruption, I could ponder great thoughts, watching my county far below.

Sometimes I would even doze off for a few moments. But if my brain wouldn't allow sleep, the least it could do was entertain me by chewing on a couple of interesting tidbits.

For instance, a few days before, while I was trudging across the prairie twenty-five miles southwest of Posadas, one of my hobbies had paid off in spades. I liked to imagine that I was an observant old fart, but until that moment I hadn't been the lucky sort who could look down and pluck every damn flint arrowhead out of the prairie matrix, or find an unbroken Puebloan water jug snuggled in a cave. I didn't even find dimes on the sidewalk.

But this time, hiking an interesting section of Bennett's Trail and looking for signs of that dysfunctional pioneer family who had tried to bring large-scale cattle ranching to this tough country, I struck gold. Cresting a knoll, I had tripped over a loose rock, shot out a hand for balance, and there it was—a loaded, cocked Colt Single Action revolver, nose down in a narrow fissure.

For a dozen ragged breaths, I had just stared without touching. And then, like any good cop would, I slipped the simple little digital camera out of my pocket and took half a dozen photographs. I could savor the anticipation only so long, and I didn't even consider the dictum from archeologists and federal agencies about leaving artifacts in place. This was private property, and the owner had given me carte blanche—finders keepers. Slipping on one of my leather gloves, I wrenched the artifact out of place.

A graceful, lethal work of art when first manufactured, the handgun was now just a lump of heavily corroded steel. It had rested under the stars, sun, snow, and rain for more than a century, caught in the cleft of rocks.

My mind had instantly conjured a theory about who the gun's owner might have been, and why he managed to fire one shot but no more, leaving four cartridges locked in place by corrosion, the cylinder itself a useless, immobile lump. After more than thirty-five years as a lawman, I knew better than to become too attached to the first theory that shows its face. The gun could have been dropped by anyone—a Mexican national skewered by an Apache's arrow while hiking to a new life in New Mexico Territory; a wagon driver not paying attention as the gun worked its way out of his hip holster; a family drama where one man drew on another, shots were traded, and the Colt fell into place, dropping from a lifeless hand. That's the one that appealed to me, since I knew the legend that Josiah Bennett had been murdered by his own son-in-law. The legend contended that an axe had cancelled Josiah's dreams—maybe he'd managed only a single shot in self-defense.

To a local history buff like me, the discovery of the gun and all it meant was enough to trigger a legendary dose of insomnia. The evening after I'd found the relic, I'd read myself red-eyed, researching everything Colt from my own voluminous library. Because older Colts had their serial numbers stamped in three places on the frame and grip straps, I was able to scrape off enough rusted crud to piece together the number, a digit from here, a digit from there. The gun was manufactured in 1889. A letter to Colt's archives would find out to whom the revolver was originally shipped. That reply would take months, agony for a man who no longer purchased green bananas.

Confronted with a challenge, some folks pace the floor. Some chew fingernails. Some eat or smoke. I find a comfortable vantage point heavy with peace and quiet and let my mind wander through its files. What better reason to drive out to Posadas County's vast collection of the boonies, take the short walk to this vantage point, and gaze out across the night landscape that had so challenged the Bennetts a hundred years before. But that puzzle—the gun, the Bennett family, and their fate—was only one motivation for my trek to the rim of Cat Mesa.

In addition, my thoughts whirled around to what now was referred to in the family as *The Concert*. Not *my* blood family, of course. My four kids, now grown and deep into middle age, were scattered across the country, doing their own thing. One of them, my oldest daughter Camille, managed to call me too often, fretting that I was not doing enough to reach some ridiculous benchmark of old age.

The Concert burst upon my adopted family, the Guzmans, like a prairie fire. Like everyone else in town, I was in the blissful dark about the whole matter until two weeks before, when the first glossy posters went up. The posters appeared in several strategic spots, announcing that at 8 o'clock on Saturday night, February 9, my godson, Francisco Guzman, along with a conservatory chum, Mateo Atencio, would be hosted in concert at the high school…a *big* concert. An *event*.

The photo displayed on the poster was professional, showing the thirteen-year-old Francisco looking mature and perfectly decked out in black, one arm resting on a polished grand piano's keyboard. The slightest of smiles touched his lips, guaranteed to set young ladies' hearts pitty-patting. Standing just behind him, holding a brilliantly polished silver flute, was a lad I'd never met. Mateo Atencio could have been Francisco's older brother. Two kids, both prodigies, too young to drive themselves to the concert.

The issue wasn't that the two kids would put on a concert. That's what talented musicians *do,* and even some who aren't so talented. But genius or not, Francisco R. Guzman was but thirteen, very minor indeed. Granted, the residential conservatory that he attended in Edgarton, Missouri, stood *in loco parentis.*

But…had young Francisco discussed this event with his parents? No. Dr. Francis Guzman and Posadas County Undersheriff Estelle Reyes-Guzman had learned about the concert when the high school music teacher, Jerry Reader, had presented to them a proof of the poster in question—something he at least had the courtesy to do *before* the posters went up. The posters prompted a predictable reaction, since both Francis and Estelle were somewhat old-fashioned about such things and believed that parents still gave direction and permission to thirteen-year-olds.

Being the good detective that she was, Undersheriff Estelle Reyes-Guzman soon delved into the heart of the matter. Jerry Reader, the high school music teacher, had been contacted originally by a Professor Hal Lott from the Leister Conservatory, where the two boys lived and studied. Reader told Estelle that it was his understanding that such concerts were a requirement for senior performance majors at the school—which, at thirteen and fifteen years of age, the boys both were. Promises of concerts were not given in advance, since student populations—even those made up of gifted students—changed frequently.

But in typical fashion, Francisco had requested of Mr. Reader that news of the concert should be a surprise until posted, and not to breathe a word to the Guzmans. In his own youthful exuberance and ignorance, the notion had never crossed the boy's mind that his parents might *enjoy* a few twangs of anticipation. Fortunately for him, Jerry Reader had shown the poster proof to Estelle before it was splashed around town.

The undersheriff's next call was to Professor of Music Hal Lott, MA, MFA, PhD, and so forth. I would have liked to have listened in. Estelle would have been courteous enough, but her voice would have carried overtones that would catch Dr. Lott's attention. The good professor had explained everything, offered an apology, and maintained that he was as excited about the concert as the boys. He pointed out to Estelle that public recitals and performances of all sorts were a vital part of the young musician's education. The school, Professor Lott said, would take care of transportation, with professional drivers, two professors in company, the two young musicians, and ten student stagehands traveling in a massive RV appropriate to a rock star, in company with a well-maintained stretch van.

As a cop, I had hated vans, since I'd seen more than a few of them reduced to a collection of bent and torn parts, strewn down the highway. I was sure Estelle had shared some of those same concerns. But in due course, the details of the concert had been finalized.

The high school teacher, Jerry Reader, had fretted to Estelle about the condition of the school's piano. Estelle had suggested to him that he fret to Dr. Lott, which he did. He was told not to worry—the staging truck would follow the RV and the van, and its principal cargo was a mammoth Steinway. These guys didn't mess around.

Reader, who had never had the pleasure of trying to teach Francisco Guzman before the boy left public for private schooling, was giddy with delight. He might have experienced gifted students during his career, but never a true prodigy, never a youngster who had been featured, at age eleven, in a major national magazine after a triumphant concert in Los Angeles.

Promising further significant musical surprises that he wasn't at liberty to divulge, Professor Lott was able to add Posadas, New Mexico, a tiny village shrunken to fewer than 3,200 folks, to his list of venues…in the high school gymnasium—a place with acoustics much like a parking garage…and Reader was told not to worry about that, either.

Estelle had spent an hour on the telephone with her son, and found out a few more details, including that at least two major pieces of music composed by the youngsters themselves would be debuted at the concert. This performance would be followed a week later by a similar concert in the tiny village of Dos Pasos, Texas, Mateo Atencio's hometown. Further "surprises" Francisco refused to divulge.

What a little wart, I thought. True enough, Francisco Guzman was a genuine, critically acclaimed prodigy whose concerts up to this point had been numerous and well-attended. He'd kept his proud parents busy, traveling to venues as far away as Chicago, St. Louis, Philadelphia, and of course, the Big Apple, where he'd appeared on some public television feature. But as far as I could tell, the rave reviews and all the doting hadn't gone to the boy's head.

When I saw him at home during breaks from school, he was the same kid I'd known since his birth. He loved monkeyshines with his little brother, Carlos. He could cook up waffles that almost floated in the air, or green chile lasagna that just about reduced me to an over-eater's coma. And, being a prodigy, he would play piano for four or five hours at a stretch, until the sweat soaked his black hair and dripped from his chin. A short break to take a shower and gobble calories, and he would dive into another session.

As I sat on my rock pondering the logistics of all of this, I supposed that a hometown concert was logical—and long over-due. Maybe Leister masters handled this gig as a matter of course for young musicians of such prodigious talent that they surely would end up belonging to the ages. The staggering tuition the place charged should certainly cover it…that and the whopping thirty-dollar admission price.

I had offered to host the traveling faculty and stage crew at my spacious old adobe, and hoped that I'd have the chance to engage Master Professor Doctor Lott in conversation. Francisco and Mateo would take the bunks in Francisco's room at the Guzman's modest little place on 12th Street—the fate of western world music nested in a couple of knotty pine bunk beds.

Those were the thoughts running through my mind as I lounged on the rim rock of Cat Mesa that February night… musings about an old, rusty, worthless revolver plus excruciating anticipation four days before *The Concert.*

So preoccupied was I that I almost missed the two pops of harsh, white light that blinked through the uniform darkness of the southwestern prairie, tiny flashbulbs too distant for me to judge cause or detail. Had I been caught in a sidelong glance, I would have missed them. But they were enough to bring my mind into sharp focus, since the empty prairie doesn't pop with light for no good reason.

I held my breath, straining my eyes, hoping for more. The two sharp flashes had been far to the south, the angle putting them at least twenty miles away, a distance where even a pair of headlights would be mere pin pricks in the night, not bright jolts of light.

The old cop in my system awakening, I pushed myself off the Oldsmobile-sized boulder that had been my sofa and stood carefully. Inky space yawned in front of my grandstand on the mesa rim. No distant whump of an explosion or gunshots reached me as I listened, only the lightest whisper of night breeze exploring through the canyons and cliffs.

Watching my footing, I made my way back to the SUV parked in the juniper grove behind the rim. With the ten-power binoculars rescued from the avalanche of crap on the SUV's center console, I returned to the mesa rim and once more settled on the limestone boulder, knees drawn up close. Training the glasses south, I had a thousand-foot elevation advantage over the prairie. The great dome of a trillion stars ended abruptly behind the rise of the San Cristóbal Mountains marking the border between Posadas County and Mexico. The lights had flashed against a black blanket. They hadn't been my imagination.

Another flash of light winked and then I could see a halo of sorts, maybe caused by something as insignificant as a campfire. Even the heavy binoculars didn't help.

Statistics would predict that a family of illegal aliens, chilled by the clear winter night, had started a toasty blaze somewhere along County Road 14. But matches didn't produce a flair visible from twenty miles. An exploding cup of gasoline? Not likely. An explosion of two propane tanks? The fireball resulting from that would have been immense.

Puzzling scenarios were a pleasure for me, and so I sat and watched for a while. But then the campfire, if that's what the faint halo in the distance was, swelled a bit as if it had jumped the rude fire circle and found the endless, stumpy grass of the prairie.

"Ah ha," I said aloud. Something scuttled off into the rocks behind me, its beady-eyed inspection of *me* startled by a sudden human voice. Bracing my arms against my knees, I concentrated the binoculars. And then the puzzling show grew into Act Two. A pair of headlights blossomed, unmistakable twin tunnels of light heading north on County Road 14.

Chapter Two

I knew that spread of prairie about as well as I knew my own back yard. The three state highways cut the county east-west like the tines of a crooked fork, NM 56 far to the south, NM 17 west from the village of Posadas, and finally NM 78 at the foot of my mesa. County Road 14 connected all three state highways like a piece of crumpled spaghetti laid across the fork.

Shifting my view south again, I could see that the glow of fire had grown, near the scar marking the county road's swath. Fleeing north along that rough county byway, the headlights were now running faster than would be prudent on that gravel road. They disappeared briefly behind a low mesa buttress and I counted the seconds, letting the topography of that route play through my mind—not far from the spot where I'd stumbled upon the Colt revolver.

Sure enough, half a moment later, the lights reappeared. At that pace, the driver had about six minutes before reaching the intersection with NM 17, the center tine of the fork that eventually entered the village and became our main east-west drag, Bustos Avenue.

What was now clearly a young prairie fire continued to grow. Unchecked, a fire in that country could run fifty miles without a pause—maybe a good thing, some environmentalists might argue. But the occasional rancher wouldn't think so. I reached around my belt and found the little holster that contained the cell phone, an odious gift from my eldest daughter on my seventy-fourth birthday. I had promised Camille that I would always carry it. First, she had tried to get me to wear one of those medical alert gadgets around my neck. Not a chance. If I fell up here on the mesa, the buzzards' circle would be my alert. Camille and I compromised on the phone. The first auto-dial rang twice before pick up.

"Posadas County Sheriff's Department. Sandoval." Renee Sandoval sounded as if she were twelve years old. I'd known her since she was two, when Children, Youth and Families rescued her from a miserable non-home situation. I had put her dad in jail and, free of that creep and her child, Renee's mother took off for a new life, leaving Posadas and Renee in her dust. By a kind twist of fate, Renee found happiness with a super foster family and took their name, then married a solid guy well into a career with the telephone company. She doted on hubby and their three well-grounded urchins.

"Deputy Sandoval, this is Bill Gastner." I rattled off the cell phone's number, and she didn't ask me to repeat. "We have what looks like a grass fire about twelve miles south of State 17 just off County Road 14, near Waddell's place." I raised the glasses again. "I'm watching a vehicle northbound on 14 that may have been involved somehow. He's about five miles south of the intersection with 17, and I'll let you know which way he goes when he reaches the highway."

"Say your location, sir?"

"I'm on the rim of Cat Mesa about a mile in from Forest Road 128."

"Ten four." After one a.m. on a brisk February night? The unflappable Renee didn't ask. Like other members of the sheriff's department, she knew my habits well enough, even though she'd never worked for me during my tenure. And as the current sheriff, Robert Torrez, had once observed, "What's so great about daytime, anyways? You can't see anything…"

"Can you stay with me, sir?"

"Affirmative." I could hear the radio chatter, and recognized the voice of Brent Sutherland, the sole road deputy on duty. He reported from just east of María, a tiny hamlet tucked in the far southeast corner of the county. That put him twenty minutes out, even if he flogged the horses.

The cold was starting to seep through the old blanket and my down-quilted coat. The boulder had given up the last of its day-time heat storage, and I stood up to unpetrify my butt. A cup of coffee and a cigarette would have tasted wonderful, even though I hadn't smoked for a dozen years. And then I froze in place.

"Well, I'll be damned." From a mile west of Posadas, itself a modest wash of lights, the county was black—not a ranch house, not a yard light, not even the parking lot lights of Victor Sanchez's Broken Spur Saloon, far to the south. I turned carefully. The entire western half of the county was unbroken night. I'd been concentrating on one point of interest and hadn't noticed the lights wink out—there were too few to make a grand show. But sure enough, the one sodium vapor light that should have illuminated the fuel island down at Posadas Municipal Airport didn't. Much farther south, the Prescott ranch was in the dark where I knew two yard lights should have illuminated the yard and corral.

"Dispatch, has anyone called in a power outage? To the west of the village?"

"That's negative, sir."

"You might want to give Posadas Electric a buzz, then. See what they have. I don't know if it's related to the fire I'm reporting or not. And be sure to tell the deputy that the vehicle I reported heading northbound may have nothing to do with any of this."

"Affirmative." She was gracious enough not to ask who the hell I thought I was, delivering her marching orders.

Minutes ticked by. That one set of headlights followed the black contour map north. Eventually the speeding vehicle reached the state highway and turned east with a wild swerve—I didn't know any ranchers who drove like that, but their teen-aged kids did, especially after leaving a beer blast to tackle a double-dog dare.

"The vehicle in question has turned east on 17. He's moving right along." That put him eight miles due west of the village.

"Affirmative, sir. Deputy Kenderman is available. I'll have him swing that way."

"Advise him to approach with caution. Sorry I can't give him a description, but right now, it's the only vehicle eastbound on that stretch of highway." Perry Kenderman was a part-timer whom the sheriff's department had inherited when the village of Posadas gave up its remnant force and contracted with the county for police services. Kenderman was far from the sharpest tool in the box, and had had his share of troubles in the past. But when the department had only one deputy on duty in the county, it was handy to have even a part-time officer ready to take a call in the village.

The radio background told me that Deputy Sutherland was northbound toward the village from the southeast, and Kenderman was just swinging onto Bustos from Sixth Street. I could stand there on the mesa rim as a long-range bystander, but there was enough going on down below to trigger my curiosity and to remind me that the winter night's chill was winning. I needed coffee.

With a last look through the binoculars to make sure the scooting vehicle hadn't turned off as it neared the village, I left the mesa rim. In a few moments, my SUV was jouncing down Forest Road 128, brushing its fenders against piñon and juniper limbs where the two track narrowed and twisted. I drove carefully, without any great sense of urgency.

A cattle guard rough enough to loosen teeth marked the intersection with County Road 43, the ribbon that approached the village from the north, and in another three miles, gravel turned to pavement. As the macadam snaked down the mesa toward Posadas, I turned up the radio just in time to hear Kenderman's gravelly voice announce, "Three zero two is stopping a blue Nissan pickup, license not readable."

I frowned with impatience at the lack of information. Where *was* Kenderman, exactly? How many occupants were in the truck? Even if the plate was unreadable, there was more he could give us. Camper shell? Club or crew cab? Guess at vintage?

"PCS, three zero niner is five south on seventy-six," Sutherland radioed. "I copy three zero two."

Dispatch wasn't satisfied with Kenderman's cryptic radio call. "Three zero two, ten twenty? Backup ETA is six minutes." The traffic stop couldn't have been very far from the village line. Kenderman didn't respond, no doubt already out of the patrol car, flashlight in hand. I could picture him rolling his bony shoulders in that odd habit of his as if his uniform was chaffing in all the wrong places.

The driver of the Nissan couldn't know that he had been watched on his rush north across the prairie. Nor could he know that he was being stopped by a part-time cop who was both careless *and* inexperienced.

We had several minutes to wonder about Kenderman's traffic stop as his backup headed north toward him. If the truck driver was reporting a prairie fire, Kenderman should have been on the radio, relaying the information for the fire department. Maybe he was an acquaintance of Kenderman's and the two men were standing under the stars, chatting.

I had reached the abandoned Consolidated Mining boneyard halfway down the mesa when the relative peace and quiet of the early morning hours were broken by Deputy Sutherland's frantic radio call as he reached the scene of the traffic stop—a call that set off the blizzard of radio traffic that filled the air during the time it took me to drive from the mesa into the village, then head west on Bustos Avenue.

It required more self-control than I possessed *not* to hurry in response to Sutherland's frantic "officer down" call, but I paid attention to the road, muscles so tense they ached. The last thing I needed to do was collect a deer standing in the middle of the road, or some emergency vehicle headed to the scene. Just as important, I needed to stay out of the investigating officers' way, and that was the hardest of all. By the time I arrived at that lonely spot just west of town, the sheriff was already there, dressed in rumpled jeans and sweatshirt. He had no hair long enough to comb, but I knew he'd just rolled out of bed and into the first thing he could find.

Two off-duty deputies had joined him, and I pulled to a stop on the highway shoulder a hundred yards out. The real cops were on the job. There was nothing for me to do except tell someone exactly what I'd witnessed.

The undersheriff's black Charger rumbled by me, braking hard. This time, Undersheriff Estelle Reyes-Guzman didn't park. She hesitated just long enough to exchange a few words with the sheriff, then drove past the scene and headed west on the state highway. *How goddamn odd,* I thought. She hadn't even stepped out of her car before leaving the scene. And there was only one explanation for that.

"What the hell is this all about?" I said aloud. From what I could see, State Route 17 would soon be slammed shut, this patch of macadam taped off. The vehicle that Kenderman had stopped was nowhere in sight, so common sense told me the assailant was history, leaving only a victim behind.

I sat back, trying to relax but feeling that awful, too-familiar creep of ice in my gut. Kenderman's patrol car was parked facing town, front wheels cocked toward the pavement, a wisp of exhaust issuing from the tailpipes, light show in full operation. A body was crumpled in the middle of the east-bound lane thirty feet or so in front of the aging Crown Vic county car. Part-time officer Perry Kenderman's body had that flat, deflated look of the truly dead, underscored by the large dark puddle of blood spreading on the asphalt. I didn't need a closer look.

The radio jabbered some more, and I turned it down a bit. I knew the drill, and didn't need to hear all the machine gun chatter of calls. I knew what the procedure would be now. Of all the people responding to this mess, I was the last one who needed to clomp his size twelves through the evidence field. I turned up the SUV's heat a notch and sat quietly.

Every road out of Posadas County should be corked, and there lay one of Sheriff Bob Torrez's most obvious challenges.

Sure enough, cops had responded to this site without delay or confusion once Deputy Sutherland's distress call had gone out. But by then, Deputy Perry Kenderman had been dead for too many minutes. If the driver of the blue Nissan had headed for the interstate, he already enjoyed a substantial lead. If the killer *hadn't* headed to the interstate, it was anyone's game.

This computer age would assure that an APB would reach its tendrils from sea to sea, well ahead of the killer. But the loopholes were plentiful, and no computer could plug them. The killer could have headed out of the county in several creative ways, sticking to back roads until he was free of the net. If he'd headed south toward Mexico without knowing that the border crossing at Regál was closed from midnight to six, he'd flounder a little trying to decide what to do. If he was a local—and his speed maintained on the gravel county road suggested that he might be, any side street, any alley, any parking lot or garage might hide the little truck.

Dr. Alan Perrone's BMW whispered into view, and he stopped in the middle of the highway beside me, never taking his eyes off the view ahead. Sheriff Torrez waved at him, pointing at a spot on the shoulder fifty yards ahead of Kenderman's unit and the pathetic shape now under a blue tarp. As he pointed, Torrez strode down the road toward us. He paused for a moment to talk with the physician, then headed for my SUV.

"Kenderman's dead." The sheriff's voice was husky and nearly inaudible. He touched his own right cheekbone, then a spot two inches behind his left ear. When Perry Kenderman, flashlight in hand, bent his lanky six-foot three-inch frame down to peer into the driver's window of the Nissan, he never suspected a thing. He hadn't tried to jump back, hadn't staggered away. He'd dropped in place when the bullet crashed through his brain.

"He never had a chance to touch his gun," the sheriff said. "And the son-of-a-bitch drove over Kenderman's right foot when he left." Up ahead, I watched as Dr. Perrone peeled back the blue drape and then stood quietly, looking down at Perry Kenderman.

"What can I do to help?" I knew that detailed depositions of what I'd seen or heard would be required, but right now, this very dark second, there might be something more urgent that a well-trained civilian, however firmly retired, might do. Sheriff Torrez stared down at the pavement for a moment. He *had* no extra moments to waste, and I waited impatiently for him to kick into gear. The thunder of a heavy diesel interrupted us, and I looked in my rearview mirror to see the winking lights of a fire engine, and behind that in tight formation, two pickups and a couple of electric company bucket trucks.

"Tell you what…these guys need to get through. Go on ahead and follow Estelle. Jackie Taber is just about there by now." He nodded toward the approaching parade. "These guys will be right behind you." His huge hand slapped my window sill. "And be careful. We got us another one out there." *Another one out there.* I could have asked a dozen questions, but as the iceberg grew below my heart, Torrez had already straightened up and was striding back toward the first truck, radio in hand.

"You got it," I called, but he didn't pause to chitchat or explain. Nothing I could do would help Perry Kenderman. I wasn't a religious sort, but was a believer in balancing the scales here on planet Earth. To that end, my mind was already focused on *out there.*

Chapter Three

Cops don't drive away from a homicide scene to check out something as mundane as an out-of-control campfire. I had expected Undersheriff Estelle Reyes-Guzman to hit supervision of the Kenderman homicide scene at a dead run. But she hadn't even stepped out of the car. Did *another one out there* mean that some other innocent soul had walked up to the blue Nissan, this time to beg a ride, a drink of water, a spare tire or lug wrench? Like anything else, I supposed, killing grew easier with practice.

I knew every rancher in that part of the country where I'd seen the lights, and counted most of them as friends—even the high-profile Miles Waddell, on whose ranch property I had been hiking lately in my quest to investigate the life of Josiah Bennett, and on whose property the rocks grew that had sheltered the Colt revolver. An hour after finding the gun, I'd showed it proudly to Waddell, and he'd wondered right along with me what kind of story it had to tell. He had left that investigation to me, though. He was deeply involved now in a project to place an observatory on top of his own private mesa. Contractors had just finished his access road, but they weren't working there at night. I could imagine Miles, sometimes a bit confrontational, running afoul of some wacko—although what either one of them would be doing out and about at one in the morning on a winter night on the open, desolate prairie was anyone's guess. Investigators would ask me the same thing. More scenarios.

I tried to relax as the SUV held eighty-five miles an hour on State 17, but that was impossible, knowing that the two young women—Sergeant Jackie Taber and Undersheriff Estelle Reyes-Guzman—were driving into the unknown…an unknown perhaps populated by some trigger-happy freak. Of course they could take care of themselves. I'd always thought that Perry Kenderman could, too.

A mile before the County Road 14 turnoff, a pair of headlights blossomed in my rearview mirror, the grill wiggle-waggle lights frantic. In a few seconds, an Expedition proved it could break one hundred as it shot past me, driven by Captain Eddie Mitchell. Mitchell, a veteran of large metro police departments Back East before joining first the village as chief, and then the sheriff's department as captain when the village department dissolved, was cool, tough, and fearless. I felt better, and lifted my foot as up ahead the intersection reflectors popped out of the dark.

County Road 14 had been a nasty, narrow two-track until a year ago when the road was widened, graded, and graveled, pounded by heavy trucks into a boulevard as they headed toward rancher Miles Waddell's project. Traffic produced plumes of cloying dust, and now the night air was thick with it as I bumped off the state highway. Up ahead, Mitchell's lights disappeared, and then I was forced to slow as the southbound county road tackled Bennett's Fort, a ragged mesa I'd named a dozen years ago—and the same geology I'd scanned through binoculars from the distant mesa-top less than an hour earlier.

I'd seen the Nissan's headlights dodging around the curves northbound, but try as I might, I could add no information that would be useful to the sheriff. Two headlights in the dark…that was the whole of it. But Sheriff Bobby Torrez hadn't just told me to go home and crawl into bed—he hadn't told me that he'd deal with my deposition in the morning.

In another five miles, I caught still more glimpses of the rainbow of lights in my rearview mirror, the cavalcade of emergency vehicles gaining on me relentlessly. One more rise, and I saw our target…a smallish grass fire working its way to the north, running right along the county road and edging out into the open prairie. The flames licked straight up, the smoke hesitant to pick a direction. It was the sort of prairie fire you could fight with a garden hose. It didn't need most of the county's emergency services resources.

I slowed, peering this way and that into the night. Surely this show of emergency support didn't leave the scene of an officer down to respond to a grass fire—in a spot where it could burn unmolested for hours without hurting anybody or anything.

"So what the hell?" I said aloud. Undersheriff Estelle Reyes-Guzman's black sedan was parked in the dead center of the county road immediately behind Jackie Taber's department unit with Eddie Mitchell's Expedition damn near in the bar ditch beside her. A quarter mile beyond, just across the cattle guard that marked Miles Waddell's property, a pickup truck was parked facing us, headlights bright and four-ways pulsing.

My cell phone buzzed, and it took me a while to manipulate the tiny thing right way up.

"Gastner."

"Sir, it would be good if you can pull your vehicle off the roadway about a hundred yards behind mine." Estelle's voice was unperturbed. "And if I get busy, don't walk any farther south than my unit. We have a live power line down."

"Copy that." I didn't pester her with more questions. In fact, I was surprised that, upon noticing my vehicle driving up, she'd even taken the time for that brief message.

We had enjoyed no weather capable of dropping power lines, and the only one I knew about in this section of prairie was the main line east-west—wooden double poles with double crossbucks, three double heavy lines plus the ground. Double poles don't just fall over. They always reminded me of towering mechanical giants, striding confidently across the prairie, arms lugging their electrical burden. They didn't just fall over. And even if they did, cops don't leave a homicide scene to attend to the resulting power outage.

I parked where I was told, then got out and stood beside my vehicle, heavy flashlight in hand. Something popped a shower of bright white very near the roadway. In a moment, the pickup truck's headlights and four-ways switched off, and things became a bit clearer without those lights staring us in the face.

Off to my left from the east, the parade of power poles marched across the prairie. And sure enough, the symmetry of their order was broken where the lines sagged in graceful waves toward the ground. Incredibly, three sets were down, three giants toppled, including the set just off the county road.

Not possible, I thought. Over a lot of years, I'd seen errant trucks sheer single utility poles. Even careening cars sometimes accomplished that. Storms knocked them down now and then, but rarely if ever in our part of the world. Three double units in a row? The moon, working on a bright half, wasn't much help in making sense of this scene.

I'd been given permission to advance as far as Estelle's vehicle, so I gingerly picked my way to the shoulder of the road. When the cavalcade inbound reached my location, I stepped well back. One of the big Posadas Electric Cooperative Kodiak line trucks, toting its bucket lift, broke off from the pack and trundled across the prairie eastward, bucking and lurching, breaking a trail that skirted the damage by a wide margin, finally circling in to the first standing pole set where the power lines started their graceful curve toward the earth.

A state police unit and two more electric company trucks filed past, then made room for the pumper from the Posadas Fire Department. Behind them, a Bureau of Land Management yellow back-country truck idled in. We had a damn traffic jam.

Little radio traffic broke the stillness now that most of the crews had embraced the privacy of the cell phone. And sure enough, mine beeped.

"Gastner."

"Sir," the undersheriff said, "the power has been shut off back at the relay station in Posadas, so we're clear."

"Affirmative." Why she thought my needing to know that was a priority, I couldn't guess.

"We're going to use my vehicle as the command post, so if you want to make your way up there, we'll get this circus underway." I heard the tension in her voice, and knew her patience was thin. All the traffic obliterated prairie marks, pulverizing everything into the fine dust that now rose into the night. She'd done a good job of traffic directing, though. No one parked near the power lines.

"I'm on my way." *My way* was a sedate walk, since night, flashlights, and trifocals make a rotten combination. Ahead, silhouetted against the lights and inky sky, a plume of water fanned out from the pumper, and I could hear the hiss against the flames. It would have done the prairie good to burn off a few million acres, but that wasn't going to happen.

Miles Waddell, the rancher whose pickup had been blasting its lights into our faces, and who owned all the land to the south, advanced from his vehicle but stopped well short of the cattle guard where one of the twin legged poles had toppled, sprawling across the county road, one of its legs reared high in the air where it had teeter-tottered across a big juniper corner post that anchored the section fence.

The wires were a jumbled mess, and the heavy transformer complex that the pole had also carried had broken from its supports and lay askew. That's where the fire had started, the power lines arcing into the grass. And odds were I'd seen the initial lightning bolts of the short circuit from my perch on Cat Mesa, twenty miles away.

I reached Estelle's vehicle and stopped. She had parked directly across the road, and Jackie Taber was unreeling the yellow tape to keep the hordes at bay. With the power now shut down, the electric company crews still kept their distance, waiting for the word from the Sheriff to move in.

My first view through the binoculars told me that nobody was going anywhere for a while. This wasn't about the little fire, or the downed poles. A body lay in the dust of the electric company's two track along the power line, just a few feet from the last broken stump. The victim was lying on his back, arms thrown wide. In the vague, flickering light, the body had that same flat, deflated look shared by Deputy Perry Kenderman. And just beyond his feet, the stump of the electric pole had been cut off three feet above the ground, leaving sharp splinters on one side where the electric tree had taken leave of its stump. Above the dead man, the butt of the pole hung suspended, teeter-tottering over the fulcrum offered by the fence line's juniper corner post.

Even a simple crime scene gives up its details a few at a time. Some investigators would claim that, just as there is no such thing as a "routine" traffic stop, there is no such thing as a "routine" homicide crime scene. This night, the questions tumbled in one atop the next, with no coherent pattern or order.

The most obvious explanation to me, from my vantage point a hundred yards away where I leaned against the front fender of the undersheriff's Charger, was that somehow this unfortunate soul had stumbled upon the driver of the Nissan pickup, perhaps as the killer was putting the chain saw to the final pole. And like the unsuspecting Perry Kenderman, a single slug had dropped the passerby in his tracks. Nissan man had left the victim to stare at the stars. I was uncomfortable with that scenario, easy as it was. Nothing directly connected this site, this death, with the Nissan. I hadn't seen it parked in this lonely place.

But maybe…and where was the victim's vehicle? Had he been a Mexican afoot? Our harsh desert ate a few of them every season. Or had the little Nissan pickup belonged to him, only to be stolen after his murder? If that was the case, what odd circumstance had set the killer afoot in the desert in the middle of the night, so eager to kill and steal a truck? Again, someone from across the border? I grunted in disgust and dug a toe of my right boot into the dust. That scenario just didn't work, for myriad reasons. I watched the dark figures moving about in the harsh lights, and took a deep breath of impatience.

Another state patrolman arrived, a grim-faced kid who looked so much like my eighteen-year-old grandson that he earned a double take from me. Doug Posey, the local Game and Fish officer, joined the party. More Posadas Electric Cooperative hardware, a couple more of the sheriff's department's dwindling staff. Then, coming up from the south, three Border Patrol SUVs raised their own dust cloud.

We had so many flashing red and blue lights that it was impossible to find the Big Dipper.

Slipping in quietly, Dr. Alan Perrone—finished with his preliminary examination of the unfortunate Perry Kenderman—parked immediately behind Estelle's car and paused as he reached me. This time, I earned a long, careful scrutiny.

"Hell of a night." He shifted his heavy medical bag to his other hand.

"Looking endless," I said.

"Are you holding up all right? The sheriff tells me you watched all this from up on the mesa?" He turned his back on the light display and gazed off to the north, where Cat Mesa lay rugged and invisible. He shook his head in wonder.

"I caught just a couple of flashes," I replied. "My guess is that's when the transformer went down. But it all beats the hell out of me. And then I saw a single vehicle driving north up to the state highway. That's not much to go on."

He stood quietly, surveying the convocation ahead, an uncharacteristic moment of repose for the peripatetic physician. "So let's see…" He thumbed his phone. A hundred yards away, it appeared that the undersheriff had her personnel organized to allow some working room. The now-covered body lay in isolation, the black plastic tarp bathed in harsh light from a portable generator.

"Let me know," Perrone said into his phone, and listened patiently, nodding now and then as if the speaker on the other end of the phone could see him. "I can bring him in with me." The physician nodded again, glancing at me. "You bet." He snapped the phone closed. "You know, we can probably do something about that insomnia of yours."

"Maybe tonight it paid off," I said.

He chuckle didn't carry much mirth. "Are you up for a hike?"

"Hell, why not," I replied. The sheriff had sent me out here, and I had taken that as just a simple courtesy extended to a former colleague and friend—and since I'd been the only one to witness the beginning of this episode, he'd want to keep me on a short leash until I'd handed in a thorough written deposition. But the last thing I needed right now was to gawk at a corpse.

The undersheriff would have *her* reasons to invite me in, and I had the sinking feeling that the answer was obvious. I had known Perry Kenderman for years. Odds were good, in a county this small, that I would also know this pathetic figure lying here, under the black plastic.

Chapter Four

Maybe Curtis Boyd's final fading vision was the great Milky Way spreading across the desert sky. Maybe he had struggled for a few seconds to ponder his lot in life, and what he'd leave behind. All maybes that didn't concern Dr. Alan Perrone. What *did* concern the medical examiner was how a veteran Posadas County rancher's youngest son came to rest in this particular spot, dead as dead can be.

I'd known the dad, Johnny Boyd, for thirty-five years. He had already become a Posadas County institution by the time I first met him. Service as chairman of the County Fair Board back when the economy allowed fairs, member and then president of the school board for a decade or more, active on the livestock board—he and his wife had raised four kids with all the usual family triumphs and catastrophes. His older bachelor brother, Edwin, had lived at the main house too, and he'd kept the sheriff's department busy from time to time.

Curt Boyd, the rancher's youngest son, had attended his share of rodeos and county fairs as a tyke, sporting the little cowboy boots and oversized hat that scrunched down on top of his ears, so cute, cameras clicked when he scampered by. Years later, I had watched the track meet when the Posadas Jaguars took state, and it had been Curt Boyd who had hammered the pole vault, anchored the mile relay, and set a state record in the 440. He'd dominated the 4-H livestock classes at the county fair as a teenager, but with all of his big fish in a small pond success, Curt had never taken to the ranching life, hadn't beaten himself lame like his daddy with a life of livestock, barbed wire, post-hole diggers, and recalcitrant windmills.

The last I'd heard, he had settled in as a social studies teacher in Las Cruces, coaching track on the side. I couldn't remember when I'd last seen him, but this poor battered corpse bore enough resemblance to the living Curt Boyd that I had no doubts it was him.

Dr. Perrone muttered something, scrunched down and manipulated the victim's head and neck. "Is Linda here yet?" He looked up at Estelle, whose own camera had shot dozens of images while she waited for the department's photographer, Linda Real, who should have been working for the FBI, but instead had married one of the deputies and stayed home and happy.

"She's on the way."

"You're going to want to document this pretty thoroughly," Perrone said. "His neck is broken right at the first cervical. Damage right on down to the fourth. There's no sign of exterior trauma from the rear, though." He let out a long breath. "That's just about the most massive whiplash injury I've ever seen."

"He wasn't hit from behind, then."

"No. From this." He traced a line along the victim's jaw, mangled and bruised. It didn't take a physician to see that the jaw bone was smashed, with teeth splintered as if some gargantuan boxer had caught him with an uppercut to end all haymakers. Perrone probed delicately with a gloved hand, holding his flashlight close. He fished a small plastic bag from his kit and deftly snapped it open. From a spot just under the jaw line he withdrew a splinter of dark wood. "Somebody clubbed him a good one under the chin."

"Somebody or something," I said. The memory cards were beginning their long, lazy turns around the rusty spindle of my brain's Rolodex.

"Sir?" Estelle prompted.

I glanced at the undersheriff. "All this brings back memories. You remember Morris Ferguson?" No, she didn't remember.

Morris Ferguson was well before her time. But twenty-five or so years before, old Morris had won the job as Posadas' mayor. He never had the chance to lift the gavel.

"Morris went up to spend a weekend with his brother in Truchas," I said. "They went out wood cutting, and a two-foot thick aspen tree they were felling got tangled and kicked back off the stump." I looked up at the severed electric pole high above our heads, held suspended by the tangle of wires and the stout juniper fence post that acted as its fulcrum. Its marching partner, with the remains of the twisted transformer supports, lay flat in the dust. "Same thing. The aspen kicked back and caught him in the head." I touched my temple.

Estelle favored me with a bemused grimace, her dark olive skin and movie star teeth spectacular in all the surrounding lights. I shrugged. "Once in a while I remember something useful." I reached up, but stretched as tall as I could manage, the butt of the pole was still three feet out of reach, a spear of uncut wood projecting a sword's length where the pole had been jerked off its stump before the saw cut finished the job. "That would fetch him a hell of a clout."

"You're saying that the *pole* hit him?"

"I'm *guessing,*" I said. "That's all." I pointed upward. "Check that butt of the pole for tissue and blood, and that'll confirm it. But in order for that pole to end up so far in the air…see there? It jacked over that juniper corner post and boom. That would be the sucker punch of all time."

Perrone grunted something as he pulled clothes out of the way and then hiked Boyd's T-shirt up. He found not a mark on the ghostly white skin, not a bruise or nick. Rolling the corpse over, an examination of the back found only some faint scuffing, most likely from landing back-first in the gravel. One elbow had found a patch of cacti.

"And where's the saw?" I asked. "Have you had the chance to walk the line back east to the first cuts? If we stick to the tracks of the service road, we can do that without wrecking the scene before daylight." *We, we, we.* But hell, I wasn't the one who had invited me out here. "See, this whole thing makes me nervous." I turned in a semi-circle. "We have six poles down. Three sets of two. Now, you cut the first one," and I waved toward the east, "and they're just going to hang there, maybe all crooked and saggy, but they won't go down. I'm willing to bet on that."

"It takes a special kind of crazy to chain saw a major power line," Estelle said. "That's a lot of voltage hanging overhead. And you couldn't possibly predict which way they'd fall...or sag, or whatever."

"True. And even worse with the second set. You already have the weight of one pair hanging out of place, their weight on the wires. You whack a *second* set, and something is going to give way. And a third set?" I shook my head, and touched a toe of my boot to the stump. "What do you think?"

Estelle remained silent as she knelt down, holding her flashlight to illuminate the back side of the power pole's fourteen-inch diameter stump. After a moment, she turned and let the light track the few feet over to the county road. "This pole has been hit a number of times." Her voice was so quiet and husky that I could hardly hear. Maybe the thought hadn't been intended for me, but I barged in with my two cents anyway.

"You got this pull-out on the county road," I said. "A handy turn-around after the cattle guard. Miscalculate a bit and the stock trailer takes a chunk out of the pole. Or somebody backs into it trying to do who knows what." With a crackle of joints, I knelt beside her, letting my hand run over the rumple of scarred wood on the back side of the pole. "Huh. With all the damage over the years, there isn't as much wood as maybe our guy thought there was."

Estelle stood and beckoned to Linda Real, whose plump figure had materialized out of the shadows. "We need portraits of this every way you can, Linda."

"Absolutely."

"Ditto all the others. Both the stumps and the downed poles. Number them starting at the eastern-most set, one-two, three-four, and these five-six. Northern member of each pair is odd—one, three and five. And I'm more interested in the backside of the cut, how much was left when he jerked the saw out of the wood."

"You got it."

"Good close-ups of the saw cut and the break point."

Linda nodded, but she was already selecting a lens from her camera bag as well as some gadget for the strobe to mute the burst of light.

The undersheriff applied some upward force to my left elbow, and I tried to remain graceful as I rose to my feet.

"Are you up for a little walk, sir?"

"Of course," I said with feigned enthusiasm. For years, various doctors like Alan Perrone and Francis Guzman had been cajoling me to walk, walk, walk. My nature was to sit, sit, sit. It was easier to think when I was motionless. But this intense young lady always brought out the best in me. I glanced toward the county road where a fair crowd had collected—cops who wanted in, Posadas Electric crews ready to assess and repair the damage, rancher Miles Waddell still patiently supported by the fender of his truck, firemen finished with their half-acre burn. The crowd remained stationary, though. They apparently understood that if they started milling about, any semblance of crime scene would be stamped into oblivion.

Taking the damaged power poles in order, we visited each saw cut, crossing first to number five, nearest the tarp-shrouded figure of Curt Boyd, the pole that had kicked across the cattle guard as the whole mess tilted and twisted.

The initial cut was a neat job, the saw ripping through the creosoted pole to within an inch or two of completion.

"That's not much to support the pole," I said. "The least little breeze would do it."

"And no breeze tonight," she said. "Not until dawn, maybe. Between this," and Estelle touched the torn fragment that the saw hadn't finished, "and the wires themselves, would the pole stand? I mean, barring a wind or a push?"

"I would think so, but I'm just guessing. You'd have to ask Dick Whittaker. But if all six weren't cut all the way through, if they're just balancing there on a little splinter of wood…"

Superintendent of this portion of the grid, Whittaker was talking to a group of his men fifty yards away.

"I'll meet up with him in a bit." Estelle measured the wood with her fingers. "Not much left, but maybe enough." She looked off to the east. "So. Here we have six cripples, each one held by only an inch, and along comes one little morning breeze…"

"Absolutely. And it could be that the last one they cut sabotaged the whole plan. Over they went, and that last one kicked Curt Boyd." One at a time, we visited the other four poles, and all showed the same pattern: a clean cut that implied a powerful saw with a sharp chain and a confident operator. In each case, the saw cut stopped short of running through, leaving just a minimal tag to support the pole—a tag that had splintered when the poles toppled.

"Paul Bunyan gave this a lot of thought," I said. "A whole bunch of power poles standing, just waiting for daytime breezes. Can you imagine that? A bunch of wobbly giants, ready to take the plunge. And by then, our cutter is long gone."

"His scheme didn't work quite the way he planned."

I thought about that for a moment. "It worked until the last one, sweetheart. Maybe he missed a closer look at that last one, with all its nicks and bangs. Or he got a little excited, maybe a little tired and drove the saw just a hair too far. Over she goes, and with that weight off balance, the whole set rips free. A jangled mess."

"The truck you saw driving north? He couldn't have just been driving by here out of coincidence," Estelle said quietly. "If he'd been a innocent witness, he would have stopped the first cop he saw to report this. If the truck whose lights you saw was the cutter, then he took off when the poles went down. And he didn't take his injured friend with him, he didn't leave the saw behind, and he didn't give Kenderman a chance."

"And no sawdust on Curt Boyd," I added. The undersheriff stood still, gazing at me, lost in thought. "Boyd sure as hell wasn't the saw handler. Those things spray chips and oil all over the place. And by the way," I added, "I didn't see a *truck* driving north. I saw a set of headlights. That's all."

"Tell me how you see it happening, sir. With Boyd, I mean."

I took a deep breath. "I see Boyd standing a few feet behind the cutter, maybe holding the flashlight. Maybe he steps forward a little. He's done this for five poles, and so on the sixth maybe he's just a little bit cocky…a little bit off-guard. But then the pole starts to lean, to sway maybe, and dollars to donuts he just doesn't duck and run like hell. That's what the hell he should have done, of course. Instead he looks up and gapes in fascination. Maybe he tries to shout at his buddy, reaches out a hand in panic. Now in the best of all worlds, because both boys are off to one side, both poles might have tangled past them without catching either one. If the one pole gives way first, I can see the whole mess twisting before the second pole comes loose. See, they hadn't *meant* for the poles to fall just then. That's my theory. I mean, why would they? There's too much risk. But that weak pole changed all that. It crashes down on the line fence, right on that big juniper brace, and the butt end bucks up before they have time to say, 'Oh, shit.' Bucks up and back and catches Johnny's boy right under the chin on the way up. Pow."

"What a friend, just to leave him lying out here."

"Nissan man? If that's him, what a friend indeed, even though I think it would have been obvious his buddy was stone cold dead. And if he has half a brain, he knows this sort of damage isn't something that would take until morning to discover. He wants out of there, you bet. He knows folks are going to be on his tail."

I shrugged. "Seems to me that all this would explain why he didn't give Perry Kenderman a chance, didn't try to bluff his way out of a speeding ticket. He's left a corpse behind, and the death occurred during the commission of a felony—and with that half a brain of his, Paul Bunyan knows he's in deep shit. And at the same time, he had to know that no matter how fast we could respond, the odds are in his favor. He can be long gone, without a trace, if he acts quickly enough. Road blocks are a wasted effort."

She knew that as well as I did, but I pressed on. "The killer didn't spare an extra minute arguing with Kenderman. Shot him and drove away. He's got time on us. And you're not going to find someone covered with sawdust at a traffic stop. He won't be that dumb. Not if he tried to think something like this through." I watched her dark face settle into a determined frown. "Boyd was a local kid. That's a place to start. And you know, this is an interstate power line. You won't go far before you have to talk to the feds."

"Captain Mitchell has already called them," Estelle said. "And we'll have a full State Police presence in a few minutes."

"Well, then, that's good. If you want a running start, have Linda photograph the bottom two feet of number five, there, if you can figure out how to reach it, or cut it off, or something. Take some scrape samples at the same time. If Curt Boyd got himself clobbered some other way, then you've got a different game altogether. But I'll bet you a green chile burrito that nasty uppercut to the chin is how he died. Perrone found a sliver of wood in the wound, so nothing else makes sense. Not unless we find a handy bullet hole hiding someplace."

I took a deep breath and regarded the still-spectacular night sky—not because I loved star gazing, but to stop my motor-mouth from continuing to tell Estelle Reyes-Guzman things she knew perfectly well on her own.

"Two things bother me the most," she said. "One is the timing. He wanted to cut and run. With the right weather conditions, that power line might not have toppled for who knows how long. When it *did* finally go, it could have caught vehicular traffic in any number of ways as busy as this road is now. He couldn't have known who he might end up hurting or killing."

"Best laid plans. At least it's not a school bus route." Miles Waddell's mesa was dark against the stars, but come dawn the heavy machinery would bellow into life with his observatory project…machinery coming and going that would shake the ground.

"You called dispatch just after one."

"I did."

"And Mr. Waddell contacted dispatch at roughly the same time. That's how dispatch logged it. The sound of the saw woke him, he says. He said he wouldn't have called, but no one saws wood in the middle of the night. He drove across his mesa from where he was parked to the rim, looked out and saw the fire already starting. He missed the poles actually dropping. And he says he didn't see a vehicle. That's how quickly our guy decided to leave the scene."

"All right. You said two things bothered you."

She nodded. "Oh, *si*. We've been talking about Curt Boyd's partner in this stunt. There could be more than one, sir. At least two more could fit in that little pickup. Maybe three."

Chapter Five

At one point earlier that morning, Miles Waddell and I had been looking at each other from opposite ends of the county. The killer—or killers—had been sandwiched between us, scooting north to the rendezvous with the unprepared Deputy Perry Kenderman. Despite my best intentions to mind my own business, I found myself trying to imagine how *I* would juggle two wildly different but related crime scenes if that lot fell to me. It was easiest just to say, "Well, I'm retired now. Good luck, guys."

I admit that I hadn't particularly warmed to Perry Kenderman over the years. He had his share of family issues that got in his way, and on top of that, when he put on his gun belt, he developed a certain swagger that made me nervous. He had finally attended and graduated from the state Law Enforcement Academy, well below the middle of the scholastic heap. He had been a part-timer for first the village and then for the sheriff's department largely because I had had grave reservations about his sloppy law enforcement skills. On occasion, it seemed that he made laws up as he went along. I had kept him on a short leash, letting him have minor duties. Sheriff Torrez had hauled in the slack even more. None of that meant that Perry Kenderman should end up lying on the pavement, his brains and blood soaking into the macadam.

On top of that, the volatile Johnny Boyd would have to be told that his youngest son was dead, with no ready answers about why.

"What can I do for you, other than staying out of the way?" By this time, my insomnia was beginning to lose ground, and a toasty bed was inviting. I was hoping the undersheriff would say something politely dismissive, like "We'll talk later."

Instead she reached out a hand and gently took my left elbow. "Maybe you'd talk to *him*." She nodded toward the county road. I turned and saw the SUV pulling to a stop behind all the other vehicles, the winking lights playing off its red slab sides. Frank Dayan, now owner and publisher of the weekly *Posadas Register,* scrambled out and immediately drew a bead with his digital camera. What he, or the camera, could see in the light-exploded night was unclear.

"That I can do. 'Investigation is continuing,' a department spokesman said?"

"That's perfect. No one is identified until Bobby gives the okay."

I nodded. I knew the drill. "Frank will be able to figure out the 'who's who' all by himself. Is there anything special about the power pole damage you want Dayan to know?" For once, the publisher had lucked out. His paper came out on Thursday. An early Thursday morning disaster was perfect for him, a man who lived for the opportunity to scoop the metro papers and TV stations almost as much as he relished a new full page advertisement. And this story was oddball enough that the choppers would flock for *exclusive at 10* photos of downed power poles.

"Not from us, sir. He can count that there are six down. That's as far as we go." Which meant that if Dayan could pry something out of the Posadas Electric Cooperative, he was free to do so. Estelle squeezed my shoulder. "And when you're done with him, you need some sleep."

"Plenty of time for that. Not that you have time to think about it, but when does the Leister contingent roll into town?"

Estelle pressed both hands to the sides of her head in mock agony. "Ay. Sometime Saturday, I'm told. Carlos has been climbing the walls." She rested a finger on her lips, secret style. "He knows something we don't."

"Interesting conspiracy going on there," I chuckled.

"You'd be amazed," she said. "And thanks for heading Frank off at the pass."

I didn't mind the assignment, since I liked Frank Dayan, and on top of that, knew perfectly well that Sheriff Bobby Torrez wouldn't mind me taking on the PR task—anything as long as *he* didn't have to do it—a great lawman in the field, a lousy bureaucrat in the office.

When I'd been chief deputy, then undersheriff, and finally sheriff of Posadas Country, I'd enjoyed many a refreshing moment while reading young Bobby Torrez's reports—masterpieces of concise brevity. My favorite had been a report written after an intoxicated prisoner punched Deputy Torrez while being led to an upstairs cell. *"Prisoner struck deputy. Prisoner fell down stairs."* Fortunately for us, the prisoner had been so intoxicated that he remembered nothing of the episode, content the next day to attribute his colorful bruises to the blind staggers.

I made my way across to where Frank Dayan stood in company with Deputy Sutherland. Frank could have blended in on a street corner anywhere in the Middle East, even though I knew that he was the first generation of many in his family to stray beyond the city limits of San Antonio. Dark, piercing eyes were mellowed by a wide streak of indecision in his nature, with fine features and whiskers that lent a dark blue, Nixonesque shadow if not shaved four times a day. This uproar had caught him unprepared, and in the glare of pulsing lights, he looked both haggard and chilled.

"Bill, they even rousted you out of bed?"

"I wish I could say that it was their fault," I said. He pulled off a glove and his grip was soft, but he held on for a moment.

"I thought I was going to need an act of Congress to get through the road block there at the village limits," he said. "The sheriff sent me out here."

"Bobby is turning mellow in his middle age," I said. "But homicides are like that. If we don't keep a tight rein, things go missing. Like evidence, for instance."

"Someone said it was Kenderman. Is that true?"

I wondered who the 'someone' was, but didn't bother Dayan with that. His paper wouldn't be out until later, and by then, the whole world would have the identification.

"The undersheriff asked that I be the department liaison this time around," I said without answering his question. "The department is spread pretty thin just now." Even that was a bit of news for Dayan. Some police administrators would have ulcers thinking that the public might find out that the department had a weakness, but what the hell. It was true.

Dayan peered past me, trying to make sense of the tangle. "Do I see three sets of poles down?"

"You do. Dick Whittaker will talk with you about that when he can break loose."

"How did they do that?" The lens of Dayan's camera twitched as he went to the maximum zoom, trying to see through the darkness.

"A chain saw."

He lowered the camera. "A chain saw? You've got to be kidding." He jotted something in his notebook. "At least two people involved, then?"

"Investigation is continuing."

"Well, you have one lying there," and he nodded in the direction of the tarped victim. "Right? Do we have an identification yet?"

"Investigation is continuing."

Dayan looked pained. "Bill…come on. Is this somebody local?"

"We'll…*they*…will have that for you later in the day, Frank."

"Shot, or what?"

I hesitated, actually eager to give Frank *something*, anything that would reward his answering a winter night's call. "It appears now that one of the poles might have struck the victim when it kicked off the stump as it twisted and fell." I held up a cautionary hand. "That's preliminary supposition, Frank. And it's supposition from me, your basic 'unnamed spokesman,' not from the S.O." The newspaperman saw all the pieces tumbling into order.

"You found the chain saw?"

"Not as far as I know."

"Or a vehicle?"

"Not yet."

"That means that there *was* somebody else. So they high-tailed it out of here and were stopped sometime later by Deputy Kenderman."

"I don't hear a question in all that, but let me caution you that as of now, there is no connection between the two events."

Dayan grimaced. "You're as bad as the sheriff, Bill."

"We have to be careful until we know what we're talking about." I was fully aware that this 'we' business was becoming too easy. "Just between you and me, off the record, and blah, blah, blah, it *appears* that's what happened. They don't have an actual link yet, so don't jump the gun."

"Chainsaws are noisy, though."

I held out my arms and turned in place. Not a single porch light winked. Had the electricity been on, the sight would have been the same. True enough, chain saws were noisy, but the sound would mellow and fade, the direction hard to pinpoint out on this vast prairie.

"What actual damage was done?" He held up his hands like blinders, trying to see past the kaleidoscope.

"Again, Whittaker will have all the numbers. They dropped three sets of double supports—double poles. They went down, along with all the associated high voltage lines and at least one transformer. Something in all that mess shorted out and started a little fire. The Posadas Fire Department responded promptly and had it out in minutes." Didn't I sound like the polished PR man, though.

Dayan took a deep breath. "What's Waddell say?"

"I haven't talked to him, Frank." At least not since the day before, but that was none of the public's business. Across the way, the rancher was still posted at his truck, but now two other figures kept him company.

"I need to show you something," Dayan said. "Do you have a couple of minutes?"

"Sure." I followed the newspaperman back to his little SUV, and Deputy Sutherland, who had remained at a discreet distance while we talked, returned to his post in the middle of the road.

"I just received this yesterday." Dayan leaned into his car. He emerged with a file folder and extracted a single sheet. I took it and focused my flashlight on it. "They want to run it as a half-page ad."

"'They' being…" and then something twanged in my head, a warning that I was treading on slippery turf. Just as the sheriff's department didn't share the files of its daily workings with the public, Frank Dayan's world was governed by similar constraints. I had no intention of falling into the middle of something where I didn't belong. I extended the paper to Frank, but he waved me off.

"No, no. Go ahead. I was going to hunt you up today some-time anyway. I've already made up my mind that I'm not going to accept the ad."

"This came in the mail?"

He shook his head. "Door drop. Along with cash to cover four weeks' insertion."

"Cash?" I adjusted my trifocals and maneuvered the flash-light. The format of the ad was professionally printed, with "1/4 page, 4 wks" written in the top margin in pen. The content was one of those wordy diatribes that folks like to run in small rural newspapers announcing that THE END IS NEAR, or ONLY 5 DAYS LEFT TO FIND JESUS. This one had nothing to do with religious fervor, though. The headline left no room for doubt: THE GOVERNMENT IS WATCHING AND LIS-TENING TO YOUR PRIVATE CONVERSATIONS!!! NO CELL PHONE IS SAFE!!!

The headline, complete with exclamation points, snaked around a photo of a radio telescope much like the ones at the Very Large Array northeast of us near Magdalena. Stealing and modifying a scene from a recent hit film, a black Suburban was parked near one of the antennas. A black-suited man had his briefcase open on the hood, headphones snuggled on his ears.

THEY'RE NOT LISTENING TO THE STARS...
THEY'RE LISTENING TO *YOU!!!*

"What amazing bullshit," I said. What followed, in only marginally smaller print, was a diatribe against government in all forms, the feds in particular. Also targeted was the United Nations, with WORLD ORDER NOW DICTATING THE AMERICAN WAY OF LIFE!!!

Despite the sobering nature of the night so far, with two corpses and an eco-thug stunt that wasn't any brighter than most such, I still managed an amused chuckle as I read on. Then the chuckle died as the silly manifesto became a personal attack.

> DON'T BE FOOLED BY WHAT'S GOING ON IN SOUTHWESTERN POSADAS COUNTY. THAT'S **NOT** AN INNOCENT OBSERVATORY CURRENTLY UNDER CONSTRUCTION ON THE MESA. DO YOU WANT A UNITED NATIONS LISTENING POST AND COMMAND CENTER IN YOUR NEIGHBORHOOD? DO YOU WANT FOREIGNERS CONTROLLING YOUR LIFE, YOUR COMMUNICATIONS, EVEN YOUR EVERY THOUGHT? DO YOU WANT A RUNWAY FOR MILITARY JETS AND SURVEILLANCE-ATTACK DRONES IN YOUR BACKYARD?
>
> JOIN THE FIGHT NOW. TAKE THE FIRST STEPS WITH US IN OUR RESISTANCE TO THIS INTRUSION. FIGHT FOR YOUR RIGHTS!

"Christ, now we've got the 'resistance,'" I muttered. At the bottom of the ad was the admonition, JOIN WITH US TO DRIVE THE FOREIGNERS FROM POSADAS COUNTY. RETURN YOUR HOME TO **YOUR** CONTROL. ENJOY PEACE, PRIVACY, AND ABOVE ALL, **HOME RULE.**

Centered on the bottom margin, PAID FOR BY THE COMMITTEE OF AMERICAN VALUES didn't include a name or address. So what did one join, and with whom?

"Dropped off, you say? You obviously didn't see who it was."

"Nope. Dropped in the mail slot through our front door. That and twelve hundred dollars in cash. All hundred dollar bills."

"Twelve hundred bucks. Not bad, Frank. That's a serious investment on their part."

"I just can't do that. Not an ad without a name and address. I mean, hell." He scratched his head. "I don't know what to do with the money. I mean, I can't return it, unless somebody comes forward. But I won't run the ad. That's final." He took the ad copy and slid it back into the envelope. It would have been easy to laugh the ad off, but twelve hundred bucks was serious ammunition. The tally was now two deaths and a heap of money. That was no laughing matter.

"You need to show that to the sheriff," I suggested. "There's an implied connection there that he'll want to see. And he'll want to process the originals. There's nothing I can do for you, except tell you to be careful. We're dealing with some serious fruitcakes here, Frank. Be very, very careful. Tell Pam the same thing." His editor didn't move from her chair often, but she was well known—and well liked—around the community.

Dayan grimaced, and I could understand his conundrum. Newspapers didn't relish collaborating with law enforcement agencies. Once independence is lost, once it's more than just buying a cup of coffee for a friend, it is hard to go back. "I thought I'd show you, and let it go at that. I can't return the cash, since I don't know where to send it. Maybe they'll come pick it up in person."

"Let's hope not," I said. "I'll mention the ad to the sheriff and undersheriff if you want me to, but beyond that…"

"Well, you know everybody on the planet, and I thought you might have some ideas who would send something like this." He offered me a sympathetic smile, but it quickly vanished. "You think this," and he held up the envelope, "is related to this vandalism?"

"At this point, I wouldn't hazard a guess, Frank." I reached out and tapped him on the chest. "But you be careful."

He puffed out his cheeks in exasperation, then shook his head. "You haven't had such good luck staying retired lately."

"I'm just being helpful right now," I said. "I don't know anyone who would write nonsense like this. But do talk to Bobby or Estelle. They both understand the ticklish position

you're in. That's my advice." I hesitated. "Between you and me,
I got roped into this mess just because I was sitting up there
on the top of Cat Mesa," and I turned and gestured toward the
northeast, "stargazing and pondering deep thoughts. I saw the
flash of the transformer when it hit the ground, and gave the
S.O. a shout. And here I am, a material witness now. No good
deed goes unpunished, Frank." As compelling as it might appear
in print, I did not add that I'd also seen a vehicle leaving the
scene at a high rate of speed.

I nodded at the envelope. "If you want me to talk to Bobby,
may I have a copy of that ad?"

"You can take this one, if you want. I have the original in
our safe."

I held the envelope up so the lights caught it. No printing or
label on it whatsoever. "Is this the original envelope?"

"Yes. I took the ad and cash out."

"Who else besides you has handled this?"

Frank looked uncomfortable. "You mean, like fingerprints?"
I nodded. "Nobody other than you. I picked it up off the floor
below the mail slot. Nobody else in our office touched it. I
didn't show it to anyone, because I didn't want office rumors
spreading something."

"Good man. Then it's got your prints and mine, and maybe
of someone else interesting." I held the envelope gingerly by the
corners. "You just never know. Leave the money and paperwork
in your safe. Don't mess with it until you hear from the Sheriff."

"I haven't had the chance to talk to Miles Waddell yet.
Should I?"

"Well, let me ask you a favor. Of course, you're free to talk
with anyone you want, Frank. But it seems to me that the tighter
we keep this just now, the better off we are. Let me take this,
show it to Bobby and Estelle, and maybe talk to Miles. Whoever
wrote this nonsense is talking about Waddell's property, and
he should be up to speed on what's going on behind his back."

"You'll keep me in the loop?"

"Of course."

"And no word yet on the victim?"

"Estelle will release all of that as soon as she can, Frank."

He turned and looked east. Dawn was thinking about it. "I'd like to try for some pictures in a bit."

"Suit yourself." The image of a power line leg kicked high on top of an old juniper post, with a crowd of folks with bags under their eyes, might make for good camera fodder. I didn't need to be included.

I left Frank with Deputy Sutherland as his escort, and trudged over to the second set of power poles. Undersheriff Estelle Reyes-Guzman was kneeling at the remains of one of the poles, in conversation with Dick Whittaker, superintendent of Posadas Electric. She would pump him for every scrap of information he knew. When she had to testify, she'd know more about power lines and all their accoutrements than most veteran linemen. Whittaker, a stump of a man with prematurely snow white hair that sprayed out from all sides of his baseball cap, rose and offered a hand as I approached.

"I understand you've been sleepwalkin' again, Bill." The crinkles around his eyes faded. Nobody was much in the mood for humor. "Bobby tells me that you saw all this go down."

"Don't we all wish that," I said. "I saw the flash of the transformer when it hit the ground. And that was from where I was sitting up on Cat Mesa, twenty miles away. That's it."

"Well, this son-of-a-bitch used a good, sharp saw. I'd guess a fair-sized one, too, lookin' at the size of those chips. Creosote-treated line poles aren't the easiest firewood to take, I'll tell you that. Your man came ready to do business. Damnedest thing. I tell you what, I've known Curt Boyd since he was this big," and he held his hand at knee level. "Never figured him for something like this."

"I'll bet you the farm that Curt was just a bystander," I said.

"You think?"

In all probability, Estelle hadn't mentioned the accomplice in the speeding truck. She pushed herself off her knees and looked quizzically at the envelope I held.

"You have a minute?" I asked.

She nodded. Whittaker swept his flashlight toward the downed transformer. "I'll see how the boys are comin'."

The two of us watched Whittaker make his way around the clumps of cacti and stunted prairie grass, and when he was out of earshot, I said, "Frank passed this on to us. To you, I mean. I'm just the postman." Estelle read the ad copy, sharing with so many people the odd habit of starting at the bottom, skimming here and there, and finally returning to the top of the copy, her flashlight ambling down the lines of type as she read.

"I wonder if Mr. Waddell has any idea what he's set in motion," she whispered. A couple hundred yards away, the rancher was still rooted in place, now with two or three shadowy figures I couldn't make out.

"Without a doubt. Small as this county is? I'd like a dollar for every time somebody's asked me what the hell Miles Waddell was building out here. I tell 'em that as far as I know, he's erecting an observatory, and the response is usually a scoff of disbelief. 'He ain't puttin' no telescope up there,'" I said, mimicking an atrocious drawl, "'not with that fancy road.'"

"When was the last time you were in this area, sir?" I'd known Estelle since she was a child playing in the Mexican dust, adopted by an aging school teacher, and in all those years, my name had never passed her lips—at least not in direct conversation with me. She chose *Sir* or Padrino, the latter being the rough equivalent of *godfather*, which I was to her two boys, Carlos and Francisco.

"As a matter of fact, yesterday afternoon. This past afternoon. I was doing my daily constitutional, checking out a piece of prairie behind Bennett's Fort. I told you I found that old revolver? I had to see if there was anything else in the same spot." The rugged little mesa to the north had captivated my attention ever since I'd found an axe-head there the previous summer that was the right vintage to belong to a homesteader—perhaps Josiah Bennett himself. And with it sprang the intriguing idea that the axe-head *might* have some century-old blood on it. Pulling in a few favors, the resulting lab tests had been negative.

"You didn't see anyone?"

"As a matter of fact, I did. Waddell and I talked for the better part of an hour." I pointed at the cattle guard. "Right over there, where he's standing now. It was so quiet we could hear the transformer humming. He told me the power company has him scheduled for a new one. Bigger and better. A whole goddamn substation. You need to talk with him."

"No one else?"

"Nope. No figures skulking around with a concealed chain saw. And you know, on the way back into town yesterday, I caught a glimpse of Perry Kenderman. He was just pulling out of the parking lot behind the dry cleaners." I winced at the memory. "You never know, do you? You never know when it's the last time you're going to see somebody."

And that prompted the thought that within minutes, if he hadn't already heard, rancher Johnny Boyd would learn that his son was lying dead on the prairie, sucker punched by a utility pole. I wondered what father and son had talked about the last time they were together, whether they had argued, reminisced, planned for a big day sometime soon…all those things humans do.

"This sort of night makes me want to crawl back into my cave," I said, and Estelle smiled in sympathy. She reached out a hand and held me by the elbow.

"Thanks for coming out, Padrino. Remember we had green chile stew and corn bread planned for tonight. Six o'clock…or so."

I sighed. "We might make it. You're going to be out here a long time, sweetheart." She had never minded my pet name for her, used in the privacy of our own company. I guess I could have called her *ahijada,* the Mexican for *goddaughter,* but "sweetheart" was easier to pronounce. "Bobby has the road into town locked up. Who the hell knows what direction this is all going to take. I'll be around later in the day to type up a formal deposition. That won't take long."

"There's always time to eat."

"I'm glad to hear you say that. And I look forward to coaxing some of these deep, dark concert secrets out of Carlos." I touched the button on my watch and saw the faintly illuminated 4:41 a.m. The Don Juan de Oñate restaurant's back door would open in another hour as Fernando Aragón, his wife and daughter, arrived to start prepping for the day. They'd find time to make me a proper breakfast. Maybe that would suggest some sleep.

"Can you spring Waddell free for a bit?" I reached out and touched the envelope I'd given to Estelle. It now resided in a large plastic evidence bag. "You know, when Miles and I met out here yesterday, we didn't talk about this. He might not even know that he's in the cros-hairs. He was so excited about a new telescope he's wheeling and dealing for with some folks out in California, that's all we discussed—other than my Bennett project."

"He's been reminded that he'll need to come in for a deposition as well," Estelle said.

"You don't mind me prowling around a little? I'd like to know more about that." I nodded at the envelope. "I know a lot of people, but not a soul who would pull a stunt like this. Most people only rant and rave when it's free. I mean, people enjoy silly rumors."

"Sir," she scolded. "You prowl all you want."

Chapter Six

Fernando Aragón admitted Waddell and me through the back kitchen door of the Don Juan de Oñate restaurant with the dawn, and despite his good-natured grumblings, I knew that we wouldn't have to wait more than ten minutes before Fernando served up the sort of breakfast that warmed the cockles—whatever *they* are. Part of it was curiosity. From the Don Juan, the light show of emergency vehicles was just a quarter-mile down the road. It was too bad that *he* didn't have insomnia. Had he been standing in his dining room, looking out the west window, he might have witnessed Kenderman's ill-fated traffic stop.

Returning to town, I had been able to navigate the roadblocks, but Miles Waddell hadn't. He'd left the scene down at the northern border of his ranch and driven the long way around to Posadas—first south, then twenty-eight miles to the village by way of State Road 56. He was still stopped three times.

When the rancher-now-developer sat in the booth across from me, he stood his impressively buttoned cell phone on the table beside his napkin, turned so that the screen faced him. His trademark purple neckerchief nicely complemented his smooth, tan skin. Somehow, the New Mexico sun, wind, and single-digit humidity had never wrinkled him.

"So how much do you want to know?" Waddell hunched forward, both hands curled around his coffee mug, voice lowered to a husky whisper. "They hauled your ass out of retirement, now? And what the hell were you doing up on Cat Mesa at one o'clock in the morning, for Christ's sakes?"

"It was a beautiful night," I replied. "Who would want to miss that? At least until about twelve minutes after one. Then it went all to hell."

Waddell leaned back and swept an arm up to rest on the booth's plastic back. "You can't imagine how *far* to hell this is going." He patted the neckerchief at his throat as if an errant breeze might have blown it askew. Natty was the word for Miles, with his scarf, pressed shirt, and *almost* creased blue jeans. His expensive boots carried just enough dust, with honest-to-God scuffs above the heels where his spurs fitted. Deep crow's feet around his eyes broke the mahogany of his tan only when he smiled—and he wasn't doing much of that this morning—he'd show a set of teeth just crooked and just white enough for strangers to peg him as a Hollywood character actor.

"Are you…" and he made a come and go motion with his hand, "with the department for this?"

"I have to write a deposition, same as you. I saw the flash when the transformer popped, and I might have seen a vehicle leaving the scene. And that's just between you and me."

"That's all?" The crow's feet deepened, and the light-blue eyes regarded me with amusement.

"No, that's not all. But nothing formal. I told Estelle I would talk to you."

He ducked his head and leaned out of the booth, mimicking a search for a hidden microphone.

"Are you okay with that?" I asked.

"Sure. Why the hell not? So the ground rules are that anything I say to you might well be passed on to the sheriff's office."

"Yes. That's a good way to go. If I think they need it."

"Better them than some others I can think of," he sighed. "I haven't even seen Torrez around."

"He spent most of the night just down the road." I nodded out the window. "Likely he's gone fishing down in Cruces. That's where Boyd was teaching, and he'll be checking connections down there."

"Hell of a thing, just cold-blooded..." He let that trail off, then added, "They said it was Kenderman." Waddell shook his head wearily. "Young, skinny fella?" I nodded. "He tried to give me a ticket once. He didn't like one of my stock trailers. Said the license plate was obscured."

"Can you imagine?" I laughed. "And was it?"

"Sure. In all fairness, it wasn't on the trailer."

"And he let you talk your way out of it?"

Waddell grinned. "Sure. I had it under the seat of the truck." His face lost all humor. "Were there signs of a struggle?"

"No."

"Well, Christ." He lowered his voice and leaned forward. "Related to the shit down at my place?"

"If I had to guess..."

Fernando brought two loaded plates, enough breakfast for four people.

"You got enough of everything?" he grumbled. "How come you're out so early?" His accent was thick, even though he'd been north of the border for half a century.

"Because we're hungry, Fernando."

He grinned at that and waved a hand. "You holler at me," he said. "Jana will be in before long." The sheriff's cousin had waited tables at the Don Juan for twenty years, and was one of my favorite people. If she had saved all the money I'd dropped on her in tips, she could buy a new truck.

"I wanted to show you this." The rancher had carried a slender attaché case with him, and around the first bites of his breakfast burrito, slipped a hand in and retrieved a newspaper clipping. "Actually, I have two things, but the good news first." He passed a folded newspaper page across the table. I saw it was a tabloid from a San Francisco suburb well inland from the bay. The lead headline announced that folks weren't happy with the public school budget. Were they ever?

Down at the bottom, a modest double column headline announced that "*Origins* Project Finds Home." I read the headline aloud, and glanced up at Waddell. "And *Origins* is...what? That deal you were talking about yesterday?"

Reading a bit further I answered my own question. "A sixty-five meter telescope...my God."

"The old classic at Mt. Palomar is one hundred inches. Imagine sixty-five *meters,* if you can."

"I can't. That's a lens more than two hundred feet across."

"Two hundred fourteen feet, actually. And it's a radio telescope, so there's no lens as we know them," the rancher said with relish. "Just a big round dish that collects sounds from a gazillion light years away...which means a gazillion years in the past. Imagine that? All the way back to what they call the original microwave background out there in deep space. It's not just a big slab of ground glass."

I smiled at his enthusiasm. "Has Frank talked to you yet about this?"

"He called me, and we'll get together today sometime. Other than that, not a soul yet." He reached across and tapped the top of the newspaper page. "And notice that it wasn't important enough to rate the top spot—and the *Chronicle* and the *L.A. Times* haven't run with it. It's in the *who cares* department."

"I would think the good folks at Walnut Haven would be loath to see a project of this size leave their community."

Waddell shrugged and shoveled more burrito. "You can have a sky full of smog and junk," he said around the food, "or you can have the heavens open for viewing. It's hard to have both. They have lots of coastal haze, lots of smog, lots of politics. That's probably the worst polluter. Me, I have clear nights, no traffic, and free land."

I scanned the rest of the article. "'A ranch in southern New Mexico.' No mention of you."

"That's part of the deal."

"You're going to let them install this monster on *your* mesa?"

"Yep."

"That's got to include a large building, with all the computers and control room and this and that."

"More like huge," Waddell said happily. "And some housing."

I recalled an earlier discussion with Miles Waddell when I'd just come out and asked point-blank what his plans were for the mesa. He'd mentioned an observatory, but implied a private one. The new road up to the top suggested a lot more. Rumors had been rife, of course.

"I've signed a ninety-nine year lease with them," Waddell lowered his voice. "A seventy-five-acre patch on the southwest corner of the mesa-top. Got 'em to go for a buck a century. They agreed, and now it's official."

"Well, sure. How could they refuse a deal like that?"

"Exactly the point. No traffic, no lights, no pollution. Flat, dark, and apparently perfect orientation for whatever portion of the night sky they want to listen to." He glanced toward the kitchen as Fernando appeared with more coffee, and we waited until he'd left us to our little dark corner.

"See, they even drilled a couple exploratory holes in the mesa-top to make sure we weren't sitting on top of a limestone honeycomb. From a geological point of view, it's an unshakeable location, even with the limestone caverns at the north end of the mesa that the BLM is interested in developing someday."

"As unshakeable as anything is on this old planet," I observed. I read the story again. "Christ, Miles, it's going to cost a fortune to bring that monster up to the mesa-top. What's it weigh… five hundred tons?"

The rancher settled back and carefully balanced his fork on the edge of the plate. "Actually, I know *exactly* what it's going to cost." His tone was cautious, and he'd shed a little of his rancher's accent. "To sweeten the deal for them, I'm paying a portion of the transportation costs." He held up a hand. "Just a portion. Sure, it'll take a fair chunk of change. That baby weighs nine hundred and sixty tons, Bill. That's when it's all bolted together. Still, there'll be sections of it that come up to thirty tons or more.

That's why the new road. You haven't been up there in a while, have you? That old gun you found has you occupied."

"The road is gated," I said wryly, not that I was ever averse to slipping over a fence or through a stock gate.

"We'll get you up there."

"And here all this time, I imagined you were going to buy yourself a ten-inch reflector and a lawn chair."

Waddell laughed loudly. "You ain't seen the half of it, my friend. But what's keeping you busy after all this?" He held up another loaded fork. "Other than writing a deposition or two? They got you working this case? Or are you settling in with a box of fresh pencils and a stack of legal pads to write your memoirs?"

"No. I told Estelle I'd help where I can, but this is a young man's game. Hell, by the time the morning's over, they'll have *federales* involved, every state agency there is, and enough overtime requisitions to make the county legislators quake in their boots."

"I guess we can expect all that." He opened the leather case again. "You ready for the bad news?"

"Whether I am or not…"

"See, you mentioned rumors before." He hesitated with papers half out of his briefcase. "What's your favorite?"

"You mean the most ridiculous one?"

"I'd like to hear that."

I stirred a puddle of green chile juice with my fork. "I'd have to say that whatever it is you're doing up there is designed to support a United Nations peacekeeping and drug interdiction force, with massive programs to randomly tap cell phone traffic. And on top of that, an airbase for surveillance drones. That tops my list."

"Mine too." Waddell slipped another publication out of his briefcase, this time a glossy, well-funded conservative Colorado publication that I recognized. "Friend of mine with the Colorado Livestock Board sent me this." He had folded the paper so page seven prominently displayed the headline, *"Foreign Domination of Ranchlands Gains Another Foothold."*

"Oh, for Christ's sake," I growled. Posadas County's desiccated desert and short bunch-grass prairie country was conspicuously mentioned in the first paragraph, but Waddell was not mentioned by name—much like the ad that Frank Dayan had showed me. Written to imitate a breaking news story rather than a diatribe, the article still accomplished the same thing… spreading nonsense.

"How did they find out about the Walnut Haven project? And since when is California *foreign?*"

"It's not?" Miles laughed. "But look, somebody knows somebody. And you know, that doesn't bother me. It's all coming out here shortly. I plan to let Frank in on the whole thing, by the way, and let him scoop the other papers. I mean, the big dish is hot news, Bill. They'll employ two dozen people, from telescope gurus to janitors." He took a deep breath and looked out the window at the blank, cold sky. "The thing that irks me is trying to figure out why a project like this has to be a clandestine scheme of some sort." He turned to look at me. "Why it can't just be what it is?"

"Because most people are devoid of that kind of imagination, Miles," I said.

"Wish to hell I really did understand. Seems like if it's something that *they* can't imagine, then somehow it must be something dangerous and a threat to truth, justice, and the American way." He grinned ruefully. "I didn't figure on that at the beginning. I figured they'd just say, 'Well, that's crazy Miles, but it's his money.'"

I leaned back, letting the pool of chile settle. I had wondered now and then about Miles Waddell's source of income—he didn't earn it punching a small herd of cattle. But that was none of my business. "You know, I've heard a few folks talking about the mesa project. When they ask me what I think is going on, I tell 'em that I've heard you say you're building an observatory of some sort. And that's it."

Waddell squinted one eye like a wild schemer. "Ah…but observing *what*…that's the paranoid part. Look," and he laid down his fork. "You have some time this morning, before all this deposition shit lands on our heads?"

"A little time. The depositions are critical, Miles."

"Run out there with me. For just a few minutes."

I glanced at my watch and saw six o'clock straight up. The sun was just touching the tops of the buildings across the street. "We can do that."

"See, I want to show you the plan for *NightZone*, but up there, where it makes sense. The whole dream. It'll blow your socks off."

Swimming the last bite around the platter, I sighed with contentment. "All right. Let the day begin."

"You can leave your rig here if you want," Waddell offered. "I have to come back to town anyway."

I pushed myself out of the booth and slid two twenties under the edge of my plate, waving off his offer as he dug for his wallet. "Tell you what," I said. "Let me follow you out. With the mess we have this morning, I never know what's coming up. I need my wheels." I grinned. "My mobile office."

"Hell of a retirement you've got going," Waddell said. "I'll meet you at the gate."

And that should have been simple enough.

Chapter Seven

State Highway 56 approached the village of Posadas from the southwest. It was heavily used by Posadas standards, carrying not only the rumble and clatter of local ranchers with their stock trailers, but traffic to and from Mexico and from southern Arizona. Snowbirds with enough spirit of adventure to pull their big RVs off the interstates used it, as did the burros who pulled used cars in tandem for sale in Mexico. And one way or another, a flood of illegal aliens used the highway, walking its shoulders, stuffed in vans or trucks, or driving their own well-worn piece of the American dream.

I turned south on Grande Avenue toward State 56, letting Miles Waddell cruise on ahead. I didn't need to eat his dust when, in twenty-six miles, we would turn off on County Road 14. But I didn't even make it out of town. I was still a quarter-mile north of the Posadas Inn and the interstate's overpass when I saw Waddell's brake lights flash, and then another light show of a different sort. A mammoth RV trundled northbound toward me, passing under the interstate with a sheriff's patrol unit glued so close to its back bumper that the county unit might have been a vehicle in tow.

Sergeant Jackie Taber, having already worked most of the night out at the crime scene, was starting her day shift by catching a speeding snowbird. By the time I passed McArthur Circle, the first street a long block north of the interchange, the RV had heaved across my path and into the Posadas Inn's parking lot, angling far off to one side. It halted beside one of the towering light poles. Taber followed in close formation, and as the RV came to a stop, pulled forward and to one side so she had a clear view of the RV's front door.

I glanced ahead to see Waddell's ranch truck enter the sweeping bend to State 56 far ahead, a burst of dark exhaust telling me that he had his foot in it. I was poking along, true to habit. As I came up on the parking lot, I looked across and saw that Jackie Taber had gotten out of her car and was moving around the driver's door. The door of the RV had opened, and I could see a figure on the top step, bare knees and shins just visible.

Body English is everything. Even at a quick glance, I could see the tension in Taber's body. Left hand extended in the universal "halt" gesture, right hand drifting back toward the butt of her service automatic, her knees had flexed as she turned. And sure enough, the figure in the doorway of the RV appeared to be holding a weapon of some sort. That's what I saw, and that's what I acted on.

Too late to turn into the parking lot's last entrance before the interstate interchange, I braked hard and cranked the SUV around to the left, executing a U-turn directly under the overpass. The turn continued, bringing me 270 degrees around to face the parking lot entrance. And there I had an unobstructed view of the huge, square ass-end of the RV, tinted windows revealing nothing inside. Ahead and off to my right was Jackie Taber, hand on gun and barking orders. The bulk of the RV hid the doorway from my view, and I swung right just wide enough that I could make out the figure standing there. Stopping well to the rear and just to the left of Taber's unit, I slammed the gear lever into Park.

I knew all the ways a civilian could get himself into trouble by arriving in the middle of a crime scene, running the risk of upsetting what might be a delicate balance established by the responding officer. Who knows what the mind-sets of those involved might be. At that point, I acted out of that zone that cops sometimes call "trained instinct."

My Dodge Durango was bright red—not obviously a police vehicle, but who the hell knows these days. With an armed confrontation going on, I wasn't about to look the other way and cruise past. Nor could I just sit in the car and wait and see what transpired. The sheriff's department radio that was bolted under the dash was silent, the idiot light dark, and I didn't take the time to reach down to turn it on. No doubt Sergeant Taber had called in the stop, and even as I got out of the SUV, I saw her left hand snap up to the little microphone on her shoulder epaulet.

I had time to take two steps forward, putting me immediately beside the left front fender of my SUV. The figure in the stairwell of the RV shifted position, and I saw the long barrel of a gun swing down. Distinctly, I heard three words, barked out in command by Sergeant Taber.

"Put the gun…" and that's as far as she got.

The blast was incredibly loud and sharp, and Sergeant Taber disappeared from my view. As if acting entirely on its own, my right hand swept back and found my stubby magnum, nestled under my jacket. As the barrel of the assailant's gun swept toward me, I drew and fired. The man—now I could tell that's who it was—was in quartering view to me, still on the steps of the motor home. Even as I pulled the trigger the first time, he was starting to turn awkwardly. The recoil of the .357 was harsh if I thought about it, but during that episode, I never felt it. I continued to fire until I saw the assailant's shotgun clatter to the parking lot and he crashed onto the RV's steps, one leg angling crazily out the door.

Motion to my right became Jackie Taber, picking herself up with one hand on the bumper of her vehicle, the other holding her automatic pointed in the general direction of the RV. Still thinking on their own, one of my hands opened the cylinder of the Smith and Wesson and pumped out the five empties, and the other groped the Speed Loader out of my left jacket pocket. By the time I realized what I was doing, I'd advanced a step or two, and could see the man writhing on the steps of the RV, blood pouring down his Hawaiian shirt, across his snow-white Bermuda shorts, and onto the chrome of the RV.

He made no move toward the shotgun, and I closed the distance in a few strides.

"Oh, my God," the man gurgled. There didn't appear to be another weapon within his reach. I chanced a quick glance to the right, and saw Jackie advancing, automatic extended. The swell of relief was palpable. She was up and efficient again.

"Secure the shotgun, sir," she barked at me, with no quaver, no hesitation, no gasping for breath. Without having to worry about her, my brain was free to do something constructive. I didn't want that gun—and I could see it was a fancy, long-barreled thing—to move an iota from where the assailant had dropped it. Once a crime scene is altered, there's no going back.

In the distance, I could hear two sirens, so I stepped to the shotgun that lay well out of the wounded man's reach and just stood there, looking up at the dark side windows of the RV above me. I saw no motion, no shadows. I heard no latches snapping open, no one crawling out a back window.

"Sir, try to hold still." Taber's voice was still heavy with command, but now tinged with a little bit—a very little bit—of concern. I turned and saw that her uniform blouse—despite the nip in the February air, she hadn't been wearing a jacket—was pocked with a couple dozen pellet tears. On the left side of her jaw bone, a little pimple of blood beaded.

Her assailant moaned something, trying to shift position. "My hand…"

Well, sure enough, his right hand had seen better days. It had been gripping the wrist of the shotgun when one of my bullets blew his thumb off just above the base joint—and not a neat job, either. That didn't concern me as much as the mat of blood that was soaking the left side of his shirt just below the armpit, and another leak from his right hip. He moved a little, eyes trying to focus, and when he did, I saw a puddle of blood on the step behind his head.

Neither Jackie nor I was about to clump past him into the RV to rummage for clean towels. The EMTs would be on-site anyway soon enough—that plus the little matter of *securing* the RV. We didn't have a clue who might be inside, or what their intent might be.

"The ambulance will be here in a minute, sir. Just try to hold still." I managed to sound concerned too, but my concern sure wasn't directed at him. With that threat neutralized, Sergeant Taber was headed up into the RV, gun leading the way.

"Tisha," the man said clearly, and then his eyes rolled up in his head and he sagged against the aluminum door frame, out for the count. His breathing was strong, and I saw no red fountains, so there wasn't much for me to do except stand there, revolver in hand, trying to slow my own pounding heart.

The thirty seconds was an eternity while Jackie was inside and before the ambulance appeared in a great cascade of winking lights. Farther up the street another vehicle bellowed, siren loud and piercing. Sure enough, Undersheriff Estelle Reyes-Guzman's Charger overtook the ambulance, and braked hard to swing into the motel parking lot.

I head Jackie's soft voice behind me as she appeared in the doorway.

"...CYF officer ASAP," she was saying, and I saw her wipe the blood off her chin as she holstered her automatic and switched the phone to her other hand. "One juvenile, looks to be three or four." And sure enough, the little flaxen-haired girl, eyes like saucers, stood in the small space behind the driver's seat, shielded by Jackie's husky figure. The deputy bent down and scooped the child up. Quick to recognize where safety was, the tiny arms locked around Jackie Taber's neck.

First impressions can be wonderful, I suppose. As the undersheriff swerved into the parking lot, and what did she see? An old man holding a .357 magnum, and his target collapsed on the steps of the RV, a Bermuda-shorted snowbird punched full of holes. Above them on the RV's steps, Sergeant Taber holding a child. I had no doubt that Estelle's analytical gaze pulled in all the details.

"The RV is clear," Jackie announced.

I took a deep breath and holstered my revolver. Now that there *was* time for both a breath and some reflection, I knew that every step, every word, every action that came next would be scrutinized six ways from Sunday. As my first sheriff, the late Eduardo Salcido, had been fond of saying in tricky situations, "Make it right."

Carrying the child, Jackie maneuvered down the RV's stairs past the leaking guy in Bermuda shorts, and met Estelle halfway. The ambulance stopped behind the undersheriff's sedan, and the two EMTs waited for some sort of cue. It was their scene now, but they needed to know that the bullets had stopped flying.

The sergeant and the undersheriff conferred for just a handful of seconds, and then Estelle was at the wounded man's side, beckoning the EMTs. She didn't say anything to me, knowing that I wasn't about to go anywhere. At that precise moment, what had happened…the *how* of it all…mattered not a bit. If the child was safe, that was number one. The rest of the team would work on saving the shooter's life.

Staying well out of the way, I watched the EMTs work, and felt a small—very small—surge of optimism. I could see that the head shot was a glancing gouge just above and behind the man's right ear. If he was lucky, the slug hadn't cracked his skull.

The wash of blood soaking his Hawaiian shirt came from a six-inch laceration where a hollow point had ploughed first across the flab of his upper left chest, then took a chunk out of his left biceps.

He awoke enough to emit a pathetic groan as they lifted him onto the gurney. One of the EMTs rigged IVs and took vitals while the other looked at the hip wound—probably the worst of the lot. It was a clean, straight-on puncture on the front upper hip well below the beltline, which meant that the slug most likely had wreaked havoc somewhere inside the old guy's bowels. No exit wound meant that slug had caromed around inside his pelvic girdle—a wound that could be fatal as easily as not.

A little white SUV pulled into the parking lot, and I recognized the pudgy figure of Jerri Jaramillo, one of the reps from Children, Youth, and Families. To arrive so quickly, she must have been just up the street. The little girl was our main concern, and Jackie Taber hadn't relinquished her hug on the child since carrying her off the RV. The transfer took only seconds, the child shielded from the curious, from the blood and violence.

I remained near the shotgun and watched as Estelle conferred with Taber, at one point examining the pellet wound on the sergeant's jaw. The recently arrived second team of EMTs did their own examination in the discreet cover of the ambulance, making sure that none of the other shotgun pellets had missed Taber's vest. I don't care how tough you are, when the bullets stop flying, there's a trauma that goes beyond the physical wounds. After some hushed consultation with her boss, Jackie Taber agreed to ride to the emergency room in the ambulance for a checkup.

Estelle Reyes-Guzman took a circuitous route back over to me. "One of the pellets glanced off her badge and cut her jaw. Just a nick." The undersheriff looked hard at me again. "You're okay?"

"Absolutely fine."

She looked down at the shotgun as if she were examining a recently axed rattlesnake. "He shot just once?"

"Yes. The expended shell casing is right there." I nodded to my right, where the red hull lay on the asphalt. I wasn't about to blab on. She didn't need a gusher from me just then. When she wanted more information, she'd ask.

Taking two steps, she moved to the ejected shell casing, knelt, and cocked her head to read the label on the side of the shell. "Number eights." By her demeanor, I never would have guessed that her night and day were well blended. She gave no sign of fatigue, or that we were in the middle of anything other than a serene mid-winter morning.

"And that explains a lot," I said. "She took a charge square in the chest." I thumped myself for emphasis. "Right on the ceramic plate. Bird shot isn't going to hurt her much, other than a hell of a thump."

Estelle still knelt by the shell casing, looking over at the RV's now empty doorway. I could see her measuring, computing. "So Jackie was twenty-five feet or so from the RV when he fired."

"About that. Directly in front of her vehicle."

"Did she have time to give any sort of verbal commands?"

"Yes. 'Put the gun down,' or some such. He fired without warning, and then started to turn toward me."

She pivoted and looked at the scatter of empty .357 cases that I'd pumped out onto the parking lot in front of my own SUV. She didn't question those, or why I'd even been on the scene in the first place. Nor did she explore the obvious first question: Who the hell fired first? All of that would come out in excruciating detail.

A small crowd was beginning to assemble over by the Posadas Inn's portico, and one set after another of red lights arrived as officers tried to realign themselves from one active crime scene to another.

I sighed, feeling weary but, I had to admit, not the least bit repentant. My relief at Taber's good fortune slowed my hammering pulse. I scanned the parking lot, letting the events settle in my mind, and realized that the undersheriff was watching me.

"Are you all right, sir?"

"Just dandy," I said. "It's just going on eight o'clock, and I'm already wondering if this day is ever going to end."

"You were going home?"

"Actually, I was following Miles Waddell. We were headed out to his mesa project. He had some things to show me. I'll catch him on the phone here in a few minutes."

She nodded slowly. "So, in a nutshell?" And I knew that she meant that.

"I saw Jackie northbound on Grande, following the RV with her emergency equipment on. They turned into the parking lot in front of me. As I was driving by, I saw the officer assume a defensive posture consistent with being confronted with an armed suspect. I turned my vehicle around in the street and returned, pulling into the parking lot right there." I pointed where the SUV remained parked. "I had time to step out and then I saw that the man on the RV steps was holding a weapon. Jackie told him to drop it, and the next instant, it went off."

"Had the sergeant drawn her own weapon?"

"No. Her hand was on it, though. That's how fast it all happened. When he fired, I drew my own gun, and as he turned his shotgun toward me, I fired."

"Had the sergeant regained her feet?"

"I don't think so, but of course I wasn't looking her way. It was my impression that she was down for a couple of seconds."

"You fired how many times?" She knew there were five expended casings on the ground, but it was a way of determining how discombobulated I was.

"Five. All that was in the gun. And then I reloaded." I unbuckled my belt and slipped the holster free, extending holster and gun toward her. "It's still loaded."

"I don't need that, sir," she said.

"Oh, yes you do."

She took it without comment. "Are you headed over to the office?" She was being needlessly polite and deferential. We both knew damn well that's where I was going, and whether by invite or order didn't much matter.

"I'll get started on the statement," I said. "And I want to know who that son-of-a-bitch is."

"I'll be in when I can." Estelle, knowing my propensity for roaming the county, added, "If you'd stay within earshot, I'd appreciate it. Feel free to use my office when you settle in to write the statement." What a polite way to tell me to enjoy informal custody. She actually smiled. "Remember we were going to have green chile stew and corn bread tonight. We need to make sure that happens."

I grumped. "You know, at the rate we're going, the whole goddamn county is going down the tube. It's going to take a month of Sundays to clean this up. Any word from Bobby?"

"Not yet, sir. We have a team on the way to Cruces now."

I didn't share her optimism, except that if Waddell's project—whatever the hell it was—turned out to be Paul Bunyan's ultimate target, he'd be back. If he'd seen his friend killed by a freak accident and then on top of that shot a law officer either by tragic accident or to cover his tracks after fleeing the scene, the killer had too much invested now to back off.

On top of that, I knew full well into what sort of a mess I'd managed to put myself.

Chapter Eight

"You don't stay out of trouble long, do you?" Miles Waddell laughed in wonder, but I didn't share his humor. I knew how detailed and excruciatingly accurate a good deposition had to be—over the years I'd ranted at my deputies to put their best into the paperwork, since that's the part that formed the foundation of future court cases. And when the rancher's telephone call jarred my concentration, I managed to strike half a dozen unintended keys on the computer.

He added, "You were a couple of blocks behind me, and then you disappeared."

"Yeah, well. It's turning into that sort of day. I was going to call you, and I got distracted." I listened with only half an ear, the rest of me concentrating on the words on the screen.

"I got as far as the saloon, and stopped to pick up some bottled water. They'd been listening to the whole thing on the scanner. So I headed back." Victor Sanchez's Broken Spur Saloon rose out of the dust beside State 56 twenty-five miles or so southwest of Posadas. Life was slow if all the few patrons had to do was listen to the gibberish on the police radio. And even the age of 10-4's, or 10-9's or 10 anything was dying as the cell phone made life so much easier—and more private.

"Hurrah for spectators. I meant to give you a call. I really did."

"Not a problem, sheriff. Are we going to be able to get together today? Or are they keeping you in the slammer?"

"The day is yet young. If I can, I will. But Miles, you need to buttonhole either the sheriff or undersheriff and bring them up to speed. No telling what might tie in."

"I'll do that. You're going to be all right, though?"

"Don't know."

"You sound pissed."

"I am, Miles. Shooting people does that to me."

"So you really did that, eh?"

"I really did."

"You're all right, though."

"So far."

"Anything I can do?"

"Don't suppose so. They'll be interested to hear from you about when and where you first saw the RV and the deputy."

"They came in on 56," Waddell said. "I met 'em right after the interchange, right on the curve."

"The sheriff is going to want every detail, Miles. Every damn thing you remember."

"I never did see the RV pull over, though. Maybe he thought the deputy would just go on by."

"You need to come on down to the office and offer a formal deposition to that effect. Every little piece is important, Miles."

"Sure. I can do that. That's the guy you shot, though? The old fart driving the rig?"

"That's the guy."

"It looked like Jackie Taber coming up behind him."

"Sure enough."

"She's okay, though?"

"I think so."

"That's good to hear. What a goddamn bizarre world. Look, I've got a couple of things to do, so I'll get out of your hair. I'll catch you after a little bit."

"Don't let this slide," I said. "If you've got something going on that's attracting these chain saw bozos, we need to know about it." *We.* "And by the way, they'd be interested in any sort of communications you've received lately that might be out of the ordinary. The sheriff will need to know anything along those lines."

I hung up the undersheriff's desk phone and leaned back in her comfortable chair, regarding the prose locked on the computer screen in front of me. I could have settled for *he fired, I fired, the end.* But the district attorney would want a little more than that. By the time I'd finished, the damn thing ran two pages. I read the epistle about eight times before sending a copy to file and print.

My door—the undersheriff's door—was cracked, and I could hear the jabber from dispatch and the incessant ringing of the telephone. The lights on Estelle's fancy phone flashed and blinked and died in a fascinating pattern. Nothing motivated me to move, the long hours of the night finally catching up with me. I heard a helicopter in the distance, and wondered if it was the Med-evac, airlifting the former shotgun-wielding, now much punctured, snowbird to more advanced treatment in Las Cruces or Albuquerque.

Had my aim been a little steadier, my target group a little smaller, it would have been his mortal remains heading to autopsy. Now, with him surviving to testify, his family could concentrate on deciding how many millions to sue me for. That didn't worry me much, at least not yet. I'd been sued several times before as folks tried to shift blame. Adults have a marvelous capacity to screw up, and it would not be me, or Mr. Shotgun, who suffered the most from all of this. It would be the tiny three-year-old, who had huddled in terror, while her captor pulled her world down around her terrified little head.

I was daydreaming thus in the undersheriff's office, taking advantage of her hospitality, one image after another parading through my tired brain, head supported on both hands, when Sergeant Jackie Taber appeared in the doorway. Now in civilian clothes, including blue jeans and a western-stitched denim shirt, the only visible sign of her experience was a single small bandage along her lower left jawline.

"Good morning." I sat up straighter. "You cleaned up nicely." She smiled at that, her heavy, square face softening. I touched my own jaw. "What was the deal?" We shouldn't even have been talking, but I was glad to see her up and about and refreshed.

She held thumb and forefinger together. "A little, flat pellet fragment, is all. The tetanus booster hurt more."

"And what's the deal with the child?" I relaxed back in the chair and latched my hands on top of my head…a pose that I'd assumed half a thousand times over the years as I waited for one of the deputies to explain things to me.

"There was a computer hit out of San Diego, their version of an Amber Alert, sir. The shooter is a sixty-eight-year-old grandfather, Nathan Baum, out of Orlando, Florida. He apparently abducted his granddaughter Patricia from her daycare in San Diego and was headed eastbound to rendezvous with the little girl's father. There's a custody suit going on between the girl's mom and the dad. Mom has custody, dad wants custody, and granddad decided to get right in the middle and make things worse. It's my understanding that mom and dad don't like each other much, and *granddad,* the gentleman you ventilated, absolutely hates his daughter-in-law. She never was good enough for his son."

"Ah, one of those. The kid's dad lives in Orlando, too?"

"Actually, he lives in El Paso."

"But it was the grandfather, this Nathan Baum, who drove all the way from Orlando to pick up the kid in San Diego, and then was going to do what…drop her off in El Paso or something?"

"I believe that's essentially correct."

"And I'm supposed to understand all this?"

"I don't think anyone does, sir."

"Do we know yet why he opened fire on you?"

"Sheriff Torrez has a theory, sir. He's working on it."

I covered my tired eyes with both hands. People pulled triggers for all kinds of reasons, but the most common was that during a moment of stress, they didn't know what the hell their trigger fingers were doing. "Sheriff Torrez is working on a lot of things at the moment."

"Yes, sir, he is." She settled her hand on the doorknob and studied the carpet, an industrial shade of brownish green that no one was supposed to notice. "The district attorney and an investigator from the State Police would like to talk with you now, sir." She smiled, a delightful expression that she should have used more often. "Don't blame the messenger. But they're set up in the conference room, and wanted me to tell you they were ready, if you were." What a deferential invitation to the rack *that* was.

I glanced at the clock. They hadn't wasted any time. "Have *you* talked with them yet?"

"No, sir. I suppose shortly."

"I'm surprised they didn't keep us quarantined," I muttered. I made sure my computer file was saved and closed, and pushed up from the desk.

"Thank you, sir."

"For?"

"Stopping when you did."

"I wish I could claim that it's my wide heroic streak," I chuckled. "But it was pure reflex. I didn't even think about it. And I'm glad I didn't." I followed Jackie out of the undersheriff's office. "Let's see what his nibs wants from us."

Chapter Nine

Dan Schroeder looked as if he'd spent the night out on the prairie, far from coffee or comforts. No doubt Sheriff Robert Torrez had kept the district attorney busy. With two and a half corpses, that was to be expected, especially since it was virtually guaranteed that the riddled Mr. Baum would sue us for about the national debt, even though the whole sorry affair was his fault. If he died, the family could have a field day. Schroeder was a good prosecutor, but lawsuits scared him…about half as much as they scared the county legislators.

Usually impeccably turned out, this morning the district attorney was a bit on the scruffy side. Even a hint of peach fuzz touched his cheeks below the black bags under his eyes. He nurtured what little hair he had left in one of those 50s buzz cuts, so *that* wasn't out of place. With his straw-colored suit, Schroeder reminded me of a college singing group's lead tenor—slim, bland-faced, too blond to be true.

He had positioned himself at the end of the small mahogany conference table, a collection of papers and photos spread out before him. A second officer—I couldn't recall his name—regarded me with beady blue eyes caved under a forehead whose supra-orbital ridge looked as if it had borrowed some simian heritage.

Without lifting his head from his hand, elbow planted on the table, Schroeder looked up as I entered.

"Good morning, gentlemen," I said, and Schroeder unwrapped himself, rising as if every joint in his body had failed him. I skirted the table and shook hands.

"Thank…" he started to say as he attempted to generate some grip. He cleared his throat. "Thanks for coming, Bill." He waved a hand under his nose. "Excuse my frog. Something out in the prairie set off my sinuses." He turned to his partner. "You've met Paul Mellon, I'm sure."

Mellon. I'd known Paul Mellon since he was a rookie state policeman patrolling out of the Quemado district, trying to find things to do. He'd become desperate for action a time or two, wandering south to my turf. Most memorable—and it brought a smile for me just then—was his traffic stop of a young off-duty Deputy Robert Torrez just west of Posadas. Bobby's aging, smoking, disreputable Chevy pickup looked as if it belonged hidden behind a barn somewhere, and Bobby himself was a perfect match. Fresh off an interagency drug interdiction deal, the young deputy was unshaven, long of mane and short of temper. The traffic stop with Mellon hadn't gone so well.

A big, raw-boned man, Mellon rose with grace and extended a mammoth paw. As he did so, a smile chased all of the intimidation from his features. Dimples, even. The deep-set blue eyes twinkled.

"Sheriff, it's always a pleasure," he rumbled. With that voice, he could have been a television evangelist. I took my time settling into one of the oak chairs, reminding myself that no amount of *bonhomie* would disguise why we were all here. I had shot a man, and when I did that, I had set in motion the vast complex of legal proceedings. I made a quick resolution to mind my manners.

"Lieutenant Mellon will be the lead investigator this time around." Schroeder scribbled a note on his legal pad. "Are you all right with that?"

Was *I* all right with it? Schroeder was trying to be his soothing best, why I don't know. No elections loomed on the horizon. Both Bobby Torrez and Estelle Reyes-Guzman were conspicuously absent from this little deal, but figuring out why wasn't rocket science. Schroeder would make every effort to assure that his ass was covered, and Mellon's presence, rather than members of the Posadas department, would assure objectivity—perhaps.

"You bet," I said. Lieutenant Mellon apparently didn't believe in paperwork. The table in front of him was bare save for one little yellow pad. A BIC lay capped beside it. Maybe the state cop had already made up his mind, and expected to hear nothing new.

"Tell us what happened," Schroeder said.

I launched into my recitation without preamble, probably sounding rehearsed. I didn't consult my notes, since the episode was engraved in my memory. "After having breakfast at the Don Juan, I was driving southbound on Grande. I observed a large RV northbound on Grande, and saw it pull into the Posadas Inn parking lot. One of the sheriff's department units followed, lights on. By the time I reached the scene, Sergeant Taber was out of her car, and the door of the RV was also open. I saw that Sergeant Taber's hand was resting on her service weapon, and her left arm was raised as if she was issuing commands of some sort. That's all I saw as I passed the scene. I did a U-turn on Grande, and looped back into the parking lot."

Mellon leaned forward, cupping his hands together. "Why did you stop, Sheriff?"

The courtesy title was ubiquitous. Once a Marine, always a Marine. Once a sheriff, always a sheriff.

"It appeared that there was some sort of confrontation. Sergeant Taber's hand was on her weapon, commands were obviously being given. It was not possible to determine how many people were involved—how many might be inside the RV."

"Did you hear Sergeant Taber radio for backup?"

"I did not."

"Was your radio operational?"

"It was not."

"So you didn't hear whether or not Sergeant Taber called in for backup?"

"No." Ask a third time, it would be the same answer.

"At what point could you clearly see that Mr. Baum was holding a weapon of some sort?"

"As I pulled to a stop in the parking lot. He was standing in the doorway of the RV holding the shotgun."

"You immediately recognized it as such?" Mellon sounded a little skeptical.

"Yes."

He picked up the BIC and took his time removing and stowing the top. "When you pulled into the lot, did you actually see Mr. Baum pick up the gun?"

"No. He already was holding it at high port when I arrived."

"When you *first* drove by, was he holding the shotgun?"

"I couldn't see all of him, I couldn't see it."

"But by the time you pulled in, you could see the shotgun clearly?"

"Yes."

"Aimed?"

"Not directly at Sergeant Taber. When I first saw it, it was in the hunter's 'at ready' position, barrel up slightly and to the left."

He made a "go on" gesture, the pen oscillating between two huge fingers.

"I got out of the car, and had time to hear the sergeant shout, 'Put the weapon down.' Or some such. Without warning of any kind, Baum fired. That knocked Taber off-balance, and she stumbled backward directly in front of her patrol unit. Baum started to turn toward me, and my assumption was that he was turning to fire again. I drew my weapon and fired five times."

"Five?"

"That's what the revolver holds."

"Not six?"

"I keep an empty chamber under the hammer. So five."

"Ah, the old west." The crinkles deepened around his eyes. "And at any time did you see motion or activity in the RV? Did you have reason to believe there might be someone else inside?"

"No."

Mellon drew a little squiggle on his pad. "You believed that your field of fire was unobstructed?"

Well, so much for resolutions. I felt my blood pressure surge with the wave of irritation. "I didn't have time to attend a goddamned NRA safety seminar, Lieutenant. I had a clear and threatening target. I saw no one else, no shadows, no motion. I most certainly felt threatened by the shotgun, and at that point didn't know the extent of the sergeant's injuries. I had the clear shot, so I took it."

Mellon reached down beside his chair and rummaged in his briefcase for a moment. He brought the crime scene drawing up and spread it on the table. I saw that fine red lines marked the supposed trajectory of my five rounds.

"A twenty-seven-inch group." He touched the red lines that formed the pattern of my shots. "At twenty-five feet with a stubby magnum, from a draw, rapid fire and under duress…hell of a performance, Sheriff."

I didn't know what Mellon was fishing for, or if his compliments about my shooting were specious or genuine. I settled for silence.

"You were wearing your gun at the time, or carrying it in the vehicle?"

"Belt holster."

"So, concealed carry."

"No. I was wearing a short jacket, but I made no attempt at concealment."

"You have a c.c.p.?"

"I don't consider that germane."

Mellon frowned at his empty pad. "This is apt to go easier if you just answer the questions, Sheriff."

"It'll go how it goes." I knew full well that one of the functions of the interview was to make me angry so that I'd say something stupid and reveal my inner self. So be it. "Whether or not I have a concealed carry permit has nothing to do with the way I might, or might not, have responded in this situation."

Mellon's intense, beady little eyes regarded me for a moment. Eventually he dropped the BIC on the table and folded his hands. Apparently whatever mental tussle he was engaging in resolved itself.

"At any time, did you issue verbal commands to Mr. Baum?"

"No."

"He pointed the shotgun at you and you fired."

"It appeared that he was moving in that direction. If I had to put numbers on it, I'd say that the muzzle of the shotgun was halfway through the arc from the sergeant to me. So yes. I fired, and I fired before he had the chance to bring the gun fully to bear."

Mellon paused again. Dan Schroeder had maintained his studious silence, letting the investigator have the run of the place. "How old are you, Sheriff?"

"Seventy-four."

"Do you still carry a current sheriff's department badge and commission?"

"Yes." Whether they were honorary or functional hadn't been asked.

Mellon waited a few seconds for me to pad my answer, and when I didn't, allowed a trace of a smile to deepen his dimples. He drew another little squiggle on the pad. "When you first saw the RV coming northbound on Grande, did you recognize that there was more than one person onboard?"

"No."

"And so your actions yesterday were based entirely on what you saw as you drove by, and then by the events that transpired after you stopped."

"Yes."

"And what was your intent when you fired your weapon?"

I almost grunted, "Duh," but I knew what Mellon was fishing for, so I gave it to him. "My concern was to end the confrontation, to do whatever was required to take Mr. Baum and his shotgun out of action before he fired a second time."

"Thinking in retrospect now...were you able to revisit this incident, is there anything that you would have done differently?"

"Not a thing. I might make a resolution to practice my marksmanship."

Mellon actually chuckled, showing a line of uniform overly-white teeth. He tore off the doodled page, smoothed a fresh one, and the pen hovered. "Let's run through this one more time," he said.

Chapter Ten

It wasn't just "one more time," and by the third recitation, my blood pressure had spiked and my hands were clamped tightly enough that I was in danger of squeezing the arthritis right out of them.

Lieutenant Mellon had found himself a bone, and he wasn't about to let it go. I knew the drill, though, and took several deep breaths to help wait it out. He was entirely justified, and I knew it. I didn't have to like it.

"When you first drove by the scene, Sergeant Taber was issuing some sort of verbal commands," he said slowly.

"It appeared so."

"You had time to drive a few feet, turn your vehicle in a U-turn on Grande, and then pull into the parking lot of the motel."

"Yes."

"And on top of that, you had time to pull to a complete stop, and then get out of the vehicle."

"That's right."

"How many seconds was that, do you suppose? The whole episode."

"Not very many. A few."

"A *few.*" Mellon tapped the pad. "And it wasn't *until* you arrived and got out of your vehicle that Mr. Baum brought the shotgun to bear, and then fired the single shot. Until that time, Sergeant Taber had control of the situation."

"Control? You don't know that, I don't know that, and I wouldn't be a damn bit surprised if the sergeant didn't know that either. Had she not *seen* a weapon, or heard confrontational language of some sort, there would be no reason for her to back away, hand on gun in a defensive posture. If Mr. Baum had piled out of his RV waving his hands and obviously perturbed, the scenario could well have gone down differently. The fact that Sergeant Taber appeared to be at the ready, hand on weapon, indicates that she perceived a clear threat."

Mellon mulled that for a few seconds and jumped to another road. "I understand you tend to spend the nighttime hours out and about. In fact, I'm told you even witnessed the incident out on the prairie where the young man was killed after cutting a power pole."

"Yes. From twenty miles away, if you want to call that witnessing."

"How did that happen, exactly? You on top of the mesa... pretty desolate place for one o'clock in the morning."

"There is no law, or even code of behavior, that dictates where and when I have to be anywhere," I snapped.

Mellon smiled and held up a placating hand. "So you're out in the boonies, just looking for something to occupy your time. At one o'clock on a February morning."

"You should try it. It's good for the blood pressure."

He ignored that. "When you saw the flashes of light, you immediately drove down the mesa, alerting dispatch as you did so?"

"Not immediately, no. I watched for a while. When it became apparent that there might be a prairie fire, and when I saw a vehicle headed northbound that *could* have been at the scene, yes. Then I called the S.O."

"Why did you feel you needed to do that?"

I took a few seconds to frame my answer, then replied, "Something had obviously happened out on the prairie. There appeared to be a vehicle speeding away from the scene toward town. That's what I reported to dispatch. The whole scenario deserved a look by somebody."

"By you?"

"No. I just sort of gravitated toward town. I was starting to feel the chill a little, and a cup of coffee seemed like a good idea."

"You weren't headed out to investigate those flashes of light?"

"Hell, no. I figured that if the incident actually turned into something—which it did, obviously—that investigators would want a deposition from me. Which they did."

"At what time did you decide to drive out to the electric-line site to see for yourself, then?"

"I didn't decide that. Sheriff Torrez asked me to."

"He was where at the time?"

"On west Bustos, out at the scene of the Kenderman shooting."

"And you arrived there shortly after the event."

"Yes."

"Now who asked you to go *there*? To the site of the officer's shooting?"

"No one. I went on my own. By that time, I was listening to dispatch, another deputy had responded, and I knew something had gone down. As it turns out, I was probably the only person to see the suspect's truck northbound from the power-line site, heading into town. I told dispatch he was headed toward town, and dispatch asked Officer Kenderman to intercept. So…" I let the rest of it go. Had I not called the sheriff's office, Officer Kenderman might still be alive. But that's not the way it worked.

"I see. And hours later, as you were heading home after a very long night, you see another deputy in what you assume is jeopardy, and you stop to render assistance."

"Sure enough. Except I wasn't heading home. I was on my way out to talk with a rancher friend of mine."

"But a long night before that, nevertheless. And yet you claim that you don't roam the county at night actually *looking* for…" and he waved his hand in the air, "*episodes* that might demand your attention."

When I didn't answer, he carefully laid the BIC down again and folded his hands. "Sir?"

"I roam when and where I please, Lieutenant." If I clenched my jaws any tighter, he would have heard enamel chipping. "I go out at night because it's more pleasant than lying in bed alone, staring at the goddamn ceiling. That's one of the joys of insomnia, Lieutenant." I took a long, slow breath. "The very fact that at one o'clock in the morning, I was sitting on a favorite rock way the hell and gone on top of Cat Mesa, looking at stars and thinking great thoughts, would indicate that I wasn't looking for 'episodes' demanding my attention. On the other hand," I said, and then stopped, choosing my words carefully. "If I happen upon something, upon some situation that demands response, I don't like to think that I would hesitate to render whatever aid I could until the appropriate authorities arrive."

Dan Schroeder shifted in his chair and cleared his throat. "Bill, when you drove by the motel parking lot, was Sergeant Taber out of her vehicle?"

"Yes."

"But at that moment, there was no other officer anywhere in the vicinity. At least to the best of your knowledge."

"That's correct."

"Huh," the district attorney grunted. He shook his head. "You have a sheriff's radio in your personal vehicle, do you not?"

"Yes."

"But it wasn't turned on?"

"No."

He frowned and spun his pen between two fingers. "Was there any way for you to tell whether or not the sergeant had walked over to the RV and engaged in an argument of some sort with the driver?"

"I don't think so. There wouldn't have been time. I never actually saw her approach the RV, counselor. Not during the brief time that I could see her as I drove by. She positioned herself toward the front of her Expedition. That's what I saw her do. By the time I turned around and then arrived in the parking lot myself, she was putting space between herself and Mr. Baum. That's what she's trained to do when there's a threatening situation with a weapon involved. So no. I don't think she'd had time to walk over to the RV."

"Could the discharge of the shotgun have been an accident?" Mellon asked.

"Doesn't matter to me," I said. "He had it pointed for action, that's all I know. If he was worried about firearm safety, the gun would have been unloaded and in a gun case back under his bed. But it's obvious to me that he brought it out to use it, loaded and locked and ready to go. *That's* what counts."

"Before this incident, you were eating breakfast at the Don Juan, weren't you."

"Yes."

"Again, alone?"

"No."

"Who was with you?"

"Miles Waddell, a local rancher."

"Ah," Mellon said. "You two discussed the investigations currently underway down at his property?"

"We did not. He knows better, and so do I."

"What did you talk about?"

"That would be none of your business."

The wrinkles around Mellon's ice-cube eyes deepened a touch. "Just a companionable breakfast with old friends."

"Correct."

"And all this at the culmination of a long, difficult night."

I had had worse nights, but I couldn't recall the exact circumstances. I remained silent.

"Let me remind you of what people are going to think," Schroeder said, the politician's side of him finally surfacing.

"I don't care what they think," I snapped, but the district attorney held up a mollifying hand.

"I'm sure you don't, Bill. But with the circumstances…" He pushed his legal pad a few inches away as if it were beginning to smell. "They're going to see you as out hunting something to do. First you arrive on the scene of the fatality down by Waddell's—"

"No, I didn't. I called in curious activity from a vantage point on a mesa-top twenty miles from that power line. By the time I was *sent* to the scene by Sheriff Torrez, several regular officers were already there, including Undersheriff Reyes-Guzman. I had stopped at the scene of Kenderman's murder, but didn't get out of my vehicle. And then," and I held up a hand to fend off the district attorney's poised remark, "I was assigned to talk briefly with Frank Dayan, which I did, telling him essentially nothing. Okay? Then I went to have some goddamn breakfast, and shared a table with Waddell. I then intended to visit a project of his out on the mesa. I was following him out of town, in point of fact, when I stepped in the middle of the Baum incident. Now, I *could* have looked the other way when I drove past the scene of Sergeant Taber's traffic stop, but I didn't. I'm not wired that way." I straightened a crick out of my back and tipped the empty coffee cup, hoping that more coffee had somehow generated itself from the trace of sludge.

"As *you* well know," I directed at Mellon, "when someone fires a shotgun at a peace officer, or at anyone else for that matter, you don't just stand there with your head up your ass, waiting to *see* if the creep is going to fire again. You don't politely ask him what his intentions are. *If* he had dropped the gun and locked his hands on top of his head, I wouldn't have fired. He didn't do that." I picked up the coffee cup as I pushed my chair back, rising stiffly. "Somebody in this place has to have some."

The opening door damn near knocked the cup out of my hand. Sheriff Torrez loomed, tagged shotgun in hand. I was surprised to see Torrez, since as far as I knew, Kenderman's killer was still on the loose, and that would be priority one with the sheriff, not monkeying around with Baum's duck gun.

"Fresh one." He nodded at the coffeemaker behind dispatch.

I held my cup up toward the others, but apparently they were interested only in business. By the time I returned to the conference room, Mellon was examining the shotgun. The sheriff had stood the gun upright, recoil pad on the conference table.

"Estelle happened across this." Torrez's remark was directed toward me, barely more than a whisper. He reached over and pulled the charging lever back sharply. Hesitating only a second for all of us to see that the gun was empty, he released the bolt and let it slam forward. Had there been rounds in the magazine tube, one would have been chambered.

Lifting the shotgun six inches straight off the table, he held it thus for a moment, then let it slip to thud against the wood. The click of the internal hammer falling was loud.

"Screwed up somehow," he said. "It don't take much of a jar to set it off."

"Wear and tear?" I asked.

Torrez shook his head. "Don't think so." He turned the gun and pointed at first one screw and then another. The screw slots showed signs of an ill-chosen screwdriver, the buggered metal in sharp contrast with the rest of the gun's choice condition. "Joe Hobby got in there, is what I'm guessin'."

"Could that damage account for it?" Schroeder pointed at the butt stock just behind the receiver where one of my rounds had gouged the wood and removed the shooter's right thumb at the same time.

"Don't think so. Anyways, it's something we'll look at," Torrez said. "He's got other problems, too. Late-stage pancreatic cancer, for one thing. Docs say that his odds are slim and none." He looked at me as he hefted the shotgun off the table. "Your shots maybe will speed up the process a little. That's about all."

"Have you talked with his son yet?"

Torrez shook his head. "CYF is goin' into that right now. It's a mess. All we know is that Baum picked up his granddaughter in San Diego where she was living with her mom. Took her from the neighborhood daycare. They were headed to El Paso where the son lives. Maybe. CYF hasn't found him yet as far as I know."

"Did Mr. Baum know that he has pancreatic cancer?" Schroeder asked.

"Yep. He was under treatment by the Cancer Center down in El Paso. Until last week, when he skipped his chemo treatment and headed out on his own."

"Stupid, stupid," Schroeder said in wonder. Then he frowned. "I want the son—what's his name?"

"George Baum."

"George—I want him in custody ASAP, Sheriff."

"We're workin' on it," Torrez nodded. "Maybe stupid runs in families. He shouldn't be hard to find."

"What's Nathan saying, anyway?" Schroeder asked. "Did the son put him up to this or what? Is this just a wild ass stunt to break the daughter's custody of the child?"

"Don't know. Baum's not in any condition to talk with us yet. He's still under."

The district attorney glowered at the table, shaking his head slowly. "Is this one of those suicide-by-cop deals? You think that's what he wanted? He knows he's caught, so…"

"He sure as hell was unlucky, then," I said.

The paperwork and conferences stretched the day into a never-ending mess, and I lost track of whether I was coming or going. The District Attorney and his investigator hauled Miles Waddell in for a tete-a-tete, to find out what the rancher had seen or heard. They even persuaded Frank Dayan to come in for a chat, exploring the issue of the proffered advertisement that had never seen the light of day. I would like to have sat in on that one, but didn't—and didn't press Frank later to see how quickly he'd folded, telling the cops everything he knew.

None of the roadblocks succeeded. The killer and his little Nissan pickup had faded away as slick as you please. I was sure that Bobby Torrez would continue the effort at least until dark, but after that, there was no point in corking the roads. The killer was long gone, and that left us—them—with little to go on. A blue truck, no tag number. No year. No definitive description. No radio conversation. No recovered slug or shell casing. Just a dead cop on a lonely road.

But we—and this time the "we" was accurate—*did* have a description of where the Nissan had *been*. I had seen it north-bound from the felled power poles, had witnessed it turning east on the state road, speeding toward town. That little snippet of an image screened itself over and over again through my mind, even upstaging the sorry incident with Nathan Baum.

Chapter Eleven

I needed to be doing something physical, to keep my assaulted brain from stewing itself into a puddle. Since my luck hadn't been so wonderful last time, this trip I allowed myself to be chauffeured. The rancher drove south from Posadas on NM 56, speedometer pegged just below ninety, the big diesel sounding as if it were locked right in the glove box, clattering away. I relaxed back in the plush seat and let Miles Waddell worry about critters stepping out into the road. I could have dozed off in all that velour comfort, but what he had given me to examine was more interesting.

Someone had cut the front off a Frosted Flakes cereal box, and in neat block letters printed a message on the back: *Cattle yes, U.N. no!* A nail hole top and bottom marred the smooth, thin cardboard.

"That was nailed to my gate post," Waddell said. "Real professional job, eh?"

"Bobby should see this."

"I suppose he will." He slowed hard as we came up behind a little sedan poking along at the speed limit, and when the road straightened out beyond the Rio Salinas bridge, passed with a hearty bellow of turbo-diesel. I slid the crude sign up on the dash and settled back.

We approached his mesa from the south, cutting off the state highway onto County Road 14 just southwest of the Broken

Spur Saloon. If he ever forgot exactly what he was building, Miles Waddell could stop in there and hear a dozen versions.

As we turned onto the dirt, my cell phone chirped. I'd promised Estelle Reyes-Guzman that I'd pay attention to it, and sure enough, her quiet voice greeted me.

"Sir, Neil Costace is in Las Cruces. He's picking up one of the Homeland Security guys, and they'll be heading over in an hour or so."

"Good afternoon to you, too," I said.

"I know this just thrills you to death, but I was hoping that you'd be available for a little bit when they arrive."

I was hoping. Never was an order from the undersheriff of Posadas County couched in more gentle terms. Flattery would get her everywhere.

"Nah," I said. "Waddell and I are headed to Vegas right now. Don't know when we'll be back. We're going to spend some of that money the United Nations is paying him."

"Sir," the undersheriff's voice remained gentle and patient. "There are FBI offices in Vegas, too."

"You're no fun." She also didn't have time for shit from me. "We're out at the mesa. You want me in town, or what?"

"We'll come out. And dinner is still on, sir."

"You dreamer."

A road beaten to dust wound a half-mile off the county thoroughfare, then turned abruptly toward the foot of the mesa where we encountered the gate, the sort of structure that, in a world of rambling barbed wire and juniper pole enclosures, was guaranteed to set folks speculating. Waddell stopped the truck and found a remote wand in the center console. With the push of a button, the black gate with its bright-yellow caution stripes rolled aside.

"Works off the cell phone, too," he said with satisfaction. "We're leaving most of the downside construction until later. We'll concentrate topside, then work on the tram and base house," Waddell said, twisting around to survey the generous, dust-beaten parking lot behind us. "Less to draw the curious that way."

"If Curt Boyd and his buds were after your site, why didn't he just drive down here and take an axe to your gate?"

"Don't give 'em ideas," Waddell said. "Maybe they didn't want to get within rifle shot. Maybe they caught sight of you roaming around down here on the prairie and that spooked 'em."

"Evidently not enough." The road up the mesa was enough to fuel lots of curiosity. We drove through the gate, and I watched as it slid closed behind us. The tires whispered on silky smooth macadam. Artistic stonework graced each culvert and drain. The place reminded me of a National Park project. Unspoiled by standing signage, the road was marked European style, with reflective painted symbols on the macadam surface itself.

"One point six miles of this," Waddell announced with considerable satisfaction. "You've seen it a couple dozen times while it's been under construction. Did you think I'd lost my nut?" Before I could answer, he added, "You know, in all that time, you never asked me point-blank what the hell I was building up here. You're not curious?"

"Of course I'm curious. You told me some time ago that you were building an observatory. A man can build what he wants."

"That's what I used to think. Now I know there are folks who don't share that view." The rancher slowed the truck abruptly and pointed toward the north. I could see several vehicles still parked out on the prairie, near the fallen poles and the spot where Curt Boyd had met his end. Dust plumes marked more incoming traffic from the north.

The new macadam mesa boulevard swept upward as we continued, around the mesa's western terminus with a spine-tingling view all the way to Arizona, and after rounding a gentle curve, started on the final climb to the rim. "You haven't asked yet," Waddell said. "The question that always comes first."

"How much this road to the stars cost you?"

He smiled broadly. "That's what I like about you, Bill. Cut to the chase, no bullshit. Sure, that's what everyone gets around to asking. And the answer for your ears only is a nice round two million a mile."

He saw me glance at the odometer. "One point seven," he supplied. "This little stretch comes in right around $3.4 million."

"Christ." The notion of a cattle rancher with $3.4 million to spend on mesa access—or on anything else for that matter—was inconceivable. "You know, I can remember when you were trying to have Gus Prescott scratch a path up here with his old road grader."

"Circumstances change. Gus did a little for me, and then the project started to take on a life of its own, and he ended up with more than his share of troubles. I started to look around at other options. See, Carl Rockford and I had a long talk." I'd seen Rockford's name on enough pieces of heavy road-building equipment over the years to know that Miles Waddell had gone first class on this little private boulevard up the mesa. "Now, the story he told his crews was that I was building an enormous sand and gravel operation down at the bottom, and a housing development up here."

"It's amazing what people will believe."

"As long as it fits what they understand. Folks have seen gravel pits, and they've seen plenty of subdivisions. They can readily imagine that there might be a worthwhile investment there. So they believe it. It fits their paradigm." He said "paradigm" as if he'd just learned it. Maybe he had.

"If I had said I was building an observatory, no dice. No one would understand what the hell I would want with an observatory, or why the hell I'd spend so much money on it, because *they* don't. It's not obvious how I'd earn a return on the investment, or the expenditure." He glanced over at me. "And you gotta have that, Sheriff. You have to have a return, because no one does anything anymore just for the fun of it." He shrugged. "Isn't that depressing? And because they don't understand it, they'd ask, 'Where the hell did Waddell get all that money? Must be into drugs or something.'" He laughed. "Or funded by the United Nations conspiracy." He tapped the newspaper on the center console. "That's the new theory."

"I heard the one about the gravel pit and the housing development topside. Didn't believe it, but I heard it a time or two."

"You didn't believe it because you have more than half a brain. I mean, come on. A housing development? Can you imagine school buses winding up and down this road? It'd be a hell of a commute to work for the parents. But see, with an observatory, and with that big array from California, *this* is where the work will be."

The roadway abruptly crested and I could see the breathtaking sweep of the mesa-top, so flat it appeared to be laser-leveled, the rim an abrupt and clean transition from brown earth to blue sky. From civil cases involving this desolate place and former owners, I knew that the mesa-top included more than 900 acres.

"As good a spot as any," Waddell announced as he parked in a dusty patch, the thin mantle of topsoil beaten raw by machinery. We faced north, uncomfortably close to the vertical rim rock. When he dismounted, the rancher immediately walked to within a single step of eternity.

"How's this for a grandstand seat?" The breeze touched his purple neckerchief. I zipped up my jacket and got out, running my hand along the fender. I could imagine my ankle twisting and me taking wing over the edge. Far below and to the north, the vehicles looked like Matchbox toys, the downed power poles like toothpicks cast willy-nilly. Somewhere hundreds of feet under our boots were the string of limestone caves that the Bureau of Land Management was thinking of developing. Telescope on top, caves underneath—it would be a hell of a tourist attraction.

"But you know, for all this, Bill, the real view is up here." He swept his arm to take in the heavens, a full dome with a slightly rippled edge south at the San Cristóbals and another to the north marked by Cat Mesa outside of Posadas.

He dropped his arm. "Hell, you've seen it. You get yourself Orion just coming up in the early morning sky out there to the east in late summer, with all the planet traffic? Why, it's enough to take your breath away. And then come winter the Milky Way turns around and cuts the sky in half. You know, I've seen

SkyLab go over half a hundred times, and *every* time, I swear I can see 'em waving out the window."

He gazed up into the sky. If he did it much longer, the sun would fry his retinas like bacon rinds.

"You're too damn polite to ask, but you'll want to know." He turned and faced me, feet planted hard as if he expected me to take a swing at him. "Do you know what my mother said to me two years ago, just before she died?"

"I have no idea."

"'Go ahead and do it.'" It was that simple to her. I'd talked to her about all this, and she said to just do it. I explained the whole concept, and she tells me, 'If it doesn't work out, you'll have tried.'" He shook his head slowly. "I never could work for her, all these years. I tried, back in the seventies. But Chicago wasn't my idea of heaven."

"This is, though?"

"Damn right. At least, it's where I'm going to build heaven. Let me show you."

He stepped to the truck and pulled a large cardboard tube out of the back seat. As he was working the plastic cap off, he looked across at me, eyes assessing.

"How are you weathering this shooting mess?"

"Mess is the right word."

"I talked with Schroeder for a few minutes, after we were done with Fish-eyes in that inner sanctum," Waddell said. "It almost seems like he's trying to combine all three incidents—the Boyd kid's death, the cop's shooting, and then the thing with Jackie and the creep in the RV."

"Two out of three, maybe," I said.

He rapped the tube gently against the fender of the truck. "The family will sue you?"

"Oh, probably. That's par for the course in these things. They look for somebody to blame."

Waddell smiled in sympathy. "How many times in all your years with the department has someone tried to collect a pound of flesh from you?"

"Too often." It wasn't the sort of accomplishment I wished to inventory at that moment, so I let it go at that. Waddell regarded me solemnly.

"Jackie is a lucky young lady."

"Yes, she is."

"And Baum…that's his name? He's going to live, you think?"

"It looks that way."

"So you're not as good a shot as you used to be." He took a deep breath and turned to survey the mesa. I waited for a welcome change of subject, and it wasn't long in coming. He still held onto that cardboard tube, and my curiosity was building.

"What does our good sheriff think about young Boyd's misadventure?"

I was sure "young Boyd" would call it worse than that if he could. "The sheriff doesn't confide much," I said. "I'm certainly not on his short list."

"You'd probably be surprised at how close to the top of that list you really are," Waddell said. "Did Estelle speculate?"

"Even less than the sheriff."

Undaunted, Waddell tapped the tube on the hood again. "And what to *you* think?" he persisted.

"I'm not paid to think anymore. But I'll say this…there's nothing random in this gig. Boyd and whoever was with him picked a spot where they could work without interruption, with a pretty good plan of attack."

"Boyd obviously wasn't alone, though. We know that. Someone made off with his vehicle, that's for damn sure."

"Between you and me…" I stopped, because ships have been sunk with simpler little slips. Waddell didn't need to know that Boyd's clothing hadn't borne the absolute evidence of creosote-stained sawdust. "Let's just let it go at that. He had help, and they'll catch the son-of-a-bitch."

Waddell shook his head in silent disgust while he fished a can of Copenhagen out of his hip pocket. He concentrated on taking a delicate little pinch, placing it just so behind his lip. After he'd stowed the can, he turned to lean his back against the fender of the truck. "You know, I just don't know how people hear about all this stuff. I hadn't talked much with anybody, and already I have those assholes chainsawing down power poles. I have newspapers in Colorado ranting about conspiracies. Hell, I've even have a private security firm up in Denver shooting me proposals for when I'm up and running." He grinned. "And that's not even counting the dumb ones. You heard the rumor about the military, I'm sure. Do you know how many folks think that those big radio telescopes are actually used for earth-based listening? Like we're going to monitor your damn cell phones?"

"Sure. I've heard that." The rancher's serious, pensive expression drew me up short. "You're not taking them seriously."

"Not the rumors, but the jerks who spread them? Damn straight. I am taking them seriously, as a matter of fact," Waddell said. "And look where we are…the Boyd kid is dead, isn't he. That's how serious all of this is, Bill." He paused, eyes squinting into the distance. "Have you ever visited the VLA up north? The Very Large Array?"

"Sure."

"So you *know* that there are folks who think *that* installation is just a front for clandestine listening…satellite spyware at its best. And always *clandestine,* of course. First they listen in, then they'll take your guns, then they'll be after your pickup truck."

"Pickups?"

"Hell yes. Anti-green, gas hogs that they are. Plus, in the Middle East, what do the rag-tags use as military vehicles?" He wagged a finger. "Pickups."

"I refuse to be paranoid, no matter how many people are chasing me," I laughed. "Life is too short for this kind of shit."

"Well, sure enough it is." Waddell heaved a huge sigh. "So… is this a warning to me?" He jerked his chin toward the ruined power poles far down below. "That's the way I see it. I mean, who the hell else would be affected by cutting the power? And what asshole with half a brain is going to think dropping a few power poles will stop this project? Come on. I told Bobby Torrez the same thing." Waddell thrust his hands in his pockets. "Goddamn freaks with too much free time."

No hard evidence had surfaced indicating that Miles Waddell's project, whatever it might be, was drawing fire, but it was a logical assumption—and enough to cause sleepless nights, I was sure. I nodded at the cardboard tube. "So what's the deep, dark secret?"

He popped the top off the tube. "This is a hell of an undertaking for a country boy," he said. Adopted country, maybe, I thought.

"My mother was ninety-one when she died," Waddell said. The rolled plans, if that's what they were, remained half in the tube. "Still sharp as a tack, still hating most things about life since my father died thirty years ago. I showed her this set of plans, and she didn't say much. But I saw her eyes twinkle. The day—the *day* before she died, she sent this to me." He handed me a single sheet of neatly folded correspondence. In violet ink, the writer had printed two sentences: *Let's see what you can do with it. Make it worthwhile and be content.*

I read it twice, then handed it back. "That's it?"

"That's it. Well," and he waved a negligent hand, "you know all the legal paperwork. The lawyers have to carve out their pound, Bill. But when all said and done, yeah. That's it."

"I should ask what the 'it' is," I said.

"I was her stepson, too, you know. Goddamn *stepson*. I guess I'm the only souvenir of the man she loved."

"And what's the *it*?"

"Just between you and me?"

I glanced around us as if checking for eavesdroppers.

Waddell patted the tube and its partially withdrawn contents. "Let me show you. It's easier." He collected the tube and moved to the back of the truck, dropping the tailgate. Spread out on the gate, the architect's rendering was large, fully three by four feet. I held one side as the breeze touched one corner.

"Jesus," I breathed, and Waddell let me examine the rendering without comment. I saw not just one modest observatory, but an array of buildings dominated first by a modest radio telescope in the center of a courtyard, a telescope about the size of the units at the VLA, and then farther to the southwest, not far from the edge of the mesa, the installation of a much larger dish—I guessed it to be the California project. It dwarfed the control building, the cars, and people.

"You've been thinking about this for some time," I said.

"Sure enough."

"I had no idea."

"The ten-cent tour." He bent forward and guided me around the plan. "Computer center for the big guy," and he touched the California dish. "Then over here is a theater linked to the eighty-inch housed in this dome. That's what I call my 'first look' scope. Hell of a program to orient visitors to the facility and the heavens. It's like one of those big-screen theaters you see in museums where they show the movies. Curved screen, the whole bit. But it's a live feed from the telescope, mixed with some canned stuff. And really much, much more that that." He looked across at me and grinned. "I mean, we *might* have a cloudy night some time."

He charged on. "Now *this* should appeal to you." He touched an attractive building shaped in a crescent. "Five-star restaurant. We'll pay special attention to the green chile burritos. I'll hire Fernando Aragon as a consultant, if I have to." *Ah, the power of money,* I thought. He touched what appeared to be a glass dome on the restaurant's roof. "Peel that back, weather permitting, and you can sip your soup and watch the heavens slide by."

He swept his hand across two other buildings whose roofs appeared to slide apart in sections. "Four sixty-inch units, each one viewing a separate section of the heavens, image projected on giant screens in a comfy auditorium, live narrative when appropriate, and on and on." He straightened up. "You impressed yet?"

"'Flummoxed' would be a better word. Why haven't I heard about all of this?"

Waddell shrugged. "I've been keeping it close, Bill. I wanted to go through all the planning stages before anything went public. Once I *go* public, with all the permits and shit like that, there'll be no secrets."

"Public access?" I leaned across and touched the site of the California project.

"Ah. Probably not. That's up to them, I suppose. They're a bonafide research facility. Their primary target of study right now is the deep space microwave background. The fundamental stuff."

"More fodder for conspiracies, Miles."

He held up both hands in surrender. "I know. I know. But I don't have time for that."

"Is this what I think it is?" A tramway cabled its way up the steepest section of the mesa's northwest rim, originating from a single large building and parking lot down below. "I see it, but I don't believe it. Do you have any idea how much a funicular costs, Miles?" It was a silly question that popped out of reflex, and if I hadn't understood before, the scope of Waddell's problem became clear now.

"Tramway," he corrected. "Fully enclosed cars riding on suspension cables. It's short enough that it doesn't need a mid-point support tower. The cable is made in Switzerland. And yes, Bill. As a matter of fact, I know *exactly* how much it will cost."

I leaned close so that I could read the label for the building complex where the tram docked on top. "Resort and hotel."

"I haven't come up with a good name for it yet. Some folks might want to come stay here just for the desert bird-watching down below. That's fine, too. Some of the best mountain bike trails on the continent. Horse rental. You know, the possibilities are really endless if you focus on how to attract the wide-ranging clientele. No tunnel vision." He held up the tube and shook out another rolled document. "But I just found this..."

"You've got to be kidding." The 18 by 24 photo montage showed a fetching little narrow gauge locomotive pulling four passenger cars and a flame red caboose. Smaller photos layered around the central image of the locomotive showed close-ups of the unit's various features.

"Natural gas?"

He nodded happily. "That smoke plume is pure steam. Chuff and puff just for looks. I've scouted out a nifty route from Posadas around behind Prescott's ranch, cutting across some of the most impressive arroyo country."

"Chuff and puff," I mused. "Nobody runs cabooses any more, you know."

"I do. Train's not a train without one." My frown must have alarmed him. "I've thought this through, Bill. I really have."

"Okay," I said slowly, and peered at the logo at the corner of the blueprint. "Powers, Broyles, and Hadley…who the hell are they?"

"A bunch of kids," he replied proudly. "Hadley's the son of a former girlfriend of mine. *Former.* We parted on the best of terms, thank God. He's the oldest of the trio, twenty-eight and smart as a whip. Broyles and Powers were classmates of his at the University of New Mexico. I wanted architects who have some imagination but who can follow directions and keep their mouths shut. Hell, they're going to make mistakes, but that comes with the turf." He laughed. "Hell of a first job, huh? But what's important is that they'll deliver what *I* want, not what *they* want. That's the heart of their marching orders, and they understand completely."

The breeze touched the rendering again and Waddell rolled it up neatly and stowed it in the tube. "Are you ready for the exciting part?"

Chapter Twelve

"I need you."

"Like a goddamn hole in the head," I scoffed. "You might need a good therapist before all of this is finished." I brightened. "You need an old, crusty engineer to drive the train? *That* might appeal to me for a day or two. And by the way, Miles…I didn't ask. Where the hell does the train *go?* You mentioned the Prescotts. There's a fair list of properties between Posadas and your mesa, including theirs."

"I've planned a thirty-two-mile route. A little longer than necessary to pull in a *great* mountain bike course that's on a piece of property I happen to own. Another little detour to take in some scenery at the southwest end of Cat Mesa. There's a great birding spot up there. But, seriously…"

"So you actually have all kinds of people who know a little bit about this project. You can't talk to neighbors about railroad easements without word leaking out."

"A few know bits and pieces."

"And that's all it takes. Somebody knows more about this project of yours than you think."

"And that's why I want you to work for me, Bill." He held up a hand as if to ward off my incredulous response. "Let me tell you what I need, Bill. Really. I need someone who likes to cruise around the desert, looking at stuff. I need someone who drives around at night—maybe just with the light of the moon, or that little 'perpetrator light' you used to use behind your front bumper."

"That was Bobby's idea, not mine," I said. And it was a good idea—a single tiny bulb down low between bumper and front wheel, throwing just enough light to mark the side of the path on a moonless night.

"I need someone to sit in on some planning sessions, who'll give me his opinion when I need it, probably more often when I think I don't. I need someone to be around, on no particular schedule, to check that when a shipment of a hundred yards of gravel is delivered, I *get* a hundred yards. I need someone to chat with folks on an informal basis. I need…" and he held up his hand when he saw me about to interrupt. "I need someone to talk with Frank Dayan, Bill. I want to make sure we keep him happy. He's got a big story breaking in this week's edition. The California folks had some neat glossies they provided, so it'll make a splash. I want to be sure that continues with all the media, but I also want to make sure he scoops the big papers regularly." He paused for breath. "The easiest way to keep them all happy is to advertise, advertise, advertise. When I do that, goddamn right they won't ignore me. See? I *have* thought this out."

He turned and sat on the tailgate, boots dangling a couple of inches above the dust. "There's something else I didn't mention."

"Several little things," I replied, "like a really basic little thing." He looked puzzled. "I don't care if your mother left you ten million bucks. That won't pay for all of this. And when you can't pay, you're going to end up with a bunch of abandoned foundations and broken promises, and maybe a locomotive they'll call *Waddell's Folly.*" He looked pained. "You could run cattle on the tramway up to the mesa-top for skyline grazing, I suppose."

"'Skyline grazing.' I like that. And you're damn right. I can't build this for *fifty* million. For one thing, I don't want to do this project in slow stages, finishing up when I'm a hundred and eight. I want it done right, and I want it done now. And I can pay for that. This whole deal," and he swept his arm to include the mesa-top, "is a three-year project, start to finish. That's the challenge."

"You think?"

"How does three hundred and thirty-eight million sound, Bill? After taxes, that is." He obviously enjoyed the expression on my face. "That's a third of a *billion*, my friend. And in addition to that…" He punched the air with a forefinger, "in *addition* to that, throw in a whole superblock of downtown Chicago real estate. Good stuff, too, if you like Chicago. High-rises with marble foyers and all that. Fortune 500 companies as tenants. We're not talking crumbling adobes here. What I *am* talking about are the results of a long, long lifetime of high finance. And you know what? I don't need a single brick of it. Not one little office. All of it goes. All of it on the block. And that's almost another billion. *Billion,* with a 'B'. I'm not about to sit around and wait for all those fancy buildings to start crumbling." He reached across and patted the cardboard tube. "This is what I want. This is what I need to do."

"Well, damn."

"Well, damn is right. Let's do it."

I looked out across the mesa with a jarred perspective. "You sure have a way of bringing the world to your doorstep."

"You don't think it will work?"

"I think that lots of people would like to have your problem, Miles. Or share in it, anyway. Half of the world's crazies will think you should give the money to them for *their* pet projects. Half will think you should just donate all your inheritance to charity. Half will want to screw you out of it with all kinds of scams. Half will want to just stick a gun in your ear and steal it outright."

"That's a lot of halves."

"It is. And on top of that, a tiny, *tiny* fraction of one percent of the population *might* understand what you're doing and why. You'll find a few astronomers who might be willing to jump into bed with you for a hand in all of this. A few will want to work with you. The dangerous ones are the ignorant sons-of-bitches who think that *you* should think like they do."

"Will you work with me?"

"Miles, I have enough to keep me happy right now, thank you. A lawsuit now and then to keep me interested." I shrugged. "I don't have the energy, the expertise, or even the time left on Earth to be of any use to you." I saw his shoulders twitch. "And what's this 'something else' that you forgot to mention in all this deal?"

He grimaced and hunched forward, both hands planted on the tailgate. "There are really two things I should mention, and I need your advice about what to do. I already mentioned the first one. A couple of days ago, this impressive as hell packet arrived by certified mail—from a security firm in Denver. I don't know how they got my name, or how they got wind of what I was doing here, but they offered to negotiate a comprehensive security contract with me. On-site during construction, and then a permanent part of the facility afterward."

"There you go," I said. "Word gets out, no way around it. Maybe they heard about the California project. Maybe they read that same article about the feds moving in…about the UN establishing a beachhead, so to speak. Professionals might be the best road for you, because you're sure as hell going to need security of some sort. Have I heard of this outfit?"

"United Security Resources. USR."

"Huh. I don't know them."

"But see, how appealing would that be? I mean, imagine Bob and Ginny and the three kids coming from Columbus, Ohio, to enjoy this installation. To ride the train, ride the tram, have their breath taken away by the dark zone up on top. And the first person they meet is some uniformed storm trooper riding around in a black Suburban with air-raid slits over headlights, telling them where they can or can't go. I don't think so."

I laughed. "And don't forget, Miles…whole sections of the night sky will be off-limits to civilian stargazers. You have to control where you point all those telescopes. I mean, you can't just look around willy-nilly, you know. You'll need security to make sure the telescopes are all pointed the right way."

"That's depressing, Sheriff. Don't even think about starting *that* yarn."

"Be prepared for your full measure of crazies, that's all I'm saying, Miles. But look. In an installation this huge, you're going to have to have some security. A lock on the gate down below isn't going to be enough. I mean, think of the complications. Some old fart has a heart attack at this altitude, you're going to need some organization to handle it. Someone takes a fall on the rocks. Someone steps on a rattlesnake. Someone vandalizes—we know *those* nitwits are out there. Break-ins. Shoplifting. You name it. You have to have some sort of infrastructure to deal with that, even if every member of your security squad is in plain clothes, made up to look like innocent college professors."

"That's an idea." Waddell looked at me shrewdly. "See why I need you?"

"I'm flattered, Miles. But I think you'll need a good deal more than some old retired fat guy."

"You bet. But I need that old fat guy to help me keep my feet on the ground. I need someone to talk to without having to worry that what we say will get dumped into the rumor mill. I don't want an asskisser, and I don't want Gestapo. Just someone I can trust for an honest opinion. I've watched you work over the years. And maybe most important, I don't think money impresses you much. You can't imagine how important that is to me right now."

I sighed. "I don't need a job, Miles. I really don't. I have my own projects." That was mostly true. "I'll be around off and on, and I'll be delighted to be a sounding board any old time you can catch me and buy my lunch. If you want to give me the combination to that gate down below, all right. Let's keep it informal. How about that?"

"If I have to settle for that, I will. All I'm asking is that you just…*be around,* on an unannounced basis. No clocking in and out. Just a set of savvy eyes that isn't busy with other concerns. I mean, right now, this project is no problem for me. I can cover all the bases. But that's not going to last. We'll have a fair-sized village being built here. You'll be a welcome sight, moseying around the place."

Turning a full circle, I once more drank in the sheer enormity of that mesa-top. "I'm already curious enough to be out here from time to time."

Waddell nodded vigorously. "That's a start. Can I make you an offer?"

"An offer for what, Miles? I don't need or want a job."

"But this is different."

"At the moment, maybe. But you know as well as I do that these things have a tendency to grow like kudzu. First thing you know, you'll ask me to do something that'll conflict with plans I've already made, and there you go. Hell, I might want to take two weeks to head north to Fort Sumner, or Fort Union, or one of those interesting places. Or a month fishing in Montana. Or six months visiting the kids."

"You don't fish, Bill. And when this is up and running, your kids will be beating a path to come *here*. And what the hell. When you're not here, why that just fits in with the random nature of your job."

"*Job*. Even the word has a repulsive sound, Miles. I've had *jobs*. Years and years and years of jobs. I don't want another one."

"You know…" He sounded so cagey that I knew what was coming. "We haven't even talked about remuneration."

"Because that assumes some figure will impress me. I already told you, Miles—I don't need the money. I'm content the way I am."

"You think?" He readjusted his Stetson and zipped up his jacket. "This has the potential to be a life-changing deal, you know. I mean, this isn't just a little eight-inch reflector telescope mounted on a flimsy tripod. We're talking a state-of-the-art facility here. We'll attract visitors—even researchers—from all over the world. We're talking about an infrastructure so complete and diverse that we can connect with other installations around the world." He held up a hand as if to ward off my interruption.

"And all *private* enterprise, Bill. That's the thing. No government grants to hog-tie us. No approval from some NSF hotshot for funding." He smiled tightly. "No UN asking for a link tie in with one of our instruments."

"With something that big, you sure as hell don't need me in the way."

"Shit, what have I got?" He swept an arm in a wide arc that included acres of open mesa-top blossoming with half a thousand red surveyor's flags. "A three million-dollar road. Enough surveying done to make somebody's career. I have preliminary state approval for both the granddaddy of all septic systems up here, and another one down at the gatehouse. I have two building permits…I'll need fifty by the time I'm through."

"And all somebody has to do to get what he wants—to force-fit his agenda into yours—is to hold up one of those permits. Pull some strings. Call a buddy in Santa Fe or Washington."

"I think we can keep everybody happy, Bill. And I think that because we don't have any hidden agendas. Big as it is, this is just a theme park of sorts. It's a tourist attraction on a mega scale."

"And the California project already has their foot in your door, Miles. *They're* not a theme park."

"You think that was a mistake?"

"Time will tell, won't it?"

"I've stayed below the radar, but that won't last long. So far, it's ninety percent ideas and planning. It's easy to do that under the table. But when the earth starts being pushed around, or when pieces of that big radio telescope start rolling through town, then watch out." He pointed to the east. "See over that way? Go all the way to the rim. We'll have our own gravel pit and portable crusher plant for a while. Won't have concrete trucks battering my road to pieces. It's all right here."

"The California folks are in agreement with you about the whole thing? Tourists, publicity—all that? They haven't tried to change any of your plans?"

"The more the better as far as they're concerned." He held up two fingers. "Number one, more publicity means more access to grants and funding. They need every buck they can scrounge. And two, the more publicity, the less of this conspiracy shit there is to muddy the water. And that won't go away unless the whole thing is public—wide open. Tours for them are essential. The public just doesn't get to *use* their monster, is all. You'd have to be a trained astrophysicist to understand what the computers are listening to, anyway."

"That's a tough nut," I said. "People who believe stupid things are the last to admit that they might be wrong."

Waddell nodded. "I'd be an idiot not to think I've got a whole sea of hurdles to face," he said. "Maybe I'm smart enough, maybe I'm not." He pointed to the west, where a tiny tan SUV had crested the access road and rolled quietly toward us, a plume of rich red dust rising behind as it turned off the macadam.

"What was I saying about a lock on the gate not being enough?" I said. "How did they get through the gate? You locked it behind us."

"Yet another glitch to fix. Closed, but not locked. All you have to do is push. You know these folks?"

I squinted as the vehicle drew closer. "That's Neil Costace driving. You've met him, I think."

"The Federal Bureau of Investigation? You're kidding."

"Decision time, Miles."

"Decision?"

"Now you need to decide how much you want to tell the feds." I shook my head slowly. "It starts early and never stops. You want me gone so you can have some privacy?"

He regarded the approaching SUV. The driver and passenger appeared to be in animated conversation.

"Do you think I'm nuts?" The rancher asked quietly, ignoring my question. I looked at him quizzically. "I mean this whole project. Spending the money like this."

I reached out a hand and clamped his shoulder. "Stop it. You're stepping in the most common trap there is. If you spend your money the way *other* folks think you should, you're courting misery, Miles. I'll give you all the help I can, short of being on the payroll."

He smiled. "Let's not be courting misery, then."

Chapter Thirteen

Just as the district attorney had been comfortable to let the state investigator do most of the grilling during my earlier interrogation, Neil Costace had brought along his own hired gun. Costace had never impressed me as being a stereotypical Hollywood-style G-man. No dark suit, no beady eyes, no arrogance. He no doubt had access to the stereotypical black Suburban, but even that had been upstaged this time by a little tan Jeep Patriot sporting a New Mexico plate. He stepped out wearing worn jeans, salmon-colored golf shirt, and a quilted vest. He ruined his cover with the black ball cap with three-inch gold letters that announced "FBI", the kind that wannabes like to adopt.

The young man with Costace climbed out of the SUV carefully, watching where he put his feet. In New Mexico, that's not a bad idea. So skinny that I could see joints poking at his jacket, he sported chinos, blue polo shirt, and a New Mexico State University ball cap. With his New Balance trainers, he might have been a graduate student in astronomy, even though graduate students generally didn't carry guns. This kid's howitzer was a concealment challenge.

"You turn up in the damnedest places." Costace gave me a two-handed shake, and I appreciated that he stopped just short of crushing my joints into little arthritic granules. His amber-flecked green eyes—very un-FBIish—scrutinized me. I'd known the agent for fifteen years, and I'm not sure what new detail of my physiognomy fascinated him this time. There was even a hint of sympathy in his tone.

"This is Richard Hotchkiss." Costace held a hand toward his partner.

"Rick, this be the legendary Bill Gastner, guardian of the purple sage, recently retired New Mexico livestock inspector, former Sheriff of Posadas County, and the man who knows more about this country than all the rest of us put together." He drew himself up and shook his head. "Bill, you've had a hell of a time these past forty-eight hours."

"It's been interesting." Since he'd brought it up, I assumed he knew the details. He would already have talked with the sheriff and undersheriff, perhaps even Schroeder, the district attorney.

Costace regarded me with a wry smile. "Takes guts to draw against a man with a shotgun."

"He had already fired the damn thing once, Neil. I didn't have much choice. I didn't want him to shoot again."

"I suppose not." As if he'd noticed my companion for the first time, he thrust out his hand to the rancher. "Miles, how are you?"

That Neil Costace knew Miles Waddell didn't surprise me. It was a tiny county, without many clumps of sage, purple or otherwise, behind which to hide. But I filed the interesting association away for future reference.

"You want to watch your step, hanging out with this guy," Costace added. "Agent Hotchkiss here is with Homeland Security," he continued without giving Waddell time to respond. Posadas County included a number of residents who would hear that and react as if Costace had said, "Agent Hotchkiss carries smallpox." I sympathized a little bit. When a sheriff introduced himself, you knew that he had a neat little book of county statutes that he was enforcing. The State Police or the Department of Game and Fish had well-established guidelines. But I always had the feeling that the folks at Homeland Security were making it all up as they went along, with no clearly apparent limit to their authority. And when the agent in question was a kid without the wisdom of the ages, that made me very nervous indeed.

Hotchkiss shook hands without a word, his grip gentle and polite. He let a pleasant nod suffice.

"So…" Costace began, and then stopped, gazing off to the north, hands on his hips. He squinted into the distance, and I knew he was examining the dark outline of Cat Mesa north of Posadas, twenty plus miles as the raven flew. "The sheriff tells me that you were sitting on top of the Cat. And when things fell apart down here, you saw the action."

"That's a little over-dramatic," I said. "I saw two flashes of light, Neil. That's all, at first. I assume now that what I saw was the transformer shorting out when the poles went down. I could see another pinprick of light that I think was the grass fire started by the short. And a few minutes later, I saw headlights northbound on fourteen. I called the S.O. at that point. He—or she—drove north to the state road and turned toward town."

"Two little blips of light."

"That's it."

"What was your first thought about what was going on?"

"Most likely? Just some unsubstantiated, wild guesses. None of them turned out to be true."

He continued scanning the mesa-top. "So we're not actually looking at a direct connection between that speeding vehicle that you saw and the pickup truck that Officer Kenderman reported stopping. It's an assumption that they're one and the same."

"That's correct. A strong assumption."

Costace turned and regarded Miles Waddell. "And you?"

Waddell raised an eyebrow, but didn't respond.

"You were out and around during all of this? The sheriff said you might have heard something. The saw, maybe."

"I was in my camper," the rancher said. "Parked way over there, near the south rim." Costace shielded his eyes, squinting into the distance. The travel trailer was a dot near the mesa rim, a modest little domicile for a billionaire. Waddell's home, a sprawling ranch house twenty miles north of Lordsburg, saw its owner rarely.

"And first?" Costace waited patiently, content to draw Waddell's answers out one at a time.

"I heard a chain saw. But it was off in the distance, and I didn't bother to investigate until I heard the ruckus. Maybe it was the power lines crashing down. I went to investigate, and sure enough. I drove down, got close enough to see the damage, and thought I saw a body. So I called the S.O." He held up both hands. "That's it. In a few minutes, the emergency vehicles started arriving. The distance plays tricks. I couldn't tell for sure at first where the noise of the saw was coming from."

"That's odd, though," Costace said. "At that hour."

"Yeah, it's odd," Waddell laughed. "One o'clock in the morning? Not to mention one little point—there are no trees worth firewood down there. We don't get many firewood cutters in these parts."

"But you didn't get up to investigate right away?"

"Well, sort of. I could hear the saw, so I went outside to listen. That's when I could tell they were off to the north, not too far away. Then I heard the crash…more like a *whump*. I drove over to the rim to look, and I could see the fire. It was just a little scatter of flames at that point."

"I was surprised to hear it was Curt Boyd," Costace said. The agent had had a run-in or two stemming from the family's interest in military weaponry. Every one of their fully automatic weapons—even a rare Lewis once mounted on a World War I biplane—was fully documented and taxed. I had tried my hand with the big .50 Browning during one memorable July Fourth shindig at the ranch, and did myself proud, reducing a '62 Chevy to scrap metal at 500 yards. Then there came a time when another rancher had taken a wild shot at a low-flying airplane and in a one-in-a-million fluke had actually struck the pilot. For a while during the investigation that followed, it might have seemed natural to suspect the Boyds.

But machine guns are like a mesa-top observatory in at least one way. No one believes that you own all those automatic weapons without some hidden agenda, and rumors fly.

"I've known Boyd since he was a kid," I said.

"Sure," Waddell added. "In fact I saw him a couple of weeks ago, and we chatted for a bit. He was hunting prairie dogs north of here." Waddell turned to me in question. His memory was accurate. I'd been hiking the Bennett Trail and seen first the young man with the Mauser 98 World War II sniper's rifle, and then, a few minutes later, Miles Waddell himself, repairing a short section of barbed wire fencing.

"You mean he wasn't using a Thompson on the dogs?" Costace laughed.

"Ah, no," Waddell said. "What the hell was it? I'm not much of a gunny."

"A German sniper's rifle," I supplied. "Not antique, but historical. A little overkill for prairie dogs, but effective. He was hiking by himself, and wasn't anywhere near the power lines."

"So," Costace mused. "You went to have a look-see. You saw the truck leaving the scene?"

"No. Sure didn't."

"Any ideas who Boyd's associates might have been for this deal?"

"That's the question, isn't it?" I said. "When the sheriff has time to deal with the Las Cruces end of things, maybe we'll find out. Curt had been teaching and coaching down there, so that's a place to start."

"We've been there, and will be again." Costace apparently was unconcerned that he was blabbing his intentions in the presence of a couple of civilians. "It makes sense to me that if Boyd was tied in to the school's schedule down in Cruces, his associates might be in Cruces as well." He studied the ground at his feet. "It's a crap shoot, though."

"His associate could have been living in Calcutta," I remarked. "With the Internet, or e-mail, you can command-center from anywhere in the world. They could have planned to rendezvous here for this little gig."

"If Boyd's vehicle shows up in Posadas, I might buy that," Costace said. "Otherwise, it makes sense that they drove up here together."

"So what's your interest in this?" I asked Hotchkiss. I knew exactly what his interest was—sabotaging interstate power lines, maybe any kind of power lines, was a federal matter, and would spike all kinds of interest. But the young man had kept his own counsel so far, and I admired the zipped lip.

"An attack on interstate power lines is a serious matter," the young agent replied as if he'd heard my prompt. That was an entirely adequate explanation, and he didn't embellish it.

"Somebody's dumb prank," I said, and didn't believe it.

"Were that the case, they'd have taken out something closer to town, where more people would actually see their handiwork." Costace looked hard at Waddell. "Pretty close to you."

"And they wouldn't kill a cop if it was just a prank," Hotchkiss added, the first time he'd offered an independent thought. I didn't agree with him, since many a prank had turned needlessly tragic.

The wind was picking up a chill, and Costace zipped up his vest. "It bothers me that someone is out to disrupt your power up here," he said. "If that's what this is. Could be just coincidence, but who the hell believes in those? They picked a spot where they could work *without* drawing attention. It almost worked, if you'd been sleeping a little harder." He smiled at Waddell. "There's not much up here yet, but it sends an interesting message, don't you think?"

I wondered what the official FBI thinking was about Waddell's undertaking—of course, they would know something, even if it was wrong. They had access, if they so wished, to all the permits that Waddell had filed. They would know about the California outfit and the huge radio telescope.

"There are all kinds of rumors," Waddell said carefully.

Hotchkiss prompted, "For instance?" His voice was reedy, reminding me of a bassoon playing in its tenor register.

Waddell turned guarded. "Just all kinds of things."

"A United Nations listening post up here, maybe?" Hotchkiss managed to say that with a straight face.

"You've heard that one, too," Miles said.

That didn't appear to surprise either agent. "And are you?" Hotchkiss asked.

"There might be some good rent to be had for that."

Hotchkiss didn't look amused. "What *are* you going to do for power up here? One little transformer stepped off that line down there doesn't seem adequate for what you have planned."

Waddell pulled out the little tin and took his time loading his cheek with another neat pinch. "And just what *do* I have planned, Agent Hotchkiss?"

"Just in a manner of speaking," the young man said, with no hint of apology, "what you do is your business within the parameters of law, but the road up here bespeaks *something*, it seems to me. This isn't just pasture."

For a moment, Waddell fell silent, and then sighed as he reached a decision. "Let's make this easy, gentlemen." He uncorked the tube once more. "Maybe knowing what's going on will help find these jerks." In a moment the two feds were examining the plans and the architectural rendering of the completed site.

Costace whistled in amazement, and the rancher let them look without comment, until the FBI agent straightened up. "I have a nephew who would give his left nut to work in a place like this."

"Tell him to watch my website for progress reports." He extended business cards to both agents. "The application process will be posted." *How odd,* I thought, *to hear this rancher talk in terms of "posting" and "websites," a rancher whom I'd known by way of cattle counts, freeze-snapped fences, or vanishing groundwater.*

Hotchkiss was glued to the rendering, eyebrows furrowed together, head shaking slowly from side to side. "Who's funding all this…I mean, we're talking millions and millions."

"I'm funding it," Waddell said easily. "I'm sure your agency has tendrils into the IRS vaults. Go there, and you won't have to take my word for anything." They didn't protest, even weakly.

After another moment scrutinizing the plans, Hotchkiss nodded. "You're going to be a target, sir." He looked satisfied to be able to say that. Maybe it was a form of job security for him.

"Tell me why?"

Hotchkiss hesitated, and Costace didn't come to his rescue. "Well, for one thing, it's the money. You can't dump this kind of money around without attracting the kind of attention you don't want."

"All right. We've come to that same conclusion. I was planning on shooting a few of 'em and hanging their corpses on a pole, down there at the entrance way. Do that a few times, and it might put a stop to all the nonsense."

Hotchkiss looked pained. "You're going to need security, for a start. But that's not the real issue."

"And what is?"

"Folks are going to think you're up to something else."

"I've been told that. I'm hoping some well-targeted publicity will smooth things out. That starts this week. Otherwise, I don't care what people think."

The agent looked dubious. "If someone is upset enough to cut down your power poles, it isn't going to stop there. You can be sure of that."

"Well, *one* of 'em got himself permanently discouraged, and *that's* a fact. And his partner's a fugitive. His life is over. If there are others, that's why we pay you the big bucks."

"You can bet that we're interested in who they might have been working with," Hotchkiss said.

"If they were," I said.

Costace shot a quick glance my way. "We're almost sure of it." He pulled a small notebook out of his pocket and jotted a note or two.

"Let me ask you something, then," I said. "It doesn't require a rocket scientist to take a chain saw to a wooden power pole. Make that six power poles. Any airheaded teenager could do that. How does this stunt lead you to think it's some big conspiracy?"

Costace laughed gently. "You know, maybe it's just a form of job security for us." He turned serious. "A teenager would cut a pole closer to town, where he could see the results. This was done with a purpose—and it makes a hell of a statement to drop six like this."

Hotchkiss drew a circle around the mesa-top installation with his index finger.

"How many acres?"

Waddell started to say something, and bit it off. I saw his jaw muscles clench, why I don't know. The kid from Homeland Security had had the time to scrutinize the drafting, and pick up all kinds of details. But apparently the rancher had reached his limit.

"A few," he said.

Hotchkiss glanced up at him, clearly puzzled at his reticence, then turned his attention back to the drafting. "But this is the only access to the mesa-top." He swept a finger across the rendering to the access road.

"How about that," Waddell said dryly. He didn't offer to educate the young agent. Both the rancher and I knew that there was the remains of an old mining road on the southeast side. At the moment it could be used for a world class championship 4x4 course. But what the hell—maybe another million would make it passable.

Hotchkiss straightened up. "Can we get a copy of this?"

"No, you can't." Waddell deftly rolled up the rendering and the multiple sheets under it, and Hotchkiss watched with a stone face as the rancher slid the plans into the cardboard tube. They *could* get a copy, of course, from any number of sources, the state building inspector being the simplest. But at the moment, Hotchkiss remained polite.

"We can't help you if we don't have the information we need."

Waddell laughed. "How about when I want your help, I'll call *you?*" His tone was perfectly pleasant and reasonable. He looked across at me. "Isn't that the old joke? 'I'm from the government and I'm here to help?'"

"What do you folks know that we don't?" My question took the two agents by surprise. "Your response time was pretty good for a case of vandalism."

"We were headed this way," Costace said.

"The California deal?" That earned a sharp look from Hotchkiss and a smile from Costace. "Why do you say that?"

"Makes sense. You've got some folks out there who have announced that they're moving a half billion-dollar radio telescope out of their state to New Mexico. California is not going to take the loss lightly—and only a few folks in New Mexico are going to welcome the project, at least until they find out how many people are going to be employed here. The rest would prefer the rumor—that it's the government, once again here to help."

"I think you're overreacting to the rumor," Costace said. "To rumors and old, bad jokes."

"And yet, here *you* are. The sawdust down below is still fresh, and we've earned a visit from both the Federal Bureau of Investigation and the Department of Homeland Security."

"We were around."

"And that's pretty lame," I said. "Did Sheriff Torrez call you?"

"Yes, he did. Listen, Bill," and Costace took me by the elbow as if he wanted to lead me out of earshot of the others. I didn't take the hint, and he relaxed his grip. "Look, I don't know what your stake in all this is…"

"No stake."

His eyes twinkled. "Right. That's why you're sitting on a mesa-top at one in the morning."

"Not this mesa, and when you're pondering deep thoughts like I do, you gotta sit somewhere lofty."

"If something comes to your attention that you think we ought to know, will you call me?"

"You're on the Rolodex, Neil."

He nodded, and Hotchkiss took the opportunity to hand me a card. I extended it to Waddell without looking at it.

"Good luck with all this," Costace shook hands with me and Waddell as if he meant it. Hotchkiss' grip was still polite, but a little tempered this time. We watched them trudge back to their sporty little SUV.

"I should have locked the gate down below," Waddell quipped, and I laughed. "You never know who's going to drive in."

"See? We're just as paranoid as everybody else."

Miles Waddell, rancher, entrepeneur, dreamer, once more implored that I consider his offer, and as I left the mesa that afternoon, I thought about the mammoth design of his project, and the odds of it actually seeing fruition. Small to none, was my pessimistic conclusion, and I kicked myself for falling so easily into that trap. I felt a pang of sympathy for him. And the second thought was one of irritation. Why *shouldn't* Miles Waddell be able to build his castle in the sky? Why should boneheads stand in his way?

Chapter Fourteen

I spent the rest of the afternoon at the sheriff's office, reviewing my depositions to make sure my less-than-acute memory hadn't botched it. The account of my nocturnal mesa-top observations was brief, but the paperwork I cranked out for the shooting of Mr. Nathan Baum spelled out that incident in excruciating detail. I knew damn well what was coming from that one.

Listening to dispatch with half an ear, I followed the manhunt for Perry Kenderman's killer. The unsuccessful roadblocks were lifted shortly after four p.m., but they'd become useless long before that. By four-thirty, the investigation out at the power line was closed, with a depressingly brief list of evidence. Heavy equipment from both the local Electric Cooperative and from the grid had arrived and were allowed to move in.

Evidence was scant. We—they—had a corpse with a broken neck and crushed jaw, some sawdust from a chain saw, a few scuffs in the gravel, and six downed power poles. One witness had heard the chain saw. Another had been watching from twenty miles away.

The list for the Kenderman site was equally brief: a corpse with a through-and-through head wound with no bullet or shell casing left behind, a brief radio broadcast, and some scuff marks in the gravel.

The shooting of Sergeant Jackie Taber and Nathan Baum was as well documented as the Boyd/Kenderman tragedy was obscure. The only lingering question was why Nathan Baum hadn't tried to sweet-talk his way out of the initial confrontation with the sheriff's sergeant, instead of confronting her from the get-go with a shotgun. Did he actually expect that the officer would take one look at the gun and say, "My mistake. You can go now."?

The sheriff and half a dozen other officers of various jurisdictions clumped through the office at various times that afternoon, all grim-faced and frustrated. I didn't know where they were coming from or going, and didn't ask. It wasn't that I wasn't curious—I was, acutely so. But I was also aware of how in the way I could be.

Because I had a standing offer to use the undersheriff's office, I relaxed there, with a nice view of the neighboring county buildings and Cat Mesa beyond. Musing was a great way to spend time, and I was good at it, my thoughts free-ranging.

"Are you ready for a ride?"

I startled so hard that I yanked a muscle in my neck.

"Sorry, sir," Estelle Reyes-Guzman said. "I didn't realize you were asleep."

"I wasn't," I grumped. "I was thinking." I glanced up at the wall clock and saw with some astonishment that it was late afternoon...I'd been thinking, all right. And hopefully not snoring.

She regarded me silently for a moment. "I'd like to talk with Johnny Boyd," she said. "He's home now. Bobby talked with him out at the site, but I wanted to follow up on a couple of things that Boyd mentioned out there. He asked if you were around, too."

"I'm around, all right. What's Johnny need from me?" Counseling the bereaved was not my favorite pasttime.

"He wants us to understand what his argument is with Miles Waddell."

I looked at her quickly. "I didn't know that there was one." And if Johnny Boyd had a beef with Waddell, why would Boyd care what *we* thought? Or more specifically, what *I* thought. The answer was painfully obvious. Another loop of the lasso was trying to tie itself around my feet. The little word "no" would solve that.

"Sure, I'll ride out with you." I pushed myself out of the chair, and then hesitated as my brain began to sift through all the files that included assumptions about the father-son relationship between Johnny and Curt Boyd. "What was your impression?" I knew the flashpoint of Johnny Boyd's temper was low, and he wasn't quick to forget and forgive. Losing a son was fundamental, but I couldn't see how Miles Waddell could be held responsible in any fashion.

"I got the impression that Mr. Boyd saw something coming," Estelle said. "That maybe he was resigned to something like this happening."

"So you think Johnny knows more about his son's home terrorist activities than he was willing to admit to the sheriff?"

"That's a possibility, sir. I know he's comfortable with you, though. He doesn't warm up to the heriff much."

"Old harmless me," I laughed.

There were two routes out to the Boyd ranch northwest of Posadas, and both of them fell into the "you can't get there from here" category. The shortest route was up and over the east end of Cat Mesa, then winding down the dusty ranch roads for twenty miles to the Boyds' back gate. On a rapidly approaching February night, even one studded with moon and stars, that wasn't my choice of roads for a high-strung sedan.

I felt a twinge of relief when Estelle turned her new Charger west on the state highway that ran past Posadas Municipal Airport. That civilized route was twenty-five miles longer, exiting the county to the north and then looping back through the tiny hamlet of Newton, followed by four miles or so of washboarded gravel.

The car's stiff seats didn't do my backside any good, but I suppose that in a high-speed chase, I'd be glad for them. The stiff suspension telegraphed every tar strip in the highway. We sped north, and "sped" was the operative word. The thumping tar strips became a rapid staccato as the massive hemi engine found its comfort zone, and I relaxed.

"How do you like this crate?" I asked as we slowed for Newton fifteen minutes later.

"It won the low bid," she shrugged, then grinned. "The boys like it."

"They would," I scoffed. Francisco, now a sage thirteen, and Carlos, sprouting up at nine, had pleaded for rides and pouted when their mother refused. I didn't know what youngsters called vehicles like that nowadays, but I suppose it was cool, boss, wild, bad-ass, or whatever. I preferred my rides to be sedate and cushy. "What else have you heard about the concert?"

"Absolutely nothing," Estelle replied. "Carlos is so excited he can't stand still."

"He never could."

There wasn't much of Newton left to attract tourists. Maybe two ranching families still lived there, along with half a dozen vacant buildings. We crashed off the pavement and swung past a road sign that announced that county maintenance ended. The dirt lane was smooth as long as we went fast enough to keep the tires on the tops of the bumps. In two miles, we passed under a laser-carved metal archway that announced the Flying B ranch of J.R. Boyd and Sons.

Like most ranches, the owners had found a sheltered spot to build a home. Boyd's was tucked against a low mesa, protected to the north and west. As we approached, Johnny was standing on the front porch, out of the halo of light from the kitchen door. His cigarette glowed bright, and then extinguished as he ground it out under his boot heel. The porch light flashed on, and Johnny half turned toward the house in irritation. The light went out.

Two Aussie heelers danced circles as they charged across the dusty yard. Johnny snapped something, and both dogs stopped as if they'd come to the end of their invisible leashes. Unsure of just how to herd us, they retreated to the porch.

"Evening." There wasn't much warmth in the greeting, but he stepped off the porch and extended his hand—gnarly and hard as seasoned juniper. "This ain't the easiest thing for you, I guess." He nodded at Estelle. "Come on inside. Startin' to get a bite out here."

Low of ceiling and small of window, the Boyds' living room was dominated by a wide fieldstone fireplace centered on the east wall, and a couple of large piñon logs smoldered. I'd been here a number of times, and knew that the place could look a whole lot brighter. Now a heavy flannel blanket of tragedy smothered the home.

Maxine Boyd, short and stocky but trying to be sporty in crisp jeans and a flowery western shirt, appeared from a side room. Her face was puffy and one hand carried a wad of much-used tissue. "Hi, guys." She sounded cheerful but brittle, as if she'd greeted one well-meaning neighbor too many. Then to her husband she said, "Don't leave the girls outside now."

Johnny grumbled something and turned to the door. The two heelers slunk in, casting accusatory glances our way. They settled in twin doggy beds behind a green Morris chair.

The rancher gestured toward the well-worn sofa. "You'd have some coffee, I expect," he said, and without waiting for our response nodded at his wife.

"I have some nice tea if you prefer," Maxine Boyd offered. I'd seen Estelle drink coffee once in all the years I'd known her—and maybe that was inaccurate. I'd seen her *hold* a coffee cup once.

The rules of hospitality observed, Boyd settled his scrawny frame on the forward edge of the Morris chair and stared at the apathetic fire, hands clasped tightly.

"You was out there today?"

"I was."

"What'd you see?" That was a tough question and Boyd corrected himself. "I mean from up on the Cat. I heard that's where you was first."

"I didn't see much, Johnny. Two flashes of light. That's about it. I'm guessing that's when the transformer hit the ground." And that would have been a second or two after the butt of the power pole had kicked back and killed his son.

Boyd got up and bent over the fireplace, stabbing at the logs. He had the magic touch. Flames erupted and a small puff of fragrant smoke escaped into the room. For a while, he leaned against the fireplace, staring into the flames. Maxine delivered coffee and one tea, along with a generous plate of sliced spice cake. She moved as if that simple hospitality had used up the last of her energy reserves. She settled in a straight chair near the dark wood gun cabinet, home to a portion of their son's interesting arsenal of military collectibles.

"Curt didn't think much of Waddell's railroad idea," Boyd said abruptly.

"What was his objection?"

Boyd returned to his chair, hands once more clasped tightly. "The whole damn project, from one end to the other. Why, Waddell's got who the hell knows who comin' in from California, he's got a road better'n most public highways. But a *railroad?* Why, hell. I got to agree with my son on that. It's going to scar up the land, for one thing. Once something like that settles in, it's there forever. And I don't much like the notion of a whole train-load of tourists staring up the valley at our place. I mean hell, that thing will be runnin' day or night. I don't care if it's propane, electric, or even coal—it's going to be noisy and scare the shit out of the cattle."

He wound down a little, and I asked, "And that was it?" The railroad would pass nowhere near the Boyd ranch—perhaps within a mile or so of one section that wrapped down around Cat Mesa. They'd certainly never see or hear it from this house. The cattle wouldn't care one way or another.

Boyd fell silent and I waited without pushing him. "You know why he wants to build a goddamn railroad track? I mean, ain't the big line enough?" He looked across first at me, and then at Estelle as if he'd noticed her presence for the first time.

"It's great country, Johnny." A scenic ride through the scarred country would be like stepping back into Hollywood's wild west. There were even places for an impressive trestle or two. At night, other than an occasional ranch, the darkness would be incredible, even threatening, to some city folks who were used to the constant wash of light pollution. But...I could understand Johnny's hesitation to embrace the project. Sure enough, the hooded lights of a locomotive would pierce the darkness, startle the wildlife, break the mood.

And noise? There was bound to be some, perhaps significant. Locomotives with a train of cars didn't pussyfoot through
the countryside. Clattering, clacking, the whistle and hiss of
steam—trains announced themselves.

"But hell," Johnny said, "I probably wouldn't have stood in
his way. I mean, he offered me a fair chunk of change to lease
a route through the south acres, there down beyond the mesa.
That's out of sight, and far enough away. He wants to avoid the
National Forest, though, and I can understand *that*. I mean,
hell, the paperwork dealin' with the feds would take a lifetime."

"You and he had discussed the project in some detail, then?"
Estelle asked.

"Couple times. Hell, no big deal to me, when it comes right
down to it. And like I say, he laid a lot of money on the table.
Old train…picturesque, I guess." He sighed. "Now the boy—he
saw right away. You could haul some fair payloads on a train,
even narrow gauge. Stay off the highways and such."

Haul payloads? I thought. *Payloads of what? Tourists, yes, a fair
payload of excited people.* "Johnny, let me ask you something,"
I said. "Do you seriously think that Miles Waddell is building—or cooperating to *have* built—some sort of clandestine
installation on top of his mesa? You remember the brouhaha
when they tried to build a heli-tach base out to the west of here
for fire suppression."

"Yep. I remember. Hell no. I don't think Waddell is in cahoots
with some New York mayor or some ambassador or nothin' like
that. I think he's got grand ideas about some sort of telescope,
usin' it to attract tourists. Maybe it will, maybe it won't. Ain't
much exciting about a damn telescope, in my book."

Johnny Boyd obviously hadn't seen the plans drawn up by
Waddell's imaginative architects, including far more than "a
damn telescope."

"But your son…" I prompted.

"My son had his own ideas about all this. With so many
things that could use the money, he don't see why Waddell wants
to waste it on something that nobody, and I mean nobody, is

going to use. You think folks will come out to the top of some mesa, lay themselves down in the cactus, and stare up at the stars? Hell, you could do that anywhere."

"He disagreed enough to disrupt power. What did he think that would accomplish?"

Boyd looked pained. "I can't tell you that. I don't know what he was thinkin', Bill. Don't know why he was there. Maybe he didn't know…"

"You know," I said, "Waddell is playing his cards pretty close to the vest. How would your son have heard about the mesa project?"

"Couldn't tell you."

"Did he ever discuss the project with Waddell? With him directly? Did he ever talk about that?"

"I guess you'd have to ask Waddell that," Johnny said.

"He said there was no way a single person could do something like this mesa project," Maxine said softly. She shifted uncomfortably. "It's just too much money. I mean, no one has those kinds of resources without the government being behind it. That's what Curt said. Nobody in country like this."

It's so easy to be wrong, I thought.

"Mr. and Mrs. Boyd," Estelle said, "did your son ever talk to you about any sort of disruptive activities? Did he discuss the possibility of somehow targeting Mr. Waddell's project?"

"Not directly," Boyd replied. "He was concerned. Maybe more than that. He was angry." Boyd sat back in the chair, spine stiff. "See, he grew up in this country. He hunted and rode all over these millions of acres. I guess he's kinda like me in that respect—always assumed that the land would be the way it was. Too far away from the cities for any kind of development." He almost smiled. "Ain't going to ever be no box stores out here, you know what I mean?"

"So he saw Waddell's project as an intrusion?" I asked.

"Sure enough. Traffic, tourists, trains—hell, tour buses, even. And that's just the start. You get houses, now. I mean hell, his employees will need places to live. They ain't going to drive to hell and gone out here from town every day. First it'll be a sea of trailers, then a goddamn subdivision if the thing works out." He managed a bleak smile. "And you know what's next. A goddamn *convenience* store."

I saw a flush creep up Johnny Boyd's leathery cheeks. "My son didn't cut those poles, Sheriff. Without even bein' there, I can tell you that. They say he wasn't the one using the saw. Hell, you don't know. He might have been trying to *stop* the deal, for all we know. Maybe he was just in the wrong place at the wrong time."

"Odd place to be at an odd hour."

Boyd shook his head slowly. "I'll give you that." I saw the wrinkles around his eyes deepen a little. "'Course, you've been known to prowl some, too."

I stared down into my coffee cup. Maxine hadn't offered a refill, and I had the impression they were just waiting us out. It wasn't clear to me why Johnny Boyd had asked us to visit—he hadn't exactly dropped a ton of useful information on us.

"Your son believed that a man ought to be able to do whatever he wants on his own land?" I asked. "Without government intrusion?"

"Fair enough," the rancher answered.

"That would apply to Miles Waddell as well, wouldn't it? Regardless of his wealth?"

"Depends who he's in cahoots with," Johnny said, and we were right back at the beginning.

"And your son thought Miles Waddell is in cahoots with somebody, is that it?"

"Hell, you've been up there. You don't think so?"

"What I think doesn't matter, Johnny. But just for the record, to set your mind at ease…no, I don't think Waddell is in league with the devil, no matter how you color him. I think he's becoming a victim of a rumor without substance or logic or even common sense. I mean, be honest. What's there to listen to in this part of the world? Hell, I'm not into all this new technology, but I know that satellites have made any ground-based communication limited to the point of being useless. What, do we think that they're going to point one of those huge radio-telescope dishes at Las Cruces and listen in while Benny tells Bob about the new elk rifle he's going to buy?"

Boyd's lip quivered and he rubbed his face hard. "Well, he's got more money than sense," he managed.

"So what? It's Waddell's money. It's his land. He doesn't need our approval for what he does. There are no neighbors close by down there, so even his loud music—if he chooses to play some—won't keep anybody awake nights. And if he wants to step outside his travel trailer and let loose a magazine or two from a World War II machine gun at jackrabbits, that's his business. That doesn't make him an anarchist or a collaborator, does it? Any more than your son's historical hardware is any of the government's business."

"Did your son bring any of his friends or acquaintances out to the ranch?" Estelle asked, and I was glad she did. I didn't need to bore these folks with my own soapboxes.

"He brought Kiran out for Christmas Day," Maxine said. "That's one of his roommates."

"One of them," I prompted.

"Well, four of them have rented this old adobe house over in Mesilla. It's just a beautiful spot. They even have water rights off one of the irrigation ditches."

"Kiran's last name?" Estelle asked.

Maxine's brow puckered and she looked at her husband for help. He shrugged helplessly. "Some damn foreign thing," he muttered.

"Oh, stop. No wait. 'Bhutan'. That was it. He's from New Delhi and studying agricultural engineering at State. I believe he's a PhD candidate. Just a very nice young man. I don't think I've ever met anyone so polite and well-spoken."

"But you've never met the others?"

"I haven't. And Curt hasn't been home enough to really talk about them. I know that one of them is also a coach—soccer, I think. I don't know about the fourth. Oh…and the young man who plays soccer? He's from Kenya."

"Kenya," I repeated in surprise, although why I don't know. All university towns have a large contingent of foreign visitors, and Las Cruces was certainly no exception. "Curt had a real international house going. So India, Kenya, and the other?"

"I just don't recall," Maxine said.

"Mrs. Boyd," Estelle asked, "did you contact any of his roommates or friends this morning when you heard of your son's death?" *Not that it would matter much at this point,* I thought. Sheriff Torrez and his multi-agency task force would have long since had the place blanketed. There'd be a warrant to sift through Curt Boyd's belongings, search the house, talk to the roommates.

"We haven't talked with anyone."

"Any other close friends?" I asked. "Did Curt have a girl friend? Fianceé?"

"He spoke of Julie Warner as if the two of them were making plans." Maxine looked embarrassed. "We've never met her, but…" She rose quickly and walked across to an elegant rolltop desk where she collected a section of newspaper. "I don't know why all the hush-hush, but I happened to see this in the paper."

She handed the photo to me, out of deference I suppose, and I promptly passed it to Estelle. She looked closely at the photo and article, then passed it back to me. Coach Julie Warner was caught in mid-yell, shouting encouragement or instructions to her volleyball team from the bench.

"Attractive young lady," I said. Slim, trim, with a long pony-tail of dark hair, Julie Warner even made the grimace of a coach's holler look good.

"You've never met her?"

"Hell no," Johnny Boyd said. He stretched one leg painfully. "You know, my son has his own life now, and it ain't what he grew up with. He don't confide much."

"Did the two of you argue about Waddell's project the last time he was here? At Christmas, maybe?"

"Nope."

"Did he talk about any other people with whom he might be associating—anyone with similar sentiments?"

"You're talkin' about somebody who might talk Curt into taking a chain saw to power poles? Not hardly, Sheriff."

"What was on his mind when he visited at Christmas?"

"Can't guess. He talked about his coaching season…he was pleased goin' into the second half of the season five up, I guess. Mostly he went on about a new gun he found. Hell of a deal. He'd bought a handful of shells for it, and was tryin' to talk this Kiran fellow into goin' out to the range to try it out. The kid wasn't much interested."

"What did he find?"

"One of them French Chitchats. That's what I call it. It's over in the cabinet if you want a look." He didn't wait for me to accept the invitation, but rose as quickly as his bashed knees would allow, as if eager for the chance to dwell on something other than the death of his son.

The large gun cabinet beside the fireplace wouldn't have been my choice for secure storage, but I knew that the half dozen barrels standing upright were a small fraction of the young man's collection.

Johnny opened the glass door and hefted out a bulky, awkward-looking weapon with a massive crescent magazine.

"I'll be damned," I said with honest admiration. "Where did he find this?"

"Don't know. But there she is." He handed it to me, the first time ever that I'd handled the French light machine gun with which allied soldiers had struggled during World War I. The thing was a horror of awful engineering and crude manufacturing, but it's what they had.

"Cost him some," the rancher offered.

"I don't doubt that." After a moment, I handed the gun back. The Boyds had a paperwork snarl ahead of them if they wanted to keep their son's collection. As far as I knew, each fully automatic weapon in the collection was papered to the young man.

They couldn't just be sold to a neighbor, or given away. Johnny would figure it all out when he could settle his mind.

"This Kiran fellow was one of Curt's roommates, right? Was he the only one who came out with him at Christmas?"

Boyd nodded. "Seemed like a nice-enough fellow. Quiet as hell. I was hopin' that Curt's girlfriend, there, would come along, but she was visiting family. Back in Michigan, I think it was."

We probed this and that for another fifteen minutes, and then took our leave.

As Estelle idled the stiffly sprung sedan out the driveway, I tried to make myself comfortable. "And I apologize," I said as we passed under the metal archway that capped the front gate. "I was going on and on there."

"That's all right, sir."

"Well, no, it's not. But…" I reached out and slapped the dashboard in frustration. "It's harder than hell to stay on the sidelines with something like this. I've known the Boyds for years. One thing I know for damn sure—it wasn't Johnny Boyd who was with his son last night."

"It would be easy to invent," the undersheriff said. "Curt had surrounded himself with foreign roommates—Indian, Kenyan, and Ecuadorian. He…"

I interrupted her. "*Ecuador?* I didn't hear that mentioned."

"His name is Roberto Esquibel. He's a senior majoring in child psych. He's also a licensed practical nurse."

I looked at her with amusement, once again left behind by Estelle Reyes-Guzman. "And the guy from Kenya?"

"A junior majoring in physical education. I'd have to read my notes to get his name correct."

"You're slipping, sweetheart." And she hadn't blabbed what she knew to the Boyds, either, letting me charge ahead, bull-headed and out of order. "So we have a household full of inter-nationals. Let's stretch the loop a little and include Julie Warner. What's the surprise about her?"

"Originally from Toledo, Ohio. Graduated from New Mexico State two years ago in El Ed. Teaches and coaches varsity volleyball."

"No surprise there. We've got an international house, and a fair young lady. Any of them wearing chain saw dust?"

"I doubt it, sir."

"Hot arguments over dinner about the United Nations invading the United States?"

"That may be."

"None of them owns a Nissan pickup truck?"

"Curt Boyd does. Or did. Color blue, 2009 model, Golf Lincoln Foxtrot Seven Niner Seven."

I sighed. "And we don't know where it is at the moment, do we?"

"No, sir."

"There's a connection, then. You have a guy or gal driving it with creosote sawdust spattered on his trousers, splatter of bar oil, maybe some spilled gasoline. Then there's sawdust in his shoelaces, red sand ground into the floor mats, all kinds of shit. And a chain saw in the back. And if he shot Kenderman, then you can mix all of that in with some nitrite residue from the gun shot."

"And the direction. When he left the scene, he headed north on the county road, not south. Had he gone south, you wouldn't have seen him. You wouldn't have called it in."

"True…but he couldn't have known I was stroking my insomnia up on Cat Mesa. Which way he headed was a flip of the coin."

"Unless he was an outsider and didn't know better. If Curt Boyd drove *to* the site because he was familiar with the country, then it makes sense his partner would take the same route going out."

The reflectors along the side of the state highway flashed by altogether too fast as we headed into town.

"So now what?" I asked.

"Bobby has a meeting called for nine o'clock." The digital clock on the dash showed we were well past civilized dinnertime already. "You're welcome to come." She smiled. "Encouraged to come, in fact."

"I'd rather sleep," I said. Even insomniacs eventually collapse, and I was reaching that point. Only the whacking of the tar strips on the highway was keeping me awake. "And I need fuel," I added. "I remember vaguely a promise of green chile stew and corn bread."

"Yet another in a long string of broken promises," Estelle laughed. "Carlos is going to be furious." Her youngest son had an affinity for experimentation in the kitchen, and the nine-year-old's creations were sometimes delectable, sometimes awful. He did hold dear the old-fashioned notion that corn bread should be golden, crumbly, and touched only by real butter, melting down the sides.

"You need rest more than the chile," she added. "How about cashing a rain check tomorrow?"

"I'll check my busy schedule."

I knew there were going to be lots of bags under lots of eyes before the sheriff had this mess cleaned up. If the killer had been driving a truck that belonged to Curt Boyd, that closed one loophole, but didn't get us far. Didn't get *them* far. Curt Boyd's companion at the fatal power pole party remained a shadow. It was hard for me to believe that the young teacher would be able to live one life with roommates and girlfriend, and another entirely separate life with a cold, calculating eco-terrorist and killer. Some how, the two paths must cross, or at least touch.

Back at the Posadas County Sheriff's Office, and with a little bit of reluctance, I took my leave, so weary that for a moment I forgot where I had parked. That wasn't a difficult mystery, since there were only a half-dozen vehicles in the lot, all but one with government plates.

I settled into my SUV, started it, and waited until all the digital nonsense on the dash had calmed down before pulling it into gear. I wanted to go home, and I didn't. The night, clear and calm, was so damn comfortable that I knew I sat on the brink of waking fully. I didn't fight it. With an evening where things out of place would shout their existence, I was loath to ignore the opportunity. So I compromised.

Slouched comfortably in the fancy any-which-way power seat, the police radio turned low, I took "the loop," a path I'd worked out years ago that allowed me to cover most of the village without retracing or crossing my own path. The hunting would have been better with two inches of fresh snow, but the brilliant night sky that would have warmed Miles Waddell's heart didn't promise moisture.

As the clock ticked past eight that evening, the village was already winter-night quiet—a few kids out and about, one or two renting videos at Tommy's Handi-way convenience store when I paused there for some of his awful coffee. The First Baptist Church parking lot was empty, but there was some life at the VFW, a squat, ugly little building up on North Fourth that used to be the Baptist church's home.

No one was parked in the abandoned drive-in theater out on County 43, no one was trying to cut a late deal at Chavez Chevy.

I lowered the window and dumped out the last of the fetid coffee as I turned south on McArthur Street by the Hamburger Heaven. Business there was as slow as anywhere else, but it only took the aroma of a single broiling burger to waft out, setting off the hungries. Not to succumb to the temptation this early in the evening meant I was seriously off my feed, but I wasn't sure I had the energy to chew.

The struggle to keep my eyes open kept me occupied as I drove home to my own comfortable burrow on Guadalupe, no longer trying to X-ray every shadow or peer behind every building, no longer trying to see the lurking shadow of a blue Nissan.

Chapter Fifteen

At one time, my residential lot off Guadalupe had been a five-acre parcel, worth enough to make any realtor salivate. I'd kept a half-acre and given the rest to Dr. Francis and Estelle Guzman. It had been a good move. The Medical/Dental Clinic built there had prospered, and I took a quiet pleasure out of occasionally cruising the spacious parking lot and seeing all the license plates from Chihuahua and other points south.

The attached pharmacy was still open, with two or three cars parked in front. Out of old habit, I looped through the parking lot, glancing at license plates. There had been a time when I might run them through dispatch. I returned to my own driveway. I damn near fell asleep waiting for my garage door to open, and when it scrolled shut behind me with a gentle thud, the thought occurred to me that I could just slump in my car seat and snooze without all the hassle of dismounting.

"Come on," I said aloud. Supporting myself against the wall, avoiding a rack of long-abandoned paint cans, I reached the interior door that took me into the small utility room. Moving by automatic pilot with my hand skimming the rough adobe walls, lights weren't necessary. Miles Waddell's dark zone mesa had nothing on me. The old adobe was a proper burrow, and the tiny night light on the kitchen wall—allowing me to always find the coffeemaker at the oddest of hours—was enough without polluting the whole house.

The darkest room in the house was the bedroom, and by the time I reached it, I'd shed my jacket, hat, and the replacement Smith and Wesson that had become my companion an hour after I'd surrendered the other one to the undersheriff for the sort of pointless testing that only lawyers love. I sat on the side of the bed for a moment, considering. Then I just let gravity win, using a last burst of energy to swing my feet up.

When I next looked its way, the dim three-inch numerals of the clock on the bureau said it was nine thirty p.m. I'd slept for less than an hour or for a full twelve—either way, I felt as if I weighed three hundred pounds. The expensive pillow-top mattress that my eldest daughter Camille had insisted upon had a firm grip on every stiff joint. So why wake up? Why not just roll over and sink once more into a few moments of oblivion? I had started to ponder that very question when the phone rang.

My land line—the one making all the racket—was out in the kitchen, by design. If it were bedside, I'd answer in my sleep and probably embarrass myself. This way, if the caller let the phone clamor long enough, I'd get up, find it, and be coherent enough to swear fluently.

The ringing passed five, and I heaved out of bed, making my way through the short hall and around the corner.

"What?" I growled.

"Got two things," Sheriff Robert Torrez said, and his voice was so soft that I had to cover one ear with my free hand and stuff the receiver into the other.

"They better be good, in the middle of the goddamn night."

Bobby didn't rise to that. Instead his tone sounded as neutral as if I'd said, "Why, thanks. I was expecting your call."

"Estelle and me are going to run over to Deming. Thought you might want to come along."

"For what?" I looked outside and saw pitch black. The nap had been less than an hour.

"Deming PD found the truck."

"No shit?"

"No shit."

"And why do I need to see it? All I saw was headlights from twenty miles away. What am I going to recognize?"

Silence, so I let him off the hook. What the hell…I enjoyed their company.

"All right. That's just what I need right now, a ride to Deming."

"We'll be by in about five minutes."

"Yup." I sounded as if a late night road trip outbid the pillow top. But if I hustled, the coffee would be done in time.

"Nathan Baum died, by the way."

That news punched me silent. No wonder Bobby had called.

"I guess a blood clot," the sheriff added. "Something like that."

Normally, the sheriff's vintage understatement would have amused me—Baum died, "*by the way*…a clot, or "*something like that.*" I didn't try to find the right thing to say.

"I'll be here." I hung up. I would have liked to say that I swung into action like a well-oiled machine. I fumbled the coffeemaker, forgetting the filter and spilling the water. But what's better than gritty cowboy brew in the middle of the night? While it gurgled, I charged around my face with an electric razor and, knowing I'd be stuck in a vehicle with others who might not appreciate a storm of perfume, settled for a little witch hazel aftershave.

As I poured the coffee into a large Thermos cup, I heard a vehicle crunch on the gravel in front of the house. I had almost reached the front door when I remembered the four-inch Smith and Wesson, and found it tucked under my jacket on the foyer bench.

The sheriff was driving one of the new extended Expeditions, and Estelle got out as I emerged from the house. She held the SUV's front door for me. "I curl up easier than you do," she said. "Did we wake you up?"

"Thank you. And yes."

As I slid into the big tank, the sheriff did an unexpected thing: he reached over, extending his hand. His grip was powerful but not crushing, almost as if he was trying to transmit a little sympathy with the greeting. He watched as I managed the shoulder harness, and didn't ask about my hardware which the short jacket didn't conceal very well.

"Schroeder said nothing's changed," he said, leaving it to me to figure out to what he might be referring. I assumed it was Nathan Baum's death and my contribution to it.

"Clot broke loose from the surgery?"

Estelle leaned forward, no doubt pleased that the security cage was *behind* her seat, not in front of her. "Francis said the autopsy will clarify it, but he thinks that's likely. Probably from the massive hip surgery. For a few minutes, they thought that they could bring him through it, but it didn't work out that way." Her hand touched my left shoulder. "The cancer was advanced, by the way."

"The way it goes," I said. "He didn't have to offer an invitation with that shotgun." But no matter what the Monday Morning Quarterbacks who hadn't been there said, there was a monumental difference between wounding someone—causing a world of hurt and complications—and *killing* them…no more phone calls from granddaughter, no more pride in what the son might be accomplishing, no small satisfactions, no good coffee, no more Christmas mornings with the family. Just dead.

"So where's the kid?"

"She's back with her mother."

"And the father?"

"Don't know," Torrez interjected. "That's one of our problems. But we got some paperwork now." We swooshed up the interstate ramp, and it was evident that we weren't going to waste a lot of time in transit.

"It turns out that there was a restraining order filed against him," Estelle explained. "Against the son. Apparently George Baum originally had visiting rights on a regular basis, and blew that this summer when he took off with the little girl to visit Grandpa. Mom went ballistic and won the court order after he punched her. She wouldn't press charges."

"Ah…that kind of guy."

"Lots of education, lots of computer savvy, and unfortunately lots of temper. He's talked himself out of a string of jobs over the past couple of years. From what we're told, George Baum is the sort with all the answers, and everyone else is an idiot."

"You've been busy," I said. "So where is he, do you think?"

"I wish we knew. All we know for sure is that he isn't at his home in El Paso. One of the nurses *thinks* that he came to the hospital in Las Cruces briefly. They're not sure. He wasn't allowed to see his father. The old man was in the operating room at the time. George ranted and raved, and made a few threats. Your name came up."

I lurched this way and that, trying to get comfortable with seat belt and coffee mug. "I'm sure he just wants to thank me. What can I say." I nodded and sipped the awful coffee. "Now Deming."

"Curt Boyd's truck is parked in a storage unit there, just off the main drag," Estelle said. "DPD says the unit's renter is as puzzled as we are. He's the one who called police."

"After touching everything that could be touched," I added cynically.

"Actually, no. The lock was off, the door open a few inches. That tipped the owner off. He called DPD without touching a thing. Without going in. And as soon as the officers saw that the truck was a candidate for our BOLO, they contacted us."

I watched the lane markers and signs blur by, trying to imagine why Perry Kenderman's killer had chosen a little rental cave in Deming to ditch the truck. A portrait was beginning to emerge, and this killer was quick to take action, quick to think his way out of the box when he made mistakes. "This guy makes me nervous," I said, and twisted around to look at Estelle Reyes-Guzman. "What's the team in Las Cruces sending you?"

"Mitchell went down earlier," the sheriff said, and I guess that covered it as far as he was concerned. Captain Eddie Mitchell was a no-nonsense kind of guy, a creative and fearless investigator, and "procrastination" wasn't in his lexicon.

"I hear the feds already talked with Boyd's roommates?"

"In the process." Torrez braked hard as a motorist carrying Arizona plates on his Pontiac pulled out to pass a tractor trailer truck just as we rocketed up behind them in the passing lane. The sheriff knew the vehicular confrontation was his fault, given that he was running far too fast without his emergency equipment switched on to clear the path. We sat patiently at 75 until the Pontiac, safely past the truck, pulled back into his lane.

When we passed, I could see the shadow of the driver and hear his thoughts about government officials traveling on junkets at taxpayers' expense. The sheriff let the big SUV creep back up to 90 again, and five miles out of Deming, a west-bound state police cruiser in the far lanes winked his red lights at us.

"You're expected," I said. Torrez didn't reply, but of course he was. Every cop within two hundred miles stood on high alert, without the luxury of diving into a pleasant nap. And sure enough, as we shot down the Deming exit, there was a city PD cruiser parked on the shoulder. Torrez reached down and turned on the red lights, and as we drew up behind the cruiser, the cop pulled out to lead the way.

Chapter Sixteen

The storage units were off on a side street south of the main drag. Two long buildings housed two dozen units, and the entrance was blocked by a second city police cruiser. Behind him was a Border Patrol unit and a newer model pickup that I knew belonged to Sheriff Blair Escobedo. As we pulled to a stop, a New Mexico State Police cruiser joined us.

"Too many people," I muttered.

Torrez laughed, his handsome face breaking into a rare smile. "This is the age." It had taken him two decades to accept interagency cooperation, and then to actually work to enhance the process. Gone were the days of jumping astride a good horse and thundering across the prairie, alone after the bad guys. Too damn bad.

A Deming PD lieutenant approached, and he walked with one hand on Sheriff Escobedo's right shoulder as if he had to hold the sheriff in place to finish a conversation. I knew Escobedo well, a law man with a tough county to shepherd. There were rare times when he even worked hard at it. A former Marine, former county commissioner, former a lot of things, he'd tried for years to hire Robert Torrez away from Posadas County. I forgave him that, and chalked it up to good sense in choosing his officers. But he had no patience with the federal government, holding all their agencies in almost bigot-like contempt. When you're in a county squatting right on the border, forced to work alongside the Border Patrol, Immigration Services, Federal Bureau of Investigation, and on and on, that's a painful quirk to nurture.

The sheriff didn't look in a mirror often enough, either. Togged out in one of those quasi-military uniforms with the circle of five stars on each collar, Escobedo looked less like Commander of Allied Forces Ike Eisenhower than he did a character actor portraying a Mexican Federale *jefe* in a grade C spaghetti western. I was a large, too-heavy fellow myself, but Escobedo's belly made me look downright anorexic. It hung over his Sam Brown belt in great slabs.

The lieutenant wound down in his lecture to the sheriff as they drew within hand-shaking distance, and the five of us went through the formalities.

"You knew my dad," the lieutenant said to me, and I scrutinized his name tag again. He was as trim and fit as Escobedo was a slob.

"Colin Martinez?"

"That's him," Lieutenant Paul Martinez beamed.

"What's he up to now?" Colin and I had worked some interesting interagency drug stuff years before, and I always was pleased when the operations ended and I could go home. Colin Martinez believed that if he thumped enough heads, the drug trafficking problem would fade away.

"He retired last year and moved to Tampa," the lieutenant said. "He's heavy into the swinging widower scene." The son had inherited his looks from his father, who no doubt was cutting a swath.

"Ah," I said. Somehow, Martinez's comment about the "swinging widower scene" sounded like something my eldest daughter would say, ever hopeful that my social life might blossom. Thank God she lived halfway across the country.

"So," Sheriff Escobedo rasped. "Tell me about all this. What did Kenderman walk into? Took him by surprise, or what?"

"Yup. Traffic stop." Torrez pointed his own index finger at his skull and pulled the trigger. He nodded toward the storage building, in no mood to stand and chat. "Show me what you got."

"It hasn't been touched," Lieuetenant Martinez said as he led us to the right-hand row of units. *That in itself was a miracle,* I thought. Mid-way between two of the outdoor security lights, number eleven's door gaped open a foot. "The owner says this is exactly the way he found it." Martinez stopped a pace short of the door. "He walks up and sees the door is open, and then sees the lock on the ground over there. He forgot to snap it in place. The latch wasn't tight in, and the door drifted up." He pointed without moving forward, and the beam of his flashlight haloed the brass padlock that had been dropped into the corner of the doorway. "So he rolls the door up some more, he says without handling it, sees this strange truck parked inside, and then sees that his motorcycle is gone. So he calls us."

"He," Torrez prompted.

"The owner's name is Brandon Smith. Brandon C. Smith. Lives over on Fairway. Just a couple of blocks."

"Where is he now?"

Martinez turned and pointed across the street. On the front porch of a modest little block home, half a dozen people had gathered. "A biker buddy of his lives right over there. I told Smith to stick close until we get to him. You want to talk to him?"

"Yup. Not now." Torrez knelt in front of the door, regarding the plastic bag that now covered the lift handle. Someone, not trusting even a responding cop's impulse, had protected the handle from unthinking fingers. Torrez nodded in satisfaction, and then dropped down to a push-up position so that he could peer under the door…a tough maneuver for such a big man. Supported on toes and elbows, the sheriff swept his flashlight this way and that. Finally satisfied, he arose with a grunt.

Using his flashlight, Torrez lifted the door until it rolled all the way up. The light switch was immediately inside to the right, and Lieutenant Martinez started toward it. Torrez held out a hand.

"Wait a sec." Without stepping into the storage unit, Torrez let the flashlight beam roam, digging into all the corners. The place was neat and clean. It appeared that the owner was using the unit as storage for a significant collection of paint cans, a handy inventory if he was a landlord.

The Nissan Frontier had been driven in nose first, and I could see only one set of truck tracks in the fine dust on the floor. Another set, this a single track, exited the unit along one side. A blue tarp, maybe one that had covered the motorcycle, had been tossed carelessly in the corner.

"And well, well, well." Martinez pointed, and his body language said that he *really* wanted to step into the unit. On a side shelf formed by one of the braces between upright support girders, a well-used chain saw rested, along with a quart of oil and a small red gas can.

"Now why would he do that?" Estelle murmured.

"It might not be the one." Torrez bent down and placed his flashlight on the concrete floor immediately inside the door track, then rolled it with his toe so that the beam shot a glancing pattern across the floor. He stopped when the beam reached a spot on the floor directly under the driver's door of the Nissan where a collection of shoeprints were visible on the dust-covered concrete. "What do you think?" He looked at Estelle, who had already unzipped a bulky camera bag and was attaching a large flash unit to her digital camera.

"Iffy," she said. "Certainly not enough to identify anything beyond size. Maybe brand."

"We'll do those first from the outside," the sheriff said. "We got us a wait for the van anyway." It turned out to be not much of a wait. Estelle had taken a series of exterior shots and was positioning herself with a telephoto to tackle a nice angle shot of the faint traces on the floor when the enormous black-and-gold State Police crime scene van oozed into the side street. That prompted a derisive groan from Sheriff Escobedo, who so far had been content to stand to the side, arms crossed comfortably over his mammoth belly.

"Now we'll be here all night," Escobedo muttered. "I don't see nothin' we can't do right here ourselves without making a big state deal out of it."

We? I thought. So far, Escobedo's efforts had equaled mine, but Torrez ignored him. If the world of county sheriffs was a close brotherhood, I think that Bobby Torrez considered Blair Escobedo an embarrassing idiot brother—if he considered him at all. Of course, to Sheriff Escobedo, Perry Kenderman was just another name, another county's problem. I knew that in the past, Escobedo *could* be thorough and meticulous in the best of times, but this chilly night, he wasn't in the Posadas County sheriff's league.

Bobby Torrez might not have been able to quote Locard's Exchange Principle, but he sure as hell understood the Frenchman's concept that no one can commit a crime without leaving *something* behind at the scene—if not tracks, then fluid traces, prints, fibers, hairs, smudges…all of which could be easily missed or dismissed by investigators.

When the killer had driven Curt Boyd's pickup into this rental unit, and then stolen the motorcycle stored there, he'd obviously been stealthy and careful. He hadn't awakened the entire neighborhood, even though his heart must have been pounding in his ears like a kettledrum. I didn't know what model the motorcycle was, but if it was a big Harley, or even a snarling two-stroke dirt bike, its departure might have attracted some attention. That wouldn't have escaped Bob Torrez's attention.

If the chain saw carried the reddish sawdust of power poles, why leave it behind? The simplest reason was that he couldn't carry it on the bike. By off-loading it from the pickup, sloppy cops might assume that it belonged to the unit's renter.

Without doubt, the faint shoeprints left in the dust wouldn't be the killer's only mistake. If the saw was his, fine. In addition, there would be other evidence that he'd been in that small, plain chamber, and the crime scene techs and Estelle Reyes-Guzman would find it. I needed to stay out of the way, but I wasn't in the mood for chit-chat with Escobedo or anyone else. I considered sinking into a quiet, dark corner by the Dumpster, but the sheriff's Expedition was handier and a hell of a lot more comfy. I settled in to wait.

The French forensic pioneer Locard never said that humans would leave a *lot* behind. After three hours of fine-toothed combing, when the rest of the city had long since gone to bed after the late show, the list of evidence was predictably and depressingly short.

We had faint, ghostly shoeprints of the sort left by those fancy trainers, and I predicted that the photos of those, despite the angled-light tricks and enhancement toning, would reveal little beyond what Estelle had predicted. Dusting revealed a few decent latent fingerprints, including a clear set of three from the top of the truck's door—a natural place to touch and an easy spot to forget when giving the vehicle a quick wipe down. If the killer had worn gloves, the prints would belong to the truck's rightful owner, Curt Boyd.

I had watched them gather a fair selection of hairs from both front headrests. And, like the latent prints, if we had a killer in custody, matches might be possible. Without a killer, hairs and prints would molder, useless in their envelope in the evidence locker. If the killer had been fingerprinted before, there would be a chance that a match could be made. If.

"Not a hell of a lot," Lieutenant Martinez mused as he strolled over to where I sat, door ajar. "Gloves or a wipe down. I'm betting gloves. Truck is dusty as hell, and a wipe down is going to leave lots of traces." He'd spend several moments enjoying watching Estelle and one of the State Police techs working the cameras. "But we got us some big questions."

Sure enough, we did. Like *why, why, why*. I'd been brooding about that very thing, but no epiphany had bloomed other than the obvious. The killer needed to dump the Nissan, and maybe it was as simple as finding a storage unit door ajar. If he could park inside and then snug the door down, who knew…it might be weeks or months before the owner showed up. And the killer had struck gold by an easy change of vehicles, if he could find the keys. Only the saw had been a complication.

I watched the sheriff across the street, where he had isolated one witness after another. Now, he and a huge, spade-bearded guy had ambled down the street away from ears, now standing on the dirt sidewalk. I assumed that this might be Brandon Smith, storage unit eleven's tenant. As Smith talked, I could see his beard bob up and down. The beard was one of those wonderful creations that would catch the wind and make moves of its own as its owner rode the bike.

The sheriff took notes in his bold, blocky printing, but I tried to stay optimistic. What was to find here? The killer took a bike, and in moments, Torrez would post that APB. By the time the bike was found, its rider would have commandeered yet another vehicle, and so it went. But we were establishing a trail, however faint.

What we needed were the connections. How did the killer find this spot, this empty cubbyhole where he could make a quick change? That was one corner of the puzzle. I leaned back against the cushy seat and mulled that for a while. My first conclusion was just too easy. Find an open unit, ditch the truck, take a bike conveniently ready for him? I wanted to plunge into that conversation the sheriff was having with Mr. Smith, but resisted.

I glanced at my watch. The cold had begun to seep into my joints, and I considered firing up the Expedition. I needed something to do, or I needed to be snuggled into my burrow, one or the other. The longer I sat and watched, the more I wondered about Sheriff Torrez. Estelle hadn't called me with the invite. It had been the sheriff himself, a man usually willing to let others deliver messages. And as far as I could see, he didn't need a damn thing from me.

I stayed out of the way and waited. Somebody found coffee, and a Styrofoam cupful found its way to me. Somewhere about halfway to the bottom, I dozed off, and then awoke with a snap as the tipping cup drizzled its contents down my pants leg. I straightened up and, human nature being what it is, swore eloquently and glanced around to see who might be a witness.

The sensible thing for a tired old man trapped by circumstances was to commandeer an empty back seat and curl up for a nap. Of course I didn't do that. Nor did I find Estelle or Bobby and suggest that we go home—we…they…had scrubbed this place until half of the State Police Crime Scene crew now stood around unemployed.

Finally, on his way back across the street, Sheriff Torrez walked head down, cell phone pasted to his ear. I had the awful thought that it was Captain Eddie Mitchell checking in from Las Cruces, and that Bobby would announce that we needed to drive down there.

He corralled Estelle, and they conferred for a while. The smart thing for me to do was force a recharge, pry myself out of the truck, and look productive. I was in the process of prying when the two Posadas cops found me.

"You okay?" the sheriff asked as he and Estelle climbed into the SUV.

"Fine," I lied. "I was about to look for a couple of toothpicks." If he understood the lame joke, he didn't react, but I earned a sympathetic smile from Estelle.

"Mitchell has a list of names to work on," Torrez said.

"I'm eager to hear about that," I lied again. Raising a hand to include all the human shadows still drifting here and there, I added, "I'm not sure why you dragged my sorry carcass all the way down here. What can I tell you?"

"Any ideas are welcome," Estelle said.

"If I had any. You have a clever, opportunistic son-of-a-bitch at work here. I have to wonder how he knew that this place was even here—unless he lived in Deming. If he didn't know the bike was inside, what was the attraction, other than a place to ditch the truck that *might* not be discovered for who knows how long? And when he sees the bike, he dumps the chain saw, the devious little bastard. What, he's planning to come back for it? And I have to wonder, now what? Where is he headed on that Harley? I assume that's what it was, since old gray beard over there doesn't look like he'd own anything else. And our man is an experienced rider, obviously, since a neophyte doesn't just hop a Harley and avoid killing himself in the first hundred yards. And that's if he can even get it started." I took a deep breath, more of a sigh. Estelle and Bobby waited patiently. "I assume you have all the particulars on the bike from its owner."

"Yep."

"Stored with a full tank? Key in the ignition?"

"Damn near." Torrez gazed at me thoughtfully. "He had a spare key in one of those little dealios stashed in the saddlebag."

"Clever. I would always do that, myself."

"Natural enough to look there," the sheriff observed, not responding to my sarcasm.

"How did he pop the door? What's the owner say?"

"He forgot to lock it."

"*Forgot?* With a twenty thousand-dollar bike inside?" I shouldn't have been surprised—I'd forget my middle name if it weren't secured on my driver's license. And I'd misplaced that more than once, too.

"He says that if it isn't locked, the door will eventually drift up a bit. Wind buffets it."

"So our man turns off the main drag, because why?"

Torrez shrugged. "Maybe he saw a cop car. Maybe he wanted a cup of coffee at the Miami." From where I stood, I could see the coffee shop at the intersection with East Pine Street. Had the killer pulled in there, or swerved out of sight there, about the first thing he'd see was this storage facility just down the street.

"A quick thinker," I said. "He's got to know that Kenderman would have radioed in *something*. I mean, a description of the vehicle is pretty basic. The killer feels exposed, and wants to get rid of it just as fast as possible. Things worked out for him."

Torrez grunted something uncomplimentary.

"An APB is out for the Nissan," Estelle regarded the storage unit skeptically. "Up to now, anyway, no one's going to give a Harley a second look, so a trade makes sense." She turned and nodded at me. "He knew this was here, didn't he?" Seeing my raised eyebrow, she added, "Head straight for Deming after the shooting. That's what he did. He knows he needs another vehicle. He *can't* know that Kenderman called in such a vague description, so he assumes we're looking for him. He didn't find this place by accident."

"Why not steal a car in Posadas?"

"Exactly so. He didn't run that risk. Maybe he didn't know how."

"Not everyone does," I said. "Hell, I couldn't. I'd scrunch down to look at the snarl of wires under the dash and get stuck there. It only works in the movies."

"We got us a new direction to go," Torrez announced abruptly, and he sounded more confident than I felt. "Smith is sweatin' it out."

"Steal a man's Harley, and he's not going to be a happy camper."

"Yeah, well, that's one story," the sheriff said. "He had a little trouble finding the registration, but he finally came up with it. When he handed it to me, his hand was shakin'."

"You make people nervous, Bobby," I said, but I knew where he was headed with this. "You think the bike wasn't stolen?"

"Nope. I think our boy knew the bike was here."

"The door unlocked just for him?"

Torrez nodded. A little tingle of progress does great things for the attitude, and I found myself jolted wide awake. "Now wait a minute," I protested. "That means the killer *knew* there was a chance that he might need wheels—something beyond his friend's truck. Why something like this that might just as easily screw him up?"

"It might not have been planned this way," Estelle said quietly. "He didn't plan to see Curt Boyd die at the scene. That was a freak accident. They had planned to cut, and run." She held up a hand. "And Curt dies, and at that moment, that very moment, his whole game plan had to change. He's near to panic. If he can just get out of town, maybe he can cover his tracks. So that's what he does. He leaves the scene, concentrating on that. And what happen?."

"Kenderman," I said.

"That's right. And remember, here's a guy with a lot to hide. The killer can try and talk his way out. When Curt Boyd died, that *does* make him a killer…the simple route of death during a felony, which chopping poles certainly is." I had rarely heard Estelle so adamant. "Our man has a gun, just in case. And that takes us right back to the whole issue of having nerves and triggers. He might not have *meant* to shoot Kenderman, but the gun went off one way or another."

"I'd go for that," Torrez agreed. "Like Baum shootin' Jackie… maybe."

"Everything goes to hell, and now he's got a cop shooting on his hands," I said. "What if that's the time that he uses his cell phone and calls his buddy, Mr. Smith. Cruces is too far, too much exposure on the highway. Deming is close. It's a good gamble he can make it before the net closes. The rest follows." I looked across at the storage unit. "Better to hide it here than just park the damn thing on a side street, I suppose."

Across the street, the group of observers were still enjoying the show. I could see Smith, his beard flopping as he no doubt recounted his conversation with the Posadas sheriff.

"Except numb nuts over there called the cops to report his bike stolen," I said. "Why would Smith do that, except maybe a clever move to get himself off the hook?"

"He ain't too clever," Torrez said. "But I think that's exactly what he did."

"Especially when he comes to understand what the words 'conspiracy' and 'complicity' mean. You're going to pull him in?"

Torrez looked at his watch. "This is the lieutenant's turf, so he's going to organize a little party for us. We'll give Smith a couple of hours to sweat, and then Martinez will give him a back-seat ride down to the P.D. We'll see what we can get out of him." He almost smiled. "We'll see if he understands those fancy words."

I felt a weary, sinking sensation blossom. The sheriff and undersheriff would want to be in Deming when Brandon Smith took the hot seat and spilled the beans, and there didn't seem much point in a fast twenty-minute return trip back to Posadas, unless they were just extending the courtesy to me. That was a good idea, come to think of it.

"So," I said. "What did you actually want from me? I wasn't much help to you."

"Thought you might be interested," the sheriff said lamely.

"Horseshit," I scoffed. "You don't drag somebody out of bed in the middle of the night just because he might be *interested*."

Bobby actually checked his watch, apparently to see if my "middle of the night" estimate was accurate. He glanced in the rearview mirror at Estelle.

"One of the nurses at Las Cruces told the cops that she talked to a guy who fitted George Baum's description just a few minutes before his father died," Estelle said. "He wanted to get into the I.C. to talk to the old man. They wouldn't let him. There was a bit of an argument, apparently."

"That's what Bobby told me over the phone. So we know where he is now."

"No, sir, we don't. The nurse did say that in the heat of the moment, George Baum became verbally abusive and she was about to call hospital security when he left abruptly. Lots of threats, sir. He ranted about the shooter taking a walk away from charges. That would be you, sir."

"Yep, I do that all the time," I said. "Comes with the turf."

"That's true. But he said something about not letting that happen this time. Until we know where *he* is, we'll feel better knowing where *you* are."

"What, he was threatening me? Surely not," I said in mock horror. If I had a dollar for every time I had been threatened in my long career, I'd have a hell of an IRA.

"This could be serious, sir. The nurse heard him mutter, 'The man who did this.'"

"It never occurred to him that his dad earned what he got?"

"I'm sure the discussion with the nurse didn't go there, sir. And I'm considering George Baum's track record for bad decisions when it comes to relationships."

Irked, I shifted in my seat. "What, I need babysitting now?" Somehow, hearing myself sound angry and petulant made me even more so, but Bobby Torrez, never a talker in the best of times, said just the right thing. He huffed what might have been a chuckle, and glanced my way.

"It's for his own safety," he said. "If he does something stupid…"

"He'll cool off," I said.

"We can hope so," Estelle said. "In the meantime, it doesn't hurt to be careful."

"We don't want him becomin' another notch on your six-gun," the sheriff said.

Chapter Seventeen

Now that the possibility of a threat lingering in the shadows had been mentioned, I had no trouble staying wide awake for the rest of the ride to Posadas, brief as it was. I wasn't worried about George Baum—statistics said that nothing would come of his threats as time scabbed some of his emotional wounds. There wasn't much I could do about his threat anyway, other than stay vigilant.

I did stew about a killer on the loose. If the bearded idiot in Deming, Brandon Smith, was a fat-faced liar and indeed knew the killer, why didn't he just help him ditch the truck somewhere innocuous, and then give him a ride back to Las Cruces—or whereever it was that he wanted to go? Because a man on a motorcyle raised fewer suspicions? Perhaps. I had a hard time imagining a Harley owner loaning out his bike to anyone other than a cherished best friend, another veteran bike rider.

Decades in law enforcement had taught me that people often did really, really stupid things, especially when under duress. Unless Perry Kenderman's killer was a habitual assassin, then he certainly was under duress. He'd seen the blood and brains fly, he'd seen the officer stagger a step or two backward, already dead before he toppled to the ground. Plenty of duress. When the killer drove away into the night, it's a wonder that he was even capable of shifting the little Nisssan. His breathing would be coming in gasps, with heart pounding, blood pressure off the scale, his hands sweaty. All of that would work in our favor.

But…did one man willingly let another take his Harley? More likely to loan out his wife. He did have the presence of mind to remove the saw, puzzling though it was that at that moment, the saw loomed as so important to save. Maybe he had other poles to whack.

The dash clock announced 4:00 as we wheeled down the Interstate ramp into Posadas. Grande Boulevard, a four-lane artery designed and built in grander times, was empty. Torrez swung off and wound through the naked cottonwoods to Guadalupe, and pulled into my driveway.

"You're headed back to Deming right away?" I asked. Torrez had already opened his door even before I'd managed to release my shoulder harness. Maybe he was inviting himself in for coffee.

"Pretty quick," he said, and shot the beam of his flashlight into the shadows beside the garage and through the grove of runt elms and brambles that formed my elegant landscaping and windbreak. He slipped through the gate to my courtyard and tried the front door.

"I have keys," I called.

"Just hold your horses."

I turned and looked at Estelle, who was busy listening. The sheriff slipped around behind the house, and reappeared from behind the garage.

"Okay," he said, and halted at the front door.

"You really think so?" I smiled at him as I jingled the key ring. The front door opened with its usual loud wail of dry hinges. The sudden discharge of air from the quiet adobe told me only that I'd left the coffeemaker on.

"What were you planning to do today?" Estelle's voice was quiet at my shoulder, and she knew me well enough to know the answer to that question. I didn't schedule my days, instead welcoming the sometimes unexpected flow from one thing to another. "It might be good if you were to stick close to home."

"So I'm easier to find, you mean?"

She touched my arm gently. "At least keep your radio handy."

"That I can do."

"Dinner tonight?"

"You bet. But first it's breakfast. And then I'm thinking I might cruise on out and have another talk with Miles Waddell. I have lots of questions, still." I followed her into my house, and she did a quick circuit from room to room.

"I feel as if I'm enrolled in the Witness Protection Program," I growled. "You can stop snooping for hidden contraband now. And Baum will never find me out on the mesa."

"Did you know your coffeemaker is on and dry?"

"Yes." I shucked my coat and slipped the holstered revolver off my belt. It hit the hallway bench with a heavy thud.

The sheriff appeared in the doorway. He glanced at his watch and then beckoned Estelle. And then he paused. "You going to take Waddell up on his offer?"

"Which offer is that?"

"Workin' security?"

I laughed. "No. I don't know what you heard, or from who, but that wasn't the offer. He wants me to just roam around the project, keeping my eyes open."

"Security."

"No. You know, he's already heard from one firm—some company up in Colorado that wants that job. And I told him that's the direction he ought to go, but," and I shrugged, "he doesn't want a bunch of storm troopers."

"Long as we don't have to run out to that mesa every ten minutes." He started to close the door. "If you head out that way, watch your step." He nodded at the holstered revolver snuggled into my wadded up jacket. "And don't leave that at home."

As the heavy Expedition crunched out of my driveway, the old house fell deeply silent. Heavy lidded, I caved in to the decadence of doing it right. I even shucked my clothes and tossed them in the hamper for my housekeeper to find, relishing the cool sheets and soft pillow. Insomnia lost that round.

I awoke so hungry the pillow might have tasted good. And no wonder. The bedside clock announced that it was ten minutes after twelve, and the little amber am-pm light said afternoon. My bedroom was so dark, and on the northwest side of the house, that the sun didn't intrude through the single window with its heavy royal-blue curtains. I'd missed breakfast, and if I didn't stir soon, I'd miss lunch.

After shower, shave, and fresh clothes, I looked and felt ready to greet the day. The scorched coffee carafe went in the trash, a new one from the stash in the pantry, and I was in business. The mail had already arrived, and among the avalanche of catalogs and grocery store flyers was the *Posadas Register.*

"Oh, come on," I grumbled, because there I was below the fold, in a candid photo snapped who the hell knows when, talking with the sheriff, who towered over me by a foot, and State Police Lieutenant Mark Adams, who was wearing his grim state investigator's face as he looked over his left shoulder at something. Just visible to one side was the mammoth slab side of Baum's RV. The photo was all right—I looked more or less alert, posture pretty good. It had been taken long after both the shooter and Sergeant Taber had been removed from the scene. The headline had prompted the groan.

Shotgun blast Wounds Posadas Deputy,
Former Sheriff Shoots Armed Assailant

I flipped the paper over and there was the rest of the day's happy news, blared in a screamer headline and kicker that stretched across six columns.

Local Man Dies During Attack on Power Grid,
Long-Time Posadas Cop killed as Terrorist Flees

Reading as I returned to the kitchen, I saw that Frank Dayan had gathered his facts pretty damn accurately, and his chair-bound editor, Pam Gardner, had penned the thorough story with a minimum of editorial intrusion.

I skidded to a stop toward the end of the Baum story. "Well, shit," I muttered.

County Commission Chairman Dr. Arnold
Gray has announced that he will be seeking a commendation for Sheriff Gastner's
quick response as a civilian.

"Although this is a tragic incident, it could have been far worse had Sheriff Gastner not responded as he did. To step into the line of danger is downright heroic, and Sheriff Gastner deserves our sincere thanks."

"Well shit," I muttered again. "Just leave it alone." The lead story—it had been a great week for Dayan's little newspaper—was liberally laced with "allegedly," "according to…" and "police said." And small wonder, since the story was such a tangled web.

"Police said" that Curt Boyd was working with an accomplice, and "allegedly" whacked down three sets of power poles carrying 42,500 volts on six lines. The resulting damage, "police said," had caused major power losses for all of western Posadas County, and much of southwestern New Mexico and portions of eastern Arizona.

"Investigation is continuing" into Boyd's death, although "Police said" that it appeared Boyd had been somehow struck by one of the toppling structures.

Two dramatic photos were featured, including one of the massive, jagged power pole balanced precariously over the fence post near the cattle guard. Another showed Estelle examining one of the stumps.

What was missing from the story was the "why." Dayan and his editor had refused to speculate on the reason for the vandalism, but they hadn't missed the possible connection with Miles Waddell's mesa venture.

On the left side of the front page, a showy little story, boxed in a fancy border, announced that the power line vandalism would not slow Miles Waddell's *NightZone* project. The brief story ended with a little italicized squib directing the reader to *"see related story, page 3."* Dayan was getting a metro paper complex.

I opened the paper and my eyebrows shot up in surprise. Miles Waddell had obviously come to some decisions, going on the offensive. A full page headline bellowed, *"NightZone Attracts Power Scope Project!"* An exclamation point, no less.

Settling at the little counter with a full cup, I scanned the article, which featured a canned photo of the California radio telescope, noted as being "identical to the historic dish in Lucerne, Switzerland." With a dish spanning sixty-five meters, and with an on-line weight of 1,150 tons, the telescope would be the largest of its kind in the continental United States. Always the good news for strapped communities, as many as twenty-two people would be eventually employed at the radio telescope facility.

Several "Waddell said" paragraphs announced the proposed restaurant, the museum, the theater, the five linked observatories for tourists' viewing, the tramway to the mesa-top, the basic plans for coping with the combined challenge of tipsy tourists and darkness. The rancher had spilled his plans to Dayan, holding nothing back. There was so much detail in the story that I suspected Waddell must have talked with Dayan long before the rancher corralled me on the mesa-top. Why hadn't he just said so? That irked me a little, and I wondered what other details had been withheld from my confidence.

Whether such complete publicity would be a strategy that worked to Waddell's advantage, or gave his opponents plentiful ammunition to kill the project, only time would tell.

I noticed that no mention was made, in any of the stories, about a locomotive chugging across ranch land to the *NightZone* mesa. Miles Waddell was becoming adept as a politician.

Chapter Eighteen

It's easy to allow oneself to dwell on events about which nothing can be done—but life goes on. I turned another page of the *Posadas Register*, and was startled again. There, nicely printed, was the concert poster photo of Francisco Guzman and Mateo Atencio, with a three-column headline running underneath. *Concert Debuts Two Works,* the bold print heralded. Were the two youngsters "the works?" I scanned the story and chuckled. Dayan had seen the posters, talked with the school's music teacher, Jerry Reader, and maybe even called Leister Conservatory. But he hadn't found out anything new. He hadn't been able to talk with the child musicians. He'd missed having the story in the previous week's paper, since the posters hadn't appeared soon enough.

Here again, patience was forced upon me. Sure, I could call my godson, and I didn't doubt that Francisco Guzman would talk to me, his *padrino*...after a vow of secrecy. But I wasn't about to intrude there, either. I could wait, like everyone else. Damn it.

A big week for the *Posadas Register,* though. Dayan would be swelling with pride. The concert story should have graced page one, but I knew I would have had a hard time convincing the publisher of that. Crime sells. Classical music concerts are lucky to make it out of the classifieds.

Finished with the paper, I settled in the big leather chair down in my library, and picked up the rusted hulk that used to be a Colt Single Action Army revolver.

The trigger, which in the flower of youth was a slender little sliver of polished, blued steel, had rusted away, leaving only a little nub projecting from the frame. Interesting that the sear, protected in the gun's guts and perhaps bathed in oil, hadn't rusted away too, allowing the powerful hammer spring to slam the hammer down. The whole mechanism was one big lump of corrosion.

Was the original shootist killed while holding the Colt at full cock, ready to defend himself? Had he fired once, and was ready to put a second slug into his victim? What stayed his hand? A slug in *him,* most likely.

I turned the gun this way and that, enjoying both its heft and history. To whom had it been shipped? Was it a single-gun shipment to an individual, or one of several to a hardware distributor? The one compartment of my mind not occupied by other things contemplated all that.

I put the relic back on the shelf, found my notebook, and with a coffee refill, headed out the door, grateful for my burst of ambition. With no phone messages from the sheriff, the State Police investigator, or the district attorney, I opted to continue enjoying the day with a project that was solely mine. I made sure I had the County Assessor's map portfolio that I'd managed to copy years before, and piled into my SUV. Posadas sheriff's dispatch sounded politely interested when I informed them of my location and intentions.

Intuition had rarely done much good for me—I didn't have Estelle Reyes-Guzman's finely tuned dousing rod. But powered by professional-quality wishful thinking, I knew without a doubt—no doubt whatsoever—that the Colt had belonged at some point to someone from the Bennetts' camp. The wrong caliber to be a military issue, the gun was certainly civilian, and its loss would have sparked a panicky search…unless its owner had been dead by the time the revolver had clunked down into the rocks. The gun had been lost exactly where I proposed Bennett's Trail—named by me—to pass through that rugged country.

Within rifle-shot distance of Waddell's project to the south, I had found the revolver on the south-facing slope of the "fort," that rough mound of rock that had protected travelers from the wind and weather. When dropped, the Colt had most likely been only a year or two old—still a treasure, and still worth a month's pay in those days. Junk or treasure, I'd added the relic to my collection of artifacts from that portion of the county. Every single one added something to the legend of the Bennetts...at least to someone like me, with an active imagination.

My objective on this clear, brisk day was a small trash dump that I'd found late one afternoon several weeks before, discovered when I'd been ready to head in to town for dinner. I hadn't taken the time then to do a proper survey as the light failed, and I hoped this was just the therapy I needed. I couldn't quiet the unanswered questions about the weeks' events that persisted in my mind, too many avenues of investigation that I wished—all right, *longed*—to pursue. Too many people deserved answers.

Instead, I tried to force my attention to this small scatter of junk. A tin can was an interesting artifact, believe me. If the label was paper, it was gone in a year or so, remnants turned face down lasting a bit longer. Printing on the metal itself faded evenly with time. After only a year, a bright Coke can will fade to a soft pinkish. The metal of the can itself hadn't been *tin* for generations, and the steel corroded at a sedate pace.

At one point, cans were sealed with a drop of solder in the fill hole—not exactly high tech, but it worked. As these older cans turned to deep rust, almost black, what did remain, happily, was that little touch of solder. That solder plug dated the can's remains back to the latter years of the 19th and early 20th century. That wasn't exact archeology, but it was fun. What I hoped to find was a fragment of *something* that shouted out, loud and clear, "Eighteen Ninety-one," the last year I'd been able to find any trace of Josiah Bennett being in Posadas County. His name was on a property claim. Unfortunately for him, he hadn't lived long enough to make his mark on the land, but there his name was, in beautiful script, in one of the musty old county ledgers. The ink had flowed on *2June1891*.

It was easier to hike across the rugged prairie than to drive, so I parked on the county road. Major construction was going on at the power-line site down by the cattle guard south of me, with half a dozen big rigs and a towering crane. Through binoculars, I could see a flat-bed truck loaded with the transformer jugs. Not far from the scorch of the fire, a chain-link fence with top strands of barbed wire was being erected around an area a hundred feet on a side. Miles Waddell was getting more than just a little gray bottle hung from a cross buck. His development would drink juice at an astounding rate, and the new substation would supply it.

Picking my way with care, I climbed the south slope of Bennett's Fort, scanning every pebble, chunk of dried cactus, or stump of creosote bush. What I really wanted was a pack rat's den. Those little critters are an archeologist's best friend, right up there with skeletons and fire circles.

The can scatter was where I had remembered it, on the east slope where the sunrise would catch it. Just downgrade was a gnarly juniper with multiple stumps and shaggy, long strings of bark. It had seen and heard the whole tale, but it wasn't talking. Mounded around its roots and stumps was enough detritis to suggest a pack rat at work.

The first can to attract my attention was two-thirds buried, its punched top open, the dirt cascading inside. Easing it out of the ground, I could make out the ghost of its embossed metal announcing KC baking powder. You gotta have biscuits. KC cans were scattered across the entire Southwest, right along with cans that had once held peaches or pears, and a few years later, Prince Albert's finest.

What I wanted was a circle of stones, natural or otherwise, with charcoal inside the ring. Locate a camp's fire circle, and the odds of finding other artifacts escalates exponentially. A group of folks takes their ease by the fire, and trouser pockets point the wrong way. A coin slips out, or a pocket knife, or a comb. And in the toss-perimeter around the campfire, the empty bottles land, sometimes to smash, sometimes only to chip. The French investigator Locard was right. You can't pass this way without leaving something behind. Early campers didn't even try.

I picked at this and that, making a mental note to build a screen sifter someday. The trouble with a sifter, though, was that it presumed *digging,* which presumed a *shovel.* Next thing you know, you have *work.* Pretty soon somebody stops by to see what you're doing, and the trance is broken.

That idea had no sooner crossed my mind than the distant chuff of a diesel and the faint crunch of gravel alerted me. I'd been sitting with my back to the afternoon sun, soaking it in like a grand old lizard, and I turned when Miles Waddell pulled his big pickup truck to the shoulder of the county road a hundred yards away. Sure enough, he'd found me. He parked immediately behind my SUV, and dismounted. He had company. A vehicle I recognized as the courtesy car from the airport, an aging, sun-faded Chevy Malibu, parked in trail.

I admitted to being a creature of first impressions, and I watched as Miles and a statuesque woman advanced across the prairie. She was of equal height to Miles, but a trifle stouter—*powerful,* if it was appropriate to apply that term to women. A dark blue monogrammed cap was pulled low over her eyes, double concealed behind a pair of aviator-style sunglasses. Hair just a shade off white was cut pixie style, long enough to look nice, too short to grab.

Rising to my feet as they approached, I saw that they were in no hurry, and the rancher was clearly in motor-mouth mode, the murmur of his explanations floating across to me. She walked with her hands slipped into her hip pockets, and that pulled her shoulders back enough that the open quilted jacket proved my first impression correct. In addition to a spectacular figure, the open jacket revealed something else—a moderately sized automatic in a high-rise holster.

Cop. With a half dozen agencies currently at work in the county, which one was she? And why the hell did she need the airport's long-of-tooth heap? She smiled at something Waddell said, and then the two of them hit the scatter of rocks and boulders on the hillside. Steep enough that he had to attend to business, I saw Miles lean forward and work at climbing, his hand occasionally dropping down to a rock as an assist. She followed, obviously waiting on the rancher. Had she wanted, she could have danced up the hill.

"Thought we'd find you out here," Miles called. I didn't reply, but waited as he panted the last few feet. "You sure can find the spots," he added. He reached out to shake my hand, turning as he did so. "Bill, this is Lynn Browning. Mrs. Browning, this is Bill Gastner," and he added the list of titles, former this and that, that people always seem to think important.

"A pleasure," Mrs. Browning said. Her voice was a throaty alto. *Mrs.* was an old-fashioned label I hadn't heard much lately. "I saw the article in today's paper. I hope the Baum case will resolve itself for you." She took off her dark glasses and let her interesting, just-off-gray eyes bore into mine.

"One way or another," I replied. "And you are with…"

"Lynn is CEO of United Security Resources." For someone who hours before had been so dead set against a private security army, Miles sounded pleased with himself. "Out of Denver," he added. "They're the ones who contacted me earlier."

"Uh huh." Astounded, I wondered what she had told Miles to effect such a complete switcheroo in a matter of hours. I settled on the tried and true. "You folks have had some winter."

I'm sure Lynn Browning hadn't flown 700 miles to discuss the weather, especially since Denver *always* had winter.

"For a little while, I wasn't sure we were going to get out of town," she replied. Her bright smile was sincere and charming—melting, one could say. "By the time we crossed into New Mexico," and she made a curtain rising motion with her hands.

"That's the way we are," I said.

"You are fortunate." She pivoted at the waist to survey the prairie. "And just look at this," she said in a reverential whisper.

She turned back and studied me with blue-gray eyes. "Are you looking for something in particular, sir?"

"Pack rats would be nice," I replied.

"Industrious little collectors." I was pleased that she hadn't instead asked, "What are they?" Instead, she'd instantly made the correct connection, and I was beginning to understand the wily Miles falling under this young woman's spell. Although now, at close range, I saw that I would be hard-pressed to make an accurate guess at her age—thirty-five, perhaps. Forty, maybe even forty-five. The fine skin around ears, eyes and mouth hadn't been ruined by smoking or sun-worshipping.

"Mr. Waddell tells me that you're working to trace the movements of a frontier family that might have passed this way."

Miles Waddell shifted when I looked at him, glancing off into the distance as if thinking some version of the modern lingo, "*my bad.*" How effortless it was to share information with someone who first appeared congenial and…attractive. And in fact there was nothing wrong with Lynn Browning knowing what I was doing—except the principle of the thing.

"Sure enough. A grand waste of time, no doubt. It's just a curiosity of mine."

"Puzzles can become consuming." She sounded as if she really meant it. "How do you know they came this way, these people?"

"Well, actually, I don't," I sighed. "Little pieces here and there. An educated guess."

"And their significance?"

With a laugh, I said, "Absolutely none. It would be nice if I thought he'd left a chest of gold bullion behind somewhere, but as far as I can determine, he died nearly penniless, bludgeoned to death by his own son-in-law."

"Right on this spot?"

"I doubt it. Family legend places the murder up north somewhere." I shrugged. "I don't think anyone knows." We had tested Miles Waddell's patience to his limit.

"In light of what happened in the past couple of days, Lynn came down to express her company's interest in person," Miles said. "I have one of their packets over in the truck. And you know, regardless of what I was saying the other day, it sounds like a pretty good deal to me."

That was fast, I thought. "More power to you."

"I wondered if I could get you to take a look at it." He managed to sound as if I'd already agreed to do such things for him. I decided not to argue, not to play hard to get. A more sincere entrepreneur than Miles Waddell there never was, but I had the feeling he was going to have to work hard to avoid being skinned. Someone as attractive, smooth, and sweet-talking as Lynn Browning could pull the wool over his eyes with a few elevated heartbeats. More importantly, I was curious.

"I'm not familiar with United Security Resources," I said to Mrs. Browning. "How about a company capsule in fifty words or less."

She smiled, but it was a practiced delivery. She slipped the earpiece of her sunglasses into her pocket, and her gaze was direct and unflinching—almost as if she knew exactly what impact those eyes had on men, and wanted their full effect turned loose on me.

"We employ two hundred and forty security specialists around the world, almost always in small teams. We work entirely with private enterprise. No embassies, no politics, no celebrity security. One of our newest contracts is with a small container shipper, placing two employees on each of their seven container ships. We have people with a contractor on the ice roads up in the north country. We have two people helping with a massive university study in Peru at Machu Picchu. There is a team at a major health facility that's being built by one of the big computer companies in Zimbabwe."

She paused, maybe to see if I'd been counting words. I hadn't, and looked expectant.

"Our primary interest is providing security for very special needs. We do not do box store parking lots at Christmas, or provide ride-along armed services for bank couriers. As I said, we do not stand guard for celebrities or politicians."

"You pick and choose."

"Yes, sir. We do."

"You flew into Posadas today?"

She nodded. "The new airport paving job and runway extensions are impressive, by the way."

I picked up an abandoned zip top lid that had faded to a nice soft silver. Trash or artifact—it was only a matter of perspective. "And what challenges does Mr. Waddell face that your firm is eager to help with?"

"He and I discussed some of the commonly held impressions the public might have about private security firms," Lynn said. "First of all, we are not a gang of thugs. We don't stand in the corner dressed in black, glowering at folks while every once in a while talking into a little wrist radio. We learn the entire operation, and then we phase into it in the most seamless and effective way possible." She clasped her hands together. "We like to be proactive, not reactive." She smiled. "We *can* react, if the need arises. We prefer to make confrontation unnecessary. We do that by making sure that *our* employees have a sincere interest in the project to which they're assigned, and understand its unique challenges."

"That presupposes a hell of an educated, trained staff," I said.

"Two things are absolute for our hires," she said. "One, a four-year college degree in something useful." She smiled. "One of our newest hires has a bachelor's in music from Ithaca College in New York. Second, we require successful completion of a reputable, nationally ranked law enforcement academy. We pay for that if it isn't already on the resumé. Our folks need a clear understanding of what their boundaries are."

"Lots of cops don't have that," I scoffed. "Military experience?"

"That's usually a plus, but not always, and not required."

Mrs. Browning seemed entirely comfortable with being interviewed in this remote spot, and in no hurry to be elsewhere. She clearly understood why Miles had hiked her up the side of the mesa to talk with me. And I was impressed that she wasn't glued to her cell phone.

"Do you feel you have a fundamental understanding of what Miles is undertaking here? I mean, the *scope* of it?"

"I showed Lynn the blueprints," Miles offered quickly. I looked at him in surprise.

"You say you have a proposal from her firm in the truck?"

"It's not so much a proposal as it is an introduction to our company," Mrs. Browning said. "We can't make a formal proposal, a bid, until we know the details."

"Ah," I said. "Of course." I selected just the right limestone chair and relaxed back. "So you've seen the blueprints. All the projects?"

"A great deal, anyway. The train, the tram up the mesa face, the restaurant, the California project, the various sized telescopes and dishes linked to the big-screen theater…most ambitious."

"Yes."

"I would expect many interesting challenges posed by all of that."

"Yes again," I said. "And most of all, that it doesn't become a case of good money just tossed away."

"Certainly that, especially during the construction and development stage. I was impressed with the California project."

"The big brute."

She squatted, balancing on the balls of her feet. "We look at the little things, too. Like the logistics of no outside lights after sunset." She made a face of consternation at that, and added, "Wow."

"We have those little solar-charged path lights…they'll be like the aisle delineators in a movie theater," Miles said proudly. Mrs. Browning smiled at him.

"And like I said, that's a small thing. But there will be hundreds, maybe thousands of *small things,* and we will have to pay attention to them all—and how they interface with the public." She took a breath. "That's why we advocate an open-ended contract, sir. We're not here to duplicate what the sheriff's department does, or the State Police. We'll be looking to prove our worth to Mr. Waddell every step of the way. And if we don't… well, then, he tells us to take a hike."

"What's your take on our recent events?" I pointed off toward the electric company's construction site.

"You know," she said, "I've read the newspaper accounts that have just started to come out, especially out-of-state. Some of it is troubling. Some of it is just thoughtless people making grandstand statements. About as important as some guy standing on the street corner with a sign protesting big SUVs. All I can say for sure is that there is *potential* for trouble there. And I mean beyond the damage to the power line. You know," and she looked down at the ground, frowning, "one of the recent issues we've been following with increasing interest is this secession idiocy."

"You're kidding?" I had written off the whole group as just a bunch of spout.

"No. A lot of it is nothing more than what my husband calls red-necked bellyaching about big government." Something must have vibrated in her pocket, because she drew out a little gadget, glanced at the screen, and put it away. "But it's also an opportunity to make a lot of money. There's a lot of money to be made pandering to people's fears. Like selling boatloads of generators before every hurricane. The quick buck crowd." She grinned, but her mouth was hard when she added, "One step up from the folks who peddle canned, dehydrated water."

"You see a lot of that?"

"No, not a lot. But enough that it troubles industrial investors thinking to move ops to the Southwest. They want a good workforce, good utilities and infrastructure, maybe some state or local tax breaks. They *don't* want some doofus sawing down their power poles." She rose to her feet, gracefully, without the popping of a single joint. "I'm not saying that's what you have here, either. But all the grandstanding articles we've read shout the same anti-government sentiments, one way or another. It's rare that somebody takes overt action like this." She turned and watched the county road.

"I don't know if paranoia is passed through drinking water or what," she said, "but there it is. And even without *any* of that, Mr. Waddell is going to face some security issues with his development. Part of it is because millions and millions of dollars are involved, and when you spill that much honey, it draws lots of flies. Part of it is genuine paranoia about new development in their backyards. Part of it is just because the world is full of nuts. What we've learned over the years is not to underestimate."

The county road was sending up regular plumes of red dust, one truck after another, and as the flow continued, Miles Waddell glanced at his watch. In the distance, I saw a vehicle or two heading up the mesa boulevard. The rancher was going to discover the true joys of trying to be in several places at once.

My own phone chirped, and I ignored it. What did attract my attention was a tan-clothed figure trudging across the prairie toward us. I hadn't noticed her when she joined the parking lot down below, and what Undersheriff Estelle Reyes-Guzman wanted with us was anyone's guess, but I soon found out. Lynn Browning followed my gaze and cracked a huge smile.

"Company," she said. "I wanted to talk with her today, but I didn't expect she'd find us out here." Browning didn't just stand there and wait. Instead, she set off down the slope at a brisk almost-trot.

"What do you think?" Waddell asked.

"About?"

"Mrs. Browning."

"I'd like to meet *Mister* Browning."

"He usually flies the chopper, but couldn't make it today." Waddell said. "So she flew herself, and I met her at the airport. Mighty impressive, Bill."

"If she's got a helicopter, why not just land out here?"

Waddell shrugged. "I suppose she has her reasons. Maybe it's more discreet this way." He laughed. "Maybe she doesn't want to get their fancy bird all dusty."

Down below, the two figures merged with first a vigorous handshake and then a hug. "I'll be damned," I said. "Life is full of surprises."

Chapter Nineteen

As they almost sauntered up the hill, I could see that Lynn Browning was doing most of the talking—no surprise in that. The undersheriff absorbed like the best ocean sponge. And Mrs. Browning was giving her plenty to absorb. On the county road, a flat-bed tractor-trailer hauling three large spools of something raised a mammoth, billowing cloud. The truck slowed for the power line repair site, then motored on toward the mesa access road. It was going to take months for the air to settle out all the crap raised by the construction.

"Tell you what." Miles glared at his watch as if it were lying to him. "I need to be down there. Look, if there's anything else you need from me…" He turned and regarded Mrs. Browning and Undersheriff Estelle Reyes-Guzman as they approached. "You'll let me know what you think?"

"Sure enough. That part is easy."

His meeting on the trail with the two women was only the briefest of pauses. I saw Miles motioning toward me, and then ducking his head apologetically as he made his exit. I might have resented the hand-off, were the folks in question not Estelle Reyes-Guzman and her friend. They were going to be hard folks to refuse.

As the pair made their way up to my vantage point, I had the thought that now would be a perfect time to go on vacation, far, far away. Waddell's world was growing into a beast that could suck me in, multiple investigations were swirling around me, and not least of all, my godson was soon giving a formal concert that promised surprises. My world would have to stop spinning to miss that performance, but all the rest?

I put on a cheerful, welcoming face and extended a hand to Estelle. Her grip was strong and warm, and she drew me into a powerful hug and held it long enough that I wondered if I was under arrest.

"Hey there," I managed.

"Carlos was badgering me to remind you about tonight." She finally drew back, but didn't let go of my hand. She had always been more attentive than I deserved, but doubly so after the Baum shooting.

"Wouldn't miss it." I glowered and grumbled, "And we've heard that before."

"I've asked Lynn to join us."

"Absolutely."

"I wanted to talk with Estelle about two things," Browning said. "That's actually what prompted the trip at this particular time, although I wanted to see the *NightZone* site before we formulated a final proposal for Mr. Waddell. The weather is supposed to be perfect tomorrow, and we'd like to shoot a series of aerial photos of the mesa…the road approach and several other physical features that might impact what we do."

"Good idea," I said. "Look, you two have a lot to talk about. But before I hit the road, I have to ask how you two come to know each other."

"Nothing more complicated than roommates in college," Mrs. Browning replied. "And our paths manage to cross now and then—not often enough."

I laughed. "I had a roommate once…can't even remember his name."

"We've stayed in touch over the years. You know, until today I've never had the opportunity to visit Posadas. Everything just fell into place. And that brings me to number two."

She smiled at my puzzled expression. "Number one was the aerial photos. I wanted the S.O. to know whose helicopter was snooping over private property. You know how rumors go. And now, I'm wondering if *you*," and she touched my left shoulder, "can break away and join us? I could use a tour guide, and Mr. Waddell won't come. He says that he gets airsick, but suggests that you might be persuaded. He claims you know every rock in Posadas County."

"I've turned over a few," I said. "I'll check my busy schedule, but I'd be happy to." *And that's how all this suck-in works,* I thought ruefully. The inability to use the simple word *no.*

"Eight o'clock?"

"Sure. Assuming the district attorney doesn't have other ideas."

She nodded gratefully. "The other thing I wanted was to develop a feel for how the local agencies are viewing this project." She looked hard at Estelle. "Especially the S.O."

"I'm not so sure that the sheriff has given Mr. Waddell's project much thought," Estelle said carefully. "Everything is still so tentative. As the construction really starts rolling, if this project is to be anywhere near the scope planned, we'll have to develop carefully thought-out strategies."

"We can help with that," Lynn Browning said eagerly. "Let's find some time this afternoon to talk about it." She made a gesture that included me, and I held up both hands.

"I'll see you for dinner. This afternoon, I really need to get a few things done."

Mrs. Browning nodded graciously. "I hope you find your pack rat." She sounded as if she meant it.

Estelle drew a business card out of her blouse pocket, and jotted on the back. "This is the vehicle registered to George Baum." She passed the card to me. "It's troublesome that he's managed to stay below the radar. His soon to-be-ex-wife said that George and his father were close, but she thinks that maybe taking the child was Mr. Baum's idea, not George's."

"And maybe they'll win the family of the year award." I shrugged. "We'll keep our eyes open. That's about all we can do." Knowing what car George Baum drove might be a help, but half the cars on the road were silver, and a fair percentage of them were late model mid-sized sedans. I wasn't about to waste my time surveying parking lots or camping in my rearview mirror trying to spy just the right Camry.

I earned another hug and a handshake, and the two women left me to my pack rat hunt. The mound of rock-strewn prairie I was exploring produced a .270 rifle shell casing, new enough to be from a hunt within the past couple of years. I'm glad the shooter had been concentrating on his prey and not searching crannies. It was amazing to me how an artifact, especially one as spectacular as the old Colt, could remain undiscovered for so long.

The possible camping site yielded nothing other than an empty can or two. For a long time, I stood on the apex of the highest rock pile. Cat Mesa would have stood in Bennett's path, forcing him to cross to the east or west of it. Without a path of artifacts to mark his way, it was a fifty/fifty guess. I needed an eyewitness. Bennett had sired a daughter who married the man who killed him. If the homicidal young man and his wife had produced children before he was hanged for his father-in-law's murder, the Posadas County court house had no records of it.

I took a deep breath and stretched my back, turning in place. My phone did its irritating little noiseless dance in my pocket, as if knowing that I had paused in my endeavor and might deign to answer the damn thing. I fumbled it out and turned so the sun wouldn't blank the screen. Sheriff Robert L. Torrez never called to chat, to pass the time of day, or to try out a new *app,* whatever those are.

"Gastner." Nothing happened, and I turned the gadget over. "Gastner."

"Where are you?"

"Well good afternoon to you, too," I said. "I'm standing out here on Bennett's Fort, thinking great thoughts and enjoying summer in the middle of winter."

We enjoyed silence while the sheriff digested that. "Did you get that letter sent off to Colt?"

"Yes. We'll know to whom the gun was shipped in a month or so."

"Huh," Torrez grunted, having exhausted his apparent interest in that topic. I could hear quiet radio traffic in the background.

"Did you do any good down in Cruces?" I asked.

"Just got back. Found out a name, anyway."

Pry, pry. "That's a start. Whose?"

"Ever heard of Elliot Daniel?" That the sheriff hadn't recognized the name was the reason behind the call. I might not remember what I had had for breakfast—or *if* I'd even eaten it—I often could dredge up a name from the distant past, and once I had the name, all the family connections fell into place.

I thought for a moment and came up blank.

"The girlfriend met him a time or two," the sheriff added.

"Boyd's girlfriend?"

"Julie Warner, and the first thing she told me was that he's a wild-haired asshole."

"Nothing illegal about that."

"Yeah, well, I'm not sure she means it. This Daniel guy is Brandon Smith's nephew."

"You're kidding." I don't think Bob Torrez had ever told a joke in his life.

"He used to live up in Portillo, Smith says. According to him, Daniel has been trying to go to school some."

"Trying?"

"Military took him, then he managed to wreck an eye. Not service related. He's been tryin' to get on with a couple of security firms."

"Huh. Now isn't *that* interesting."

"Anyways, we got Smith locked up on charges of conspiracy and harboring a fugitive. Their DA down there is more of a wuss than ours is, and he'll probably cut Smith a deal so that he walks. But not before we find out all we need to know about his nephew." The sheriff abruptly fell silent.

"They're not going to cut any deals when the murder of a cop is involved."

"Make you a bet?"

I wasn't about to go there. Conspiracy was one of those slippery charges that frequently got nowhere in court.

"Any ideas where Daniel is headed?"

"Only that he's on his own bike now. MVD says it's a 2010 Kawasaki 1100, black and gold. The girl—this Julie Warner—told us that she'd seen him on it from time to time, when he visited Curt Boyd. And we found Smith's Harley parked in one of the general lots at the university. Switcheroo."

"Did his uncle want it back?" I jested and Torrez scoffed. "Clever guy, this Daniel," I added. "He gets rid of the Nissan, then the Harley. If you have a name, you have everything else about him, Bobby. Good work."

"Yup."

"A current address?"

"An apartment in Cruces. The PD has it under surveillance."

"Then it's just a matter of time." I knew that Robert Torrez hadn't called me just to chat. And I was sure he felt no great compunction to keep me abreast of developments. "What do you need me to do for you?"

"What's United Security doin' in Posadas?" He didn't volunteer how he knew that they were in town, although a parked helicopter with a bold logo printed on the side took away all the guess work. If he had talked with his undersheriff, he knew damn well what the security firm was doing in his county.

"It's USR's boss lady herself," I said. "A gal by the name of Lynn Browning. She's talking with Miles Waddell, shooting him a proposal to provide security. Tomorrow she wants to photograph Waddell's mesa from the air. She invited me along."

"Interesting that she shows up." Torrez's voice wasn't much more than a whisper. "Doesn't seem like her kind of gig."

"You know her?"

"Yup. We've met." He didn't explain where or when. Instead he said, "Estelle's going to be asking her what she knows about Elliot Daniel."

"Browning would know him?"

"I'd guess so. He wanted to work for USR."

"How do we know that?"

"That's what one of Boyd's roommates said. Daniel said he read about 'em on the Internet, and got all hot to trot. He came over one night lookin' to ask Boyd for help with the job application. The roommate remembered because Daniel was askin' how much stuff he could just make up. The two of 'em talked about how good that would be…for Daniel to be workin' for USR and have inside information about just what was goin' on up there."

The sheriff gave me time to mull that over. I could see the web glimmering, tendrils touching here and there. What better way for a prospective employee to impress a potential boss than to encourage a new contract…bring in the promise of a large payoff with the application. A little eco-terrorism should have gone a long way toward spooking Miles Waddell into seeking security services. That was but one possibility. They all made me nervous.

"I'll be at Estelle's for dinner here in a little bit. Browning is going to be there as well. And tomorrow, we're flying a survey of the mesa."

"Okay. Watch yourself." The phone clicked off.

Chapter Twenty

"Frankie is coming tomorrow," nine-year-old Carlos announced in a grave imitation of a butler. He held the door for me and bowed ever so slightly. "Welcome, and may I take your coat, Padrino?"

"What TV program has been frying your brain, Bud?" I asked, and swung out of my jacket. I kept the quilted vest.

Teresa Reyes, Estelle's mother, offered me a nice smile of recognition. She was engulfed in a colorful afghan, nestled in her favorite rocker near the fireplace. It seemed to me that the favored chair grew larger each time I visited and saw the tiny woman sitting in it. Two more years, and the grand old lady would hit the century mark. Twenty years before, I would have predicted death's door any day for her, but that door had slammed shut, locked, and bolted, and like a piece of petrified heartwood, her dark brown skin just kept adding polish to the wrinkles and crevasses. Estelle's stepmother had me by twenty-four years, and damned if in all likelihood she'd probably outlive me.

I crossed the living room and with a hand on the arm of her chair and another on the back, bent down and pecked her on her high forehead. "How are you doing, Teresa?" I asked, looking forward to the standard answer.

"Too old," she whispered. She patted my russet vest. "That's a nice color on you." She gazed up at me, and I'm not sure just what her dark eyes saw. The left was starting to cloud, and the coke-bottle glasses that hung around her neck would do little for the macular degeneration in her right eye. Losing the ability to read had to be a deep sadness for her—as would an unclear, smoky vision of her two grandchildren.

"What do you think of this, *Francisco*?" she asked as I straightened up, emphasizing the proper name for Carlos' benefit. Not waiting for my answer, she added, "So young for such a thing."

"I'm looking forward to the concert," I said. "Quite a production they've planned. Our old gymnasium is going to shake to its foundations."

Carlos reappeared after stashing my coat. He folded his hands reverentially. "May I get you something from the kitchen, Padrino?"

I regarded the kid soberly. Sprouting up now, developing some muscle definition, Carlos Guzman was every bit as handsome as his older brother. And, I had always thought, in his own way just as much a prodigy. For the past couple of years, he had developed an unshakable interest in designing anything that soared upward—buildings, bridges, aircraft—and despite being an otherwise normal nine-year-old, could concentrate on a project from start to finish…that same gene for concentration that guided his brother Francisco through five or six hours of nonstop piano practice.

I'd never met a kid with a wider imp streak. Now, Carlos the Butler waited patiently for my answer. He'd be disappointed if I demurred, so I screwed on a thoughtful expression. "What I'd really like…"

"Yes, Padrino?" He had settled on a modified British-Mexican accent, in itself quite an accomplishment.

"A cup of properly aged coffee, if you please." I noticed that Addy Sedillos was peeking around the kitchen corner. Like her older sister Irma, who had worked for the Guzman corporation for years, Adorina had no trouble managing the household, regardless of the bizarre hours demanded by a doctor and an undersheriff.

"No cream, no sugar, but the oil skim on top should reflect aging in the pot for at least ten hours."

Perfectly sober, Carlos allowed his face to fall, despite the twinkle in his eyes that he couldn't suppress. "I'm sorry, Padrino. All we have at the moment is a nice dark Sumatran blend that will finish brewing in another minute."

I sighed mightily, trying not to laugh at a nine-year-old saying the words 'Sumatran blend.' "I'll just have to settle for that." I glanced at Addy. "How are you doing, doll?"

"We're surviving," she said, and advanced with a hug. "Estelle just called a few minutes ago. She'll be home around six. The doctor is in surgery, so..."

"Life as usual," I laughed. "Thank you, sir," I said to Carlos, who handed me a mug of dark, aromatic coffee and a small saucer heaped with gingersnaps.

"My pleasure, Padrino."

I settled in a well-broken-in spot on the sofa with an end table near at hand. "So tell me what you're building at the moment."

The boy's shoulders relaxed, and he became an excited nine-year-old rather than a reserved member of the household service staff. Perching on the sofa beside me, his hands were animated. "Have you seen the inside of the gymnasium?"

"Sure I've seen it."

"The sound is going to be awful, Padrino. It will echo like some old cave."

"Huh. So what do we do about that?" A Carlos without a solution was unthinkable.

"And Mateo plays the flute. *That* sound isn't like some orchestra or something. It'll just go out and get lost in all those trusses."

Trusses. Such a nine-year-old's word or concept. "Have you met this Mateo guy?"

"Yes. He's..." and his voice dropped and took on an awful Texas twang, "a cool dude, man." The boy's hands drew something in the air, his forehead furrowed. "They need to hang acoustical baffles," he said. *Acoustical baffles?* It was hard to keep a straight face, so I sipped delectable coffee and then tried a gingersnap. "I made those," Carlos announced, and pushed himself off the sofa. "I have to show you something." He vanished.

"This boy." Teresa's whisper was hoarse.

This boy returned immediately with a large sheet of paper, and I tabled my cup so he could spread the rendering across my lap. I recognized the sketch as the inside of the gym, the elevated stage at one end, four basketball backboards cranked up against the ceiling, an electronic scoreboard at the end opposite the stage. It was the sort of do-all gymnasium designed in the 1950s. The rendering betrayed Carlos Guzman's age. He hadn't yet mastered how to end lines crisply at the corners.

"Why didn't they use the Little Theater?" I asked.

"Tooo little," Carlos chirped. He started to say something else and I held up a hand. He slammed on the brakes and looked at me expectantly.

Tracing the lines of the walls, I asked, "So when did you learn all about perspective?"

"Oh, that's easy, Padrino." He held his hands apart, then zoomed them together as he pushed them away from his body, mimicking a set of disappearing railroad tracks. "All you have to do is decide where you want the horizon. Mrs. Carrillo showed me that last year." He said it as if "last year" was decades ago.

"This is your solution?" I tapped one of the large tapestry-like things hanging from the ceiling, huge versions of the various championship flags that schools hang in gymnasiums. He nodded eagerly. Enjoying this peek into how his young mind worked, I asked, "What do they do, exactly?"

He frowned and took a deep breath, as if girding for the challenge of explaining something so simple to someone so dense. Touching the roughly drawn stage, he swept his fingers across the area where the audience would be sitting. "The sound can go this way," he said. "But not up here." His index finger traced several arrow-like paths upward where the sound would strike the baffles. "These stop it from bouncing all around among the girders."

"Huh. I'll buy that. You know, it'll be interesting to see what the Leister stage crew comes up with."

Carlos carefully rolled up his rendering and then shrugged expressively. "I faxed Francisco a copy of this," he said. "They'll have to do *something.*"

Silly me. Why *wouldn't* a nine-year-old know all about acoustical engineering, or copying and faxing and the like? What did I think he would be doing, riding a bike all day? Or playing basketball? Or hiking?

As if reading my mind, he asked, "Were you out at the fort today?"

"Yes, I was."

"Will you take me out there again sometime when you go? I mean, when I don't have to be in school?"

"You got it, my friend." I'd inflicted my Bennett theories on all of the Guzmans at one time or another, and both boys had tagged along with me on more than one occasion when I explored Bennett's route. Carlos had been fascinated by the Colt, and the first thing he wanted to do was haul out the can of penetrating oil and try to free up the rust-frozen hammer. My edict that the revolver be left alone hadn't made sense to him.

He leaned forward to check the coffee supply, then bounded back to the kitchen, returning with the pot. I know adults who can't pour coffee and talk at the same time, but Carlos managed perfectly.

"Will Mamá catch the guys who sawed down the power line?"

"You have doubts?"

"I guess not."

"You *guess* not?"

He sighed. "She will. Her and Big, Bad Bobby." I laughed, and the exchange earned a dark glower from Teresa. I don't know which she disapproved of more, the boy's slangy grammar or the nickname for a respected elder. Maybe both. "Do you think that someday…" He hesitated, on unsure ground. "Do you think I could talk to Mr. Waddell sometime?"

I regarded the boy with interest. "You'd like that?"

His eyes lit. "I really would like to see the plans for his idea. Mamá said that you saw them."

I nodded sagely. "Yes, I've seen them. You think you could do that and be a good listener at the same time?"

"Yes, sir." And Carlos Guzman probably could. I could imagine Miles Waddell's eyes glazing over as a nine-year-old chattered on about improbable changes to the rancher's cherished plans. The boy's welcome would wear thin really quickly, especially since Miles Waddell wasn't one of those folks whose world revolved around children. Seldom seen, never heard. If *Night-Zone* reached fruition, he'd have to get used to them—school buses by the fleet would be visiting. It would be good for Miles to see the sort of excitement his project could generate in minds other than his own.

"I'll see if I can make that happen," I said. "Not this weekend, though. We have a lot going on, don't we?"

Carlos puffed out his cheeks in a very adult expression of overload.

"When your brother was home for Christmas, he didn't say anything about the concert?"

"He's got secrets," the boy said. "I tried to find out, but he's..." and he squeezed his lips together tightly.

"As some other boys should be," Teresa observed dryly.

Headlights washed across the living room window and I heard the crunch of tires in the driveway. Carlos was at the door long before me, and I mentally thanked him for outgrowing the stage when he felt the need to screech his announcements. Now it was, "That would be Mamá." He turned to me as I crossed the living room. "Has she given you a ride in the beast yet?"

"Yes." I rubbed the small of my back. "I'm still recovering."

I stood at the storm door and gazed out. The black "beast" was parked in the driveway facing out, and Estelle still sat in the driver's seat, jotting notes in her log. Across the street, a dog launched into a frantic comment on the new arrival—a car and a person he'd seen a thousand times before. Farther down Twelfth a cat crossed, just touching the cone from a streetlight. Pausing in mid-stride, the cat turned to look back at the brainless dog, then ducked under the back end of a parked car. That didn't draw my curiosity until I looked back at Estelle, now getting out of her vehicle. Then it felt as if someone had snapped my head back against a rubber band tether. A silver, mid-sized sedan. And inside, just visible under the streetlight, a single figure sat at the wheel.

A few seconds later, the airport courtesy car eased around the corner from Bustos Avenue, looking exactly like the cop car it had once been as it slid to a stop just beyond the Guzmans' driveway. As Lynn Browning parked, the silver sedan fired up and pulled away from the curb, disappearing down the first cross street.

Chapter Twenty-one

"That's Arturo Salazar," Estelle said as she approached the front steps. She had seen my attention diverted by the departing sedan and guessed the reason.

"Junior," I added, a little embarrassed at how easy it was to jump to ridiculous conclusions when the nerves are wound. Arturo Salazar had died the year before, but his son, who lived just two doors south of the Guzmans', continued the family funeral home.

"How did your day finish up?" I held the storm door for her and her attached son.

"Some progress." Estelle turned to wait for Lynn, who hustled up the sidewalk and joined us. She'd had time to change into casual jeans and a white sweatshirt, comfortably rumpled under a short down jacket. "And yours?" I added for her benefit.

"My day was spectacular," Browning said. "More vacation than work." She hefted the slender attaché case. "And the weather tomorrow is supposed to be just what we need. You still up for a little flying?"

"Sure."

She turned her attention to the others as Estelle made introductions, and the usually ebullient Carlos appeared captivated. "Do you need to shed some weight?" Estelle asked. "I'll put your jacket in on our bed." As she slipped out of her coat, Lynn Browning unclipped the holstered handgun from her belt and tucked it in the jacket before handing it to Estelle. The movement wasn't lost on Carlos. She kept the attaché case.

"What agency are you with, ma'am?" he asked, the picture of polite curiosity.

Lynn regarded him with interest as she first shook hands, and then held his for a longer moment. "I'm with United Security Resources out of Longmont," she said, without adopting the overly sweet "everything must be a learning experience" tone that so many adults favored with kids. "We're a private company."

"Just outside of Denver," Carlos clarified.

"Correct. We're down for a couple of days to meet with Mr. Waddell." She crossed to where Teresa sat in the rocker and combined a differential half-bow with a gentle two-handed shake. "Mrs. Reyes, what a pleasure. Do you remember that we met a long time ago? When Estelle and I graduated from the police academy?"

"I wish I did," Teresa said dryly. "These days, I do well to remember where I am. But you're welcome here."

I watched the undersheriff shed gun, cuffs, and a few pounds of other junk as she relaxed into another life. When she returned from the bedroom, I asked, "Did you folks make any progress today?"

"We have some contacts out of state that are checking out possibilities," Estelle said. "Mister Daniel wasn't someone who spent his life lurking in the shadows. He's left pretty big footprints, at least up until a couple of days ago. We were successful in opening up his credit card records, and Tom Mears is on *that* trail. We have both land line and cellular accounts." She held both hands up as if holding an invisible basketball. "In short, he's going to find life as a fugitive a challenge."

"My sympathy goes out," I scoffed. It would be perfect justice if Elliot Daniel didn't enjoy a single peaceful moment until such time as a cop slapped on the cuffs. We—I—wanted him looking over his shoulder every minute. He'd make a mistake, and that would be all it would take.

Unfortunately, such mistakes could be long in coming. There were fugitives under every rock, and some of them had evaded law enforcement for years, even decades…even a lifetime. But now, relaxed in this warm house with good food on the burner, I didn't want to waste another moment considering the fate of Elliot Daniel. He'd find his own rock, and I hoped his life would remain bleak and empty.

"How did he come to know Boyd?"

"They both took the same adult ed computer class at the college. Similar interests, I guess. Similar politics. Boyd became fascinated with European politics between the two wars. His girlfriend told us that. He was incredulous at the way Hitler was able to come to power."

"Ah. The old 'those who don't learn from their mistakes are bound to repeat them' thing."

"Perhaps so, Padrino."

I didn't want to weigh down a nice evening talking about a killer's motivations. "And anything new from the pianist?" I asked.

Estelle laughed. "Ay…we'll know tomorrow, Padrino. This has been an interesting experience." She flopped onto the sofa after hugging her mother, and when settled, reached over to take the old woman's left hand in both of hers. Lynn Browning had taken the rocker on the other side of the fireplace, the attaché case on the floor by her chair. "Parents are supposed to wean children, not vice versa." Estelle shifted position slightly and touched the back of her mother's hand to her lips. "I know more than I did a few days ago, at least."

"I'm glad someone does."

She smiled at her youngest son and reached out to accept a cup of tea that he delivered. Mother first, then company? What would the butler's book say about that? He turned to Lynn. "What may I get for you, ma'am. Tea? Coffee? White or red wine? We'll be serving smoked salmon under a dark chipotle sauce in a few minutes."

Lynn pondered for a long moment then held up her thumb and index finger about an inch apart. "This much red would be wonderful, thank you."

"I believe it's a Merlot."

"Perfect." She watched him exit. "He's nine?" Estelle nodded, and Lynn added, "Going on thirty."

"Under the current fascination, he hasn't been able to decide whether to study as an executive chef or an architect," Estelle said. "These things change weekly."

"He could design restaurants," I said.

"One of the concert posters was prominently displayed in the motel lobby," Lynn said. "They look very much alike, your two boys. I wish I could stay for the performance."

"You should make a point to," I said. "This sort of thing doesn't come around very often. I'm about as musical as a fence post, but I know musical genius when I hear it." Estelle made an impatient face, but didn't disagree.

"Maybe I will. What does he play? I mean, piano, of course." She reached out and patted the flank of the grand piano that rested in front of the living room window. "But what's he studying?"

"Everything from A to Z," Estelle said. "From the squarest classical to his rendition of desert car crashes to contemporary jazz."

Carlos reappeared and delivered Lynn's wine, then made a quick stop at his grandmother's, leaning against the arm of her chair for a few seconds.

"And you're committed to silence, right?" I said to the boy. He grinned and ducked his head.

"I really don't know," he pleaded.

"Do we have a polygraph around here someplace?"

"No, I really, really don't."

"He hasn't let on what the surprise is?" Over Christmas, I'd heard Francisco during several of his practice sessions, and the kid's progress was astonishing. His technique was now driven by all the energy of a powerful teenager, but tempered so that his range of emotion was startling. His slender fingers were capable of caressing the keys so gently that I had to strain to hear. But none of that was a surprise. Since age seven, the kid had been soaring, his progress upward like the brightest comet. It all made me nervous.

"Not a word," Estelle replied.

"How did all this come to pass?" Lynn kept looking at the closed piano as if it was about to speak.

"Leister Conservatory encourages each one of their advanced performance majors to arrange a hometown concert." She set the cup down on the end table carefully. "After Posadas, the kids go to Dos Pasos, Mateo Atencio's hometown in Texas." She smiled. "If you think Posadas is small…"

"You've met Mateo?" Lynn asked.

"We have. A quiet, immensely talented flutist. He's a first-generation Texan who likes Italian food. That's the extent of what I know. As for the rest…" She held up both hands in surrender. "There's nothing we can do from our end about this concert, so other than saying 'no', which I'm not about to do, I guess we'll just wait and see."

As if the aroma of the dinner reached out and drew him in, Dr. Francis Guzman's SUV pulled into the driveway, and in a moment *Oso,* as his wife fondly called him, appeared at the door in time to grab the knob before Carlos had a chance to fully open it. They tussled for a brief moment, and then the burly doctor appeared, grabbed Carlos and upended him under one arm, threatening to pound the youngster's head into the parquet.

"About one more year," he said with a cheerful grin. "Then the brute is going to be doing this to me." He dumped the youngster unceremoniously on the floor, earning gales of laughter, then extended a hand of truce. "Sorry about that," he explained when he noticed company other than myself. "It's all part of the male-dominated tribal ceremony."

He crossed to Lynn Browning. "I'm Francis Guzman. And I've met you before."

"How good is your memory?" she said, rising to extend a hand. She allowed the physician a few seconds to try his recall. "Lynn Browning," she prompted. "Your wife and I went to school together."

"Ah! Well, that's been a while. Welcome back." He slipped behind Teresa Reyes' chair and enveloped her in a massive hug.

"Oh, now," the old woman protested, obviously delighted.

Estelle intercepted her husband as he was headed my way, and he swept her along with an arm around her waist. "I have about twenty minutes," he said. "Blown appendix, but he's stable now." He extended a hand to me. "Padrino. You're lookin' good."

"For what?" I replied. He gave me that practiced survey of clinical assessment, head-to-toe in ten seconds, and looked satisfied.

"Been hikin' the mesa in the middle of the night, I hear."

"An old habit."

"I know it is. And it seems to be working." His face went sober. "Sorry we lost the shooter. I'm sure you guys would have had a lot to learn from him. Like *why.*" He shook his head in resignation.

Carlos was standing in the foyer, hands thrust into his pockets. "Dinner is served," he announced when his father glanced his way. The physician caught sight of Addy Sedillos, hard at work in the kitchen. Sure enough, he hugged her, too.

In due course, we managed a reasonably uninterrupted dinner, with the chipotle-laced salmon in a delicate crust, the huge, Carlos-required dollop of cheddar mashed potatoes, and half a dozen other garnishes. Dr. Guzman set his phone on the kitchen counter within easy reach, and the food went down the hatch so quickly that we could see he hadn't been kidding about the eighteen minutes.

Addy Sedillos, plumpish, round-faced and with an easy smile who had always seemed to me to be the definition of serenity, reluctantly agreed to join us for dinner. It seemed to me that she was still embarrassed to be included, and doubly so when Estelle rose quickly at one point to replenish the salmon servings instead of letting Addy to it.

For whatever reason, everyone seemed to be keenly interested in my study of Bennett's Trail—I chalked it up to a desire to avoid discussion of sensitive or even confidential topics, and it was convenient to spend the thoughts in another time and place. That was all right with me, since there aren't many folks on Earth who don't like to discuss their current, consuming hobby.

"Will Colt actually *know* about the gun?" Francis asked at one point.

"Their archives are actually pretty good," I said. "But…" and I captured a Brussels sprout that no longer looked—or tasted, thank God—like a sprout. It was actually delectable. "Most of the time, the original sales and shipping records don't mean much. I mean, we find out what caliber, and barrel length, and stocks, and finish and all that, but we usually don't find out where it went *after* it's shipped to the jobber. They might sell it anywhere. Although," and I paused, savoring, "back in those days, they were more apt to ship to an individual. No paperwork, no restrictions." I held up a forkful in salute. "And Addy, this is masterful. All of it."

Lynn Browning clasped her hands in front of her, elbows firmly on the table, fork dangling. Teresa wasn't impressed. I saw the slight twist of her lips, just a little purse of disapproval at such casual manners.

"And when you're convinced that the Bennetts did whatever they did along this trail, what then?"

I looked puzzled. "I don't guess there *is* a 'what then.' Mostly, it's just the knowing. And if that's his gun, then that's another puzzle piece. If that's his gun, something happened on top of that little hill. And then I work on *that*."

"You might never find out. I mean, after all this time, what are the odds?"

"That's true. And that's part of the charm." I smiled at her. "The journey, not the destination."

On that note of heavy philosophy, Francis Guzman patted the table and announced, "If you folks will excuse me, I need to get back." He rose and held out his hands. "Don't let me interrupt the party." He kissed his wife and said *soto voce,* "It's going to be a while, *querida.* We have an eleven-year-old who tried to tough-out appendicitis, and it's nasty." It had to be nasty to leave before dessert. He made his exit, escorted to the door by his son, who returned shortly to serve the key lime pie, so sharply tangy that it almost cut the tongue.

I expected Lynn Browning to make her exit as well, but she relaxed as Carlos refilled her coffee cup. With the boy and Addy busy over in the kitchen, she toyed with the cup for a moment, then opened both hands, her frown deepening.

"We're in an interesting situation," she said. "I wanted to run this by you."

"Now might be the time for me to say good night," I said, but Lynn held up a hand.

"I'd like your thoughts."

"About what?"

She took a deep breath. "Just a sec." She rose and retrieved the attaché case from the living room. "We're in a bit of a pickle," she said as she sorted papers. "This is what I mentioned when you and I talked." She selected a sheet and slid it across to Estelle. Nosy as ever, I leaned against her elbow and read the letter of application. Dated in early November of the previous year, the letter was professional in appearance, nicely centered and free of blotches and strikeovers, although in this computer age, anyone could be a perfect typist.

What interested me most was the closing. Elliot Daniel's signature was neat and intelligent, devoid of any extraneous swirls or embellishments.

"Well, son-of-a-bitch," I said. Teresa shifted a little at my unchecked language, but she'd heard it all before. The letter's return address was the apartment in Las Cruces. Daniel's list of previous experience was brief, limited to fourteen months in the Air Force, four months with the United States Forest Service, and three as a private contractor for security services to Benson Fort Resort in Benson Fort, Florida. No education beyond high school was mentioned.

"As you can see, we received that on November 11th. We took no action on it other than a short form letter that basically said

USR wasn't hiring at the moment." She handed us another letter. "This one arrived in mid-January of this year."

In the same professional format, this letter promised something specific: Miles Waddell's *NightZone*. *"Although I am currently prepared to work anywhere in the world in security operations, should United Security Resources extend service to the new mesa project in Posadas County, New Mexico, I would be in position to offer my immediate expertise to your firm."*

"What was your response to that?"

"A polite e-mail of disinterest," she said. "Nothing more. Now, as it turns out, we had already posted Mr. Waddell a preliminary correspondence to express our interest in his project. There are some really interesting challenges there. But we're not hiring yet, or assigning existing staff in anticipation of anything. We haven't reached any sort of agreement with Mr. Waddell. At this point, all he has is a nice roadway up to the mesa-top, and several hundred survey flags stuck in the ground."

"By the end of summer, it'll be a different story," I said.

"Indeed. We hope so. It has potential to be a great addition to the county. And that puts us in a conundrum. First of all, we're not in the habit of sharing personnel files with law enforcement. Now granted, we're not priests or lawyers." She smiled. "The notion of confidentiality is a little more fuzzy with us. But more important, I don't want Mr. Waddell to think that we're a bunch of vultures, jumping at the chance to make a profit out of someone's misfortune. He may not want—may not even *need*—what we're offering...*if* we make an offer."

I stretched back. "It's apparent that he'll need something. There are rumors aplenty floating around the county, Mrs. Browning. If this power line incident is not just an isolated prank carried out by a bunch of jerks..."

"It's our impression that the anti-government movement, if it's serious enough to call it that, includes more blow-hards than not. A few of 'em will pick up the editorial pen, but there aren't many people who will pick up a gun, or a chain saw, and do the dirty work. This is what I think: I think that Mr. Daniel decided that if his prank delivered Miles Waddell's account to us, Daniel would stand a good chance of being hired. He's obviously had troubles keeping a job, but he's a calculator."

"I'm curious how Daniel found out about the project," Estelle said. "It's been my impression that Mr. Waddell has been just about as private as he could be with all of this."

"If he talked with Boyd, there's a connection," I said. "Boyd would know, since Waddell had talked with him or his father, or both, on more than one occasion. And really, all he needs to do is type in 'security' on his search engine, and there we'll be. We don't hide." She smiled. "Sometimes, I wish we did. We hear from some *unusual* people."

"What does United Security want from us?" Estelle asked. "We're not even sure what Miles Waddell is going to end up with. If anything beyond a fancy roadway."

Lynn nodded at the folder. "First of all, that's yours to keep. It includes everything we have, or received, related to Elliot Daniel. If it does you some good, fine." She regarded Estelle thoughtfully. "I want *you* to know…the sheriff's department to know… that after talking to Mr. Waddell at some length out at the site today, that *NightZone* is a project that we're keenly interested in. It appears to us that he's making every effort to appeal to a broad base—not just a few stargazers, and not just a university program that's limited in scope. If Mr. Waddell accomplishes only a small fraction of his entire dream, it will be an impressive installation." She nodded. "It'll also take some time for the general public to accept it for what it is."

Estelle nodded, but said nothing.

"When the project is up and running, it's going to put stress on your department," Lynn continued. "We can help with that, but it'll work better, more efficiently, if it's a coordinated effort."

"In your mind, what form will that coordination take? We're a government agency, after all. You're a private company."

"I don't know. I just want you thinking about it. How we can help you, how you can help us." She looked hard at me. "Mr. Waddell thinks very highly of you, Sheriff."

"We've been friends a long time, and Miles still has a hard time remembering that I retired a long time ago."

"I think he knows that," Lynn laughed. "He doesn't *like* it, but he knows." She slipped a business card out of her case, and printed two names on it before handing it to me.

"That first one is a state fair organization," she said. "Piers Smith is the general manager. The second is one of our shipping contracts. You might want to chat with both them about United Security. I know that Mr. Waddell is going to ask for your opinion."

"He already has," I said. "Many times."

"There you go." She took a deep breath and stretched backward. "Beyond that," and she indicated the folder that included Daniel's file, "is there anything we can do for you?"

"We have the address that's listed in here, and it's a dead end," Estelle said. "Mr. Daniel could be anywhere. I think we're going to have to wait him out. Wait for him to make another mistake. He's not using his credit card, and there's been no bank activity. He's just," and she spread her hands out, "disappeared." She gazed thoughtfully at me. "In that, he's really remarkable. A friend dies, and he panics. He kills a cop, and at *that* point, he gets either clever or lucky. He manages to slip away. He could be in North Dakota by now. Or Mexico."

"That's the wonderful thing about computers," Lynn Browning said. "It's a small world. It's hard *not* to leave any traces."

And yet, I thought, *that's exactly what Elliot Daniel had done.*

Chapter Twenty-two

Saturday dawned bright and cheerful. Lots of good food, lots of sleep, and I was a new man. On this momentous day, Francisco Guzman and his caravan would arrive from the Leister Music Conservatory. They'd spent the night in Socorro, and expected to roll into Posadas by mid-morning, giving them enough time to prepare their stage.

The concert had earned some big-league attention. I didn't care if they announced that an asteroid the size of Virginia was going to crash into the Earth. I was going to the concert. If no one else came, then I'd ask Francisco and his partner to play a concert just for me.

The Albuquerque paper had splashed the story down two columns on the back page of the Arts section, including one file photo of Francisco performing when he was so small that his feet didn't touch the floor under his piano stool. Posadas itself earned mention by the writer as 'a tiny, dusty border town, sandwiched between Deming and Lordsburg.' Well, sort of. To my relief, the paper *didn't* mention our escalating crime rate.

Over coffee I read and re-read the article, wondering where Posadas High School would seat everyone if all of Albuquerque showed up. Two dozen at the concert would be more our style. The phone jangled, and I reached across and snared it.

"Gastner."

"Sir, do you happen to have a copy of the Albuquerque paper?" Estelle Reyes-Guzman's voice was pleasant and without urgency, and I assumed that she was reading the same article I was.

"I'm looking at it, sweetheart," I said. "I'm enjoying the spread on your number one son."

"They'll be here in a couple of hours," Estelle said. "Then they'll all be over at the high school if you have a yen for mayhem."

"Ah…maybe a bit later. I'm meeting Mrs. Browning at the airport a little before eight. I wanted to talk with Miles Waddell too. I promised him I'd give him an opinion this one time, and I might as well get it over with. Who the hell knows? Maybe he'll buy breakfast…"

"You might want to take a glance at the Letters to the Editor section on B-3, sir. There's an interesting letter there from M.C. Todd."

"Who the hell is that?"

"I was hoping you'd know, sir."

"Well, I don't. Just a minute." I fumbled pages and found B-3. M.C. Todd's letter was lengthy, and I skimmed it. According to Todd, the "Posadas Astronomy Project" was planning on drilling a series of six deep water wells around the base of the mesa, to "satisfy the potential needs of the project at the mesa-top." Todd's concern was for the fragile cave system that supposedly underlay the mesa, a formation much like Carlsbad Caverns in southeastern New Mexico. Damage to underground formations that depend on a consistent water flow will be "incalculable," the article said. I grunted something and read that part again.

"I always thought 'incalculable' meant it couldn't be calculated, big or small, lesser or greater," I said.

"Had Mr. Waddell spoken to you about drilling wells?" Estelle asked.

"No. He may have applied for permits, although why I don't know. He's got a gusher in that one well that he's always had, just east of the new parking lot."

"If you see him, you might ask about it," Estelle said.

"We can call this whole project *La Brea Junior*," I muttered. "Every time I turn around, I hear this great sucking sound as I'm pulled into the goddamned tar pit." When the undersheriff didn't respond to that, I added, "What's the department's interest in Waddell's wells? Or well, as the case may be? If he has permits from the state engineer's office, he can drill to China if he wants."

"We have no interest in some rancher's wells," Estelle said quietly. "My interest is in *anything* that appears in print that can be construed as a threat to any legitimate project. This whole mess is too big for coincidence, Padrino. I can't believe Mr. Todd's letter has nothing to do, *nothing* in common, with the complaints and rumors we've heard about the mesa project. This comes right on top of Daniel's stunt. Way too coincidental."

"You think? Why not just a case of the public finally finding out about the project and venting their disapproval every which way they can?"

"I searched the state engineer's website for listings of drill permits issued. Miles Waddell isn't on the list. No one in that section of Posadas County is on the list. Not one. Nothing issued."

"And requested?" I laughed. "Forget that one. That's what you want me to ask him. The state knows the answer to that one, too, though."

"A non-official request, sir. I can't just barge onto his ranch and ask him his business."

"I don't know why not. Everyone else will."

"I hope you'll talk with him about it, Padrino. This is one instance where we really have to be proactive."

"I'm Teflon today, sweetheart. I don't want to get involved in anything that's going to interfere with tonight. I agreed to this damn helicopter ride, but that's it. What time are Addy and Carlos coming over here, by the way?"

"Mid-afternoon or so. Francisco doesn't want any big fancy to-do, so they won't have a lot to prepare for the reception."

"And there's nothing I need to do, other than leave town?"

Estelle laughed gently. "You'd have two devastated *niños* if you did that, Padrino. But no…there's nothing to do. What

Carlos forgets in all his excitement, Addy will remember. She's the perfect hostess. The reception will be quiet and cozy."

I looked across at the stove clock. "I'll be back at home no later than two," I said. "If you need the house for anything before then, showers, stuff like that, you have the key."

"Sir, thank you for doing this."

"My pleasure, and I'm not just saying that." Although how I was actually going to enjoy a mob scene in my dark, quiet home was still up for debate.

"You're going out to the airport now?" Estelle asked.

"Yep. Then to meet with Miles."

"Be careful, sir."

"You bet." I hung up, ripped M.C. Todd's letter from the newspaper and folded it into my battered aluminum clipboard. What did I care if some nutcase was writing letters to the editor with fabricated information? For one thing, Undersheriff Estelle Reyes-Guzman, as either law officer or damn near adopted daughter, didn't ask for many favors. Sometimes I wished that she would. So I jumped at the chance to be of some small use.

Besides, we were in the same boat as knowing that more than a hundred years ago, some cattleman had tried to scratch out *his* dream somewhere along Bennett's Trail. It's just a compulsion to *know,* I had decided long ago. Sometimes the knowing brought me pleasure, sometimes I wish I'd never snooped.

Chapter Twenty-three

The Jet Ranger was appointed in corporate swank, but it was working swank, wear and tear just beginning to show around the edges. Lots of insulation helped cut the shrieking of the turbine, not like the head-splitting racket of the bare metal military Hueys I had experienced a couple of lifetimes ago.

Lynn Browning was in no hurry, and I sat patiently as she examined every square inch of the bird, then finally climbed in and did the same micro-examination on the inside. The checklist seemed to be reams. At last she picked up a headset, plugged it into the radio console and handed it to me. As soon as it settled on my ears, I heard her calm voice say, "…ive by five?" The headphones' voice-actuated 'on' feature wasn't quite fast enough to catch the first letter of what was said, but it was comfortable not to have to scream "WHAT?"

For a full five minutes we sat in place, the big, flat rotors slicing the air and a stream of Jet-A exhaust drifting up into the faultless sky. Lynn positioned a small copy of Miles Waddell's map on her knee clipboard, on top of her aero chart.

Finally satisfied, she looked toward the FBO building as if airport manager Jim Bergin could read her lips through the windows.

"Posadas Unicom, USR Three Seven Zero One will be taxiing to the active."

"Seven Zero One, active is currently two eight zero, winds two niner zero, gusting to five, barometer three zero six zero.

Traffic is the UPS Bonanza inbound from the west here in about five minutes."

Even as Bergin said that, and I could picture his wrinkled face cracking at his own joke about the wind 'gusts', the Jet Ranger went light on its toes as the rotors bit the air, and we slid across the parking area macadam, our skids maybe an inch off the ground. She took the first intersection, angled out to the runway as she scanned the sky, and then tracked west down the centerline as the nose dropped and we climbed rapidly, the airport dropping away behind us.

Seconds later, rising in seamless, velvety air, we could see the tan kidney-bean shape of Waddell's mesa. To the south, the steel-blue highway cut the prairie, and I could see a dust cloud on one of the spurs off of County 14.

"Basically what I'm after," Lynn said, pointing to the south as if she had seen something else, "are coordinate photos of the mesa, from just far enough away that we can capture the entire formation." Finally I saw what she had pointed at as the sun glinted off the bright metal of a single-engine plane coming in from Lordsburg, fast and low. Almost immediately we heard the chatter on the radio as everyone announced themselves.

She answered my question without my asking. "We just need to know what's *there*."

"There are actually a couple of spots where there is access to the mesa-top from down below," I said, and she nodded. A few moments later, Prescott's ranch passed under our nose, and we skirted the south side of the mesa. Near the rim, I could see Waddell's RV trailer parked, a choice spot. The rancher's truck was gone, and the angled sun highlighted the tracks.

We stopped, the tail swinging around fast enough that part of my stomach sagged behind. When we were facing north, she used a small digital camera to snap photos from her side window, at one point actually backing up until she could frame the photo of the south-east mesa corner just the way she wanted.

"How long have you known Mr. Waddell?" the disembodied voice in the headphones asked.

"Long time."

"Where does he actually *live?*"

"He's got a nice place north of here. Ever since he started this project, he's been spending most of his time in that little travel trailer."

She nodded and banked the chopper sharply as we skirted west along the mesa edge, holding far enough away that she could capture her panoramas.

"This is the spot where California is setting up?" she asked.

"Approximately so. I think."

"He told me that he's paying some of the transportation costs."

When I didn't answer, she glanced at me. "Any idea what those are?"

"I have no idea. You'd have to ask Miles." Then, more to be conversational than anything else, I added, "I'm sure it's plenty."

Where the new access highway joined the mesa rim, she hovered in close, documenting some of the fancy rockwork that kept the road sides in place.

"When he built this road, what was your understanding about the project?"

I took a moment to separate in my own mind what Miles Waddell had told me in confidence, and what was for public consumption. "I always thought he was building an observatory," I said. "Obviously more than that."

"But you've seen the architects' rendering?"

"Sure." I reached over and tapped the small version on her clipboard. "Just the big version of that. The whole dream, minus the train."

We whupped up the air above the parking lot. First taking a photo to the south, she then pivoted the chopper smoothly so that she could shoot to the north, toward the construction of the new power substation. Despite it being a weekend now, five vehicles were at the site. No wood this time, I noticed. So what had the vandals accomplished? The new substation framework looked like something out of an Erector set.

"He never mentioned his budget for the next three years," Lynn said. "From the activity I've seen so far…wow." She smiled over at me, looking almost apologetic at her fishing.

"From what I know of Miles, he won't build anything he can't afford," I said.

"It's amazing to tackle something like this without partners—without an organization to fall back on."

We made our way now east, and in the shade of a dense grove of junipers, I could see his wellhead, the well itself protected by a little concrete bunker he'd built a dozen years before with a steel-framed windmill presiding for the stock tanks.

"Just the one well?"

"As far as I know," I said. "Have you actually sat down with Miles and gotten all the answers you need from him?"

"I plan to do that this afternoon. We have lunch planned."

"That's the best thing. I'm sure he'll provide all the Dunn & Bradstreet info you need if it comes to that."

"Sometimes a second opinion is helpful," she said.

"I suppose so."

"On a scale of one to ten, how optimistic are you that this project will succeed as he envisions it?"

"Me, personally?"

"Yes."

"I'll go for the old saw, Mrs. Browning. Miles Waddell can have anything he wants…he just may not be able to have *every-thing* he wants. I have no idea what kind of tourist traffic he can attract to pay for the operating costs. No idea."

"He strikes me as being shrewd," she said. "Excited but shrewd."

"That's a fair assessment."

For the next forty minutes, we orbited and shot, and despite the smooth air, I began to regret not having a full breakfast—too much coffee sloshed around in an empty belly.

"I'd like an overview," my pilot announced, and even as she spoke, the mesa fell away. We climbed as smartly as the lightly loaded Jet Ranger could manage in the thin, high-prairie air, and circled slowly, enjoying the full panorama. To the south, I could clearly see the pass through the San Cristóbals, and could count three vehicles in the twenty-six miles between the pass and Posadas to the east. As we reached 9,000 feet and turned, I could see over Cat Mesa to the north. It would be interesting to be able to pen the route Waddell was considering for his train. What did narrow gauge railroad bed now cost per mile?

Looking at the rugged mesa and all the arroyos and gorges cut in its flanks, I thought that a railroad that looped *around* Cat Mesa would be spectacular, the tracks heading out of Posadas to the east and north, reappearing around the west end of the mesa. Fifty miles of track, maybe. Mere pocket change. Wonderfully empty country, it all was. In the entire panorama to the north, I could see a single billow of dust from a vehicle northbound off of State 78, following what would become one of the jarring Forest Service roads near the west end of the mesa. A woodcutter, perhaps. Or Johnny Boyd taking the rough route home.

"Is there anything else you might like to see?" Lynn asked. "And by the way, I'll be happy to send you a packet of the best of the best."

"I'd appreciate that. And I'll buy breakfast, if we're headed back."

She had seen my yawns, a sure sign that a flight passenger would rather be elsewhere.

"Thanks for that," she said. "But I think I'll go back to the motel room and print some of these out before I meet with Mr. Waddell." She banked gently for one more mesa view. "What a spot," she said. "What an incredible spot."

"You know, I predict what's going to appeal to the county commission about this whole thing. *Nothing* shows to the casual passerby. No excavation, no nothing. From down on the highway, you won't be able to see a damn thing. There's one spot, if you know just where to look, that you'll be able to see the top portion of the California dish. That's it. No neon, no noise, no intrusion."

"That works both ways, though. Unless he has some careful signage, *something* to announce the location, he won't attract the casual tourist…the folks for whom the mesa isn't a planned destination."

"When this is up and running, there will be so much publicity in the media, I don't think that will be a problem," I said. More likely, just the opposite, I thought. Hopefully, Miles Waddell's *NightZone* wouldn't become a Pandora's Box.

Chapter Twenty-four

My favorite back corner of the Don Juan de Oñate was as dark as the New Mexico prairie had been blinding. In retrospect, I thought that Lynn Browning had kept her curiosity pretty well in check. If I'd been willing to blab, she'd have listened and maybe even encouraged. When I made it clear that I wasn't going to offer up gratuitous information behind my friend's back, she hadn't persisted. If that had been the reason for her inviting me along, I'd turned out to be a boring passenger.

I had taken two scrumptious bites when my little cell phone vibrated, and I dropped my fork in the process of trying to fish the damn phone out of my pocket.

"Gastner," I managed around the green chile soaked egg and onion and sausage and mushrooms and Fernando Aragon only knew what else.

"Where are you?" Bob Torrez's usual quiet voice sounded loud in the quiet restaurant. For a moment I could imagine that by ducking inside the restaurant, I had escaped the eye of his pilotless drone.

"Eating a green chile burrito that won't wait for anybody or anything," I said. "And this is the second time in a couple of days that you've asked me where the hell I am. I'm on a short leash now, or what?"

The sheriff almost chuckled, a little huff of amusement. "Just checkin'." This from a man who didn't care an iota where people were, or what they were doing or saying—unless they crossed into his turf.

"Did you talk with Estelle this morning?"

"Yep. How was the flight?"

"Spectacular. What's up?"

"I just finished talking to Art Shaum out at Chavez." Shaum was the new service manager at the Chavez Chevrolet dealership, a hardwired young man who would spend his Saturday at the dealership even though the service department was closed for the weekend. My bet was that he'd end up owning the place within a year. "He's missing a vehicle."

"I didn't take it." I waited patiently, since the sheriff had more on his mind than a stolen car or truck.

"The electric company had one of their older units at the dealership for front end work. F-450 utility body, stretch cab, four by four diesel. White, with fleet number 1214 on the front fender. Gone this morning." He rattled off the tag and repeated the fleet number.

"It wasn't locked up?"

"Just in that little paddock deal by the service entrance. Key was hanging in Shaum's office."

"And it still is?"

"Yep."

"So what are you thinking, Sheriff."

After a brief pause, Torrez said, "I'm thinkin' that I don't like coincidence. This Daniel guy is switchin' vehicles left and right. And now this…"

"Bobby, get a grip. Who is going to want a flapped-out Electric Coop truck? Behemoth like that probably won't break fifty miles an hour."

"Depends on what he plans to do with it," the sheriff said.

"Like what, do you imagine?"

"I can think of all kinds of things."

"Name one."

"Who bothers to give a second look at an electric company truck out near a construction site?"

"Well, for one thing, the electric company might. They've got all kinds of people out here who would recognize it in a heartbeat."

"Plus," the sheriff pointed out, "he's got his bike with him. He used the dealership's utility ramp and wasn't too careful about leavin' tracks."

I took a moment to digest that. The sheriff was *not* imagining things if a motorcycle was involved. "Why would he stay around?" I said, more to myself than the sheriff.

"'Cause he thinks he's got a target," Torrez said. "They finished up tossing his apartment in Cruces. Interesting hobby he had. It looks like he had just about every movie or book about the French Resistance ever made."

"The *French* resistance? Like in World War II?"

"Yep."

"That's a bit before his time, don't you think?"

"Just a bit."

"Do you think that he really believes that what Waddell is building on this mesa is the vanguard of something else? Some big, secret government project? And now, like the Hollywood preview guy would say, '*only one man can stop the unspeakable evil that lurks in the NightZone.*' And I'm not trying to make light of some creep who's turned cop killer."

"Could be. I don't know what he's thinkin'. What *I'm* thinkin' is that we got us more of a fruitcake on our hands than we guessed. If he took the truck, it means he's in the neighborhood, and he still wants to do something. So watch yourself when you're out there pokin' in dark corners."

"This is a small county," I said. "There just aren't that many places to hide a big old electric company truck."

"We're lookin', believe me. Can't believe he pulled this off right under our noses."

"You weren't looking for a utility truck," I said. "It's not your fault. On a happier note, you're still planning to go to the concert with Gayle, I hope."

"We got pretty good coverage," he said, and it didn't sound like he was planning to enjoy the music. I started to say something else, but the dial tone told me that Bobby had exhausted his patience.

I heaved a sigh and went back to work just as Fernando brought more coffee.

"Long days?" he asked.

"Very long, Fernando." I watched him pour and then nodded my thanks. "You going to the concert tonight?"

His heavy face broke into a smile. "You bet. You bet. See you there, maybe."

"*Sin duda,*" I said, trying out one of the two or three Spanish idioms that I knew. I had left my phone on the table, and it vibrated in a little circle like some strange insect.

"Gastner." I raised a hand in salute to Fernando as he retreated back toward the kitchen.

"So tell me about your impression of Mrs. Browning," Miles Waddell said without preamble.

"You're in love?"

"She's a corker, isn't she? I could be, except I'm twenty years out of date to be in competition. And you know, there's a photo of her husband on one of the brochures she gave me. He's about six-six and looks like he could pound me into the ground like a fence post. Where you at?"

"Don Juan."

"Why is that not a surprise. I saw the chopper as I was driving back to the site from town. Nice rig."

"Sure enough."

"So?"

"So what?"

"What do you think? This is why I pay you the big bucks."

"Yeah. Well, if I was you, I'd ask for a list of references, and after hearing from them, I'd hire United Security." I shrugged.

"That's the plain and short of it?"

"Yep. If you're going to develop even *half* of what you've planned, you're going to need some security. I'd be surprised to hear that another private security company could offer any more than hers does. Most would offer far less."

"That's what I wanted to hear."

"The flight this morning prompted another question," I said. "How are you moving all the water this place is going to need?"

I heard a soft chuckle. "From all my six wells, you mean?"

"That's one rumor."

"And that's what it is. You must have seen this morning's paper."

"You've heard of this Mr. Todd?"

"Nope."

"Are there any grounds to what he's saying?"

There was a pause, and then Waddell said, "Absolutely none. I have one gusher well down below. You know about that one. Nobody knows how these things link up underground, but at the moment, that sucker is six hundred feet deep and giving me five hundred gallons a minute. A *minute*. A while back, I tried pumping it down. No dice. You know," he added, "The stupid part of this particular rumor our Mr. Todd is starting—whoever he might be—is that this whole project isn't water intensive. I mean, there are no big cooling towers, no huge anything. Lots of recycling, and believe it or not, lots of rainwater catchment… what damn little rain we ever get."

He fell silent and I let him think while I chased a stray piece of chile onto my fork. "I *have* been thinking of sinking another well off the south side," Waddell said. "I haven't gone after a permit or anything, but there's actually a pretty good place down on that little spit of land I bought from Herb Torrance. The well driller's dowser says a strong flow. That's the closest spot to lift water up to the university's installation that's on that edge of the mesa. Be a good backup."

"But not six."

"Uh, no. You know, I talked to one of the hydrologists from the BLM. Is my well…my wells, if I do the second one…going to draw down the underground water they think is feeding that cave formation under the mesa? Don't know. That's the only answer they give me. Nobody knows."

"No truth to any of this, then."

"None. Is that what you're doing today, scouting out all my clandestine wells?"

"Actually, what I'm trying hard to do is stay out of trouble until the concert, Miles. But someday I'm going to write the definitive book on rumors and how they live their lives. Does somebody lie awake nights thinking up this shit? I mean, I know how rumors hop from one half-listening ear to another, but this is ridiculous. This guy is citing specific numbers."

"They're as easy to make up as vague references, Bill. You know that. No easier way to rile people. What fun is it to say, 'Gosh, if he's successful, he *may* have to think about digging another well?' What fun is that?" He laughed harshly. "And what's this about the electric company's truck?"

"Bobby called you this morning?"

"You bet. I didn't think I was on his speed dial list. What's up?"

"Just what he said, Miles. It seems this Daniel character has stolen—*may* have stolen—an electric company utility truck. There are indications he's carrying his motorcycle in the back."

"How'd he pull that off, with all the cops we got swarming around the county?"

"I have no idea. But he did, last night some time. He hot-wired it. They had forgotten to lock the dealer's boneyard behind the service department."

"Well, crap. And with all the traffic lately, who's going to notice another electric company truck? Smart son-of-a-bitch. So he's still in the area."

"Maybe. He could be."

"That makes me feel really good. What makes Bobby so sure it was our man?"

"Bobby Torrez's hunch. And I agree with him. There were signs that he loaded his motorcycle in the back."

"Well, crap. And what for?"

"I don't know what for, Miles. I'm not getting anywhere trying to second-guess this guy. But he's up to something, even if it's just a free ride out of the state in a vehicle the cops wouldn't give a second glance."

Waddell sighed with exasperation, then brightened. "We'll have the foundation plans by March first for the big guy. That mother is going to loom up here so big and grand…" He laughed with delight.

"Look, here in a few minutes, I'll have a houseful. Addy and the little brother are coming over to prepare for the reception after the concert. You're going to make it?"

"You bet."

"The reception too, at my place afterward. You're most welcome."

"Thanks. I might. You know, the auditorium we'll have in the main building will make a great venue for events like this concert. I need to get the kid to write an original composition for *NightZone*. He can debut it here."

"You might as well dream big," I laughed.

"No end to it," he promised. "You'll see."

"Just don't take too long. Remember the old saw about green bananas."

"Waiting is one thing I'm not about to do," Waddell said.

Chapter Twenty-five

By the time I reached the high school complex off South Pershing Avenue, I had managed to push all the unanswered questions well to the back of my tired brain.

An enormous slab-sided RV, black with gold artwork, a veritable land yacht, was parked in front of the gym. Hitched to its back bumper was a sleek black utility trailer large enough to hold an automobile. Behind *that* were two white Suburbans and a silver Lexus. No wonder the damn tuition at Leister Conservatory was so dear.

Superintendent Glenn Archer stood on the sidewalk, locked in conversation with a man about my age but with five times as much hair, a maestro's bouffant display that would be hell after a sandstorm. Parked on the sidewalks near them was an enormous swaddled piano, tipped on edge and supported by a dolly that looked as if it were built from spare aircraft undercarriage parts.

I parked by the tennis court fence and took a moment to call the sheriff's department dispatch. Gayle Torrez was working, and she greeted me warmly.

"I'm at the high school for a bit, then home," I said. "See you tonight?"

"I wouldn't miss this one," the sheriff's wife said. "And I didn't even have to twist Bobby's arm."

"Just put the rest of the world on hold," I said.

Glenn Archer beamed at me as I approached. He'd been at the helm of this school for close to thirty years, and I'd heard rumblings of retirement rumors. He'd guided the place through economic booms and busts, failed bond issues, plenty of nasty letters to the editor balanced by a handful of supportive ones. He'd seen plenty of youngsters go on to become productive and happy, a few joining the dregs. Our paths had crossed too often on graduation or prom weekends when we pried the shattered bodies out of wreckage. He'd seen it all, handing out a couple thousand scholarships, plaques, or varsity letters. He had probably dispensed enough tissue to weepy parents to earn stock in the company.

Now he greeted me with a carefully modulated handshake, at the same time resting a hand on his companion's shoulder.

"Bill, I'd like you to meet Dr. Hal Lott. Dr. Lott is headmaster at the conservatory. Professor, Mr. Gastner is a longtime county sheriff, historian, and all-around foundation of the community."

"My pleasure." Lott's grip was one of those warm, limp things that made me think he was protecting his baton fingers. "Young master Guzman speaks highly of you." He frowned. "His *padrino?*" He pronounced the word carefully.

"We're proud of him," I said. Nodding at all the vehicles and equipment, I added, "Quite a production."

Lott turned and regarded the activity. Four youngsters, satisfied that the piano was secure, pushed the beast across to the handicapped ramp and then up the grade, putting their backs to it.

"There are times," the headmaster said with a long, heartfelt exhale, "that I am very glad that not all of our students are keyboard performance majors."

"Interesting logistics," I said. "The piano always goes along?"

"Horowitz once played on that Steinway," Lott said. "It's become a tradition at Leister."

I knew that I should show at least an eyebrow raised in reverence at the two names, but instead I said, "The tuner goes with it?" There had to be a reason that Horowitz played the piano only once.

"Oh, indeed," Lott said hastily. "Lucian Belloit has been with us for years." He smiled conspiratorially. "It's most convenient that he's also a most accomplished coach driver."

I reached across and shook Glenn Archer's hand again. "I need to check on this Guzman kid," I said. "I'll talk with you folks later." I had recognized Carlos Guzman's ten-speed stashed in the bike rack, and knew the two boys would be inside having way, way too much fun.

Carlos stood on a raised stage, hands in his back pockets, scrutinizing the placement of the enormous royal blue banners, the center one bearing the Leister Conservatory seal. Tucked right up against the ceiling, some of the banners were draped artfully to soften the angular lines of the girders. Others hung straight down to form baffles that would direct and soften the sound.

Although youngsters were performing most of the unpacking and grunt work, I noticed that the motorized scaffold, now scissored open to reach up into the girders, was operated by two elderly men from our school district, with two older students along for the ride.

"Carlos, are they doing it right?" I said, and the boy spun around.

"Padrino!" he stage-whispered. "This is just so *amazing!*" He pointed across toward the double entry doors where the mountain of boxes and crates were piled. "I can't believe how much stuff they brought with them." As he spoke, the piano eased through after a hard left off the ramp. With laughter driving them on, the four kids accelerated the piano on its big smooth-rolling wheels until I wondered if they'd be able to stop it before crashing into the stage. They managed, and then used the hydraulic undercarriage to elevate the piano past the edge of the platform. Two belts dropped away, and the piano was rolled onto the stage, awaiting its legs.

"Where's your brother?"

Carlos raised a hand close to his nose, sighting along his index finger. "Right over there, at the top of the bleachers. They're going to fold them all up in a few minutes, though."

Sure enough, right under the *Fighting Jaguars 1992*, the hunched figure blended into the shadows.

"Last minute studying?" I asked.

Carlos scoffed, a very adult sound for a nine-year-old. "He's making changes. That's what he told me. He won't let me look."

"Ah." Something squeaked behind me, and I turned to see a kid wielding an enormous wrench on a cranky bolt, securing one of the Steinway's legs in place. I glanced at my watch. Curtain time was in five hours, and by then the students from Leister would have turned this plain old gym into a colorful concert hall. "I'm going to go bother him for just a minute, and then I'll be over at the house."

Carlos sighed. "I never realized I was going to have such a famous brother." There was wistful admiration there, maybe even a little adoration, but no envy.

I punched him lightly on the shoulder. "He's saying the same thing." The second leg drew tightly in place as I stepped off the stage, and even as I plodded across the floor, avoiding banners and crew, I saw Francisco unfold from his spot, and carefully close a portfolio. I wasn't going to get to see, either.

He rose and started down the bleachers, frowning and taking the steps one at a time. I waited for him, amused at the look of intense concentration on his face. Halfway down, it was as if he turned a switch. His eyes locked on mine, a huge smile spread across his face, and he bounded the last six benches in two bounds. I didn't get a handshake. His hug was chiropractor ferocious. He buried his face in my shoulder and mumbled something, and he didn't even *smell* like a little kid anymore.

After a long moment he pushed me back, a hand on each shoulder, and I was aware of how much of his mother's eyes he had inherited. He'd filled out, too, his face growing into some of his father's almost craggy features. He transferred his grip to a two-handed shake, and the strength of that wasn't driven by a kid who spent all day at video games.

"Isn't this all amazing?" he said happily, as if it were his first concert.

I turned and surveyed the gym. "Just a few years ago, you were playing dodge ball in here."

He laughed loudly. "Oh, wow." Turning back to me, his expression went sober. "I was sorry to hear about the shooting thing. The old guy with the shotgun."

That bolt from the blue startled me. "That stuff happens, Francisco. Even when we're not looking for it, it happens."

"Shit happens."

"Yep."

He heaved a sigh. "You're all right, though."

"Just fine."

"And Sergeant Taber is okay?"

"Just fine."

"I always liked her."

"She's planning on coming tonight."

He beamed. "Oh, awesome."

"So if the concert is at eight this evening, what's your schedule?"

He glanced at his watch, one of those enormous things with half a dozen dials and buttons.

"I have some more work to do right now, and then when they have the piano set up and tuned, a little more. Mateo and I need to finalize some things." *Finalize.* I didn't even know that thirteen-year-olds did that. "And then I need to *eat.*" He said it as if he were starving in the wilderness. "This guy," and he nodded toward the approaching Carlos, "promised that he and Addy were putting out a spread. I have to eat before a concert, or I just kind of go to sleep at the keyboard. *That's* embarrassing."

"That would be."

"And then Dr. Lott requires us to go into seclusion in the dressing room for an hour before the concert. That gives us plenty of time to work up a good case of nerves."

"You never struck me as the nervous type, Francisco."

"A little bit tonight. I don't usually play accompaniment, for one thing. It's a whole different ball game when you have to play *with* someone else."

"I should think so. I haven't met this Mateo."

"He's over in the music room working on a couple of things. And then Mr. Dayan wanted to talk with him for a little bit." He reached out both hands as Carlos arrived and folded his little brother into the Guzman bear hug. After a minute he relaxed with one arm draped over his brother's shoulders. "What do you think?" He sounded as if he really needed to know, and Carlos turned and surveyed the gym's transformation, now nearly complete.

"They *really* know what they're doing."

"They'd better," Francisco laughed. We watched as a youngster with a black suitcase disappeared behind a folding screen near the water fountain—a little remnant to remind us of the buildings more usual function. "There are some neat acoustical issues no matter how many curtains they hang," he continued. "The Steinway has this great huge voice," and he spread his hands a yard apart. "And in comparison, the flute…" he held thumb and forefinger nearly touching. "When they play together, all this balance stuff has to be worked out."

"Way over my head," I said. "Look, you have work to do, so I'll see you at dinner." Before I could prepare a defense, there came that hug again.

Chapter Twenty-six

No one talked about Elliot Daniel at early dinner. To me, he wasn't worth the breath, or the robbery of a single moment spent with Francis and Estelle Guzman's two kids and the Leister guests. Dinner included Francisco's favorite, green chile lasagna with a flood of accompanying morsels. Somehow, Dr. Guzman had been overruled, and their kitchen now included a modest deep-fat fryer which produced such exquisitely fluffy, puffed *sopaipillas* that the good doctor finally admitted as he wiped a squirt of honey off his beard, "Well, maybe these *are* worth having a coronary for."

Dr. Lott had never eaten green chile, but he indulged until sweat stood out on his pale forehead. He let the conversation focus on the youngsters, as did Lucian Belloit, Leister's stage manager, chauffeur, and general field boss. Belloit, a short, burly fellow with an infectious, booming laugh, kept the mutual admiration society at bay with sparing anecdotes about talented youngsters who managed to embarrass themselves and everyone on stage with gaffes and implosions.

"And *this* one," he said, nodding at Mateo Atencio, seated now between Francisco and Carlos, "managed to drop his flute right in the middle of a Mozart cadenza. I think that was at a concert in San Antonio a couple of years ago. Remember that?" He laughed as the red blush spread up Mateo's dark face. Except for being a bit fuller in the face, Mateo could have been part of the Guzman gene pool, dark, perfect posture and poise, a gleam in the eyes that said his agile brain was up to *something,* who knew what.

"Squirted out of his hands like a bar of soap. Tell what you did then, Mateo."

The boy's voice was almost a whisper. "I caught it in mid-air."

"He *caught* it. Neatest one-handed snatch you ever saw." Belloit hesitated. "Snagged the fumble. Impressive, I must say."

"I suppose," Dr. Lott mused, ready to add a little pomp to the storytelling, "that every musician in the world has lost control of the instrument at one time or another in his career. I remember in high school, years and years ago, the A string—the top string—of my viola snapping just seconds before I was to play a solo passage. I managed the solo entirely in fourth and fifth position, and when I was finished, I was *drenched* in perspiration."

"What about Francisco's joke concert?" Mateo prompted in self-defense.

Lott squirmed with discomfort, but Belloit remained undeterred. Francisco bowed his head, covering his face with both hands. When he looked up, he beamed across at me and shrugged expansively.

"Somebody…" Belloit glared at Mateo with mock anger, "taped a sheet of really repulsive, ah…*suggestive* limericks on the music rack of the piano. We weren't using the Steinway for that one, just a little grand that the college provided. So here comes this what, eleven? Eleven-year-old kid on stage, right?" He leaned back expansively, patting his comfortably full belly. "Now we all know that Francisco Guzman can't let a catchy rhythm go unexplored, right? So he turns the page of his music, and there's this sheet of raunchy limericks, printed in nice, clear bold-face type, easy to read. He has one page of Beethoven to play before he's cast adrift…with limericks."

"There was a good fellow from…" Francisco murmured, and he grinned impishly toward his grandmother, who so far hadn't uttered a word during dinner. I could imagine what was going through her mind, though—pride in this credible grandson, tempered with the firm belief that youngsters should know their place when in company with adults.

"Now, he's halfway into this Beethoven sonata, and suddenly the music is missing. Does he miss a lick? No. But suddenly Beethoven is all improv. To this day," and he rapped an emphasizing knuckle on the table, "to this day, I don't know how Master Guzman can make a piano tell a punch line. But he did. Beethoven would have been delighted."

"You need to play that one," Carlos urged.

"No, he doesn't," Estelle said. She looked over at me. "Should we be worried, Padrino?"

"I'm not," I said, and turned to Francisco. "And you're not going to divulge what you're playing tonight?"

Francisco glanced at Mateo. "We can't, Padrino."

Dr. Lott let out a long *hmmm* of scholarly reservation. "*We're* the ones who should be worried, Mrs. Guzman." He looked at his watch. "But we need to go to the concert hall, if you'll excuse us all. We have a pre-concert session with the artists, and then some on-stage time."

The *artists*. After spending thirty-five years arresting teenagers, it was a pleasure to hear that.

My plans were to spend the entire evening immersed in jaw-dropping music. I had no plans to worry my way through the evening, not on Francisco Guzman's behalf, or anyone else's. Before leaving for school, I made sure the hostesses had what they needed at my house, and locked up a couple of sensitive items…not the least of which was the relic Colt, its rust-fused cylinder with the four corroded cartridges such a temptation.

By the time I reached the school at 7:15, I had difficulty finding a convenient place to park. I knew the numbers. The Leister crew included four adults and sixteen youngsters—counting the artists. Glenn Archer's wife Sylvia had organized the task force to find lodging for the youngsters in area homes. That guaranteed a fair audience, perhaps a hundred people. That didn't explain the packed side parking lot by the administrative building, or the clogged loop where buses dropped off students, or the ancillary lot over by the tennis courts. That left the big parking lot by the football field and track, a lengthy trudge from the gym. And it was filling fast. But what the hell. My sadistic doctor had told me to walk more, more, more. Who was I to argue with the guy who also served as the county coroner?

The interior of the "concert hall" was colorful and devoid of the normal gymnasium echo, partly because of the temporary red vinyl floor covering but mostly because of the bannered girders. Despite the sea of chairs arranged in three large islands, the concert was going SRO unless the bleachers were used. In the back corner, two school custodians were in conference with Lucian Belloit, and one of them, a jangle of keys in hand, was pointing at the last two sections of bleachers.

A small center section up front was ribboned off, and since one of the royal-blue tickets with the Leister logo was tucked in my pocket, I made for the reserved seats. Two ushers in black and white started down the aisle to greet me, the his and hers smiles welcoming.

I found my complimentary ticket in the breast pocket of my sport jacket, and the girl—she might have been fifteen—reached out and touched my hand as if she had known me since infancy.

"Mr. Gastner, anywhere in the ribboned section, if you like."

"Thank you." *How did she know who I was?* "I'm going to roam a bit first."

She handed me a program, a stiff expensive fold with the Leister crest on the cover, and the poster photo of Mateo and Francisco on the inside. "Perhaps you'd like to reserve your seat with a program."

The hum and bustle of folks in the hall was rising. "Good idea. Thank you." On stage, the nine-foot piano dominated just off-center, and I chose a seat on the aisle five rows back where I would be able to see both artist and keyboard. A bevy of tiny microphones hung from slender gaffs, and turning in place, I could see five large video cameras around the hall, including the two stage right and left.

A backstage area had been created with heavy velvet curtains, hiding the portable control panel. As I ambled off to one side, I saw Francisco and Mateo standing together behind the curtain, Francisco with an arm across his stomach and the other hand supporting his chin, a pose of deep thought. Mateo's hands were in his hip pockets as if his tux was a pair of Wranglers. Both boys were listening as Dr. Hal Lott laid down the law about something. He talked, they listened. They did not interrupt. At one point, he held an invisible basketball between both hands and shook it. Perhaps that was a rendition of what was going to happen to their skulls if they screwed up.

A good share of the performance pressure came from the expectations of others. Nobody had come to this gig thinking that they'd see a couple of kids monkeying around. Expectations were high, and the efforts of two dozen people at stake. It wasn't Francisco or Mateo arriving to play a tune or two on the school's battered Baldwin for a few friends.

I tried to estimate what this concert was costing Leister, since Posadas Municipal Schools had provided nothing other than the yawning gymnasium. The tickets were thirty bucks, a breathtaking price for country folks in this economy. With a capacity crowd, the academy might break even. I stood in one dark corner stage left and found my reading glasses. The program alone was a class act, including the names of selections as well as a short Artist's Comments for each one.

"Padrino!" The greeting wasn't exactly shouted, but I looked up with a start. Carlos Guzman looked spiffy in his black suit. He was beaming, and held his own program toward me as he made his way across the floor. "Did you see?"

"See what?" I said, and he reached across to point out what I'd already read. "Oh, that." *Oh, that* was '*Upward, Opus 7 in G Major*'. The brief student explanation explained that Opus 7, dedicated to a certain Carlos Guzman, started with the "laying of the skyscraper's foundation in the bass, gradually building story after story until the winds play around the loftiest radio antenna on top."

I looked at Carlos, whose face was radiant with excitement. "You had something to do with this?"

He ducked his head in delight. "I sent Francisco a drawing I did of a building."

"Well, wow." I skimmed the rest of the program, saving a real scrutiny until I sat down. Out in the audience, I saw that Estelle, Francis and Teresa had arrived, and one of the ushers was removing two chairs to make room for Teresa's wheelchair.

"I'm sitting right by you," Carlos said, as if that was somehow a big deal. I suppose it would guarantee that I didn't doze off. I gave the youngster a little hug and clamped a hand on the back of his neck. "I have to visit with the sheriff."

At the double doors at the north end of the gym, Robert Torrez was locked in conversation with Glenn Archer and two other deputies—the bruised Sergeant Jackie Taber and Sergeant Tom Mears. Taber was in full uniform with no cover, but Mears was in civilian garb, a gray, black, and white ski sweater, jeans, and boots.

Sheriff Robert Torrez had dressed for the event in a bright lumberjack's flannel shirt and jeans, his boots adding another inch to his six-four frame. The quilted tan vest covered most of his equipment, with the exception of the .45 automatic and the magazine pouches. This was a concert, for God's sake, but then again, who was I to talk. I wondered what Torrez knew that he hadn't passed along to me. He glanced at his watch, and out of reflex, I did the same. Fifteen minutes to pack the hall. I had intended to check in with Torrez, but decided against it

But he didn't. He caught my eye and beckoned. I made my way through an impressive crowd, many of them older folks who no doubt would have liked somewhat more cushy chairs than the steel folders. Someone had reached a decision, and folks were being ushered toward the most forward sections of bleachers.

"Sheriff, you're looking festive," I said.

"Where are you sittin'?"

I turned and pointed. "Way up front behind the ribbon. Fifth row on the aisle."

"Okay." He didn't look especially happy, but then again, he never did. He slipped a playing card-sized photo out of his pocket. "This is what he looked like a year ago."

"He?" But one glance and I knew who "he" was. George Baum stood with one arm around an attractive woman, with his daughter standing under the protection of the other arm. "Happier times."

"One year ago at Christmas."

"What a difference a year makes." I squinted up at the sheriff. "So what do you know that I should?"

"That's the trouble. We don't know shit." His gaze tracked over the growing crowd. "The last call we know that he made was to the funeral home in Cruces that did his father. He said he'd pick up the ashes after he took care of a couple of things."

"Like?"

"Didn't say." He finished with the scan and then turned to me. "Pay attention. At this point, it don't cost nothin' to be on your toes." He reached out and tapped the photo. "Keep that handy."

"It's more likely that he's headed back out to California to visit his wife and daughter," I said.

"Maybe so." He nodded at the filling gymnasium. "This isn't the best thing to be doin' right now."

"It's been planned for a long time," I said, knowing damn well that wouldn't make any difference to Torrez. "Anyway, in about twelve minutes, we'll be underway, and then in an hour, we'll be out of here."

I think the sheriff could read my expression accurately. I wanted a serene concert without incident, a concert to grab our emotions and soar up into the clouds, leaving behind all the ugliness that man was capable of concocting. I looked at faces, seeing dozens that I recognized—including State Police Lieutenant Mark Adams and his wife. Adams was in civvies, and he was paying attention.

"How many?" I asked, nodding toward Adams.

"Six. And three of our own."

"Well, then…"

"How many you got comin' to your house afterward?"

"I have no idea. Probably too many."

Torrez almost laughed. "Let's hope not." He scanned the mob scene, which is exactly what the old gym had become. Somebody squeezed my elbow, but I had no idea who as the flood of people ebbed and flowed, filling the seats and spreading now up into the bleachers—two on each side of the gym.

"I better find my chair," I said. "Enjoy." That earned a sober nod. "Come by the house after for a bit." Another sober nod.

In the distance—roughly a basketball court's worth—that I walked to reach my seat, I greeted dozens of folks, at least half of whose names I remembered. In the reserved section, Dr. Guzman and his wife were standing, talking to half a dozen people. As I slipped into the row, Jerry Reader stretched across a couple of chairs and pumped my hand. The music teacher's eyes were huge behind his thick glasses.

"Isn't this just incredible?" he shouted, and before I had time to agree, the gymnasium lights dimmed, then brightened, then dimmed again, remaining low. Twin spots lanced out and haloed the Steinway. Not a speck of travel dust remained on its polished ebony flanks. A figure appeared to stand in the dark at a lone microphone off to one side, and when most of the audience took their seats, I could see that it was Superintendent Glenn Archer.

I sat immediately beside Carlos, who squirmed down into his seat, both hands clutched under his chin in that character-istic pose of anticipation. I hadn't had time to actually read the program, and I glanced at it now, the light already too dim for me to make out the fine print. Snagging my car keys, I thumbed the tiny pen light on, cupping it to keep the glow focused on the words. The artists would open with the *Winter* movement of Vivaldi's *Four Seasons,* arranged for the flute and piano. Fol-lowing that, Francisco would play some more square fodder, the kind of music that was going to drive ranchers to turn the radio dial searching for some Reba McIntire or Garth Brooks. In this case, it was Beethoven's *Sonata No. 10 in G Major, Opus*

14, number 2. The program's notes indicated that "Beethoven loved a good laugh, and this piece ends with just that."

As if stamping their authority with a heavily classical start, the two boys would then venture…who the hell knew where. We would have a short intermission to stew about it.

"See that?" Carlos whispered, and poked my program.

"I see, I see," I said. He was so excited he couldn't stand it. After scaling Carlos' skyscraper, the concert would return with an interesting potpourri. I didn't see any surprises, but then again, I knew this Guzman kid pretty well.

Estelle sat between Carlos and his grandmother, and the undersheriff clutched Teresa's left hand in both of hers. No nerves there. The lights took us by surprise, switching off with a dull *bang* of heavy circuits, replaced immediately by a single spot illuminating the mike in the corner. Glenn Archer squinted against it. *He* was nervous, his hands shaking a little as he glommed onto the mike and its stand with both hands.

"Good evening, ladies and gentlemen. This…" and he paused to look off into the semi-dark gym. "This is quite an experience for us and we're glad you could share in it. It's always a treat when students of Posadas Municipal Schools come home for a visit. Oh, my." He took a deep breath. "I'd like to extend a warm welcome to our visiting artists and their crew, but first, I need to point out two important things. First of all, those of you with gadgets that make noise—cell phones, I-this or that, *please* turn them off. Let's take ten seconds to do that right now." He held both hands toward us, and there was a rustling as folks who hadn't been able to figure this out for themselves complied.

"Next, we originally were going to close the bleachers. They are so *noisy,* folks. But as you can see, your wonderful turnout has far, far exceeded our expectations. So, those of you *in* the bleachers, I implore you to make every effort to avoid shifting around or changing seats. And please—corral the children who are too young to understand the need for silence." He smiled benignly. "I think that concludes all the dire warnings." Looking out toward the piano, he said, "I would like to extend a heartfelt, an *excited* welcome to Dr. Hal Lott, headmaster of Leister Music Conservatory in Edgarton, Missouri."

Lott looked smaller out on that stage all by himself, but he pumped Archer's hand and then turned to the audience with a welcoming smile—and no little cheat sheet to remind him of what to say.

"Good evening. Leister Conservatory is proud to present another in our series of hometown concerts featuring the talented students we are proud to serve." He gazed thoughtfully at the piano for a moment, as if it had something to say. "You know, I had every expectation of having to make some programming changes, but the two artists assure me that what you're holding is accurate. Well…" and he let that thought drift as the audience laughed. "Your children *never* serve up surprises to you, do they." He grinned and waited for the hall to fall silent.

"From Dos Pasos, Texas, a senior flute major at Leister, let me present Mateo Atencio." He held up a hand, and when the applause died, and sounding like a boxing match announcer, said, "From Posadas, New Mexico, senior pianist Francisco Guzman." The roar of applause was enormous, and I leaned forward a bit and looked across at Estelle.

"Senior?" I mouthed. What happened to the thirteen-year-old I knew.

Chapter Twenty-seven

The applause rose as the two youngsters walked onto the stage. Both looked impossibly young, but both moved with the grace that comes with being completely at home. The spots winked off the flute that Mateo carried one-handed as if it were nothing more than a tennis racket. Francisco, nifty in a black tux and shoes so polished that the spots winked off *them,* walked to the Steinway and rested his hand on the corner nearest the lid support. As if wired together, the two kids both bowed with reserve. Francisco smiled at our section, then straightened up and acknowledged the rest of the audience.

He ducked his head again and turned to the piano. It was then that I noticed the lack of music. None on the piano, no music rack for Mateo. No wonder Dr. Lott was worried about the unexpected. I held the program again, trying to catch enough light to read the descriptive notes. Impossible. I took a deep breath and tried to relax.

Mateo had moved to the piano's curved flank and gently placed the flute on the Steinway's right candelabra shelf. Francisco waited with his hands in his lap. Withdrawing a white handkerchief, Mateo touched his nose then dried his upper lip. Just as he was pocketing the handkerchief and reaching for his flute, a cell phone deep in the audience burst into life, a warbling, raucous jangle. Without hesitation, Francisco exactly matched the pitch on the piano and began a rapid trill, at the same time turning toward the audience with his eyebrows furrowed. That prompted a laugh, of course, but the cell phone went away, with its owner no doubt wishing he or she could crawl under the seats.

Mateo nodded, and Vivaldi sprang into life, his tribute to winter. Even I could count the square four/four time, and I sure as hell was no musician. The piano sounded with a cadence that reminded me of troops rapidly double-timing through deep snow until after a few measures the flute sprang into the scene with a series of gentle but insistent little shivers. Now we had a gang of kids playing in the snow, sliding, slipping, ignoring the winter winds. That was followed by a long sequence of teeth-chattering, and regardless of what impossibly high flights the flute took, Francisco never abandoned his relentless four-square accompaniment until the last bit when everything accelerated to a manic pace.

Atencio didn't just stand in one spot and hoot the notes. He engaged both the audience and his accompanist, rocking on his feet, punching notes, sometimes the flute pointing at the floor near his feet, sometimes arching to point to the heavens. The kid was amazing, the audience struck dumb.

Between the first and second movements, we had two breaths to relieve the tension, and a few hands thought about clapping. The second movement was as lyrical and graceful as the first was maniacal, and it was over too soon—but not before the final note stretched for measures while the piano counted down, the flutist astonishing us all with the amount of air he could capture in his lungs.

He needed that air for the third and final movement when winter winds shrieked, the piano danced, and the velocity of everything accelerated to a whirlwind of up and down, the spotlight flashing off the flute, with the two performers colliding in the end with the final "big note."

The audience didn't know what to say. Mateo had time to lower his flute after the last note died, and glance at Francisco before the audience erupted with applause so powerful that I'm sure I could taste some of the dust filtering down from the gymnasium girders.

I reached across Carlos, found Estelle's forearm and squeezed it. The little boy captured my hand as I drew back, and didn't appear ready to let go.

What next? I remembered that Beethoven's ghost was in the house, and sure enough, after the bows and applause, Mateo left the stage after establishing his bona fides with Vivaldi. Francisco settled at the piano. If I expected to be able to leave the concert hall humming the tune from Beethoven's Sonata no. 10 in G-major, I had another think coming. Beethoven had other plans. I could see why the music appealed to Francisco Guzman, since it was rich with imagery. I could picture a cat chasing butterflies and a host of other cinematic clips, up and down the keyboard, all so precise, sometimes so soft that I could hardly hear it, sometimes loud enough for two gymnasiums.

The second movement, to my mind a march that syncopated the base with the upper notes, suckered me—and lots of others—into an unexpected crash of an ending so loud it shook the stage. The final movement was a delight, bass conversing with treble, triplets fast and perfectly accurate, until a surprise ending with a little trill in the bass that sounded as if the artist had bounced on a whoopie cushion.

Francisco's wide smile greeted the explosion of laughter and applause, and then the stage was empty, almost as if something had been stolen from us. All we could do was turn to each other and marvel. But beyond the artistry of the two boys, there had been no surprises as promised by the artists. That meant that the intermission, even if it was only five minutes long, was going to seem an eternity.

Old prostates can stand only so much fun, and I decided to buck the crush of people, many of whom would have the same problem. I made it as far as the last row of the reserved section before an elderly woman with two walker-canes maneuvered out to the aisle, assisted by her son, I supposed. He nodded in apology as he helped the woman maneuver, and I waited, taking the time to actually scan the crowd. They were all talking, animated and amazed.

Eventually, I was able to step on the gas. Even so, if I had turned every "Hey Bill," or "Hi Bill," or "Evenin' Sheriff" into a conversation, the trip to the far end of the gym would have taken a week. By bordering on the brusque if not actually impolite, I reached the large foyer, grateful that a long line didn't block the restroom door.

Even so, by the time I was rewarded with a turn, I was ready to start seeking out a dark corner.

"If I listened to this concert with a blindfold, the last thing I'd imagine would be that I was hearing two kids," Dr. Arnie Gray said. I turned and found the paper towels. "If I don't see you all, give the whole family my congratulations," the chairman of the county commission said.

"You bet I will," I replied. "I'm glad you could make it."

With a long way to walk, and I hoped not much more intermission to suffer, I made my way back toward my seat. The lady with the canes had reached the foyer, one hand against the door jamb for support. Somewhere along the way she'd lost her escort.

Dr. Guzman was standing by his seat reading the program, and Carlos, still wound tight as a drum, was telling him what it said. Estelle, radiant in her black pants suit and white scarf, rose as I approached. She turned to say something to her mother, and I saw the angular bulge at her belt-line under her tailored jacket—a nasty little reminder that the rest of the world still existed, regardless of how wonderful the music might be.

"This is an ambitious program," Dr. Francis said, and I pulled my own souvenir from my pocket.

"What's next?" I said. *Border Themes and Variations* opened the second half of the program, with Mateo Atencio at the helm as both composer and soloist.

"How do these guys have the time to both compose and practice as hard as they must have to?" The physician shook his head in wonder. "At their age…"

"You have the inside track on that," I said. "I guess that's what geniuses do. They work harder than anyone else." Lynn Browning, CEO of United Security Resources, was working hard too. She had decided to remain in town for the concert, and now had cornered State Police Lieutenant Mark Adams over near the bleachers. The lieutenant was doing all the talking, his pretty wife at his side nodding away, and Mrs. Browning listening attentively.

The lights dimmed then brightened, and then the big sodium lights above the sea of banners switched off with a loud *crack* of their switch.

"So now we find out," I said, and sat down next to the jittering Carlos. "What do you think?"

He made a grimace of glee.

"Did you get to visit Francisco during intermission?" He nodded eagerly. From where I sat, I could see Francisco standing behind the curtain, coat unbuttoned, hands in his pockets… again listening to Dr. Lott, nodding now and then as he regarded the floor. He looked more like a junior executive than a prodigy.

The main spotlight bloomed to encircle the piano, the remaining house lights settled, and I took a deep breath. After a few seconds, Mateo Atencio appeared by himself, the spot erupting flashes from his silver flute. He favored the curved flank of the piano again, then moved a step closer to the audience, the spot recentering. He nodded at the applause, waited until it started to die, and lifted the instrument.

Over the years, I'd managed to batter and scar my hearing, adding the constant symphony of tinnitus on top of it all, and it didn't sound as if Mateo was playing. But he was, and eventually I became aware of a note so high, so true, just touched with a vibrato, that was held impossibly long. *No one has that much breath,* I thought. But he did. The single note intensified and then did an incredible thing. Just when the kid should have turned purple and fallen on his face, the note climbed first one step, then another, becoming round and rich as if the sun had risen over the border prairie.

I had no trouble following the composer's images as they tumbled one atop the other, and was delighted at one point when the music somehow shifted into the gentle flute music known in the Indian pueblos.

The composition was long and challenging, but when the last complex arpeggio soared, we all knew that we'd heard a master at work. When Mateo finally drew the flute away from his lips, I discovered that I'd gone too long without breathing. He beamed and bowed deeply. I clapped as hard and long as anyone else, but I think little Carlos Guzman's enthusiasm was more because he knew what was coming next. And sure enough, Mateo bowed once more and walked offstage, passing Francisco and Dr. Lott in the wings…at least what passed for wings on this makeshift stage.

Francisco's hands were empty of music, and to someone who can't remember the simplest things in life, that in itself was remarkable. I had no idea how one went about recalling that many notes in some presentable order.

The program notes said that *Upward, Opus 7 in G Major*, dedicated to Carlos Guzman, told the story of the construction of a skyscraper. I had heard Francisco improvise dozens of times, always most impressive. Somehow I found it *more* difficult to picture him methodically locking the music on paper, note by note, tearing his hair now and then, gulping the modern kid's equivalent of Mozart's red wine as he worked. Who knew? Maybe, as a modern composer, he used a goddamn computer.

I was still reading when a distant throbbing interrupted me, along with a little gasp from my twitchy little seat neighbor. I looked up, surprised that someone would start a diesel backhoe right next to the gymnasium while a concert was in progress. At the piano, Francisco Guzman was leaning over the left end of the keyboard, both hands busy on a collection of notes deep in the bass. The engine throbbed and then tore into the ground, the notes racing through the bass, interrupted only by the sharp, staccato treble notes of the backup alert as the earth mover shifted into reverse to reposition itself. It didn't take long to lay the foundations, but the dust from construction hung heavy when the sprayer drove through, its plumes of water cascading down from the treble with Francisco's hands diving one over the other.

And so it went for an uninterrupted ten minutes or so. The construction motives left me behind, but I could imagine the general image of the building towering toward the sky, sun winking off the new windows, cranes hauling their cargo up past the unfinished floors. At one point, it sounded to me as if someone had lost his balance and come perilously close to diving dozens of stories to his death. I made a mental note to ask the composer how the construction worker was saved.

Finally, a light breeze tugged at the flag on the top mast, billowing it out as the building stood for all to see, great crashing chords marching up and down the keyboard. Night fell, lights came on, and the music drifted down to a tranquil closing.

I glanced at Carlos and was surprised to see the tears coursing down the child's face. *He* had certainly understood the whole thing. I held out my hand, and he shook it with a clammy little paw. "Good work, Bud." He beamed. He might not have written or performed the music, but he *had* built the skyscraper, after all.

Chapter Twenty-eight

Opus 7 was a nice surprise, and the applause for it was tumultuous. As the applause died, the stage remained empty for a long moment. Several pieces remained for the ambitious program. The pair finally returned to the spotlight, starting a new set of short pieces with a composition I actually recognized. Wolf Mozart never knew that his Concerto No. 21 in C Major had been borrowed a couple hundred years later as the theme for the Swedish movie *Elvira Madigan,* the story of a couple of doomed lovers. Mateo's flute work, with a gentle piano staying deep in the background, was heart-wrenching…he played the whole thing with his eyes tightly shut, and I wondered if he had a fair damsel somewhere who was making *his* heart ache.

He let Francisco have his own share of meditation with Schumann's Opus 15, number 7, the *Träumerei*. I don't think I had ever heard anything so unrelentingly delicate, with the enormous bass notes reined in tightly.

Mateo Atencio was too young to have served in the Middle East conflicts, but his unaccompanied rendition of Gold's *From a Distance* certainly reached out and touched some of the audience. Across the aisle to my left, a middle-aged man dabbed his eyes now and then. As applause for that died, Francisco joined his compadre on stage, and they woke us up with a driving rendition of a Spanish piece by de Falla. And then, fresh out of program, the two boys left the stage. The performance certainly was exhausting for the kiddos, but the audience refused to let them go.

They returned together for a series of bows, and then Francisco returned solo, to thrash the big Steinway with Rachmaninoff's string-breaker in C-sharp minor, a piece that told me the Russian certainly had been upset about something. Somehow the kid was able to throttle back at the end, with the final chord almost inaudible. The audience wasn't, though—a reaction that prompted an enormous grin from Francisco.

He left the stage and almost immediately returned with Mateo in tow, but this time, the two were talking about something as they approached the piano. To the audience's astonishment, the two boys stopped behind the end of the piano, and had a somewhat longer conference, Francisco standing with his back to the audience, one hand possessively on the piano's flank, doing most of the talking. He made a series of me-you gestures toward Mateo, and the older boy finally shrugged in exasperated capitulation. Just about the time my stomach did a nervous flip, sure enough, the two artists figuratively dumped the cards out of their sleeves.

Raising his eyes heavenward, Mateo handed the flute to Francisco, who accepted it solemnly. The younger boy walked in front of the piano and made an exaggerated bow to Mateo, offering the piano bench. Mateo's facial expression said, "Oh, sure," but he walked around thoughtfully and sat in front of the keyboard.

Still, no music had appeared. Taking the same position his partner had occupied, Francisco raised the flute, but even I could see something was terribly wrong.

"No!" Mateo mimed loudly, certainly for the audience's benefit. Feigning long-suffering weariness, he rose from the bench and took the flute from Francisco's hands, swapping ends so that it faced the correct, traditional direction before handing it back. As he returned to the piano bench, he looked heavenward for the audience, who now had to realize they were part of this elaborate joke.

Mateo raised his hands toward the keys, and then paused. Turning to the audience, and the gymnasium was as quiet as if there were no audience, he said, "Francisco says the flute is easy to play because there are no pedals to get in the way." He bent over and looked down at his own shoes, poised near the three brass pedals. "Fortunately, the pedals didn't exist when Bach wrote his B-minor suite."

The words drew a rustle from some of the audience, obviously more musically sophisticated than I. If I had ever heard the B-minor, I wouldn't have been able to report when or where. I didn't know what to anticipate.

The first movement combined elements of a dignified march with just about every note ever invented, and Mateo played beautifully. For his part, Francisco's flute was crisp and pure, rolling up and down and sideways as if he'd been playing all his young life. He played the major theme with back rigid and shoulders square, as if standing at attention for military inspection. I think my jaw hung slack with astonishment. But this was just the warm up. With hardly a breath between, the two launched into the second movement, an insanely fast thing that bounced down the octaves and back up again, a pure romp of joy. I had always thought of J.S. Bach as a staid old buzzard who intoned dismal things on the organ. Not this time. Not with these two immensely talented kids. They slowed only on the last six notes, and then held it, the sound rising and then becoming lost somewhere in the ceiling above us.

"Wow," I managed, but the audience made sure I was the only one to hear my exclamation. We clapped until our hands hurt, and that drew the two performers out onto the stage twice more, but no more encores were forthcoming. I turned to say something to Estelle Reyes-Guzman and saw her folding a tissue into a small, wet wad. It was the first time I'd ever seen evidence of tears in the thirty years that I'd known her.

Chapter Twenty-nine

Carlos wanted to remain at the gymnasium to help disassemble the venue, but when I told him that his famous presence was expected at the reception, he readily agreed, the little showman. There was an added incentive. Dr. Francis needed to make a visit to the hospital and his patient with the exploded appendix, and Estelle needed a few moments to confer with the sheriff before indulging herself with an evening in the role of proud mom. I offered to let Carlos accompany me over to the house where we'd be among the first on hand to welcome the Leister crew.

A chance to ride any old time in Padrino's SUV was an incomprehensible treat for the youngster, and he and I escaped out through one of the gym's side doors, the one nearest the temporary stage curtains, the one protected by the two signs, Emergency Exit Only and Alarm will Sound when Door is Opened. What a bad influence on the youth of America I was… but I knew that the door alarm *wouldn't* sound, since kids popped in and out the E-doors all the time when the gym was a gym. The door opened onto a small concrete patio that surrounded part of the gym's electrical substation, with a narrow sidewalk leading out toward the athletic field parking lot.

Carlos skipped ahead of me, still riding his *Opus 7* high. At one point I caught his eye and held up the keys, then tossed them to him in an easy, high arc. "Over by the ticket booth," I called. "Right in front of the bus." He caught them and charged off toward where my SUV was parked, thumbing the key to flash the courtesy lights half a dozen times.

I was having such a good time watching the kid's antics that my radar was turned off. He stood by the passenger door, waiting as I approached. The silly grin had vanished but his dark, deeply set eyes were hidden by the night shadows.

"Mount up," I said, but Carlos didn't move. That's when the hair stood up on the back of my neck.

"Just get in the car," a soft voice commanded. The bulk of the SUV hid the man from view, but through the wash of the courtesy lights, I could see that his hand rested on the boy's right shoulder, essentially locking Carlos between himself and the Durango's open door. Worse, he held what in the dome light's glow appeared to be a small pistol, the barrel nestled under the boy's right ear. I stopped short. What I could do if accosted on a level playing field, with both my assailant and myself armed, was one thing. Now, here I had a treasured youngster in peril. I couldn't reach either him or our assailant. And the weight on my hip? I kept both hands in the open.

"Get in the car," the dark shadow said again. "Nothing stupid, Sheriff." I heard the shake in his voice, the sharp inhalations.

"I'm not the sheriff," I said, for want of anything better. The voice wasn't familiar, and I needed time more than anything else. "And who are you?" His "nothing stupid" remark was unnecessary. What could I do, leap in a single bound over the top of the tall SUV? Somehow dive through the interior? I could feign a heart attack, and writhe on the ground. Maybe in the process, Carlos would ram a sharp little elbow into the man's *cajones*, then slam his head into the door. Sure enough.

"Get in the car."

I could hear other voices, happy concert-goers heading home, oblivious. Unfortunately, a gaggle of them was *not* approaching us…in typical fashion, I had parked off to the side, close to one of the five rugged old elms that graced the parking lot. Behind me, the driver had parked the mammoth Leister bus. He'd be coming for it in a few minutes, but right now, it provided a most effective screen.

"Put the gun away first before someone gets hurt," I ordered.

"You didn't worry about that before," he said. "Just shut up and do like I say." He might have held the gun, but he wasn't a pro at this. And that told me who he was.

"You want to talk to me, talk, Mr. Baum. We don't have to drive anywhere. And none of this is going to bring your father back. All you're guaranteeing is that your daughter will be able to visit you in prison."

He took a shuddering breath as if what he really wanted to do was cry. That was good, since he wasn't paying attention to the Leister bus. I wasn't either. But I did see the enormous dark shadow that appeared behind him, a shadow that must have used the bus as easy cover. Perhaps our assailant heard a faint noise, or felt a shift in the air. That was all the warning he had. His right arm snapped up, the pistol arching toward the star-studded sky. Then it was wrenched from his hand, to go skittering across the hood of my SUV.

He let out a strangled cry and then *he* was wrenched backward, spinning in a blur to crash against the elm's gnarly old trunk. I dove around the back of the SUV, grabbed the stunned Carlos and shoved him in the vehicle, slamming the door behind him. In those few seconds, my assailant found himself with his face buried in the elm bark, both arms twisted behind him, with the grim *snick* of handcuffs around his wrists.

"Just stand still, sir," Sheriff Robert Torrez said. And then, with one hand on his radio and the other pinning the man to the elm by the neck, he lowered his voice. "Mears, ten twenty."

For a dozen seconds, my heartbeat and the frantic breathing of the man pegged to the tree were the loudest things I could hear.

"I'm still in the gym."

"Out back by the bus. I need some assistance. And on your way, find Real. ASAP."

"Ten four."

"What do you think you're doing?" the man gasped, finding it difficult to enunciate with his face buried in the bark.

"Just relax, Mr. Baum," Torrez muttered. "You are under arrest. You have the right to remain silent." And as the sheriff went through the rest of the Miranda rigamarole, I let out a long breath of relief, which the sheriff apparently misinterpreted.

He finished the Miranda and turned slightly toward me. "You all right, sir?"

"Just fine."

"I want a photo of the gun before it gets moved," he said. "Make sure nobody steps on it."

Circling the SUV, I opened the driver's door and peered inside. Carlos Guzman's eyes were huge as he looked across at me.

"You doing okay?" I asked. He managed a nod. "Sorry I got a little rough with you. We'll be out of here in just a minute or two."

I could see the youngster trying to relax against the seat, his spine doing a fair imitation of steel rebar. He turned to stare out the window toward the tree, then back at me.

"Did you see that?" His natural excitement about life's big adventure was returning.

"I did indeed."

"The sheriff just *levitated* him." I laughed and that felt good. A rumble of gruff exhaust announced the arrival of the under-sheriff's unit, and half a second later, Tom Mears' marked county car. Before Estelle had the chance to clear her unit, the sheriff had walked George Baum over to catch his ride to perpetual care. That's when I realized that I had seen the man before.

Transferring his grip on the cuffs to Mears, Torrez nodded at Estelle. "I want photos of the gun before anyone touches it. It's on the ground in front of the vehicle," he said. Estelle's eyes weren't searching for a now-impotent gun, and if Torrez wasn't in the mood to dispense huggies, she felt the need. Without a doubt, she had been with her eldest son when the radio call came, and it must have been a wrench to leave him, only to find Carlos somehow in jeopardy.

But now, Estelle could see that Carlos was fine, the boy jittering with excitement. She scooped him out of the car, his feet airborne.

"Bobby thumped him into the tree, Mamá." He squirmed loose and dashed to the tree, patting its rough bark. I could imagine some Baum relative adding police brutality charges to the looming lawsuit mania, using the boy's description as damning testimony.

A red Honda materialized out of the darkness carrying Linda Real and her plethora of photographic gear.

"He was waiting for you?" the undersheriff asked. With one hand clamped on her son's shoulder, she reached out with the other to me.

"Sure enough." I frowned. "The son-of-a-bitch was inside the gym. I saw him during intermission. Nice guy. He even found time to help a little old lady." Baum and I, with his photo in my pocket, had been within touching distance in that crowded gymnasium. The round, bowling ball head and stumpy body were unmistakable. Had I been paying attention…and that was a sobering thought.

A camera's flash interrupted my ruminations. "The gun is right over here," I said. Estelle ushered Carlos back into the SUV, a sign that my padrino status was still worth something.

The undersheriff's flashlight beam circled the gun, and I didn't feel any better. From a distance, even a hefty automatic can look small. But its magazine held a handful of rounds, and more important, the hammer was fully cocked, poised. It didn't help my blood pressure any to realize that George Baum's shaky trigger finger had been just a few ounces from compounding his father's tragedy.

Chapter Thirty

The incident with George Baum came close to ruining the late evening. The sheriff wanted a deposition from me—the who, what, where, and when of the incident, beginning when I had first seen Baum in the gymnasium, cleverly using a little old lady for cover. Bobby was a little disappointed when I told him that I hadn't recognized Baum at first—it hadn't been a heroically thoughtful choice of mine to avoid an armed confrontation in a crowded venue. I just hadn't recognized him. And if I *had*, the audience would likely have had something to talk about besides the music.

Procrastinating with legal stuff felt good just then, so I put off the deposition until the following day when I could sit back and reflect. But at that moment, my house was full of all kinds of chattering folks. I wouldn't have trusted my home to many people, but Gayle Torrez and Addie Sedillos were two of them. They'd done a nice job planning for the reception, with a flood of goodies temptingly arranged on the kitchen counter and spread down through my sunken library. I don't know how they'd found time to go to the concert.

Francisco Guzman, who had quickly changed out of his penguin suit to blue jeans and a flannel shirt, was holding court in company with Mateo Atencio, who had been content just to loosen his tie. Francisco's brow was furrowed deeply, hands thrust in his pockets as he shook his head slowly in response to something Dr. Lott was saying. He saw Carlos and me walk in, and a look of relief brightened his features.

There had been a few minutes on the way over when I was able to coach Carlos a little. I could imagine his ebullient, story-telling nature taking the incident with Baum and turning it into a tale taller than his imaginary skyscraper.

Obviously *someone* had witnessed, or heard about the event, since it was the topic of conversation. I groaned inwardly and turned to Estelle, who had arrived just seconds after us.

"I'm going to say a few well-chosen words," I said quietly to her. "Otherwise we're going to have to fuss with it all evening. I don't want that." She nodded reluctantly.

"Good evening, folks," I said, my voice a fair imitation of a bullhorn. The place had fallen quiet when we arrived anyway, and my tone surprised them into silence. "First of all, welcome to my home. We're here to congratulate and thank two talented musicians. A stunning concert." I flashed a smile. "Thanks to them and to Leister, who did all the heavy lifting." I surveyed the expectant faces. "On the way out of the concert, we had a little parking lot confrontation with a disturbed fellow. I hope he enjoyed the concert, because right now he's in the sheriff's custody." I smiled again and shrugged. "Everyone is fine, it's all over, so enough said about that. I don't want to talk about it tonight, because this little gathering is planned to honor Francisco and Mateo. Relax, enjoy the treats that Gayle and Addy prepared for you, and leave early." When the laughter stopped, I held up a hand. "Just kidding about that. Thanks for coming. Enjoy."

I turned away in time to accept a cup of coffee and a peck on the cheek from Gayle Torrez. "Baum?" the sheriff's department's chief dispatcher whispered toward my ear.

"Yep. All done. Bobby came to the rescue." I made a chop-ping motion with my hand. "That's it. And Gayle, thanks for all this. Great job."

She patted my arm and winked at Estelle. The conversational noise in the library rose as if someone had turned a rheostat. A moment or two later, my mouth stuffed with little green chile things with a hell of a kick, I managed to avoid the knots of conversation—including the big one with Francisco and Mateo at the epicenter. I had questions and congratulations of my own for the musicians, but they could wait for private moments. And I think I resented, just a little bit, having those moments put off not so much by this smiling, happy crowd, as by the other events of the week—a week I was sure would be recorded as one of the crappiest in my autobiography.

I found a dark corner and counted. I couldn't have explained why it was important to know how many people were in my library. Too goddamned many, and they overflowed into my kitchen and down the hall toward the bedroom suite, with a group of them looking at the family photos on my hall wall. I should have put those away for the duration. I started to feel the first twinges of the need to escape.

"You look numb," Miles Waddell said. Somehow he'd managed to sneak up on my deaf and dumb side, despite hard-heeled cowboy boots on saltillo tile. A flash gun went off, and I turned to see Estelle popping photos of her sons and Mateo, and then her son and the Leister Conservatory folks. Five or six other photographers joined in.

"I am. Completely."

"I've never heard a concert like that," Waddell said. "Did you enjoy it?"

"Of course I did."

"And did you know the kid plays flute? I thought he was a pianist."

"We were all surprised, as promised." I sipped the coffee while I regarded the rancher. "If Elliot Daniel was the one who stole the truck from the dealership," I said, "number one, why? And number two, where the hell is he hiding it? That's what we need to concentrate on."

The rancher's head tipped back and he enjoyed a hearty, but silent, guffaw. "Christ, Bill, you're amazing. You can't leave it alone, can you?"

"Nope."

"Well, in a way, I suppose that's good. I appreciate it. It tells me that you're on the job, but I personally think this Daniel character has skipped the country. You kill a cop, you're on the list." He nodded grimly. "The *top* of the list. You know that better than I do."

"If he didn't take the truck, he knows who did."

Waddell cocked an eyebrow at me. "Why would that be so?"

"I don't believe in coincidence, Miles. Daniel and Boyd took down the power lines. When we get Daniel under the lights, we'll find out exactly why. But then, someone takes the time and risk to steal a Posadas Electric Coop truck…same target, same outfit. My gut tells me it's either Daniel or someone working with him."

Waddell shrugged helplessly. "Maybe so. Maybe so. Is that what Bobby thinks?"

"I've never known what the sheriff thinks, Miles. But I'll tell you one thing. Of all the hunters I've ever known, Bobby Torrez is the best. Period. Thinking all the time. This deal tonight? During intermission, I saw the sheriff in the gym foyer talking with a couple of his people." I held up a hand, two fingers extended out from my eyes. "He's looking at *everyone*. Now, if he hadn't seen Baum then, he must have seen him follow us out the side door after the concert, because that son-of-a-bitch didn't have time to squeeze in an extra fart, Miles. The sheriff materialized out of the dark, disarmed him and pitched him into a tree." I snapped my fingers. "Just like that."

"Everybody was lucky."

"Damn right. But what I'm saying is that the sheriff has had the time to think about Daniel and what he might do next. He doesn't need prompts from me."

"If I was him, I'd take all the help I can get."

"And he does. He knows how to work interagency; he knows when to scout out alone. And everything in between."

"I saw Mrs. Browning in the audience." Waddell surveyed the room. "I was hoping she'd make the reception."

"No doubt. I heard her say that she has some photos to show you, for one thing." I took a deep breath and shook my head.

"I didn't want to spend the evening beating my brains out with all this shit. I really didn't. But it won't leave me alone." Punching the rancher lightly on the chest, I added, "It's all your fault, you know."

"That means I'm making progress."

"Nothing more irritating than a goddamn optimist," I grumbled. "If you were going to hide a truck, where would you put it?"

Miles Waddell frowned. "Where there are the fewest prying eyes. The fewest passersby."

"And what would you do with it?"

He looked bewildered. "I'm not terrorist-minded. What *am* I going to do? Crash it through my gate? Into the well house? Into the new electric substation? I don't know. Roll it off the mesa-top? Sell it in Mexico for a few pesos?"

"Keep thinking. Whatever it is, it's not rocket science. Something simple. He might have been planning to use Curt Boyd's truck, but circumstances forced him to ditch it."

"So he took the first one he stumbled across."

"Well, maybe not the first. A Friday night at the dealership? He's reasonably sure he won't be spotted. He sees the truck parked behind the fence, and takes a look. The gate's not locked. No ignition keys, but he knows how to hot-wire…and that's a trick in itself. He figures no one will notice the truck's gone until Monday morning, giving him some time. He figures wrong."

A burst of laughter interrupted us, and Miles grinned. "The kids are enjoying this."

"Everyone is," I said with satisfaction, but then the itch returned. "And to me, that means Daniel was going to use the truck before Monday morning—before anybody noticed it was gone. Before it became a hot issue."

"You're saying he has something planned for Sunday? For tomorrow?"

"Maybe so. I'd keep my eyes very, very open if I were you."

"What are you going to do?"

I sighed, looking out at the folks who had flooded my home. "I have a handful of people staying here tonight, so it's really awkward for me to go missing. I mean, I shouldn't. I have some things I want to check out, but…"

"But what?"

"This 'good host' business." I held out both hands, mimicking a balance beam. "The headmaster and his crew are going to be tired, and won't want to stay up 'til all hours, answering the same questions they always hear. The boys will be over at the Guzmans." I did a quick head count and came up with forty-seven. "There's enough food here for an army, and nobody's bored. So I guess I'll go missing for a while. I've got some things I need to check out, or I'll spend another sleepless night staring at the goddamn ceiling, listening to Dr. Lott snore. So…you want to come along?"

He thought that he knew me. "Well, it's my mesa."

Chapter Thirty-one

"Promise me one thing," Undersheriff Estelle Reyes-Guzman said. She pulled gently on my arm, and we found a quiet place in the hallway leading toward my private office…what had once been my oldest daughter's bedroom.

"Just one?"

She smiled patiently. "Miles is going with you?"

"Yes."

"Will you stay in touch with the S.O.?"

"Of course."

"You'll have your radio turned on in the truck?"

"Sure. That's two things, though."

She frowned and looked out at the folks blathering away in my library. Two of them—County Commission Chairman Dr. Arnie Gray and school Superintendent Glenn Archer—were browsing along one of my bookshelves. I was long used to Estelle not sharing every thought that passed through her head, but she was certainly chewing on something. "What?" I prompted.

"You're out looking for the truck?"

I grinned. Actually, that guess wasn't much of a mentalist's trick. George Baum was history for us. That left Elliot Daniel. "Miles and I have a lot to discuss," I said. "And yes."

"Pasquale comes on at midnight."

"All right. I'll try to stay out of his way."

"I want you to touch bases with him from time to time and let him know where you are."

I laughed. "You are such a worrywart. That's unlike you."

"Don't give us any more to worry about, then. You could do the host thing, and stay here. There are a lot of folks who would enjoy talking to you."

"I get the itch, you know."

She smiled again. "I know you do. Just be careful, Padrino."

"You're welcome to ride along. You really are."

"I appreciate the invite, but no thanks. I have a child celebrity for a son, and I'd like to have the time to talk with him." She took a long breath. "For the rest of the evening, I'd like to not care about Elliot Daniel and his creepy world."

"That's what I was going to do. But…Francisco is off to Leister tomorrow?"

She nodded. I started to turn away, and stopped. "Did you know that he was playing the flute now?"

"No." That brought a smile, though. "Francis and I are thinking of driving him to the Texas concert next weekend just so we can catch up. Unless events conspire against us somehow."

"But you're going to find the time to go, certainly."

She nodded. "You be careful, sir."

"You bet."

As I turned, she patted me on the small of the back—just an informal, friendly touch, and her hand landed right on the lump that was my Smith and Wesson.

"Did you have that with you this evening? All evening?"

"Sure." I didn't bother to say that if Baum had pulled away from Carlos, and moved around the SUV to confront me, I would certainly have shot the son-of-a-bitch. And then District Attorney Dan Schroeder would have *two* of my revolvers in custody. Estelle had the good grace not to point that out.

Before we left, I had a little confab with Dr. Lott. He seemed perfectly at ease in my home, and I made sure he knew where all the bathrooms were. Addy Sedillos would be staying to tend to our guests until I showed up, and she knew me well enough not to hold her breath.

Outside, Miles Waddell was standing expectantly beside his pickup, a most agreeable hostage. I shook my head, pointing at my SUV. Waddell squirmed around a bit getting himself comfortable in the vehicle two-thirds the size of his. He watched as I scribbled a couple of notes to myself, and then looked downright amused as I turned on the radio. No radio chatter disturbed us.

"Quiet night so far," I said, and then noticed Waddell's huge grin. "What?"

"Feels good, doesn't it?"

"What's that?"

"Working. You haven't retired yet."

I sighed. "I'm trying, Miles. I'm trying. It takes time, you know. Someday you'll find that out. *NightZone* will be up and running, grandly successful, you'll turn sixty-five, and most of the people you know will start carping at you. 'When are you retiring? You have any buyers for this place?' They won't leave you alone."

I keyed the mike. "PCS, three zero zero is ten eight."

"Ten four, three zero zero. Ten twenty?" Ernie Wheeler was working, steady and unflappable.

"West side," I replied. Not that that pinpointed much. The west side of Posadas County included a whole lot of empty acres. A thought that had been gnawing was that Elliot Daniel knew plenty about this county…whether from quizzing Curt Boyd, or from firsthand experience. We headed east, until Bustos turned into County Road 43, and then north to the intersection with NM17. That took us northwest. Six miles later, I pulled into the Posadas Municipal Airport parking lot—dark, save for a double set of arc lights over the fuel island, and a bulb above the office and each hanger door. The USR Jet Ranger was parked on the apron. When she arrived at the reception, Lynn Browning would put the gathering to good use, gleaning what information and background she could.

Rummaging in the back, I came up with a plasticized county map rolled neatly in a cardboard tube.

"Your job is to remember anything and everything." I unrolled the big map with care, keeping the kinks out. "All this courtesy of the county assessor. Now, here you are," and I touched the purple striations that indicated mesa.

"You don't need to mention the assessor," Miles laughed. "We're going to be great friends by the time this is over."

"I bet. I can't even *imagine*. But I've been thinking." Sweeping a hand across the northern, empty reaches of the county, I mused, "If I wanted to hide something, what better place?"

"The power company's truck, you mean?"

"Yep. And all this is like having a bad itch. I've got a dozen things I should be doing. I have a houseful of guests, my talented godchild is visiting, and..." I waved a hand helplessly. "This is all I can think about. Where this son-of-a-bitch went to ground."

Waddell shook his head. "So explain to me why he's even in the county. Hell, he could be on the beach in Chiapas by now."

"Because he's not finished. I think it's that simple. See, when they dropped those poles, that's one thing. If it had all worked out as they planned, they'd have slipped away clean. Ready to crawl back into their holes and plan something else. Maybe *somewhere* else. But Boyd got himself killed, and then Daniel killed a cop on top of it. That changes all the rules." I looked at Waddell. "*If* it was Daniel who stole the line truck, *if*, then it makes obvious sense to me that he's got plans. Local plans. That means that he's still in the neighborhood. He's not going to risk driving that high-profile truck around in plain sight, and it makes a piss poor getaway vehicle. Our edge is that he doesn't know yet that the theft of the truck has been discovered. He thinks he has the weekend to play."

"To do what?"

"Damn good question. To do what. But see, that's my theory. He thinks he has about thirty-six hours. Monday morning, the stolen truck is discovered. That means he can't risk driving on the highway. So by Monday morning, he's gone."

"So until then, where is he, and what's he doing?"

I shrugged. "He only knows, at this point." I tapped the map. "I want to talk with Johnny Boyd again, and this is a good time to do it. No cops breathing down his neck, and I think—I *think*—that he trusts me. We'll see. This whole area?" And I swept a hand over the northern portions of the map. "Nobody knows it better than Johnny Boyd. That's one thing. Second, I want to push him a little harder about his son."

"The boy's not even in the ground yet," Waddell said.

"No. And neither is the cop that Daniel murdered. But Johnny's had time to stew about this whole affair. He may sound like an ignorant old son-of-a-bitch, but he's not. If anybody is apt to take a shotgun after Elliot Daniel, it'll be Johnny Boyd."

I rolled up the map and laid it on the back seat. The dash clock said 10:35, and by taking the state highway up to Newton and then turning south into the Boyd ranch, we'd save a little time. It would take an hour longer to wind through the maze of dirt roads north of Cat Mesa, pounding the kidneys and choking the lungs with dust.

The headlights cut a long, yellow tube through the night, every once in a while reflecting off some tiny critter's eyes or catching a jackrabbit as he ricocheted across the asphalt in front of us.

"Is Johnny going to be thinking to blame me for all this?" Waddell asked at one point.

"I don't know. Not if he thinks about it."

Waddell seemed satisfied by that, and slouched in the seat, gazing out into the darkness. I think he was asleep when the sign for Newton flashed into view. I braked and he stirred a little, tipping his hat back away from his eyes.

Just a forlorn wart on the prairie, Newton didn't even host a post office anymore. Budget cuts had closed that, replacing the building and the services with one of those ugly little cluster boxes where patrons could stand out in the wind and the rain, fumbling keys and watching ad circulars scoot away after being nabbed by a gust.

The only surviving business was Floyd Baca's emporium of junk, featuring a large sign that read only *Baca*. It would have been hard to explain Baca *what*—a few dead tractors sinking into the prairie, a collection of railroad ties too rotted to be of any use, and a mile or so of irrigation pipe in a country where no one irrigated any more. I'd known Floyd Baca well enough to shake a hand for thirty years, and I still didn't know what he did to earn a living.

County Road 805 jounced us south, back into Posadas County, and in a mile or two more, to the entry to the Boyd ranch. In the daytime, the spread of mesas and arroyos and the silvery-black winter colors of sages and creosote brush have an elegance hard to match. At night, it's that yellow tube of lights piercing the peace and quiet. Johnny Boyd would be up, I knew. His problem wasn't insomnia, but the unrelenting pain of joints broken too many times, or chilled by snow squalls, or hatcheted by arthritis. Maybe by one or two o'clock, he'd have enough Jim Beam inside to dull himself to restless sleep.

He'd seen our headlights coming in, and was waiting by the window, backlit by a single table lamp. As I pulled the SUV to a stop, he stepped away and reappeared at the door.

"What in holy hell are you doin' drivin' around at this time of night?" he asked as we approached the front step. The two cow dogs stayed at his heels, heads down, ears unsure. He nodded at Miles and offered a brief handshake.

"I'm selling magazine subscriptions, trying to earn a two-week cruise to the Caribbean," I said, and he snorted a short laugh.

"Good place to be this time of year. Come on in. Maxine's to bed, but she left some coffee on." He held the door for us, a boot expertly intercepting the dogs. "You two stay out, now." As soon as I stepped inside, I heard toenails, and an aging blue heeler appeared at the bedroom door, gazing out blindly, nose working overtime.

"Evening, Dasher," I said, and he ducked his head at the sound of his name. "Sorry to wake you up." Dasher sighed mightily and retreated back to bed.

The davenport was way too soft, and I knew I'd never escape. I took the old wooden rocker near the propane heater. Miles

Waddell risked the sofa. In a minute, Johnny returned with two cups of coffee, no offer of additives.

Johnny was used to rancher talk—the sort of conversation that winds all over the place, taking excursions here and there, maybe winding down to the point of it all after a couple cups of coffee and too many cigarettes. I decided to try the Bobby Torrez approach—blunt, hard, direct.

"I need to know when you last talked with Elliot Daniel."

The rancher didn't ask "*Elliot who?*" Instead, he walked back into the kitchen and returned with a full cup and a lit cigarette. Maxine Boyd's efforts to convince him to quit weren't making much headway. He stood by the unlit fireplace.

"Been a long, long time," he said finally. "Only met him a couple times, anyways."

"But he was a friend of Curt's."

"Guess he was."

"You know, Johnny, we—*I*—have reason to believe that the damage to the power line wasn't the end of it."

"I can't help you all that much, I guess."

"Can't or won't?"

Johnny Boyd glanced at me, his expression saying that my tone had pricked his lizard-tough skin. But he made no reply.

"Have you seen Daniel around?"

Again, a long, pensive silence as he pondered how to best build his stone walls.

He found another cigarette, and this time he didn't seem to much care where the smoke went. "This is growin' into one of them things, ain't it?"

"I think it's already there, Johnny. We have a cop shot down in cold blood. We have a hundred thousand dollars in damages to a power line. And you have a son who isn't coming home again." He flinched when I said that. "I'm the easiest one you have to talk to, Johnny, and now's the time." I leaned forward, my elbows on my knees. "Has Daniel been here since?"

A deep draw on the cigarette, and I don't know where the smoke went. He sucked it so deep I think it just seeped into his tissues. When the undersheriff and I had visited a day or so ago, Johnny and Maxine Boyd had been courteous and forthcoming. If anything, he should have been more so this night. He'd treated Estelle with deference that earlier visit—maybe because Maxine was present. Johnny had never tried to hide that he had little use for either the sheriff or undersheriff. In his mind, both of them belonged about 35 miles farther south, on the other side of the fence.

"Do you think Curt would have wanted it this way?"

"What way is that?" He gazed at me, eyes expressionless.

"Tell me what they accomplished, Johnny. New electric poles up by next week, higher rates for customers to pay for them, two men dead…you think that's a tally Curt would have been proud of?"

I could see the color spread up under the weathered skin of his neck. He stood slowly, giving each joint time to think about it. "My son did what he thought he had to do," he said slowly. "And that's as far as it goes with me. That's what I'll remember."

"Daniel is a wanted man now, Johnny. He left your son on the prairie, and then he killed a cop in cold blood. Didn't give the young man a chance. And now he's got nothing to lose. He's a dangerous man, Johnny."

"I guess he'll do what he thinks is right, then. It ain't my affair. There was a time I might have thought different, but not now." He snapped the cigarette butt into the fireplace ashes and jammed his hands into his jeans. Miles shifted on the sofa, unsure what to say. He chose silence.

"You was in on it, years ago," Boyd said. "When Sheriff Holman's plane crashed. We had every cop in the country swarmin' around here. You, the state cops, the feds, even the damn Fish and Game Department. That just proved to me that there's no where a man can live where folks will leave him alone."

He took a long, deep breath, then limped over to the door, standing by it with his hand on the knob.

"You two need anything else?"

I rose and settled my hat. "Sorry for the late night intrusion, Johnny. I just had things nagging at me, is all."

"Well, you've been down this road before. Miles, good to see you again."

"One more thing?" I said.

"What?"

"When you went into town this morning, did you come back on the highway, or take the rough ride around the mesa?"

"Didn't go to town today." I knew his wife would never take the rough mesa route.

I regarded him for a moment, and then nodded goodnight. "My best to Maxine, Johnny." We made our way across the dark yard to the truck, and Miles Waddell stood for a moment with his hand on the car door handle, craning his neck to survey the heavens.

"You know, that's all I want," he muttered. He shook his head and got in, and I settled back and jotted a note in my log.

"What's all you wanted?"

"I'm a stargazer. That's all. Did you notice you can see some detail of the Pleiades tonight? A lot of times, it's easier to see 'em if you don't look straight at 'em. Tonight, there they are. Plain as can be."

"Just off Orion," I said, and Waddell looked at me quickly.

"That's right."

"I look up once in a while."

"And now, just because of that, we have what, two killed? Power lines ruined? A crazy nutcase running around in a stolen truck, about to do who knows what?"

"That's about it."

"All because I like to look at stars."

I slipped the log back in the center console. "It's not because you look at stars, Miles. It's because there are folks who don't *understand* that's all you want. They can't imagine doing what you're doing. It's the money, the grandiose plans…they can't imagine it's all just to get a better view of the Pleiades. Their shortsightedness is not your fault."

Chapter Thirty-two

Miles Waddell hadn't said ten words at the Boyd ranch, and I knew it had been unsettling for him. I was apprehensive that he was going to cave in—throw up his hands and give up his dreams. For some folks, it's uncomfortable to be around people like Johnny Boyd, who mope through life. That might sound unfair, since the man had just lost his son, but I'd known Johnny for decades, and he hadn't changed much.

Waddell crossed his arms over his chest and watched the night pass by. For a few minutes, he didn't say anything, and I didn't chatter. Finally he asked, "So where the hell are we going?"

We hadn't headed back to the highway. Instead we continued south on the dirt two-track leading away from the Boyds'.

"Nice night for a drive," I said. "Seems a waste to go back the way we came."

"Where lies a warm bed and a good night's sleep."

I laughed. "As long as we've come this far. You know, I thought it was interesting."

"What was?"

"Boyd's mention of the plane crash that killed Sheriff Marty Holman. I don't recall if you were here then or not."

"Hell yes, I was here. Crazy guy south of here, right? Finnegan."

"That's it. Richard Finnegan. He takes a wild shot at a low-flying airplane, and by dumb luck the bullet punches through the bottom of the fuselage and then the seat, and ends up blasting a hole in the pilot's aorta. Sheriff Holman was a passenger, and didn't know beans about flying. Anyway…" I shrugged. "It was a hell of a mess, and we lost two good men."

Waddell shifted in his seat, bracing for the unending bumps. "Dick Finnegan. Johnny Boyd's brother Edwin killed him later in a bar fight. That's the part I remember."

"Saved us the trouble of prosecuting Finnegan, that's for sure. And then Edwin died shortly afterward of cancer. But like Johnny just said…we had enough feds around here investigating the air crash to repopulate the county. And because *Curt* Boyd had a houseful of machine guns, the feds put the spotlight on him. Neil Costace had a grand old time with that."

"So what's on your mind, Bill? Why are you kidnapping me in the middle of the night, bouncing my kidneys to death in his little rattletrap?"

"It's not kidnapping if you're a willing accomplice, Miles. Look at it this way. Why would Johnny Boyd be hesitant to tell us what he knows about Elliot Daniel? The guy drove away leaving Curt Boyd broken and bleeding. There was probably nothing Daniel could have done to save him, but still…just to leave him? I'm wondering if Boyd is finding a quiet way to tell us something."

"For one thing, Johnny would end up in court, testifying," Waddell mused. "Guys like him will go to some lengths to avoid that, I would think. And like he said, he just wants to be left alone."

"That's how I see it." I slowed as the two-track took a dive down into an arroyo and we kicked gravel all the way up and out. "We have two ways to get back to town, so what the hell. Like I said, why retrace our steps? We might see something."

Waddell chuckled in resignation. "You have an extra pillow in back?"

"As a matter of fact. You're welcome to use it. There's an old army blanket there with it."

"What are you looking for out here?"

"As the kids say these days, 'just stuff.'"

"Finnegans used to live down that way."

"Yep. In point of fact, it's the *only* other place other than Boyd's in this part of the county."

"She died, didn't she? The missus?"

"Charlotte Finnegan? She did. And it wasn't too long after Edwin Boyd killed her husband. She was at least half nuts anyway. And then Alzheimer's finished the job."

"Who bought their place? I never heard."

"Nobody, as far as I know. Somebody found out that among other things, Richard Finnegan had never filed taxes. So there's that snarl. I don't know if their estate was ever figured out. On top of that, their trailer burned when Charlotte was in the hospital for her final stay. I tell you, if it weren't for bad luck, that family wouldn't have had any luck at all."

A long silence followed as we both tried to keep our butts on the seat as the prairie jounced us hard.

"This Daniel guy wouldn't know about the Finnegans' place, if that's what you're thinking," Waddell said. "Hell, I would have been lost ten times already. Especially at night."

"Two things," I said. "Number one, bad as it is, this is the only road from the Boyds' to the Finnegans', if you don't count one or two little shortcuts. So it's not hard to find. Or you can come in from the south, right up County Road 43. That cuts over to this one, County 91. But see, if Daniel didn't know where it was, Curt Boyd did."

"So you're thinking he's gone to ground out here."

I shrugged. "I don't expect anything, Miles. It's just a little puzzle piece, that's all. I don't know what to do, so I roam. And this is a spot I haven't visited in a long time." I didn't explain to him the little nagging curiosity. Johnny Boyd hadn't driven into town, but I sure as hell had looked north from my vantage in Lynn Browning's chopper, and seen a vehicle northbound on 91. Just a little burr under the saddle.

"And roaming in the middle of the night is as good as any time," he said wryly.

"Patience. Patience."

We arrived at an intersection of sorts, a spot where a faint trace of lane came in from the west and joined our two-track.

"You remember over there? By the water tank?"

"Where they found the dead hunters."

"That's it. Finnegan's perfect crime. Not so perfect, it turns out."

The two-track tackled the flank of one of the scattering of small mesas, the path worn just enough to silhouette the tire tracks in the headlights. As we drew near the crest, I slowed to a stop, and then punched out the lights. There remained a veritable swath of tiny lights inside the truck, illuminating the electric window switches, the clock, the this and that. I reached down and snapped a switch mounted low by the steering column, and we went pitch dark...not a single glow. That handy switch had cost me nearly two hundred bucks to have installed, along with all kinds of dire warnings that it would void my warranty.

"There's Waddell's sky for you," I said. The arc of stars domed from horizon to horizon, with just enough moon to fuzz them a little. I took off my glasses so I wouldn't have the confusion of the bi- and tri-focals. Waddell saw me do that and laughed.

"When we end up top-side-down in an arroyo, who do I call?"

I reached down and pulled the mike off the under-dash radio and rested it in one of the center console's cup holders. "Just find that, push the button, and holler to PCS. In fact..." and I turned the volume up a little, but instead of keying the mike, hauled out my cell phone. Its digital face was painfully bright. I tapped the auto-dialer for the sheriff's department.

Dispatch was in the middle of something, because the phone buzzed half a dozen times before Ernie picked up.

"Posadas County Sheriff's Department. Wheeler."

"Ernie, this is Gastner. Miles Waddell and I are about two miles north of Finnegan's out on 91. Just wanted to check in."

"Ten four. Are you on the way to Finnegan's?"

I grinned. "Maybe so." Wheeler's passion was fishing, not geography, but he'd been dispatcher long enough to know all of the county's little nooks and crannies. "While we're at it, is the sheriff out?"

"You know, I don't know where he is. I really don't. He hasn't called in since he went over to your place for the reception."

"Ah. I missed him." That Bobby Torrez had gone to any sort of reception was news enough. Or perhaps he was looking for me. Who knew. But if he wanted to talk with me, he knew my number. And he knew I had a department radio. "Thanks, Ernie. Have a quiet night."

"Those are boring, sir."

I laughed. "I'll take boredom any time."

My eyes had adjusted to the darkness, and I could make out the two-track clearly enough to avoid the huge clumps of cacti or the occasional errant boulder that had abandoned its repose and tumbled down from one of the mesas. "Are you warm enough?" I asked.

"Plenty."

I lowered my window, the fragrant chill welcome. This unmaintained lane would ramble east for another mile or so and then join the northern tail of County Road 43, the one lane capillary up the eastern end of Cat Mesa, then on down into Posadas, its last eight miles macadam.

The old Finnegan ranch moldered in a copse of dead elms and a single spindly cottonwood, the grove once fed by a spring and Charlotte Finnegan's ministrations. She died and the spring gave up as the water table sank. The whole goddamn Southwest was withering, a depressing thought that I tried to fend off with little success.

Why, when I first came to this country forty years ago... I barked a short scoff as I chased that line of reminiscence away. Dick Finnegan had ranched and scammed in Posadas County for forty years, and never made a significant dime. His last big deal, selling illegal antelope hunts to Texans with too much money, hadn't worked out so well for him, or anyone around him.

Johnny Boyd hung on. Maybe he loved his life, loved that the whisper of dried prairie grass was the loudest voice around him on a night like this. And maybe he hated it, but was just too stubborn to give in. I couldn't imagine the game old rancher living in a retirement community in the city. But now, faced with the *NightZone* complex as neighbors thirty miles to his south—with the train, the tram, buses, traffic, strangers who dressed funny—maybe he had reason not to relish giving Elliot Daniel up to the law.

"Just over there," I said, and pointed to the southwest. The Finnegans' burned out mobile home had taken a handful of trees with it when the electrical short set the thing on fire. Burning on a still November night, the flames had shot straight up, and even the propane tank thirty feet away had been spared. Finnegan had been long dead when it happened, his wife soon to be. The fire chief figured a pack rat had nibbled on the wrong thing.

I suppose archeologists would have a field day with this site in a hundred years, because Dick Finnegan had beaten Josiah Bennett all hollow in the artifact department. For one thing, Finnegan apparently had belonged to the Shed-of-the-Month club. Outbuildings dotted the ranch, storage for all the stuff that made up his wealth. One of them had been big enough to include a single-car garage, now empty.

A few bales of worthless hay sank earthward from what might have been a neat pile beside the barn, the weather and wind battering it down and mixing dust and hay. The barn itself might have been Finnegan's pride and joy. A steel Quonset hut, not too badly rusted but dented as if he'd used it for target practice with his pickup truck, featured a large stock pen off the back, every one of the juniper uprights still standing gray and tough.

I stopped the SUV on the road. "I'd like to take a look around."

Waddell stiffled a yawn. "Of course you would."

"I just think it's interesting that Johnny Boyd brought up ancient history, that's all. On the surface, his mention of Finnegan seems apropos of nothing."

"But…" my long-suffering passenger muttered.

"Yep, but." I dug out my best flashlight and shut off the SUV. "Beautiful night for a stroll and a snoop. We probably won't even need the flashlight, but just in case."

"The inside of that Quonset will be dark as a tomb."

"That would be unauthorized entry, and I would never do that."

Waddell laugh was just a whisper. "Oh, sure. Or maybe just simple trespass."

The fresh tracks in the driveway could have been anyone's— hunters, teens looking for a party spot, run-of-the-mill vandals like the jerk who had spray-painted something incomprehensible on the big rolling door of the Quonset. Tracks stayed fresh for a long time with our stable weather, but these were *fresh*. Even the wind hadn't had a chance to play with the sharp edges where tread cut dust.

Snapping on the flashlight, I bent down for a closer look, and the hair stood up on the back of my neck. In a spot that shouldn't have had *any* tracks, this was a smorgasbord. Generic truck tires, running heavy. And cutting here and there, motor-cycle tracks—the paw prints of a big street bike. Added to the mix was a narrow gauge set of car tracks, the treads characteristic of those new hi-tech radials.

The old Finnegan place had a new life, apparently.

I turned to Miles and held up a finger to my lips. He nodded and lifted a hand, pointing his thumb over his shoulder, and mouthed, "Let's go." Good advice. I should have followed it. Instead, I gazed at the bulk of darkness that was the Quonset.

The metal structure had no windows, at least on the front and the side facing the house. For a long moment, I stood perfectly still, listening. There wasn't enough breeze to moan around the metal edges of the building, and no coyotes had succumbed to the musical urge. If the moon made noise as it rumbled through the heavens, we would have heard it. Although I had approached with my lights off, there's no way to muzzle the exhaust burble of the SUV, or worse, the crunch of tires. If there was anyone inside, they might well know we were outside, unless theirs was the sleep of the dead. I scanned the ground ahead of me, and then turned off the flashlight.

A whisper that would have been inaudible were it not immediately at my ear said, "Isn't this where we either call for back-up or *leave?*"

I sympathized with Miles. I couldn't imagine for sure what it must feel like, standing out in the strange darkness of the prairie, with a third of a billion dollars in the bank and not a penny of it able to offer, in this particular instance, either safety or assistance.

The damn fool who was Miles Waddell's companion at the moment whispered back, "I just want to check. You should wait in the truck." I didn't smell the lingering aroma of a campfire, or the dense tang of burning diesel if someone had fired up Finnegan's old heater in the Quonset. I didn't smell aftershave or deodorant or sweat or marijuana. No one snored, no one coughed, no one sniffled. I reached around and turned the volume of my radio all the way down. "Turn off your phone," I whispered. He wasn't headed for the truck, even though he wanted to be.

The front of the Quonset was a hundred feet ahead and I stayed away from the tracks that led directly to it. Miles crept along immediately behind me.

In front of the door, I could see a haze of what must have been a cluster of shoeprints—I didn't turn on the big flashlight again, but for now the moon was enough. I felt down the right side of the door frame and found a large hasp swinging free, its padlock hanging loose. I stood quietly, sorting through memory files. The last time I'd been at the Finnegans' was more than five years ago. I'd driven by a couple of times since then, but never stopped. I had no idea whether the door had been open then, ajar, closed, or locked.

Making my way toward the corner, I saw that the man-door was a third of the way down the Quonset's forty-foot length. I was about to take a step when it opened.

Chapter Thirty-three

A dark figure appeared, vaguely tent-shaped, and stopped half in and half out of the Quonset. "I don't need a flashlight," she said to someone still inside. "The moon's perfect." It *was* perfect, and if she turned a bit, she'd see me. She didn't turn, though. Confident in her solitude, she stepped carefully away from the Quonset, angling toward a fat old juniper that had been trimmed up by cattle to look like a giant lollipop. I could see that she wore a blanket draped over her shoulders. Her legs were bare and white, but she'd shoved her feet into a pair of something. Perfect mid-winter attire. As she padded away, Miles and I faded back, around the corner.

"So," I whispered. They, whoever "they" were, apparently hadn't heard my SUV. Ah, young love. I pondered some options. Charlotte and Dick Finnegan had never had children, so this wasn't a case of kids or grandkids visiting the old homestead. Hunters, maybe, except nothing was currently in season. I could think of a host of places more romantic than sleeping in the musty old building, half full as it must be of the junk that Dick Finnegan had considered his treasure. The tracks had set my imagination in gear, though. Heavy, deep tracks for the electric company's utility truck. Motorcycle tracks for Elliot Daniel's getaway bike. And the light car tracks? Certainly for the girl. I was hooked.

I heard a low grunt behind me—Miles Waddell shifting position, trying to come to terms with the spot in which I'd put him. But at this point, I was simply incapable of pussyfooting backward, slipping away into the darkness without disturbing the nighttime peeper or her companion inside. My companion was right—I *should* have pussyfooted backward and used my phone to call for backup. The reason I didn't do that was one part curiosity and one part timing. Deputy Pasquale, lead-foot that he might be, was still half an hour away at best. That seemed like an eternity.

The dark shadow that was the relieved girl made her way back to the Quonset's people door. No flash of light escaped when she ducked inside, and the door closed with a squeaky clunk. I didn't hear the additional rattle of a deadbolt or hasp.

I had taken a step forward when a strong hand settled on my shoulder.

"Don't," Waddell whispered, "you don't know what you've got."

I don't know why that jerked me to a stop. He was right. I *didn't* know what I had inside the big Quonset. The struggle between the two alternatives was much like the cartoon showing a small devil on one shoulder, an angel on the other. The angel knew my weak spot, dredging up videos of me lecturing rookie deputies: "There is no such thing as a *routine* traffic stop. We don't need heroes—we need good, solid arrests. Take time to *think*. At the end of the shift, what we want the most is to go home to our families."

And on and on as I squirmed under the decision. If Elliot Daniel was inside, he was armed. He was a killer, and would not hesitate to do so again. Whether or not the girl was an innocent party, who knew…except if innocent, she picked damn odd times and places to play nookey.

I turned and nodded at Miles, and his relief was palpable. Stepping with the utmost care, we made our way back to the SUV. When we opened the doors, the dome light didn't come on—I'd fixed that little nuisance the day after the truck left the showroom floor. We were parked seventy-five yards from the Quonset, partially behind two dead elm saplings and a mound of creosote brush. The Quonset's door was closed. With exaggerated care, we pulled the SUV's doors shut, the faintest of clicks.

While Miles Waddell worked his way through the world's largest sigh, I was finding the auto-dial on my phone. Ernie Wheeler answered on the second ring, and I cut off his greeting.

"Ernie, this is Bill Gastner. What's Pasquale's twenty?"

"Just a second, sir."

A *second?* I didn't have a second. Maybe he hadn't clearly heard my low, gruff near-whisper.

"Where are you?" This time it was Sheriff Robert Torrez, and he sounded impatient.

"We're parked at Dick Finnegan's. There's a party going on inside his old Quonset. One truck, one motorcycle, probably one compact car. At least two occupants, one of them a girl. A young woman."

Torrez made the connection instantly. "You got someone with you?"

"Miles Waddell."

"You're in your vehicle at the moment?"

"Yes. We parked under some trees just beyond the house and driveway."

"Stay there, then."

"Your best approach is right up forty-three," I said, and the sheriff didn't bark that he *knew* what the best approach was.

"I'm headin' up that way. Pasquale will be westbound on Seventeen in just a minute. Wallace is just comin' off the interstate and he'll be right behind me."

"We'll wait."

"Damn straight, you'll wait," the sheriff said. "Sit quiet. And don't go shootin' anybody else."

Anybody else. Funny man, that sheriff. He disconnected before I could think of an appropriate response. Waddell watched as I reached down and made sure the radio was off.

"Put your cell on vibrate." I glanced over at Waddell. "Feeling better?"

"Much."

"Bobby is coming up, with Drew Wallace right behind him. Pasquale is headed our way on the state highway. So we're all set."

"Wallace is one of the state cops?"

I nodded. "So much for his quiet night on the interstate."

"Quiet nights are a good thing," Waddell said. "Hey…" He pointed. Sure enough, a sliver of light shone out past the big rolling door. I pressed the button on my watch and saw one a.m. coming up.

I thumbed my phone. "Ernie," I said when dispatch picked up, "we have some lights on in the building now. I don't know what's up."

"Ten four, sir. Everyone is underway."

"We'll hang tight." The clock slowed, each second taking a full minute. Just a few of them had dragged by when the girl appeared from the side door. Too dark for details, I still could recognize that lithesome shape as she walked purposefully to the big door and leaned against it, driving hard with her shoes kicking rocks as she pushed. The door rolled smoothly enough, with a minor symphony of squeaks, groans, and deep roller rumblings.

With a smooth roar of diesel power, the Posadas Electric Cooperative one-ton utility truck appeared, its front end looking more massive in the darkness than Ford Motor Company intended. It wasn't until the truck had covered fifty yards toward us that I could see enough of the crude modification. Thanks to Richard Finnegan's vast estate of junk, eight feet of railroad tie was lashed to the heavy front bumper, spanning the width of the truck, a black mustache of creosote-soaked oak. I didn't have a lot of time to admire the handiwork.

I caught a glimpse of the girl scampering back into the barn, and then the truck was on us. The driver knew exactly what he intended, and executed with precision. He drove directly into the right front fender of my SUV, the blow crashing us sideways across the narrow lane. Tissue paper-thin metal crumpled hard against the tire, and Miles Waddell's head cracked against the passenger window.

Wasting not a second, the truck backed away, and I could see the railroad tie in the bounce of lights.

"You son-of-a-bitch!" I roared, and yanked my door open. But by the time I was clear, the power company's truck had spun around and was raising clouds of dust, running up through the gears. I yanked out my revolver, steadied it against the door frame, and pulled off five shots, accomplishing nothing more than punching holes in the darkness. The fifth round hadn't finished ringing in my ears before a goddamn Prius bolted out of the Quonset, moving faster than I thought possible. She didn't crash into me. Instead, she followed the truck, dust cloud tiny and defiant.

"Shit," I said. The shotgun was lying on the floor of my SUV, no good to me now.

I raced around the front of the SUV and looked at the bashed headlight, fender, and bumper. "Miles, give me a hand!" We pulled and strained, and finally, with the help of a length of one-inch pipe that once had been part of the front step handrail into the Finnegans' house, yanked crushed metal away from the tire.

As we remounted and accelerated away, the SUV didn't feel just right. I hadn't seen bash marks on the wheel itself, but it felt as if the crash had treated me to an alignment job.

Fighting the wheel with one hand, I snapped on the radio and fumbled the mike. "Three oh eight, you've got a white power company truck and a silver Prius headed your way. They just bolted."

"Ten four." Mr. Excitement.

"I shot at the truck five times after he bashed into me."

"You okay?"

"Yep. Miles has a sore head where he cracked the window."

"You up and running?"

"After a fashion."

"Ten four. Stay well back."

"You bet. Oh…he's lashed a railroad tie to the front. Makes an effective ram."

"Ten four."

Elliot Daniel…that's who I assumed drove the battering ram…didn't remain on County 43 for long. The road swept through a series of graceful curves and then forked, the right path a ranch road that led west past a series of stock tanks and windmills on its way along the north side of Cat Mesa. The truck's dust trail headed that way, but the Prius swerved east to stay on the wider, smoother county road toward town.

"Bobby, they've split. The Prius is headed right at you. She's just coming up the back side now."

"Ten four."

The truck's billowing clouds caught the moonshine and looked picturesque, if art had been on our minds.

Every time my SUV jounced, the steering wheel juddered, followed by an odd noise like someone's sacroiliac being thrown out.

"They're headed toward Forest Road 26," I radioed to whoever cared to listen. Like so many interesting, out-of-the-way places, the old down-east expression applied: "You can't get there from here." But Daniel had been well coached.

"He can link with County 14 up here." I had the uneasy feeling that the vehicle I'd seen from the chopper the day before had been the son-of-a-bitch practicing. Waddell had one hand braced on the grip above the door, the other clutching the center console as I took a sweeping corner much too fast, broad sliding the Durango and confusing the hell out of all its fancy computer systems that were designed to discourage just that sort of aberrant behavior.

Up ahead, the fleeing white shadow had slowed. "He's taking it carefully," I said. "That's not a good sign."

"Why not?" Miles said. "I'll accept slow." We were rocketing as fast as I dared, and the SUV's flabby and pranged suspension was protesting.

"Because. Careful means that he's not panicked. Careful means that he knows where the hell he's going, and he thinks that he's got time to get there. He didn't have time to tie on that railroad tie just now. He had it all prepared. That means he's got plans." The narrow dirt lane swept left around a massive outcropping of limestone, wound through a little spread of black lava, and then started to curve uphill, skirting the western end of Cat Mesa. I knew that our single headlight was no longer visible in Daniel's rearview mirror, and I accelerated, hoping to gain ground.

"He's going to smash my gate," Miles said matter-of-factly.

"For what? There's nothing up there." I counted on his dust plume to lead the way, and I lifted my foot a little as I crested a sharp rise. Even slowed, I could not stop in time. The big white utility truck blocked the narrow road, turned around so that the massive front fortress of railroad tie gave me a hell of a good target. He'd picked his spot well. With rocks on both sides, I had no where to go. The ABS breaking system shrieked, groaned and shuddered as my Durango slid straight into the truck. By the time we made contact, we were moving less than fifteen miles an hour, but the impact was still enough to jar the teeth and crumple more metal. My air bags didn't think it was serious enough, and stayed quiet.

I didn't have time to pull the SUV into reverse before a dark figure appeared near my door. "Hand me the keys," the soft voice waivered. Even scared as he obviously was, Elliot Daniel was a resourceful little creep. He stepped from the deepest shadows into a bit of moonlight, a large handgun pointed at my ear. He moved half a step away from my door and transferred his aim to Miles Waddell. "If you do anything foolish, I'll shoot him. Then you. But him first."

"What the hell do you want?"

"I already told you. Hand me the keys."

I eyed the gear selector. I could jam it into reverse and hope that something mechanical up front remained operable. But all of that took a hell of a lot longer than a simple pull of the trigger.

He snicked back the hammer of the double-action automatic. "Just do it. This is no time to think about bein' a hero."

He was right in that. Moving like molasses, I switched off the idling SUV and pulled out the fat plastic dingus that was the modern replacement for an old-fashioned ignition key.

"Drop it on the floor."

Far, far in the distance, I heard a police siren. The gal in the Prius had finished her end run. If the sheriff's department couldn't catch a damn hybrid, then they might as well hang up their badges. If Daniel heard the distant wail, he gave no sign.

Chapter Thirty-four

"Now who the fuck are you two?" His voice cracked, ruining his bravado, but the handgun shifted from one of us to the other and back.

"I'm Bill Gastner," I said easily. "I used to be a friend of old Dick Finnegan's. That was his property back there. Where you and the lady were camped."

"What are you after? Nobody just cruises around out here in the middle of the night." His courage was gaining some ground. With one murder already under his belt, I had no desire to underestimate him.

"We're just checking property."

"You a cop?"

"Do I *look* like a cop?" I said, feigning astonishment.

"Yeah, you do. Gimme your wallet."

"Why would I want to do that?" The gun twitched, and his finger was against the trigger. I rethought my game plan and spread both hands wide. "All right, all right. It's in my left hip pocket. You know, there's been some cattle gone missing in these parts lately. That's why we're out." I jerked a thumb at Waddell. "This is Couey Martin. We've had some trouble with the Forest Service monkeying with his livestock. Thought we'd take a look."

I handed him the wallet, and he took it with his left hand, still standing out of range of my door. He flipped it open and his eyes narrowed. Sure enough, the first thing he saw was my old sheriff's badge, and my current special commission.

"You have a license and your insurance card we can trade? We need to clean up this mess. Sorry I got in your way, son."

The affable absurdity of that request didn't seem to register with him. He tossed my wallet past my head into the back of the SUV.

"With these two fingers," and he pinched index and thumb together, "hand me your weapon." He said it as if he were reading a script, and if he could have kept the tension out of his voice, it would have sounded pretty good.

He couldn't have known that the Smith and Wesson was empty, its rounds wild into the trees around his speeding truck. He most likely would never have heard the gunshots. Incapable of walking and chewing gum, or driving hell-bent through the night prairie while fiddling with slippery cartridges, I hadn't fumbled with the speed loaders. I leaned forward and to the left, finding the gun in the pancake holster. With my left hand on the steering wheel, I said, "Okay, now. Take it easy. Here it comes. It's not loaded." I drew out the Smith and Wesson as he had suggested, holding the magnum up like a dead fish.

"Throw it in the back."

I did so, and relaxed. If he'd wanted us dead, there we'd be. Still, the underarms of his gray army-navy store bargain shirt were soaked. His case of nerves was understandable, I suppose.

"Those," he said, nodding at the center console. I assumed he meant the handcuffs that nestled in one of the bottle holders.

"Can't do that, sorry," I said. "Enough's enough. You just…" He struck so damn fast I didn't have the chance to raise a hand. The flat of the automatic connected with my left temple, and stars danced. I cursed and pressed a hand to my head, feeling the leak.

"Get out of the car." This time there was a higher pitch to his orders, a desperation. I looked at him with one eye closed, and he still had the gun pointed at Waddell. It was too dark to see if his hand was shaking, but this was not the time to play games, no time to announce that he already had a murder one rap on his sheet, and when the real sheriff arrived, there would be no negotiations. Daniel would be in custody or dead.

More important just now was that both Miles Waddell—aka Couey Martin—and I be able to enjoy breakfast in a couple of hours, all in one piece. I didn't know what Daniel's plans were, but he didn't need to know that he had *NightZone*'s creator, the man with direct connection to satellites, the FBI, the UN, and who knew who or what else, captive at his feet. I had no desire to light the kid's Roman candle.

I held up both hands again, placating. "All right. Just all right." I unlatched the door and moved it slowly, even though he was well out of its range. I outweighed him by fifty pounds, and maybe twenty years before that would have mattered. Twenty years ago I would have smacked the gun out of his hand and then broken his arm against the sharp fender of the truck. That was then.

As it was, I damn near fell when my boots touched the ground. He darted behind me and grabbed the cuffs off the console. "You," I heard him say to Waddell. "Get out. If you want him dead, do something stupid."

At gunpoint, he escorted us to the back of the electric company's utility truck—which, thanks to the railroad tie bumper, had suffered not a bit. In the back was his motorcycle, lashed down neatly so that it nestled between four 50-gallon drums.

"Get up there," he ordered, and I laughed. There might have been room for a couple of kids.

"I don't think so, sport." The utility bed had no tailgate, but still it was high off the road, and I was far past the 'hop into the back of the truck' stage. The massive bumper included a pipe-fitter's vise welded in place.

Ever helpful, he kicked the trailer hitch. "Step on that, then up. Move it." He was right. It worked. Miles Waddell followed. So far, he hadn't said a word, his face grim. "Put these on your right wrist," he said to Waddell. The rancher didn't have much experience with handcuffs, and it took him a minute to figure them out. "Give me," Daniel said. He reached up and clenched the cuffs tight, all the while pointing the gun at me. "Go to that side of the bike," he commanded, pointing to the left. "You," and he meant me, "on the right."

We each had a little alcove in which to squat. The drums filled the front of the truck bed in sort of a "U," the front wheel of the bike nestled between the rear two. It was an effective barrier between us. "Pass the cuffs under the bike's fork in front of the engine and snap them on your left wrist," he ordered. This was a new one on me. Right to left, we were handcuffed and secured in position by a 500-pound rice rocket. The key to the cuffs was on my ignition ring, back in the SUV.

"Don't do anything stupid," Daniel repeated as he turned to climb into the cab.

The utility truck started with a lurch and reversed, accompanied by a tearing of metal as the embedded railroad tie took out part of my Durango's fancy grill guard. I shot my free hand forward and grabbed the rim of the nearest drum. It was heavy and cold, the aroma of gasoline pungent.

We could go down on our hands and knees, or kneel, or stand bent over in an ape posture that I'd be able to hold for about five minutes. As soon as the truck started down the narrow road, I realized how truly close to torture this was going to be.

"How's your head?" Waddell asked.

"Attached."

"You took a hard lick."

"That son-of-a-bitch has fast hands," I said.

"And who's Couey Martin?"

"Just a name," I said. "He used to work for the highway department years ago. I didn't figure this son-of-a-bitch needed to know who you were."

"What's he aim to do?"

"I don't know. But right now, he's got the cards. A good truck, what looks like two hundred gallons of gasoline, and two hostages. Go figure." I tried again to get comfortable, but the jouncing was brutal.

"Put your left hand down flat on the bed right by the front wheel," Waddell whispered. With the cab's center window blocked by the utility bed's front tool boxes, Daniel couldn't see us. But what served as his ally was the continual battering we took from the truck's impossible suspension. Try to move, and a lurch sent us crashing into the drums or the bike.

On his hands and knees, Waddell planted his right hand on the truck bed opposite my left, the two of us snuggled against opposite sides of the bike's engine. "Just lift the front of the bike. Use your shoulder, or butt, or whatever. Even a knee against the front wheel. It's on its kickstand, so all we have to do is lift it a little bit, then we slide the cuffs forward, out from under the wheel."

"And then what—leap off a moving truck into the cactus?"

"We'll think of something. Jump on *him,* maybe."

The problem with his scenario was that we had to lift the front end of the bike and at the same time, slide our hands in unison, hoping to slip the short link that connected the two halves of the cuffs under the three measly inches of rubber resting on the bed. It didn't work, despite our duet of groans, gasps, and curses.

"Why don't we just push the son-of-a-bitch out the back?"

"We don't want to go overboard with it," the rancher said. He thumped the heel of his hand against the nearest drum. "You think he's got gas in all of these?"

"That's all that I smell," I said.

I pushed the small of my back hard against the bike's engine, trying to ward off a savage lumbar kink. "Can you reach the bungees?" Two secured the back, with two more at the front. On top of that, the bike rested on its stout two-legged stand, held tightly from side to side.

A sudden lunge of the truck cracked the right side of my head against the rim of one of the barrels. Just when I thought I had my balance, we swerved left and I fell again. "I'm going to shoot this son-of-a-bitch when I get the chance," I swore. Looking toward the back, I recognized the wider, smoother surface of County Road 14. We'd turned off the primitive Forest Road, and the truck's speed picked up.

"I got it," Waddell said, and the rear bungee buckle on his side flopped loose. I don't know how he found it in the dark, but his hands were more nimble than mine. Contorted like a gymnast, he strained to reach the other. It was on my side, impossible no matter how he twisted. With my left hand held firm, I turned my back to the bike, pressing against the massive engine. This was the time when it would have been nice to have working rotator cuffs. With a review of every curse that I knew, I could reach the bungee buckle with my right hand, but could not managed to do anything with it.

"Find a purchase and skid the bike toward me a little. Get some slack in it," I said. He braced his back and pushed, and the bike gave a little. Another push, and the bungee drooped. This time I could reach the hook where it latched onto the frame of one of the utility boxes.

"Now the front," Waddell said in triumph. With our hands laced together under the frame ahead of the engine, the logistics of the front bungees were easier. We had the technique down pat. In another mile, and with a dozen more bruises collected, the first bungee parted company, and we had it made. The second followed.

"Okay," I said. "Now what? If we don't do this just right, we're taking a dive off this truck with the bike."

"Then let's do it right," Waddell said. But as he spoke, the truck slowed hard, and I rose on one knee, trying to see over the cab. Sure enough, we had reached the intersection with State 78, the highway from Posadas out through the northwest corner of the county toward Newton. That meant twelve miles to go down County 14 until we crossed State 17, and then on down the county road still farther to Waddell's holdings—if that's where we were headed.

We enjoyed the smooth transition for two blissful seconds as we crossed the pavement. Daniel hit the gravel on the far side and accelerated.

"Turn your back to it, reach down and grab something, and lift and heave forward," Waddell said.

"Remind me again why we want to do this?" I muttered. The exhaust pipe was handy. "Now!"

We heaved and accomplished nothing other than digging the handcuff link deeper into our flesh. "One more," Waddell gasped. And this time it worked. The bike rolled forward a bit, the kickstand snapped back, and the bike was balanced on its tires. And that meant that we were the ones defeating gravity.

"Don't let it lean on you," Waddell said. "We'll never get it up."

I silently blessed the county road department for keeping County 14 in some semblance of repair. A click, and Waddell said, "It's in neutral. Easy now. When it goes off the back, slap your hand down hard on the bed. Let it roll over the cuffs."

"This is going to hurt," I grunted.

"Of course. Anything worthwhile does."

"I'm going to remember you said that."

Looking like a pair of spastic crabs, we edged the bike backward. Linked as we were his right to my left, we had to crawl backward ourselves, shoulders and hips pushing against the bike to keep it upright. What seemed like a week took only seconds. We felt the back tire hit the rim of the bed, and then gravity did the rest.

"Hand down!" Waddell yanked me flat, the bike leaned sideways to rest its bulk on my hip. Then I felt it start to go. The front tire hit our shackled hands, took skin and flesh with it as it twisted away. Then it was gone, pitching back to land on the road with a satisfying crash and scatter of expensive parts that winked in the moonlight.

Waddell's face bloomed into a grin of wild glee. "He ain't going to be happy about that!"

Sure enough, the truck braked violently, sliding to the shoulder. Both of us careened forward and I dropped to my knees, banging my elbow against one of the drums, eliciting only a dull thunk.

Elliot Daniel charged around the back of the truck, his pistol waving like a conductor's baton. He ran back a few yards and surveyed the scattered bike, cursing. The machine might have been able to wobble down the road were it not for the crushed left handlebar. He kicked the front wheel savagely, then bent down and pulled several items out of one of the rear panniers. He didn't bother moving the bike from the center of the dirt road.

He stalked back to the truck, and I picked myself up. He kept the side utility box between himself and us, and the gun, as always, at the ready.

"I don't know what happened," I said. "It just went out the back."

"Give me your cuff key," he demanded.

"It's back in my truck, son."

He thought about that for a few seconds, then nodded. "You won't go anywhere." Without the least hesitation, he raised the gun and fired a single shot, the explosion loud and sharp. Miles Waddell gasped and lost his balance, dragging me down with him.

"You don't play games with me," Daniel said. "You and your buddy just…" and he let the rest of the sentence go, running out of words.

He returned to the cab, but returned almost immediately with one of those yellow fabric tow straps. He tossed it into the truck bed. "Wrap that around behind your cuffs," he ordered.

"Now wait a minute," I started to argue, with visions of him dragging us down the road. He lifted the damn gun again. I held up a conciliatory hand. "Don't do it." I looped the strap through the cuffs.

"Just give me the ends."

I thought on that. The strap was weighty, but not a good weapon. I could swing it at him, but what would that earn? Miles had regained his balance, but stood hunched, his free hand pressed against his thigh. I did as I was told, and the tow strap sawed against my wrist as Daniel pulled out the slack. With both ends in hand, he yanked the tow strap over my side of the truck and slipped both end hooks around something well out of reach, up forward toward the cab's rear door. Such an arrangement wouldn't have stopped a couple of agile teenagers, but it was effective for us. I might have been able to slide over the side, breaking only a few things, but I was cuffed to old peg-leg.

Daniel returned to the cab, I guess confident that I wouldn't drag my wounded partner out the back or down the side, or anywhere else. He evidently knew the handy utility of darkness. Even if we successfully bailed without shattering any more legs or necks, just where would we go? Stand in the dark and wait for the cops?

Daniel was digging his personal hole deeper and deeper. I wanted to be there when he hit bedrock. The truck started with an unnecessary jolt. Waddell cursed again.

"That son-of-a-bitch shot me," he said between gritted teeth. His free hand clutched his thigh.

"Bad?" The instant I said it, I realized how stupid it sounded. Even if it doesn't break bones, a hole is a hole, and all kinds of blood leaks out. Miles was just a dark shadow, though. He tugged my hand over and put it on his, halfway between knee and hip, right in the heavy thigh muscle.

"I don't think it hit the bone," the rancher said hopefully.

"Just try to hold still," I said. "Let's get a belt or something around it."

"It's not bleeding that much," he said. "Just leave it." He drew himself up a little, trying to relieve the weight on his leg, and then sucked in a sharp breath as the truck lurched and dumped us hard against the steel truck bed and the drums. "This is going to hurt." He looked across at me, his features indistinct. "It's a good thing I hired you to keep me out of trouble."

"You bet," I said. "Think where you'd be if I had left you behind at that damn reception."

He laughed, but without much humor. "What's the sheriff going to do?"

"I have no idea. The only thing I can guess is that he's got the girl. *Someone* has her. And he'll be able to guess where we're headed."

"My place."

"Yep. I mean, where else?" I rose a bit, trying to see out beyond the cab. "Get a good hold," I said, ducking back down. "The canyon breaks north of the interstate and Seventeen are coming up." He knew what I meant. We wedged ourselves as tightly as we could, at least thankful that the drums were dead weights, reluctant to slide around against their retainers. For four miles, we charged through narrow cuts in the rocky mesas, across two arroyos, and finally down a jagged slope that angled along a mesa flank. The mesa had dumped all its loose rocks on the road, and we swerved this way and that, at one point scraping the undercarriage.

The road delivered its last savage jolt, and then we were skimming across a dry sandy lake bed—the water gone about the time the mastodons left. Headlights cut the night sky, and we flashed under the interstate, the late-night tourists blissfully ignorant of what was going on below them.

Posadas County is sliced by three east-west state highways, and Waddell's holdings lay between NM 17 and 56. Once we crossed NM 17, we were headed for his home turf…and, I wagered, Elliot Daniel's grand plan.

Charging up a rise in the prairie, we reached the stop signs for NM 17. Determined to give us no opportunity, Daniel slowed the truck only a fraction, and with no headlights cutting the night to argue with him, dove through the stop sign, across the old state highway.

His view wasn't as good as ours. As we shot across the macadam, I saw the moonlight touching the white roof of a car three reflector tenth-posts to the east. As the pavement faded behind us, I saw the car pull out, running without headlights.

I knew that Deputy Thomas Pasquale often drove 303, one of the older hot rod Crown Vics. I had been in the office one day when Pasquale had gazed out the window with lust at the undersheriff's new Dodge Charger. He'd turned to Sheriff Torrez and asked plaintively, "When am I going to get one of those?"

"When you learn not to turn 'em into junk inside of a week," Torrez had said, and that ended that conversation. The young deputy's nickname, "Parnelli Pasquale," was well-deserved.

The old patrol car, still plenty peppy, reached County Road 14 before we'd gone another mile, still running without headlights. It turned onto our dirt road with a smooth power slide in the gravel that sent up billows of moonlit dust.

I sat back down. "Well, this will be interesting."

"Who do we have behind us?" Wadell asked. He could see the dust cloud now as the deputy closed the gap. If Daniel was paying attention, he might be able to see it as well.

"My guess is Pasquale," I replied, fervently wishing that my cell phone wasn't back on the center console of the Durango. "The sheriff said he was headed out on Seventeen. Let's hope he doesn't get too eager." And sure enough—the young deputy had either thought this through all by himself, or was listening to Sheriff Torrez's calm instructions. His patrol car slowed and remained a good quarter-mile behind us. Maybe we were lucky, and Daniel *hadn't* spotted him. Hopefully, Torrez hadn't just said, "Get close enough and shoot the son-of-a-bitch," although had I the wherewithall, that would have been my first choice. I was getting goddamned tired of being jounced, bruised, nicked, and otherwise assaulted by the rough, cold ride in the back of the Posadas Electric utility truck, chained to a fellow who didn't deserve a minute of the beating.

Chapter Thirty-five

I knew County Road 14 well enough that I could predict the worst of the bad spots, and now that we were drawing closer to *NightZone*, Elliot Daniel was getting antsy, pushing the truck hard. I still had no idea what he had in mind. Unfortunately for us, he hadn't been the sort of bad guy who liked to spout soliloquies about his motives. As the guy in the Italian western once advised, "If you're going to shoot, shoot—don't talk." Apparently Daniel had memorized that script. This wasn't a guy who was suddenly going to negotiate.

Far in the distance to the north, I saw the faint prick of headlights. More company.

"Whatever he's planned, he's going to have a good audience." I pointed, and Waddell nodded.

"I saw it. And he probably did, too."

"The only thing I know for sure is that Daniel thinks he can barter his way out with us if there's a problem. There's no reason to keep us alive otherwise."

"That's a cheerful thought." We jolted and Waddell let out a little yelp. "Now it hurts," he muttered.

Over the last little rise in the prairie, the new electric substation project appeared, the small forest of steel poles and transformer platforms ghost gray. With power restored on the service line, the crews had taken a Saturday night off. One of the big bucket trucks remained parked inside the enclosure with a low-boy utility trailer attached, loaded with four new transformers. As we drew closer, I could see various piles of construction junk around the site, but anything valuable—like the huge roles of copper cable—should have been locked inside the barbed wire and chain-link enclosure with the truck.

We didn't slow down until the last minute, and at the same time that Daniel spiked the brakes, I was crouched with one hand locked around the headache rack, the other with the damn tow strap around my forearm and handcuffs grounding me to Miles Waddell. Able to just see over the cab, my eyes ran from the cold. Just enough February to make us doubly uncomfortable, but not enough to throw a blizzard into Daniel's plans. The prairie was full of humps and bumps and things that showed no definition for the eye, even with the undiluted moonlight. I sat down and for the first time, I could hear Miles Waddell's teeth chattering. "You know, I never asked you this, but is there any chance you happen to be carrying a gun, Couey?"

That prompted a shaky laugh. "Don't I wish," he said.

"Hang in there. We have lots of company now." Off in the prairie somewhere, a cow bawled for its late fall calf. All the activity was making her nervous.

With exaggerated care, Daniel swung the rig into the substation's rough driveway.

"Sure enough," I said. He stopped, engine idling, with the railroad tie a pace from the locked gate. "Slide back, right against the bulkhead," I whispered. "Protect your head." I scrunched down tight beside him. Under the truck I heard a faint clunk as it was shifted into four-wheel-drive low range. The Ford jerked backward a dozen paces, and then Daniel shifted into drive and hit the throttle.

Free arm over my head, curled up with Miles like a couple of old best friends, we huddled down. The truck took the gate dead center, tearing it out from under the barbed wire strands that passed over the top bar. One wire scraped along the headache rack above us, the stout chain-link gate panels collapsed inward, ripping fence support posts on either side out of their fresh concrete beds. The whole thing snarled on the truck's grill and front bumper, pushed inside the compound, dragging chain-link and posts. He stopped when we were just about dead center in the enclosure, parked beside the electric company's bucket truck, the railroad tie butted against one of the transformer platforms.

I heard Daniel curse, then he dove out the driver's door, a small satchel in hand. I made one last frantic look around for a weapon of some sort. What I had were handcuffs, attached, and a loop of tow strap hooked under the truck.

Daniel pointed the automatic at us. "This is only the beginning!" he shouted.

"You think you're going to walk out of here?" I said, trying to stand up.

"It doesn't matter," he said matter-of-factly. He started to walk away, picking his way through the tangle of wires.

"What is it you want from us?" It wasn't so much the question, or even the answer, that interested me at the moment. I wanted him to stop and talk, to look at me, to ignore County Road 14, down which Deputy Pasquale's patrol car was approaching. A quarter-mile behind him, another vehicle was running on parking lights. The crunch of tires and burble of exhaust couldn't be disguised, though. It would be only a matter of seconds before Daniel looked up at the approaching danger.

The young man ignored me. Instead, now a dozen paces from the crushed gate, he bent down and zipped open the little gym bag. He came up with what looked like two highway flares, and my gut did a flip-flop.

He still held the handgun, and again without warning or hesitation, he fired, this time from a crouch. Daniel let four rounds off, paced as if he had a metronome in his pocket. I flinched away from the clang of bullets off to my left. He hadn't missed. The four holes punched in a vertical string down the drum, and instantly four fragrant jets of gasoline spurted out. A tiny fragment of something hit me just under the nose, stinging like hell, but the bullets—without doubt copper-jacketed—didn't spray sparks.

As if I hadn't had enough reason to think it before, the idea exploded in my mind—psychotics think up any excuse for their handiwork. Although it might have begun otherwise, Elliot Daniel didn't care if the government was taking over Miles Waddell's mesa for a clandestine fortress. He wasn't the single, selfless hero saving his homeland from some faceless threat. He didn't care who was trapped in a truck that was now a ticking bomb. He was a fruitcake, pure and simple. I'm sure his eyes gleamed when the first power pole started to topple, just as they gleamed now.

Just close enough that I recognized 303, Pasquale stopped his patrol car in the middle of the road. Certainly, he had been driving with his windows open, and had heard the shots. Coming up quickly behind him was another dark sedan. Finally, Daniel recognized Pasquale's presence. He may simply have not cared until this point. The deputy popped on the headlights, snapped them to bright, and then turned on the spotlight. Daniel was pinned in the burst of light, and for a moment he stood confused, some little circuit in his brain short-circuited.

The deputy stepped out of the car, keeping behind the lights. "Drop the gun, right now!" he bellowed. Daniel remained frozen, gun in one hand, the pair of highway flares in the other. The second vehicle slid to a stop in the gravel just behind the deputy's, and two figures got out, leaving the doors open.

"We have to go over the side," I whispered harshly, and hauled at Waddell's handcuffs. He had struggled to his feet—it was either that or lie in the growing lake of gasoline. The tow strap was stretched tightly enough that it would not reach to the back of the truck. Our choice was to clamber over the utility boxes.

Daniel raised his hand that held the flares, trying to shield his eyes. Gasoline gurgled out of the barrel, the top hole already slowing to a trickle as the level sank.

"Drop it right now!" Pasquale shouted.

I would think that it's hard to stare into spotlights and remain brave. But bravery wasn't Daniel's problem. He bent down slowly and placed the handgun on the ground.

"Oh, shit," I breathed. "Pasquale!" I bellowed as loudly as I could. "We have spilled gasoline over here!" The riddled drum was one thing—lighting off three more unvented drums put the bomb in another class.

"Come on," I urged, and pushed myself on top of the utility boxes on the passenger side of the truck, keeping my left arm on the inside, waiting for Miles. He staggered, drawing close enough that I could swing a leg over the side, searching for a toehold. Nothing at all. The truck was slab-sided, a straight drop to the ground. The tow strap was tangled around the rear brace of the cab's courtesy step.

Elliot Daniel had no where to go, but his mind was no longer sifting the choices. In fact, he had only two—and chose the wrong one.

"Don't! Put it down!" Estelle barked, now moving fully into the light. Flanking her was another figure, handgun forward. I looked over my shoulder and saw Daniel fussing with the striker, and sure enough, the flare bloomed with a brilliant halo. His earlier shooting said that he was right-handed, and it took a second or two to transfer the lighted flare to that hand. He had a toss of fifty or sixty feet to reach us, no challenge at all.

His right arm went up, he shifted his stance with left leg forward like a ballplayer readying for the pitch.

"Now!" I shouted, and hauled at Waddell's arm. I slid and he rolled, and the drop off the side of the truck was like a giant stamping on me with both feet. It didn't help that Waddell landed fully on top of me, his bellow of pain punctuated by a sharp explosion that rocked through the night.

Everything hurt, and I couldn't see what had happened. But gasoline still trickled in delicate little streams, now leaking down through the bed of the truck to spatter lightly on the ground beside my head.

Chapter Thirty-six

Undersheriff Estelle Reyes-Guzman was deft and gentle as she released the cuffs and untangling the tow strap, but the dripping gasoline lent an urgency that even spurred on the wounded rancher. He pushed his soaked carcass off of me and scrabbled away like a wounded spider, dragging his leg behind him. Lynn Browning appeared and hoisted him to his feet, letting him lean on her shoulder as they hobbled toward the gate.

"We need to get us all out of here, Padrino," Estelle prompted.

"Gladly," I managed. "But something doesn't work too well." I rolled onto my butt, sat up and winced as somebody stuck a row of needles in my left knee. "Shit," I muttered, and heaved like a wounded whale onto my right side. I managed to rise to my hands and knees, left leg awkwardly splayed. I stopped and looked out toward the road, catching my breath.

Elliot Daniel lay on his back, arms outflung. Looking like wisps of fog, tendrils of smoke rose from around his body. Deputy Thomas Pasquale stood a short distance away, the muzzle of a short magazine-fed rifle unwavering and pointed at Daniel. The handgun the young man had used to put holes in both Waddell and the gasoline drum lay two yards from the young man's feet.

"Everybody who's anybody is on the way," Pasquale said with forced jocularity. His single shot had been perfectly timed and saved lives, but I knew that looking down at your score was still a soul-jarring, sobering experience. Waddell was still hopping north with Lynn Browning, putting himself behind the lights, and well away from the explosion threat.

I stopped when I reached Elliot Daniel.

"What's smoking?" I asked, but I already knew. Tommy Pasquale needed any reinforcement he could get at the moment, and knowing how perfectly justified his shot was would help…a little.

"He fell backward on the flare, sir." A phosphorous highway flare was designed to stay lit come wind, snow, or rain. The damn thing was a danger, no matter what. Being muffled by Daniel's body was somehow appropriate. The second flare lay in the dirt, still capped.

I hobbled close enough that I could reach the deputy and shook him by the shoulder. "Thanks, Thomas." There was no need to check the victim for signs of life. The heavy .308 bullet had plowed into Daniel's body through the right armpit as he turned and reared back to throw the flare. The large wound high in his left side, and then through the muscle of his upper left arm, told me that the slug had smashed through lungs and heart before exiting.

"There are four drums of gasoline on that truck, and he put four bullets in one of 'em, so pay attention." I turned to Estelle, whose strong little hand was still clenched on my right elbow. "You have the girl in custody?"

"Yes, we do. A little bit of a surprise."

"In what way?"

"Julie Warner, sir."

I looked at her sharply. "Curt Boyd's girl?"

"Well, sometimes, apparently. She claims that she was trying to talk Daniel out of this," and she turned to look at the truck.

"Didn't work too hard at it," Pasquale said.

"She was doing her best," I said. "We found 'em in Finnegan's barn, and from the looks of things, she was giving it her all."

Far off in the night, the symphony of sirens reached us. "Fire and rescue is on the way to nail this place down." He pointed a finger pistol at me. "And they found your vehicle and secured it, sir. It's kind of battered up."

Estelle urged me toward the lights. "We need to put some space between us and that gasoline," she said. "Tom, will you get a tarp and cover him up?"

"Yes, ma'am."

"Don't turn him over yet…and can the gun."

"You got it." He seemed relieved to have something to do.

She added, "And *nobody* goes near that truck until Fire and Rescue have secured it. Nobody."

Both back doors of Estelle's car were open, and I took the side opposite Miles Waddell. I reached out and shook hands with him. "Be thinking about this escapade of ours," I said. "Both you and I are going to be writing depositions for about the next week."

"Two weeks, more likely," the undersheriff said. She walked around the car and knelt, examining Waddell's punctured leg with a flashlight. "Nice clean nine-millimeter hole," she said. "Any grating when you flex it?"

"I try not to do that," Waddell said. "But no. Just aches like hell now. Didn't hurt when he did it."

"We'll get you taken care of here in just a minute or two." She touched his shoulder as she stood up. Lynn Browning had been standing behind her, looking over the undersheriff's shoulder at Waddell. He ducked his head and looked up at her, and she knelt by the car to make it easier for him.

"You sure you want to work for me?" He laughed weakly. "And we haven't even started yet!"

"It gives me pause," Lynn said gently.

"First thing I want to know," Waddell said, "is *why* he did it."

"I think we all do, sir. For one thing, he wanted a job with us. Now, whether he thought that would give him insider information so he could play more games, I don't know."

I watched Pasquale spread out the black tarp and drape it over Daniel's body. He waited until Estelle had snapped several digital photos of the weapon, then nudged the gun into a plastic evidence bag, and then, because it was still loaded and cocked, into a stout ammo can half-full of Styrofoam peanuts. He marked the can with bright tape and label so some careless idiot wouldn't grab the gun out of the can and touch off a round.

My intent was to hobble around a little until my knee started working half normally, then hitch a ride back to my bashed SUV. Various folks had other ideas. It was Estelle who sliced open the bloody rip in my left pant leg and frowned at the impressive gouge below my knee.

"How did you do this, sir?"

"I guess bailing over the side of the truck. I don't know." As I spoke I noticed that a couple of slender fingers had a grip on my wrist, counting the pulse. With a grimace of impatience, I pulled away. "Come on, now. We're fine. What I really need is someone to run me over to my own vehicle before somebody makes off with keys, guns, and who the hell knows what else."

"It's secured," Estelle said. "It'll be back in town before you are." Headlights stabbed toward us, and in a moment Sheriff Robert Torrez's Expedition slid to a halt immediately beside Pasquale's. The sheriff got out, walked halfway toward the covered corpse and stopped. For a long moment, he gazed at the scene, then finally sighed and turned back, finding Miles and me where we now sat with legs splayed, feet on the ground.

The sheriff said something, his soft voice not carrying the twenty feet to me.

"I beg your pardon?"

"Why am I not surprised?" he repeated. He ambled over and regarded me, eyes invisible under heavy brows and the brim of his baseball cap. "You all right?" He ducked down, one hand on the roof, and looked past me to Miles Waddell. Without waiting for my answer, he said, "How about you?"

"I'll live," Waddell said. He sounded tired. Who knew why.

"He'd appreciate it if you had a morphine amp in your pocket," I said, and Torrez made a little snorting sound of amusement.

"Ambulance will be here in a minute," he said, and slapped the roof. As he pushed himself away and started to turn back toward Estelle, he added, "Don't head out anywheres."

I laughed, and Miles shifted position painfully.

"He sounds like he might be a little pissed," he said.

"If he was pissed, he wouldn't say *anything*." I nodded as we watched the big man approach his deputy and slide a hand across Pasquale's shoulder to grip him by the back of the neck, give a gentle squeeze, and turn him loose. "Pasquale is the one who pulled the trigger, and Bobby knows what's going through the kid's mind."

"Torrez never struck me as the compassionate kind."

"Don't underestimate the sheriff," I said. A brilliant array of flashing lights approached, diving up and down along the dips of the county road. "Our ride," I said.

"Oh, come on," Waddell exclaimed. "We're not going to ride all the way back in that…"

"Relax and enjoy," I laughed. "Beautiful nurses, soothing IV, warm blankets…it doesn't get better than that." As the ambulance pulled to a stop, I saw that Fred Romero and Paul Moore were the two EMTs on call. "Well, two out of three, anyway."

The warm blankets felt wonderful, the IV went unnoticed, and the pneumatic knee brace hurt like hell. The big pad of bandaging on the scrape below my knee would hurt worse when it was removed, along with the hair on my leg. I had been captive in an ambulance a number of times in my various careers, and hated every adventure. But this time, I didn't argue about anything. The gurney, cramped as it was, felt soft and wonderful. I was sound asleep before we reached the pavement.

Chapter Thirty-seven

Julie Warner had been crying like a lost puppy, but she was still cute enough to take my breath away. Not beautiful, mind you. Just plain *cute,* with freckles, dimples, a nose close to aquiline, thick auburn hair that swooshed back into a ponytail, and fair skin that hadn't been toasted to crisp wrinkles by New Mexico sun.

The photo of her that I'd seen at the Boyds' hadn't done her justice. But now she sat in one of the old oak captain's chairs in the first floor conference room, right wrist handcuffed to the hardwood arm. Sergeant Jackie Taber had been keeping her company, escorting her through the myriad interviews. She had told her story probably ten times.

As Undersheriff Estelle Reyes-Guzman and I entered, Sergeant Taber stood up, one hand on Julie's shoulder. She introduced us, not explaining who I was or what the hell I was doing there. The high-tech hinged knee brace was awkward, and the two stitches below ached, but otherwise I was fit enough to pass muster as maybe someone who should matter to Julie Warner.

"Ms. Warner, we have identified you as being in Elliot Daniel's company earlier tonight at the Finnegan ranch north on County Road 43." The girl nodded, and Estelle added, "Is that true?"

Julie's voice was hoarse. "Yes, ma'am."

"And why were the two of you there?"

Julie swallowed hard. "Elliot was preparing the truck."

"For what?"

"He planned to blow up the electric substation down south."

"The one near the development, on the county road?"

"Yes, ma'am."

"And why were you present?"

"I was trying to talk him out of it."

"Why would you do that?"

Julie's head sank down until her forehead touched the table.

"Julie?"

"Because I knew...I knew what had already happened."

"What was that?"

"About...about Curt. Curt Boyd."

"And the police officer?"

"I didn't know about him until this evening."

"Ms. Warner, when the police talked to you earlier—for the first time the day before yesterday, I believe it was—why didn't you tell them that you knew what Curt Boyd and Elliot Daniel had been planning to do?"

She didn't bother to wipe the tears away. And she didn't answer.

"Ms. Warner, why did you accompany Elliot Daniel tonight?"

The girl nodded wearily. "I told you...I thought I could talk him out of doing any more harm. I mean..." and she snuffled. "I mean, before, when they talked about dropping the power line, it sounded like just a crazy stunt. It would bring attention to a project neither one of them believed in, and Elliot kept talking about how after all this he'd be able to get this great job with a security company. And then after everything went wrong, Elliot was so dead set...so *determined*. Like he could make everything all right again."

"And even when you learned that he had shot a police officer, you still chose to do nothing. You chose not to call us."

"I thought..." She shrugged helplessly. "I thought I could persuade him. I'm *so* sorry."

"When you were outside the rancher's barn, did you see any vehicles parked on the county road?"

"I told them I did. I went inside and warned Elliot."

"Why would you do that?"

"When we talked on the phone, he'd made this grandstand

speech about how everyone was after him. But how they weren't going to be able to stop him."

"You believed him?"

"Yes."

"You knew that he was armed?"

"Yes."

"So you drove all the way up from Las Cruces just because he told you to."

"Yes."

"The thought never occurred to you to call the police instead? Wouldn't that have been simpler? You knew where he was hiding, you knew that he was alone."

Julie released a great, choking sigh. "I knew...I knew they'd kill him."

And sure enough, I thought.

Estelle looked across at me, and then beckoned. We stepped outside the conference room, and she took a moment to make sure the door was securely shut. "Do you recognize her, Padrino?"

"Ah, no. I mean, it could be the girl with Daniel. But it was dark, she was wrapped in a blanket. When I heard her speak, she was calling to him, she outside, he in. So no. I can't swear it's her. But *she* says she is, so there you are."

"She didn't sound worried, or distraught when she talked to Daniel?"

"No. If I had to guess, I'd say they might have been having a pretty good time in there."

"No arguing?"

"None that I could hear. What charges are being filed against her?"

"Conspiracy, among other things. If she's linked to any of Daniel's activities before tonight, it'll go worse for her. We just don't know yet."

"Too bad. Nice kid."

"She could have been," Estelle said, "except she had the hots for the wrong guys." She stepped farther away from the door. "Is Miles all right?"

"Just sore. The slug was full-metal jacket. Nice ugly hole, no fractures, no nerve damage. He'll use a cane for a while…a fashionable one, of course." I reached out and touched her elbow. "I wanted to ask you. Are you guys still going to drive over to Texas to see the Dos Pasos concert next weekend?"

She smiled that deep, lovely smile that she didn't offer up very often. "We were considering it. Assuming you can behave yourself for the week between now and then. We don't need any more bodies littering the landscape."

I held up both hands in surrender. "My best behavior. I wanted to ask, though. If you do drive over there, I'd like to ride along, if you can stand it. I never got the chance to talk as much as I'd like with Francisco."

"Of course. Carlos will be in seventh heaven to have you along. He *might* forgive you for bailing out of the reception."

"I appreciate that, but I was more worried about what mom and dad wanted, sweetheart."

She smiled again. "We'd appreciate your company."

"We'll talk about it, then. Do you need anything else from me tonight? I'm against the wall at the moment. I'll be in first thing to write up the depositions, though."

"Go get some sleep. You managed half an hour snoozing on the gurney. Go dive for cover now before Frank Dayan finds you."

I would have had to have put a garbage bag over my head to achieve that, since the newspaper publisher was standing at dispatch when I rounded the corner.

"Who the hell called you out?" I said with mock impatience.

He shook his head in wonder and thrust out his hand. "Are we going to be able to straighten this all out? Jeez…"

I glanced at the wall clock and saw that it was coming up on five. Fernando Aragon would be at the Don Juan prepping for his day. "Tell you what, Frank. Buy me a quick breakfast and I'll fill you in."

His eyes lit up. "You're kidding. The sheriff…" and he lowered his voice to a husky whisper, "the sheriff just told me that he wouldn't have anything until tomorrow. Maybe not even then."

"This *is* tomorrow, and I'm not the sheriff. And I can be bought with a green chile omelet." I held out a hand toward the door. "Lead on." Frank looked skeptical, but he fell for it.

Chapter Thirty-eight

Despite Grand Jury appearances that resulted in Julie Warner's being indicted on charges of conspiracy and second-degree manslaughter that would eventually net her seven years as a guest of the state, despite notification of a lawsuit from the late Nathan Baum's *sister*, who hadn't seen or talked to her late brother in a dozen years but who wailed in misery as she pleaded her case to a hungry lawyer, despite a second breathtaking concert in Dos Pasos by the child prodigies, the anticipation that kept me on pins and needles mounted with each passing week.

I returned home from lunch in mid-April, and struggled the bulky mail out of the slot. And there it was. The upper left corner of the envelope sported the legendary prancing horse with the broken spear in its mouth. My pulse soared. To my credit, I didn't rip it open then and there. I went inside, laid the envelope on the table, made fresh coffee, filled a cup, and found my silver letter opener.

Seated in my library, old Colt relic on the table within reach, I took a deep breath and examined the envelope once more. Sure enough. The opener made smooth work, and I pulled out the unfolded letter. There lay all the details.

When it left the Colt factory in Hartford, Connecticut in 1889, my Colt .44-40 sported a seven and one half-inch barrel, blued with case-hardened frame and rubber grips.

It had been mailed as part of a shipment of two to Rosenblat and Son's Mercantile in Silver City. My pulse kicked up another notch or two. In 1889, Silver City was a tiny place, home to miners and thieves and all sorts of interesting folks. On top of that, Silver City was the right neighborhood. Colt could have told me the gun was shipped to Danville, Illinois, and I would have been sorely disappointed. But Silver City? Had Josiah Bennett wandered into Rosenblat's, seen the Colt and plunked down his $17.50 then and there?

The possibilities whirled as I read and reread the short letter half a dozen times. Nothing was hidden between the lines, and of course Colt didn't have a clue to whom Rosenblat and Son might have sold the revolver. My coffee gradually cooled as I pondered that. Had Rosenblat kept records? Even if the firm no longer existed, did the old record book still molder somewhere, waiting for me?

It was the sort of stuff of which good, high-quality insomnia is made.

To receive a free catalog of Poisoned Pen Press titles, please contact us in one of the following ways:

Phone: 1-800-421-3976
Facsimile: 1-480-949-1707
Email: info@poisonedpenpress.com
Website: www.poisonedpenpress.com

Poisoned Pen Press
6962 E. First Ave. Ste 103
Scottsdale, AZ 85251